Praise for
New York Times and USA Today Bestselling Author

Diane Capri

"Full of thrills and tension, but smart and human, too."
Lee Child, #1 New York Times Bestselling Author of Jack Reacher
Thrillers

"[A] welcome surprise….[W]orks from the first page to 'The
End'."
Larry King

"Swift pacing and ongoing suspense are always
present…[L]ikable protagonist who uses her political connections
for a good cause…Readers should eagerly anticipate the next
[book]."
Top Pick, Romantic Times

"…offers tense legal drama with courtroom overtones, twisty plot,
and loads of Florida atmosphere. Recommended."
Library Journal

"[A] fast-paced legal thriller…energetic prose…an appealing
heroine…clever and capable supporting cast…[that will] keep
readers waiting for the next [book]."
Publishers Weekly

"Expertise shines on every page."
Margaret Maron, Edgar, Anthony, Agatha and Macavity Award
Winning MWA Past President

TWISTED JUSTICE

by DIANE CAPRI

ALSO BY DIANE CAPRI

The Hunt for Justice Series
Due Justice
Twisted Justice
Secret Justice
Wasted Justice
Raw Justice
Mistaken Justice
Cold Justice
Fatal Distraction
Fatal Enemy

The Hunt for Jack Reacher Series:
Don't Know Jack
Jack in a Box
Jack and Kill
Get Back Jack
Jack in the Green

CAST OF PRIMARY CHARACTERS

Judge Wilhelmina Carson

George Carson

General Albert Randall Andrews (Andy)
Deborah Andrews
Roberta Andrews (Robbie)
John Williamson
Donald Andrews
David Andrews

Senator Sheldon Warwick
Victoria Warwick (Tory)
Sheldon Warwick, Jr. (Shelly)

Olivia Holmes
Thomas Holmes

President Charles Benson
Charles Benson, Jr.

Chief Ben Hathaway
State Attorney Michael Drake
Chief Ozgood Livingston Richardson (Oz or CJ)
Margaret Wheaton (secretary)

Kate Austin
Jason Austin

For Robert

TWISTED JUSTICE

CHAPTER ONE

Tampa, Florida
Thursday 8:50 a.m.
January 20, 2000

THE BULLET THAT KILLED General Andrews was the same one that pierced my heart, although we were thirty miles apart when it happened and no blood soaked my chest. The damage was permanent, if not immediately obvious.

The new millennium was off to a disastrous start.

Thursday morning, two days before Andrews died, held the blessed promise of a return to normalcy. I had thrown myself back into my office routine, but I was entirely preoccupied by televised coverage of the most important national event since the war: Senate confirmation hearings for U.S. Supreme Court nominee, General Albert Randall Andrews.

Once the hearings concluded that morning, I naively assumed, my husband would magically transform into the man I had loved and somehow lost. After seventeen years of marriage, another woman would have been easier for me to deal with than George's passionate devotion to the greater good, working to defeat the Andrews nomination.

Seated at the battered desk in my hideously decorated chambers in Tampa's Old Federal Courthouse, I tried to focus on the draft orders that had been prepared by my clerks and appeared on my desk with the regularity of the daily sunrise. I signed the orders, again and again, methodically moving them to my outbox on the front of my desk where my secretary would pick them up.

Like other United States District Court judges here in the Tampa Division of the Middle District of Florida, I had a never-ending, boatload of work that threatened to bury me long before I had a chance to die a natural death. Already, the workload made me feel much older than the thirty-nine years reflected on my driver's license.

Regardless of what time management methods I tried, I never seemed to get ahead. I rarely glimpsed the scarred surface of the old mahogany desktop I'd inherited from the little Napoleon who'd occupied this office before me.

I read the draft order in front of me: Marital Privilege is a legal term that means one spouse cannot be required to reveal confidential communications from the other spouse. Marital privilege was a concept that didn't apply to me at the moment because my husband, George, and I weren't communicating at all. For example, I had no idea where he was that morning. I knew I couldn't reach him very easily by phone because I had already tried.

George was consumed with General Andrews and his confirmation hearings, and I was consumed with desire for the entire process to go straight to hell and leave me and my marriage alone.

Wilhelmina Carson, I wrote, pressing the pen so hard that a hole appeared over the dotted '*i*.' I placed the executed order on the top of the outgoing pile.

"Not since Clarence Thomas was appointed to the Supreme Court in 1991 has there been such a public display of outrage at a President's choice," the television analyst said. "Since General Albert Randall Andrews, formerly Tampa's highest ranking Army officer, was nominated to join Thomas on the bench, the country has resided in a state of outrage over his offensive political and ideological positions on a variety of issues."

The hyperbole brought a smile to my lips that didn't lighten my heart. I found it hard to believe that anyone was taking the Andrews nomination seriously. Andrews was a rogue. To my mind, he was such an unsuitable candidate that he should never have been nominated in the first place.

Andrews was more obstinately opinionated than a cable television talk show host, and twice as vocal about it. There was no way he'd ever do the one thing required by the job: remain impartial and consider each case individually as it was presented to him. Once nominated, Andrews should have been summarily rejected.

But that's not what happened.

The analyst continued reading from his prepared script. "Today, the crowd outside the Capitol building here in Washington, D.C. is larger than any of the earlier days of the hearings…"

I felt sorry for the protesters. It's not easy to have the courage of your convictions after standing outside for nine days in January ice showers.

At the beginning of the march, the protesters had been neatly organized, with the right-to-lifers on the left, the gays and lesbians on the right, and the anti-military group in the center, flowing out to the back. Today, the factions mingled into a single, huddled mass.

Icy rain soaked the homemade signs they carried. Blue magic marker ink ran off onto their heads, giving them an even more defeated look. Many huddled near fires in old barrels to catch a small slice of warmth. Even the commentator shivered as ice water dripped off his umbrella in the cold. I shivered, too, remembering only too well how it felt to be chilled to the bone by bitter January cold. It was a visceral memory that might never be baked out of me here in the Sunshine State.

I glanced out my window and saw clear blue skies, palm trees, and two homeless men across the street wearing short-sleeved T-shirts sharing a cigarette. It so rarely rains here in January that I leave the top down on my car for weeks at a time. The contrast between my world and the world I saw on television couldn't have been more complete. This, at least, was a fact that cheered me.

In the nation's capital, despite the horrid weather, the protesters had come and waited and every day their numbers had grown. They chanted, picketed, sang songs.

I shook my head and ran my fingers through my short auburn hair, causing it to stand straight up on top. The futility of their struggle would have persuaded me to quit long before now. I admired their determination. I liked to think I'd had that once.

When I was young and idealistic. Not anymore.

To do what these protesters were doing, what my husband had been doing, required the kind of conviction I no longer possessed. Before I was appointed to the bench, I practiced law long enough to learn that there are always too many sides to every story. I no longer believed in solid black and pristine white, self-evident truths and indisputable wrongs.

In politics, the question has always been, "what have you done for me lately?" General Andrews was probably finding that out now. It must have been a hard lesson for a popular war hero to learn.

For almost an hour, the television commentators had rehashed the entire course of the hearings and predictions of the outcome, which ranged from promises of complete victory to devastating loss for both sides. Whether the nominee would be confirmed was alternately feared or cheered, depending on the speaker's point of view.

My patience had been stretched to the breaking point by the weeks of bickering. I was sick to death of the constant analysis and conjecture. I wanted the matter to end. Confirm Andrews's nomination or not, but just finish the damn thing.

Just before nine o'clock, the Supreme Court nominee's limousine pulled up to the curb. The Capitol Hill Police personnel assigned to assure his safety surrounded the car and the passenger door opened.

I glanced up from my work to see the first man step out of the car. It was Andrews's personal secretary, Craig Hamilton, a pleasant little man almost a foot shorter than me, whom I'd met several times over the past few years.

As he straightened up and rose to his full height of five feet, he looked around at the crowd. For just a second, I thought I saw something like shock on his face as he faced the angry, chanting mob.

I thought again of Andrews. Why he subjected himself and his family to this abuse was a complete mystery to me. To what kind of man was the promise of power so seductive that he would struggle against hostile strangers to achieve it?

Hamilton reached out to accept an opened black umbrella offered by one of the officers standing to his right while I watched, waiting impatiently for the real story to start.

When Craig Hamilton stood to the side to let Andrews, the nominee, out of the car, I glanced down at my work.

I heard a loud, quick *pop, pop, pop* over the noise of the chanting crowd. I jerked my head up to see Craig Hamilton crumple to the ground. He was quickly surrounded by police officers.

Complete chaos followed instantaneously. My stomach recoiled in horrified impotence as I grabbed the remote control to turn up the volume on the set.

My other hand flew to the phone to call George, but just as quickly withdrew, as if the receiver was hot to the touch. George wouldn't be answering his cell phone. He'd be on his feet, rushing to help Craig Hamilton in any way possible. I hoped George wasn't in Washington, D.C. right now, but wherever he was, my anxiety told me, he was involved.

The screaming drew my secretary, Margaret, into my chambers.

"Willa, what's wrong?" she asked as she hurried over to me.

She put her hand on my shoulder and looked directly into my face. I realized that the screaming that drew her had been my own.

I closed my mouth and patted her hand. I nodded to the television set. Margaret watched with me as we saw falling bodies everywhere. I heard no more shots, but they could have been fired. "Just like Jack Ruby," Margaret whispered, referring to the man who shot Lee Harvey Oswald, right in front of God and everybody, on television after President John F. Kennedy was assassinated.

Americans have a long history of trying to solve political problems with guns. Presidents Lincoln, Kennedy, Ford and Reagan, among others, had all been targets of assassination attempts.

Being younger than Margaret by thirty years, my thoughts jumped to the attempt to assassinate President Ronald Reagan. The thought that sprang, unbidden, to my mind and flew out of my mouth was, "Just like Jim Brady."

Like Jim Brady, Craig Hamilton was in the way between the killer and his target.

I moved to one of the ugly green client chairs on the front side of my desk, where I'd get a better view of the small screen. Margaret continued to stand. Our gazes were glued to the television set now as the small picture divided into three sections. A commentator was featured in a small box on the top on the screen. Another small box reflected the real time events.

On the rest of the screen, a replay camera panned the front lines of the crowd. Involuntarily, I drew a quick breath when the camera spotted a man with a gun making his way up to the curb toward the waiting limousine.

The instant replay showed Craig Hamilton step out of the car. I watched in appalled fascination as the shooter raised his arms while holding a hunting rifle. The rifle recoiled three times as the shooter pulled off the three shots that hit Hamilton's chest. Watching felt nothing like viewing a Hollywood movie. This was too vivid, too close to home.

As both a judge and the wife of an influential member of the Republican party, I'm accustomed to seeing people I know on television. But viewing friends and colleagues being shot and trapped in a car by an angry mob was surreal, a familiar scene grotesquely transformed.

When we saw the shooter wrestled to the ground and taken away in handcuffs in a matter of seconds, Margaret said, "Thank God."

The picture returned to the unfolding events. We watched as

Craig Hamilton was quickly placed on a stretcher and moved to a waiting helicopter.

"Please let him be wearing a vest," I whispered.

General Andrews's famous temper would make him want to get out of that car and beat the shooter to a bloody pulp. Apparently, his handlers knew better than to let him do that. So he and his wife remained inside the limousine until the Capitol Police reinforcements marched into the street, up to the car and surrounded the passenger doors.

We saw countless replays of the shooting, ostensibly for viewers who'd just tuned in. After a while, the breathlessness I'd felt when Craig Hamilton went down began to recede.

"Will they stop for today?" Margaret asked me about an hour later. "Surely, the hearings can be rescheduled while they have a chance to sort this all out?"

More comments and discussion continued among the various commentators and official spokespeople as they debated the idiocy of continuing before they knew if the shooter had acted alone.

At least once before in the current public memory, the assumption had been made that a lone shooter had killed a president, and speculation about that continued to the present time. Had Oswald acted alone? An overwhelming majority of Americans thought not. We might never know. And no one was anxious to repeat the mistake of rushing to a conclusion too quickly.

I said nothing to Margaret, but I hoped that the hearings would not be rescheduled. These hearings had caused so much disruption in the country and in my life that I wanted them over. Now. Of course, I wanted the matter handled safely and responsibly, but if the hearings were finished, then maybe everyone could go home and calm down.

While we waited for something more to happen, thoughts

raced through my head with the speed of light. I could see the general's wife, Deborah Andrews, in the back of the limousine with him. She would be terrified. Deborah was a gentle soul, not meant for the line of fire. Long before now, the challenge of living with her husband had driven her to alcoholism and back.

When Deborah chose to marry the man she called Andy, she couldn't have known she'd be subjected to the glare of media scrutiny, pummeled by questions, even shot at. What would she do to save her marriage when forces beyond her control seemed determined to wrest happiness from her grasp?

I thought about my own marriage and knew I'd be no better suited as a human target than Deborah was. Even though we weren't communicating very well at the moment, I knew George would never put me in any situation that might hurt me, physically or otherwise.

George considered it one of his missions in life to take care of me. While his protectiveness was stifling sometimes, he tried not to smother me with it.

"George is perfect," all my friends tell me. Maybe. George was a banker when I married him. Now he owns and operates Tampa's finest five-star restaurant, handles our investments, and plays the very dangerous game of national and local politics. All our friends love George because of his courtly ways and outgoing personality, but they haven't had to try to live with him lately.

Considering the same question I'd posed about Deborah, I wondered what I would do to save my marriage if forces beyond my control snatched George away, and I pushed the question behind a door in my mind, and closed the door firmly, hiding the thought from view.

Instead, I focused on what Deborah Andrews must be feeling right now. Was she thinking about the privileges of marriage as she sat in the back of that limousine, waiting to hear whether she'd be marched through the cold rain into the Capitol building to sit by her husband as he faced his accusers under the hot television lights?

The Deborah Andrews I'd known might have coveted marriage, but would never desire the role she was now playing. All the country loved a war hero, but they didn't have to try to live with him.

A good marriage improved a woman's life in every way.

But a bad marriage was too often lethal.

CHAPTER TWO

Tampa, Florida
Thursday 1:00 p.m.
January 20, 2000

THE MORNING CREPT PAST, events unfolding too slowly. I left the television's sound muted, while Margaret and I waited by returning to work, although I checked from time to time for an update on Craig Hamilton's condition.

Except for a couple of telephone calls which I successfully ignored from the Chief Judge, the man we call "CJ" and who is the bane of my professional existence, my office was curiously quiet. I was able to make good progress on my orders. The stack in my outbox grew steadily. Margaret provided a tuna sandwich on white with iced tea for me, so I worked straight through lunch, marking time.

About 2:30 in the afternoon, Margaret, who'd been listening to the radio at her desk, came in and turned the volume up on the television set.

"After several hours of negotiation, the local authorities have agreed to allow the Senate confirmation hearing to resume," the analyst repeated.

Awash with ambivalence, I didn't know whether to rejoice or curse. The decision seemed foolhardy to me. The general might still be in danger. Why proceed now? On the other hand, I'd been wishing for the end of these hearings and I wanted them to finish. I was willing to take some risks to make that happen and, apparently, so was General Andrews. I put down my pen and gave my full attention to the news.

A dreadful *déjà vu* feeling overcame me as I watched General Andrews's limousine arrive again. If anything went wrong now, if the shooter hadn't acted alone I couldn't finish the thought, even knowing that my tension was far less than the stretched-taut nerves those on the scene must possess.

The analyst continued to whisper. "An almost invisible General and Mrs. Andrews are being hustled out into a thick corridor formed by uniformed police officers holding open, black umbrellas against the pelting sleet."

The protective parallel column of policemen resembled a human caterpillar as it slithered up the Capitol building steps and slipped inside.

The cameras picked up inside the Senate, showing us the Judiciary Committee already seated befitting their ideologies, Democrats on the left, Republicans on the right. The room must have been heated to boiling by hot lights and hot tempers. I could almost feel the electricity in the large room. I peeled off my sweater and tried to get more comfortable.

"The questioning of a Supreme Court nominee is done by seniority, alternating between the parties," the analyst told his viewers.

"More like watching a slow-mo tennis match," Margaret said,

talking back to the television as we resumed our places in the ugly green client chairs again. My gaze was glued firmly to the set, volume up, attention sharply focused. I wiped my sweaty palms against the napkin left over from lunch.

"If he is confirmed, Andrews will make law in this country until he dies or retires," the analyst continued. "We are now close to the end of the process. The decision made by this committee, whether or not to recommend a full Senate vote on General Andrews's confirmation, may change the course of our history for the next thirty years."

The tuna sandwich I'd eaten earlier now rebelled in my stomach. I'd wanted the vote to be over, but I worried that a victory for Andrews would be a hellish descent into backroom politics for George and the effective end of my easy-going husband.

His immersion in this cauldron of political soup had changed him at the molecular level, it seemed, and when he eventually emerged, I worried he'd be someone totally different, someone I didn't know and might not want to be married to.

I'd told none of this to Margaret, but she must have noticed when my attention wandered because she pulled me back to the present, saying, "Warwick is about to open the hearings."

Senator Sheldon Warwick was the powerful Chairman of the Senate Judiciary Committee, the senior senator from Florida and my brother's boss. Warwick was also one of our neighbors. But most significantly to me at the moment, he was my husband's local political nemesis. Warwick's mere presence on the small screen set my teeth on edge.

Margaret turned up the volume on the set, and we heard Warwick's oratory. "I'd like to express my personal sympathy and the committee's sympathy to Craig Hamilton's family and to

General Andrews, who narrowly missed being killed this morning."

The crowd in the gallery buzzed.

Warwick didn't wait for quiet to return, but raised his sonorous voice. "Before the decision was made to resume and finish the hearing today, we were informed that Craig Hamilton was wearing a bullet proof vest at the time he was shot. Fortunately, this has been standard procedure for controversial witnesses and their staff during these hearings. Mr. Hamilton's doctor reported that he is in severe pain. He suffered two cracked ribs and serious bruising. He is, I'm happy to tell you, expected to fully recover."

Margaret and I said simultaneously this time, "Thank, God."

The gallery, too, buzzed a little louder with this news and Warwick had to wait a few minutes until he could calm them back down to a quiet roar.

As he always does to me, Warwick sounded more than a little insincere when he asked formally, for the record, "Would you like to delay today's questioning, General? The country would certainly understand."

The question was posed merely to manipulate the public's perception, I knew. Warwick, a political animal who would stand for reelection soon, clearly wanted to be perceived as deferential to his party, the nominee and the process. Warwick was a Democrat. The President, a member of Warwick's party, had nominated Andrews to the court. For these reasons, Warwick meticulously followed protocol and made a clear written record of everything that occurred.

Nor would he show any disrespect toward a war hero. Warwick was a powerful man, and he hadn't gotten where he was today by being stupid. Regardless of his personal feelings, and

George had told me that Warwick didn't approve of Andrews, Warwick had behaved perfectly during the hearings and would continue to do so, as surely as most of us behave well when we're being watched by our bosses.

Andrews sat ramrod straight, like six feet of tall, cool granite, prepared for another round from his own personal firing squad, prepared to dodge bullets by moving only his lips.

"Look at that guy," Margaret said, referring to Andrews. "He's so stiff he could be carved on Mount Rushmore."

Margaret was right. Andrews appeared completely unaffected by what had happened outside this morning. His demeanor was the same straight-ahead, unflinching look I'd seen him display on newscasts during his war service as he addressed the nation with status reports. A look that's bred into every senior military man, it was an expression designed to quell fears and coerce submission.

"Thank you, Senator," Andrews said, anger and passion in his voice. "I'd never allow a fool like that to interfere with the regular process of government. We must continue."

His tone made me cringe. There's a reason I was never in military service myself. I'm no good at following orders and I don't relate well to people who think they can order me around.

I wondered again why the President had ever appointed such an inexperienced, unyielding iconoclast to the Court. I could think of at least a dozen more qualified, less controversial candidates, all more compassionate than Andrews. But no one had asked me for my advice.

High-ranking and influential witnesses had given acrid and bitter testimony against General Andrews for the past nine days. I'd seen much of it, either as it happened, or in summary on the evening news.

Now, General Andrews would testify, although he could not

be compelled to do so. So far, that seemed like a huge mistake in judgment to me.

Warwick recited more facts, continuing to make a crystal clear record. "The shooting incident this morning has been investigated and the shooter is in custody. The man has admitted that he tried to kill General Andrews, and he claimed to be acting alone, although his motives remain undisclosed." Warwick stopped here and took a few seconds to stare at the General with ill-concealed distaste.

Was Warwick's demeanor a product of my imagination? Anyone hearing the cold words he continued to dictate into the record could certainly have missed it. He continued, "Authorities do not believe, at this time, that co-conspirators exist. All parties desired to conclude the questioning today and not to delay proceedings any further." Again, he waited a couple of beats. Or at least, I thought he did. "At the conclusion of today's hearings, the proper authorities will resume their investigation of the attack on Mr. Hamilton."

Warwick polled every member of the committee and General Andrews. "Do you desire to continue these hearings at the present time?" Each answered a formal "yes."

Margaret turned to me while the polling was going on. "This is pretty unusual, isn't it?"

I nodded. "It's probably foolhardy, too. And the media will be all over this thing like white on rice."

"So why are they doing it, then?" After all her years as a federal employee, Margaret inexplicably still believed her government would do things that made sense.

"No one wants this situation to drag on any longer than it already has," I told her. Certainly, that was how I felt about it. If Warwick had polled me, I'd have voted yes, too.

"So the hearings will finish today," she said.

I nodded again, saying nothing. The end was in sight. As soon as the reason for George's involvement in these retched hearings was over, my life might return to normal. I allowed a small glimmer of hope to flicker in my heart.

"I'll bet I can guess what George thinks of all this," Margaret told me, with a grim smile.

I simply nodded. Both of us already knew that George is a very active, influential, conservative Republican. He would disapprove of anyone the Democrats chose, regardless of their objective suitability.

But I didn't tell Margaret that I'd heard George's voice raised in anger against Andrews more often in the past few weeks than I'd heard it during our seventeen years of marriage. His opposition was almost violent and completely out of character. Margaret wouldn't have recognized him, and I barely did, myself. Until now, I'd thought I knew my husband better than he knew himself.

The news analyst took the break created as they polled the committee to give us a whispered summary of the political climate for the benefit of anyone living in Outer Mongolia over the past few weeks.

"The Republicans control the House of Representatives. Like a winning football team in the final minutes of the Super Bowl, they are trying to run out the clock on judicial appointments by President Benson, a Democrat whose term ends in less than a year. Republicans want to stall the process of selecting federal judges until they again control the White House and the appointment process."

A second analyst added, "But they didn't foresee the retirement of their most successful judicial ally, the conservative Chief Justice. The Republicans thought they'd have the chance to pack all of the federal courts, and the Supreme Court in particular, with conservative judges. The Andrews appointment threw a serious monkey wrench in their plans."

The polling finally finished, Senator Warwick used his prerogative as chairman to complete the final questioning himself.

"General," Warwick said now, exaggerating his long, slow drawl, giving the word what seemed like four more minutes. "Why do you think that fellow wanted to kill you this morning?"

The shooter had said he was trying to kill Andrews and the confession had already been widely played on television.

"He's a baby killer," the man had said, as if that was all the reason anyone needed to justify retaliation by deadly force.

Without so much as a flinch or a pause, General Andrews said, "Why do you think he wanted to kill me? He shot my secretary. I haven't any idea why he did that. Do you?"

The conversation in the room buzzed at louder decibels. It was unlike General Andrews to sidestep any issue. Usually he confronted everything head on, loudly and with opinionated obstinacy. His opinions, frequently stated in other forums before and since his nomination, had been getting him into trouble.

General Andrews seemed to have opinions on everything. Highly unusual for a general in today's military, and likely to get a Supreme Court nominee rejected. The thing the public fears most, and his opposition hopes for, is a nominee with an opinion.

During the days of hearings on Andrews's nomination, the general seemed to go out of his way to confirm his opinions as controversially as possible, almost in challenge. Although he kept saying, "I have no personal agenda to take to the Court," every time he was asked a direct question on a controversial issue by anyone, he didn't hesitate to state his views.

This alone might not have caused Andrews's nomination to be rejected. Sandra Day O'Connor got confirmed even after she testified that she personally deplored abortion, but would not let her personal views influence her vote. Of course, she was a Republican, George said. To him, that meant you could trust her word.

But Andrews's views seemed so outrageous as to be absurd. In the few short weeks since his nomination, Andrews had incensed Democrats and Republicans, conservatives and liberals, men, women, children, scholars, clerics, radicals, gay and straight alike.

While Warwick attempted to regain order in the room, Margaret asked, "Is there anybody Andrews hasn't offended so far?"

"I can't imagine who that would be," I said.

Once he quieted the buzz of the gallery sufficiently to continue, Warwick asked a series of quick questions to which Andrews responded just as quickly.

"General, do you still support a woman's right to choose, as defined by the U.S. Supreme Court in *Roe v. Wade*?"

"Why should any more unwanted children be brought into the world?"

"And you oppose prayer in public schools?"

"We need prayer at home, where it belongs. Church and State must remain firmly separated."

Warwick looked down at his notes, shook his head as if he was having trouble believing the next series of questions that had been prepared by the committee. Then, he asked, "Do you openly advocate that the Supreme Court should make the law, not just interpret the Constitution?"

Margaret sputtered, "That's outrageous!"

Andrews replied, "This country needs help. The founding fathers died over two hundred years ago. And if they lived here now, they'd be making some changes, too."

Warwick waited a couple of seconds, then asked, "You are opposed to gun control, is that right, General?"

"Why not let the drug dealers kill each other? Save us all some money."

These opinions, contained in Andrews's public appearances over the years, had galvanized the conservatives against him early in the process. But he didn't stop there.

Paradoxically, Andrews confounded his liberal supporters when he stated far right views as well. Indeed, Andrews's opinions seemed incapable of classification. Neither side could completely support or reject him.

"You opposed allowing those with homosexual orientation to serve in the U.S. military?" Warwick asked.

"We don't need the morale problems caused by social and sexual experimentation programs in the military."

"And, the volunteer army, sir, you're opposed to that as well?"

"It's every man's patriotic duty to serve. I would reinstate the draft, given the chance, yes."

"How about allowing women to serve in combat, General?"

"Definitely not. Women in combat put our troops in mortal danger. I would not allow it."

With each controversial answer, the absurdity of Andrews's appointment was underscored. Warwick had to bang his gavel repeatedly and gestured the security officers to roam the aisles to restore order.

CHAPTER THREE

Tampa, Florida
Thursday 3:30 p.m.
January 20, 2000

ONCE HE COULD BE heard over the din, Warwick pressed on. "You favor the death penalty, is that right?"

"Prison doesn't deter crime, but death makes damn sure that particular felon won't commit another crime."

"You oppose welfare and any form of financial support for the homeless?"

"Those people would be fine if they'd just get a job and support themselves."

I shook my head in disbelief. Commentators had been airing these sound bites of old Andrews speeches over the past few weeks, so none of these opinions were a surprise. But they had drawn the ire of the people and generated angry protests, pitting many special interest groups against him and eroding support for the lame duck, President Benson, who had chosen Andrews. This one nomination, by a previously popular president, might be enough to hand the next election to George's party.

"You'd think they would have coached him more thoroughly, wouldn't you?" Margaret said. "I guess he's just too stubborn to listen."

The pundits had dubbed Andrews the Archie Bunker of the Supreme Court. To those of us paying attention, he'd become a laughingstock.

"He could actually be confirmed, you know," I told her.

"No joke?"

"These Senators answer to the voters. They might not want to take the chance of rejecting him. If Andrews was running for President, even George thinks he could win. These people you see on television are vocal activists. But mainstream voters seem to like his no-nonsense, straightforward style," I told her, allowing my amazement to shine through my words.

To a society that watched cable television, confrontational news, reality shows and read the tabloids, Andrews was viewed by many as refreshingly honest.

On top of that, Americans have had a long and justified love affair with military men. That pro-military brand of patriotism had flourished. Many young Americans had died protecting the country and everyone, regardless of ideology, supported our troops.

Americans hadn't had an opportunity to put a military hero in high office since Eisenhower. Some people thought it was time to do it again. But Andrews was no Eisenhower.

Margaret whistled. "Emotions are running pretty hot. He's lucky someone hasn't tried to kill him before."

Her comment shot straight through my composure. Worry had shortened my fuse to the ignition point.

"Don't say that!" I scolded her, too sharply.

Margaret, a lifelong Democrat and supporter of the President, startled me when she said, "Well it's true. Why in the hell did Benson appoint such a jackass?"

Uncontrollable violence injected into the process was the thing I worried about constantly. Having George involved in this dirty political game, even quietly, was frightening beyond anything he'd ever done before. We'd had several arguments about it, but they had only polarized us further and made us both miserable.

The commentator was whispering again now, bringing viewers up to date. "Andrews's nomination was controversial from the start. Many court watchers have told us that Andrews was always an unsuitable candidate to replace the ultra-conservative Chief Justice when he retired. Although Andrews has a law degree, he's never practiced law and never served as a judge in any jurisdiction."

I felt even more ashamed of my outburst a moment ago when Margaret came to my defense.

"So what?" she blurted. "That doesn't disqualify him from any federal appointment. After all," she said to me, "you'd never been a judge before your appointment, either."

I appreciated her loyalty and put an apology into my tone. "But at least I'd been a lawyer, Margaret. Andrews has never done that much."

Senator Warwick continued, just as emotionally unruffled as Andrews, but physically more rumpled. Not many older men can stay crisp under the glare of hot lights, and Warwick wasn't one of the ones who could do it.

"He's not entitled to wear that uniform now that he's retired, is he?" Margaret asked me, referring to Andrews, who was dressed in full regalia, medals and ribbons covering half his broad chest.

"No," I acknowledged quickly as I turned the volume up a little higher, attempting to silence her comments so that I could hear.

Senator Warwick's bald head gleamed with sweat now, but he was not deterred by the heat or the tension. He continued to rapid-fire questions at Andrews for another two hours, and Andrews just as adroitly shot back his answers. Instead of answering one of Warwick's questions, Andrews made a comic face that showed he thought Warwick was the one being outrageous. Court watchers in the gallery laughed.

"Jerk," Margaret murmured under her breath.

Warwick bristled at the laughter, coming as it did, at his expense. His face flushed, he frowned and pounded his gavel repeatedly calling for order. He looked like he might blow a gasket. I could almost see the steam coming out of his ears.

Sitting next to her husband, Deborah Andrews appeared a little green. When the laughter in the gallery eventually died down, Andrews replied more seriously.

Finally, out of patience, Senator Warwick asked his last question. "General, do you have anything further you'd like to say to this committee?"

Andrews's next words sounded like a prepared statement he had memorized for the occasion. "Senator, I have defended democracy and representative government on the front lines of three wars and several peace keeping missions. My patriotism cannot be questioned. When I returned from the third Gulf War, I received a hero's welcome."

He stopped his recitation here, allowing the applause to die down, and then resumed a more normal conversational tone. "This committee has attempted to suggest that I'm not popular with the people. Nothing could be further from the truth, and we all know it. If confirmed, I will perform the duties of my office to the best of my ability. Which is considerable."

"Man, he is one cool cookie," Margaret said.

"Being calm under pressure isn't enough to make him a good justice," I replied.

George had told me that many of the senators from both parties on the judiciary committee disapproved of Andrews. Mere disapproval, though, would not be sufficient to defeat his nomination, either.

Senator Warwick announced the close of the committee's business, thanked the general for coming and said deliberations would begin in closed session Monday.

"What happens now?" Margaret asked me before returning to her desk.

"The committee will make a recommendation to the Senate next week as to whether or not to have a full vote," I told her.

"I guess we'll just have to wait to see whether Andrews gets confirmed then," she said in parting.

It was hard for me to believe that the committee would consider Andrews seriously. Selfishly, I hoped for a quick defeat of the nomination and the process to continue with a more suitable candidate.

I tried to concentrate on my work, but my thoughts returned to the Andrews nomination. General Andrews had been a Tampa treasure before his nomination. He'd lived here since he worked out of MacDill Air Force Base as a part of the joint command that directed the course of the third Gulf War. He lived with his wife, Deborah, on Lake Thonotosassa, now that he'd retired. He lent his name to several charitable events.

Until his nomination had revealed aspects of his character that most people hadn't known, Andrews had vast public support for all his good works.

Even so, George had been against Andrews from the

beginning. First, General Andrews is a Democrat. To George and his colleagues, Andrews's party affiliation alone made him unsuitable for the Supreme Court. George believed absolutely in the GOP, the Party of Lincoln, the Republicans. Conservative and free-market capitalist.

George's GOP is big, inclusive, supportive and fiercely independent of big government. He didn't want a liberal Supreme Court to rubber stamp any socialistic policies that might sneak past the legislature over the next thirty years, like increased taxes and entitlement programs.

Almost the second Andrews's name started to circulate as a potential nominee, George went into high gear against him. George is active in Republican politics and extremely close to the Florida Party Chairman, in the fourth largest state in the Union. George doesn't hold an office in the Party, but only because he doesn't want to. My husband's influence was considerable and he wholeheartedly threw his weight against Andrews.

I looked up to see Margaret standing in the doorway, her purse on her arm, keys in hand. I glanced at my watch, surprised to see it was already six o'clock.

"Have a good night," I told her.

"Willa?" she asked.

"Yes?"

"If the committee recommends Andrews's nomination and the full Senate endorses it, Andrews will sort of be your boss, won't he?"

Revulsion flooded my senses. I forced down the bile. "Not really. He'll outrank me in the federal court system, but he can't tell me what to do." I am appointed for life, too. Unless I do something illegal, for which I might be successfully impeached, I will have my job for as long as I want it.

"But he can set law you'll have to follow, right?" Margaret had been my secretary a long time. She knew more about the law than most law school graduates.

"He'll have to get the other justices to agree with him first." I told her.

"Speaking of other judges, CJ called again," she told me, referring to the Chief Judge.

"He doesn't have any influence over me, either," I told her, my resignation so plain in my voice that she said her goodnights and left without further comment. What I'd said about the CJ wasn't exactly true. He had a lot of influence over administrative matters here in the Middle District of Florida.

Which was why I still labored in the equivalent of the federal court ghetto. All of my colleagues had long ago moved to the new Sam M. Gibbons Federal Courthouse down the street, while I was stuck with the historically significant but horribly rundown Old Federal Courthouse. The only benefit to me was that the CJ couldn't just drop in whenever he felt like it.

I ignored the CJ's messages and turned my attention back to my work. There was no reason for me to hurry. Either my home would be dark and empty while George was out politicking tonight, or he'd have his team there, strategizing the defeat of the nominee.

I was bone weary of the whole mess, so after Margaret left I continued working at my desk, where I had complete control of my environment, where I felt safe and secure. The law changed so slowly that it mimicked the movement of mountains. There were few chances for surprises, which was just the way I liked it.

I managed to put the Andrews nomination out of my mind until Friday night. Glad to have made it to the weekend, I walked through the front door of the nineteenth-century home George inherited from his Aunt Minnie and immediately felt the urge to leave when I saw how many people were waiting in the foyer.

Our house had been built by Henry B. Plant, a local railroad tycoon who also built The Tampa Bay Hotel, now The University of Tampa. Plant called the house Minaret because of the bright steel onion dome on the top, and the name stuck.

George's five-star restaurant occupies the main floor of Minaret and we live in the second floor flat. George's dining room, formerly the ballroom, comfortably holds about thirty round tables, all of which were full tonight. Prospective diners spilled out into the over-crowded lobby where the frazzled new hostess seemed completely overwhelmed.

I turned on my heel, intending to duck out and enter our flat through the back stairs, when I noticed General Andrews and his entire family waiting to be seated. The shock stopped me in my tracks long enough for his wife, Deborah Andrews, to see me. She gave me a wistful smile I hadn't the heart to ignore.

Stashing my briefcase behind the hostess station, I made my way toward the Andrews party, where I welcomed the general and Deborah to George's.

"Willa, what a pleasure to see you again," Andrews said, as he took my hand and kissed the cheek that I hadn't moved out of the way quickly enough. Deborah gave me a grateful little hug. I felt her too-fragile bones through the thin summer dress and noticed around her eyes the deep lines I'd missed while watching her on television the day before. Still, she looked happy, pleased to be here.

"You know our children, don't you?" Andrews asked.

Then he introduced them all to me again, the habit of a gracious man who has more than a little trouble remembering names of people he doesn't see regularly.

Andrews's sons were identical twins, Donald and David. I'd met them years ago, when they were still teens. They were both in the army, as the general had been until he retired. Both sons resembled their father: tall, dark and slight. Their mousy brown hair and striking cornflower blue eyes were Deborah's contribution to their appearance.

The daughter, Roberta ("Robbie") Andrews, and her husband John Williamson, or "Jack," as he was called, lived here in South Tampa. He was a member at Great Oaks, where I played golf every Saturday. Most South Tampa golfers were members there because it's the only course nearby. Great Oaks has a very liberal admissions policy: anyone who applies gets in. Which was a good thing for me since federal judges can't belong to discriminatory societies.

Robbie had her broad back to her family, admiring the antique sideboard George's Aunt Minnie had left us with the house. Robbie was opening the drawers, examining the brass pulls, just generally being nosy. When her father said, "And you know Robbie and Jack, of course," Robbie turned and gave me a thin smile. I nodded in their direction.

John was charming, as always. The pronounced white streak on the left of his widow's peak and his rugged features kept him a shade short of blindingly handsome. Not perfect, but he was a man who turned heads when he walked by. Everyone noticed John, men and women alike. His sweet demeanor added to his allure.

"What brings you all to George's tonight?" I asked Deborah and her husband, as if I wanted to know, when what I really wanted was for them to leave before George noticed their presence.

CHAPTER FOUR

Tampa, Florida
Friday 6:30 p.m.
January 21, 2000

DEBORAH AND ANDY STOOD close together holding hands, as if they were young lovers, not a couple who had been married over thirty years. Perhaps the rumors I'd heard about Deborah's alcoholism threatening their marriage were untrue.

Andy looked as ramrod stiff as I'd seen him on television. Deborah wore an old-fashioned blue shift and her hair, a pageboy parted on one side and held in place by an inexpensive plastic barrette, looked exactly as it must have been styled at age six by her mother.

"There's no better restaurant in Tampa than George's for a special occasion," Deborah said with her typical sincerity. "It's Andy's birthday." Her soft drawl was pleasant to my ear.

Deborah was every southern boy's fantasy wife, if the boy was of a certain age. A quiet woman, born and bred in South Georgia, she was a genuine southern belle who never said a negative word about anyone. It wouldn't be possible to dislike Deborah, even if I'd had a reason to do so. She was simply too kind for the harsh world she inhabited.

"We also thought we'd celebrate the end of those damn committee hearings," Andy said to me, as he smoothed his red striped tie over his flat stomach and closed the middle button of his navy sport coat. "I'm glad to be through with that inquisition. Next week the committee will vote and then the full senate. I should be on the job in no time at all." His confidence was solid as steel. He smiled directly toward me. "We'll have a chance to work together, Willa."

The words made my heart stop. Work with Andrews? There were very few things in the world I'd like less, based on what I'd learned over the past few weeks. There seemed to be nothing upon which we might agree. A working relationship between us would be a daily battle that would quickly escalate to a full-scale war that would make my daily skirmishes with the CJ seem even more childish.

Craig Hamilton's shooting proved that at least some of the lunatic fringe believed Andrews was about to be the next Supreme Court Justice, shifting the balance of power on the court to unacceptable levels. The little I knew about the behind-the-scenes work George had been doing told me Andrews's nomination was far from certain to be confirmed.

Then again, the latest polls suggested public opinion was still solidly on his side.

I searched my conscience for the right response but could come up with nothing suitable. I changed the subject. "I'm looking forward to the Blue Coat tomorrow," I said, referring to the charity golf tournament held each year in Andrews's name.

He gave me the same comic look I'd seen him use in response

to Senator Warwick's questions before he responded, letting me know he wasn't fooled by my tactics, either. "We should have a good crowd and it's a worthy cause."

The hostess appeared and we said our goodbyes. She led them into the main dining room. I watched heads turn as polite diners sneaked covert glances at the man who might be the next Supreme Court Justice.

Pondering Andy's self-deception, I collected my weighty briefcase filled with weekend work and walked up the winding, open stairs to our flat before someone else could stop me.

I pushed open the heavy oak door with my hip and walked into our living room and on through to the den. I dropped the heavy briefcase next to the floral needlepointed seat cushion of one of Aunt Minnie's harp-back chairs. I wouldn't lift the case again until Sunday and I glared at the file I knew was contained inside, Nelson Newton v. The Whitman Esquire Review.

I resented spending my Sunday on a case that, to my mind, was a serious misuse of the judicial process and never should have been filed in the first place. I had tried every way I could think of to settle the matter. Unfortunately, Mr. Newton didn't need the money and was interested in clearing his name. Name clearing was not an appropriate use of our limited judicial resources.

Litigants who believe it's the principle of the thing are the bane of my existence. American jurisprudence today is not about the principle of the thing. The system is overworked, overcrowded and overcommitted to handling cases that are about real injustice and real damages. We don't have time for the principle of the thing. The principle of the thing is to settle your own petty grievances and stay out of my courtroom.

Harry and Bess, our two Labrador retrievers were lying on the kitchen floor, and didn't bother to raise their heads when I came through the door.

"Can you tell by my footfalls that I'm not a burglar, or what?" I chastised them. Harry looked at me with one yellow eyebrow raised. Bess started to get up, but then she thought better of it and lay back down again.

"Nice to see you, too," I said, opening the freezer for the Bombay Sapphire to go with cold tonic and sliced lemons. I added ice and took my drink out to the veranda along with my first Partagas of the day. The remnants of a fabulous sunset settled above the waters of Hillsborough Bay.

The Partagas was the last of the limited reserves George bought me for Christmas and I'd been saving it for a special occasion. I looked at it, smelled it, tasted it, and considered whether fifteen dollars was just too extravagant for a cigar that would go up in smoke.

According to the propaganda, Partagas cigars come from the Dominican Republic and are made from Cuban tobacco. Hand-rolled and aged until just the right flavor could be experienced. It was the aging, along with the Cuban tobacco, that made the limited reserves special. I should quit, of course, but I long ago gave up trying to overcome my vices. How many vices I had depended on whom you asked.

I held the cigar between my thumb and forefinger, sipped my drink and thought about whether I really wanted to smoke this last one. George had bought a box of the limited reserves for me when we'd visited the Dominican last winter. The evening he'd given them to me had been a wonderful one.

I closed my eyes and allowed a flood of desire to overwhelm me as I remembered dancing in the moonlight, exquisite port after dinner, great sex later. The erotic vision reminded me of how special my husband was to me, how much I had missed him lately. After all these years, he was still the one. I couldn't imagine my life without him, and I wouldn't try.

George came up behind and gently put one hand over each of my eyes. Sounding more like speedy Gonzales, he said, "Ah, my leetle one. How can one so beeyouteeful be so alone?" George's fun-loving side has faded in the last seventeen years, but a couple of drinks still bring out the best in him.

Eyes still closed, "I used to have a lover, but he left me for a Democrat," I told him, not so tongue-in-cheek.

George bent down to give me a soul-shattering kiss that effectively silenced my complaints and left me hungry for more.

When he raised his head, he said, "Hitting below the belt, Willa. You of all people should know how important this nomination is. The Democrats have had too many federal court appointments in the past few years. Even suggesting that Andy can replace such a great conservative is just an outrage."

His Glenfiddich on the rocks firmly in hand, George sat down in the wicker rocker next to mine. He was dressed in a suit and tie, which meant my fantasy of a quiet evening at home was going up in smoke faster than the unlit Partagas. An involuntary groan escaped my lips, still tingling from the kiss.

George leaned over with a lighter and I put the cigar to my mouth. If I couldn't relax tonight, I really deserved this special treat, I decided.

"Craig Hamilton is recovering. They expect to release him from the hospital tomorrow." I told him after a silence punctuated with a good deal of puffing.

He bristled. "I'm really sorry for Craig, but I don't for a minute feel any responsibility, if that's what you're suggesting." He sipped. "If the nuts are excited to violence by the hearings, you can imagine what they might do if Andy's actually confirmed."

He was so touchy lately, my least misstatement angered him. I'd become tentative, wanting to avoid the explosions. But I had my own views, too.

"What is your side doing to make sure that nothing worse will happen?"

"What are we supposed to do? Advertise? Tell people to write their senators instead of shooting the guy?"

I didn't have the energy to debate the issues again, but I did believe the Republicans had been whipping up the fringe, not trying to assure them that the process would work without resorting to violence.

Saving that debate for later in the weekend, I braced myself for bad news and asked instead, "Why are you all dressed up?"

"I'm meeting Jason downstairs for dinner in a few minutes. You might want to join us." He must have sensed my instinctive refusal because his tone softened and he added, "You don't see Jason very often and I don't know when he'll be in town again."

Jason Austin's mother, Kate, took me in when my own mother died and my stepfather couldn't face life without mom. I was only sixteen then, a time that seemed light years ago.

Did I want to have dinner with George and Jason? I was ambivalent about the idea. I literally felt my head wagging back and forth, like the cartoons I watched as a child, as if I had an angel on one shoulder and a devil on the other, while I considered my answer.

It's true that I don't see Jason often, and I do enjoy his company, the angel pointed out. But he makes me tired, the devil responded. Jason's brand of brilliance is a struggle to be around and I didn't really feel up to it tonight.

Conversations with Jason involve only important matters; he thinks his work is vital to the world; the trivial has no place in

Jason Austin's life. Even trivial things like family. Jason lives in Jason's world. The rest of the 270 million people in this country live somewhere else.

If he wasn't the closest thing I had to an older brother, I wouldn't have been able to stand him.

Jason also happens to be the chief counsel to the Senate Judiciary Committee the committee responsible for Andrews's confirmation hearings. I'd seen him on television yesterday, sitting at the right hand of his boss, Senator Sheldon Warwick.

Part of my ambivalence was that I knew Jason was here to discuss politics with George and I'd had enough of that. I needed a break.

Still, the angel won the argument. Before George left, I told him I'd shower and join them downstairs. Otherwise, I'd be dining alone in my flat, again. I'd been alone enough lately. Obviously, my husband wasn't going to return to me, so it was up to me to join him.

I savored my cigar, finished my drink and undressed as I headed in toward the shower. I glanced longingly at my oversized bathtub. When we renovated Aunt Minnie's house, we added closets to replace the old wardrobes, and expanded the bathrooms and bedrooms. We replaced the plumbing, but I insisted on keeping the mammoth, claw-footed tub.

I loved that tub. It was a place to soak my cares away.

But I knew that if I got into the tub that night, I'd never get out. So I took an invigorating ginseng gel shower instead and tried to convince myself that I still had some energy left.

I dried my hair (two minutes), put on my face (three minutes) and slipped into a wine silk pantsuit with a cream chemise and low-heeled sandals (one minute). No jewelry. George says I'm fast, for a woman.

As I looked at my reflection in the full-length mirror, I noticed

I could have used a little more concealer for the shadows under my eyes. I reached for the tube, but then threw it back in the drawer. No amount of makeup would conceal those circles.

Glancing at the clock on my way out, I saw that it was just barely nine o'clock. Maybe I'd get to bed before midnight, with any luck.

I stopped on the landing to lock the door and then turned around to look into the foyer of the restaurant below. Peter, George's maître d', stood near the exit, chatting with a departing couple. Peter appeared enraptured by whatever the portly gentleman was saying while he simultaneously gave his attention to the man's equally well-fed wife. Both gazed at Peter as if they wanted to take him home and fatten him up.

Tampa's oldest five-star restaurant has been trying to woo Peter away from George for years. A Kentucky restaurant even sent Peter a racehorse for Christmas last year. He rejected all offers. He was devoted to George and Minaret. Peter would never work anywhere else. Of course, I think Peter is already employed at the epitome of his chosen field. Not that I'm biased.

I walked slowly down the stairs, watched the guests, and looked anew at Aunt Minnie's tastefully decorated foyer. When she lived here, the house was her private home and these were her secretaries, breakfronts and sideboards. Even the small butler's table and the upholstered loveseats in the center were hers. The soft blue fleur-de-lis wallpaper duplicated hers in gilded excellence.

Would Aunt Minnie be pleased to have her beautiful things returned to usefulness or horrified that strangers came into her home for lunch and dinner seven days a week?

It didn't matter. Without the restaurant, we couldn't afford to keep the house. Aunt Minnie, to the extent her ghost might still be with us, would just have to cope, I thought, as I made my way toward the dining room.

CHAPTER FIVE

I PASSED THROUGH THE foyer and waved to Peter over the heads of the departing oversized guests. The restaurant owner's wife has certain obligations that I preferred to ignore tonight, but when I was present here, I had to play the role. Most of the time, I enjoyed it.

Standing in the doorway to the main dining room for a few seconds, I was able to draw strength to pass the gauntlet of diners between here and George and Jason's far corner table.

When I surveyed the room, I noticed a number of familiar faces, not all of them welcome ones. Inhaling courage, I stepped cautiously into the fishbowl, feeling a little like a criminal in a lineup, knowing all eyes would be cast my way, making judgments.

At the Andrews's table, no one seemed to be having a very good time. Deborah threw me a beseeching glance. I hardened my heart, smiled encouragement, and kept going.

Further on, I nodded to Senator and Tory Warwick, who were eating alone at a window table overlooking the garden. My initial thought was: Why are they here?

Tory had on a red, low-cut dress by a certain designer she's favored since her breast implant surgery enhanced her figure a few months ago. I hoped she would behave herself tonight.

Senator Warwick himself looked very stylish in a gray cashmere suit, pink silk tie and the black, reverse calf, bench made shoes that are his trademark. The first time I'd seen the shoes, I'd wanted a pair for myself, until I found out what they cost. They looked like comfortable Hush Puppies to me, but Jason assures me there's a huge difference. I suspect most of the voters think they look like Hush Puppies, too, which may be the point.

"The fact is you have to be rich or have a well-employed, working spouse to be able to afford the job of civil servant," Jason had told me. Although we both knew that politicians act like champions of the poor and average income people because more of those folks vote.

I passed a few more tables and only had to stop briefly to speak to one other local couple before I finally reached George and Jason. I felt like I'd just crossed Times Square on New Year's Eve, or Ybor City's Seventh Avenue on any given Saturday night, weaving through close crowds, seeking a safe haven.

Jason stood and leaned over so he could give me a light, polite, southern hug. Kind of a lean across the body and a small pat on the upper back. This pseudo hug is the southern equivalent of the New York cheek-to-air kiss, I guess. It took me the longest time to get used to the gesture when we moved here from Detroit years ago. Jason is no more southern than I am. Maybe since a southern Democrat controlled the White House, the hug had become a politically correct Washington thing.

"Hey, Willa, you look great, as always," he lied.

I wondered when Jason had learned to lie so smoothly and why he was lying to me now. Was he so oblivious to my troubled appearance? Or did he simply not care? I thought I knew Jason well. Maybe not. Maybe none of us really knows another. Or ourselves for that matter. With renewed objectivity, I examined him closely.

Jason is a solid, dependable-looking man. He's average: average height (5'10"), average coloring (brown hair, hazel eyes) and an average dresser (Brooks Brothers). Actually, on the dressing thing, he could get the same suits at Stein Mart for half the price, if he had more imagination.

"Thanks," I said, kissing him on the cheek. Then, seeking to encourage more candor, I told him, "You look as tired as I feel. Don't you ever get a break?"

He failed to take the opportunity I offered. "When I accepted the job, the title sounded so good, I just thought it would improve my resume." More lies. Jason had never leapt without looking in his life and I knew he hadn't done so when he accepted the job of chief counsel to the senate judiciary committee at Senator Sheldon Warwick's request. My radar, already up and humming, sharpened considerably.

Jason had worked as Warwick's aide for the previous ten years. The chief counsel position was a promotion, of sorts, and for a politically ambitious man like Jason, a very powerful post. His ability to participate in and influence the selection of judges who might serve on the courts of the United States for the next twenty years was more than just a resumé builder.

Before we could sit down again, Frank Bennett, one of our local television anchors, approached our table. Ignoring the kick I gave him under the table, George invited Frank to join us. It seemed everyone who had gathered in Tampa for tomorrow's Blue Coat golf tournament had planned dinner here first. But then, George's was the best restaurant in town. Where else would they go? Maybe for the first time ever, I wished George owned a waffle house.

Once we were all seated, Jason asked, "How'd you get the night off, Frank? It's a busy time for you reporters, with the nomination and the assassination attempt and all." His tone implied annoyance, or maybe something closer to anger.

"I covered all that at six," Frank responded. "I'm working on the President's trip to Tampa later tonight. I thought if I came over here, you or George might give me something I can use for the eleven o'clock news." Frank looked around, then said, "It was just luck to find all the main players in the Andrews debacle in the same dining room."

Luck had nothing to do with it. The local media, like everyone else, knew Washington-based Tampa residents had planned to play in the Blue Coat charity golf tournament tomorrow. But someone must have tipped him off that all of them were sitting in this one dining room. I don't believe in coincidence.

"Wait a second," I said. "Why is the President in town? Didn't anybody stay in Washington this weekend?"

"Apparently not. They just moved the judiciary committee here, I'd say." Frank glanced around the room and let his gaze rest pointedly on General Andrews's table and then Warwick's.

George and Jason exchanged a look I couldn't decipher and George said, "You'd better not have a camera in here, Frank," with the sternness he usually reserves for misbehaving Labradors.

"Of course not." Frank managed to sound wounded before he grinned. "I got the footage when everyone crossed the bridge as they arrived. The camera crew is still over there, waiting for the departures. Where we can bombard them with questions." He stopped a beat for effect. "We wouldn't think of bringing a camera in here."

"This is private property, Frank," I reminded him.

"Is it? I thought it was a public restaurant." Frank said too sweetly, before he turned to Jason. "Hasn't anyone told your boss that he and the nominee are on the same team? Warwick and the other Dems seem to be going out of their way to make George's team the winner here."

Jason looked down at his heavy crystal wine glass, studying the circles the red wine had made on the cream damask tablecloth. He seemed to be considering Frank's question, but probably was only timing his answer.

Senator Warwick and the other Democrats on the Judiciary Committee had been openly hostile to Andrews's nomination on national television for the past three weeks. Yesterday's questioning was the topper. Every news reporter had made more than one comment about it on every newscast, news magazine or teaser since the televised hearings began.

Jason must have strategized a well-prepared response, although he acted as if he was thinking about it for the first time.

The curious thing was that the committee's hostility hadn't dented Andrews's popularity in the daily and weekly polls that controlled everything in political America now.

Like everything else inside the beltway, I viewed this as one great political game that usually made me yawn. If General Andrews got Borked, the insiders' euphemism for a nominee being attacked and rejected by the committee instead of being submitted to the full senate, the story would be over.

And it was all old ground between George and Jason. They'd argued every angle endlessly for weeks now. My interest had long since evaporated.

But Frank was still looking for his sound bite. The trick to dealing with the media is to ignore what they ask you and answer their questions with what you want them to repeat. Jason had lots of experience at this and finally delivered what I was sure he'd planned to say all along, something he knew Frank would air. "Senator Warwick supports the President, Frank," Jason said. "What the President wants, we aim to deliver."

Both Frank and George seemed satisfied with that, which was curious, I thought at the time. But I noticed that Jason didn't say what the President wanted them to deliver.

After Frank left us, he stopped briefly at Warwick's table and then the general's. The tension in the room was as thick as concrete.

George said, "Why don't we talk about something besides politics?" He flashed a wicked grin. "Jason, anything new on the romance front?"

Jason smiled wanly and I laughed at their antics, even though I knew they were purposely designed to relax us all.

"Way to go, George," Jason quipped back, "Choose a comfortable, non-controversial topic, why don't you?"

Jason's bad luck in love was a family joke. He always seemed to choose the wrong woman, one way or another. He kept us amused with his self-deprecating accounts of failed relationships for the next hour while we consumed the heavenly cuisine for which diners are willing to pay George's exorbitant prices.

We ordered the chef's special Grilled Beef Tenderloin with Marsala Mushroom Sauce, Roasted Garlic and Brie Soup and dill bread. By the time we got to the Coconut Cardamom Custard Tart with Oven-roasted Bananas, our fatigue and all bad humor had completely dissipated. Even the tension seemed a little lighter. Anger starves on heavenly food.

"Coffee and cigars on the veranda of the Sunset Bar?" George suggested. When I hesitated, he added to entice me, "It'll be quieter. And there's a full moon tonight casting a shimmering trail over the water."

We started toward the door, coincidentally following Senator Warwick and his wife, Tory. The Warwicks didn't see us and we were about to pass safely out of the dining room, when they made a tactical error. Warwick turned to avoid a tray sitting in the aisle and walked within six feet of the Andrews's dinner table.

That was when General Andrews glanced up and saw us. He raised his voice almost to the shouting point. "I'd sneak on by if I were you, too, Sheldon. You've always been a coward."

Senator Warwick, perpetually cognizant of his public image, said, "Andy, now is neither the time nor place to discuss this. Why don't you come by the house in the morning and we'll talk about it." That was the wrong tone to take with a general, even a retired one, and apparently the wrong thing to say as well.

Andrews's next statement was even louder. "Sure, Sheldon. Then you can blow smoke up my ass in private instead of saying whatever it is you have to say in front of everyone here."

Abruptly, Andrews rose, knocking the chair over backward as he stood. He threw his napkin down on the table by his plate and started to move toward Warwick, who was now almost all the way past the table.

"It hasn't bothered you to attack me in front of the entire country in those damn hearings you're heading up. Why should it bother you to have it out, here and now?"

Deborah Andrews placed a restraining hand on her husband's arm, but he shook it off.

"This doesn't concern you, Deborah," he snarled.

"Do you want to step outside, Senator, and settle it right

now?" General Andrews challenged, his chin high, with the air of a man accustomed to fighting his battles with his fists.

There was no way Sheldon Warwick could beat Andrews, if it came to that. I noticed Tory Warwick's nostrils flair and her eyebrows come together over her perfectly sculpted nose. Tory was the wildcat, everybody knew. She'd been raising hell in Tampa all her life.

By this time, we had reached the Andrews table and both George and Jason tried to calm things down while all eyes in the crowded restaurant watched the show. George walked toward Andrews and Jason approached his boss.

Deborah's eyes had widened to the size of cornflower blue saucers. She'd be blaming herself for this, I knew. Deborah believed everything her husband did was her fault. The twelve step program she'd completed hadn't been able to change her basic personality.

Calmly, quietly, George said, "Gentlemen, please. You're upsetting my guests. Why don't we just—"

Before George could work his magic, Tory Warwick had had more than enough. I glanced up and noticed Frank Bennett standing in the doorway, taking it all in.

Which is why I didn't see Tory Warwick reach over, pick up a full lead crystal water glass, draw back and throw it with all her strength at General Andrews. If she'd hit him, it would have knocked him cold, she'd thrown the heavy glass with the force she'd perfected as the baseball pitcher she'd been in college.

Unfortunately, Tory's aim wasn't improved by her alcohol consumption and she missed. The next thing I knew, I was flat on my butt on the floor.

Tory didn't knock me out, but I definitely felt dazed. I reached up and felt the tender spot on my forehead, just in front of my right temple. A small "Oh," slipped from my lips. My first thought was how Frank Bennett would report this scene on the eleven o'clock news. At least it wasn't on film.

The spot swelled rapidly. Someone handed me a linen dinner napkin filled with ice. I couldn't open my eyes because the subdued light in the dining room was blinding.

There was nothing wrong with my ears, though. I heard George shouting. In public. Angrier than I'd ever witnessed. Through my slitted eyelids, I saw George's red face as he gave Andrews a push toward the door that landed Andrews against Warwick and nearly knocked them both down on the floor next to me.

"Get out! Get out right now and don't any of you attempt to come back here! Andrews, Warwick, I'm disgusted with both of you!"

Andrews reached for his wallet, but George waved him away. "Forget the checks, just leave. And do not try to make a reservation here again."

George turned to his maître d'. "Peter, these people are leaving and they are not to return. Ever."

The Andrews family hurried to rise and leave the table, glancing down my way. Tory tried to reach me to apologize, but Jason grabbed her arm and pulled her toward the exit.

George bent down to me then. "Are you all right?"

Still feeling dazed, I tried to get up, glad I'd worn pants tonight and wasn't sitting with my legs splayed open in front of half of Tampa.

"It was an accident. Tory meant to hit Andrews," I said.

This made George even angrier. I guess it would have been okay if she'd been trying to hit me. Go figure.

Peter ushered the Andrewses and the Warwicks out and Frank Bennett followed them. He must have been tickled pink to have been witness to a brawl involving high level politicians in Tampa's classiest restaurant.

Tory tried to reach me again. "I'm so sorry, Willa," she apologized while Jason kept moving her toward the door.

CHAPTER SIX

Tampa, Florida
Friday 11:10 p.m.
January 21, 2000

PETER RETURNED AND BEGAN to placate the remaining diners, who were openly staring now. I heard him offer apologies and a dessert of their choice, compliments of the house.

After a while, I could stand up without feeling too dizzy. We walked over to the Sunset Bar, the big white ice-filled dinner napkin pressed against the rising lump on my forehead, George holding one elbow and Jason close beside me.

"I cannot believe that woman," George sputtered, although his color had returned to normal.

"You know she wasn't herself," Jason soothed.

George wouldn't be calmed. "So when she's herself, I suppose her aim is better? Then she could have beaned the next justice of the Supreme Court? That's just great, Jason. Just great."

"What do you want Sheldon to do? He can't hang around at home with her every night he's in Tampa and he lives in D.C. as much as possible," Jason retorted. His defense of Warwick was nothing if not consistent.

"Well, they can both go somewhere else to eat from now on. And I don't need that hothead Andrews in here, either. Tory wouldn't have thrown the glass at him if he hadn't started a fight. I meant it when I said neither one of them is welcome here again." He turned toward me, his anger renewed by the sight. "If Willa's seriously hurt, it'll be worse than that. For both of them."

George seemed really pissed, and it scared me. He rarely displayed a temper. My husband is the most civilized man I know.

To my George, violence is a bad thunderstorm. Who was this testosterone-laden, protective male next to me, anyway?

I felt as if my entire world had become a strange foreign land where I didn't understand the language or the customs and from which I might never emerge. My eyes started to tear. Great. Just great.

Judges don't cry, I told myself.

I blinked back the water and took a deep breath.

"Look," I said. "You two need to calm down. Everybody's gone now. I'm still living. And I'm thirsty. Where's that drink and cigar you promised me?"

They gave up their bickering reluctantly. The passion they'd both been feeling over Andrews's confirmation was intense. The steam had blown past their control here tonight, but the controversy was still boiling under the lid, threatening to spill over again if we dropped our guard for more than a few seconds.

I fingered the tender lump on my forehead, now about the size of a small spoon bowl. It would look awful in the morning. How in the name of heaven did I ever get involved in such a mess?

George and Jason had calmed down but they didn't pretend to

be interested in anything else now. They took up the political discussion they'd wanted to have at dinner but hadn't been willing to risk being overheard.

"How is the committee vote going to go? Any idea?" George asked, anger still heating his tone.

Jason visibly resisted a sharp retort and replied, "Some of the senators have declared themselves already. Some did it in their opening statements and others have formed their opinions during the questioning."

"Do you know?" George demanded. "Or not?"

Jason gave him a look that would have quelled a lesser adversary. "There are still enough that are at least undeclared to make it a horse race. Right now, I'm not sure how it will go. Fifty-fifty, maybe."

"What does Warwick think? He's the chair of the judiciary committee. He has some influence," George said with exaggerated irony.

"He has a lot of influence," Jason snapped. "But the Democrats are not the only ones who have a say in this."

"You can't seriously think any elected Republican would cast a vote for that ignoramus," George shot back.

I felt a little like a spectator at a wrestling match. Jason must have known more than he was willing to share with George, and George was determined to find out what Jason knew.

My head really started to throb. I hoped that, eventually, this too would pass. I had committed to the golf tournament tomorrow and I didn't want to cancel over a headache. I called it a night and left them deep into their argument. When I went up to bed, they hardly noticed.

I should have stayed up for the late news, just to see how bad Frank Bennett's report really was, but I couldn't face it. The story would be repeated *ad nauseum* anyway. Bad news usually gets worse in the night.

I hate thinking I'm powerless over events like what happened in the restaurant tonight, even though I know I can't control everything and especially can't control everyone. If George had wanted me to know what was going on in his political scheming, I realized he'd have told me long before that Friday. I fell into troubled sleep, promising myself that I'd fix everything tomorrow, which never works.

CHAPTER SEVEN

Tampa, Florida
Saturday 6:00 a.m.
January 22, 2000

THE ALARM WENT OFF at six o'clock. When I rolled over to turn it off and snuggle up to George for a few more winks, my hand felt only the cold, empty sheets on his side of the bed.

George never gets up before six o'clock. We're both owls. We detest those bright-eyed larks with their worm fetish.

No matter. I snuggled down into the covers instead.

The confirmation hearings were over. Our lives would return to normal today. We had survived George's single-minded pursuit of Andrews's defeat.

With the release of all that tension, perhaps George just couldn't sleep and I'd find him in the kitchen. I sniffed the air but couldn't smell an aroma of brewing coffee.

An uneasy feeling crept into my body but I pushed it away with the covers.

In the bathroom, through tired eyes, I examined the big purple egg on my forehead where Tory Warwick's glass missile had hit me. In total denial of the pain in my head, I shrugged into my running clothes. With Harry and Bess at my heels, I shuffled through to the kitchen, planning to tell George where I was going. He wasn't there.

Harry and Bess refused to tell me where he'd gone, but there were only so many places he could be. Not too worried, I expected to find him outside on the veranda with his newspapers.

When I glanced up at the clock, I realized I had only about an hour to get ready for the golf tournament today, so the dogs and I rushed down the back stairs to the beach.

Harry and Bess ran way ahead of me. When I'm in good form, I do an entire lap around our island. Sometimes two laps. Other days, I just do half a lap and take a golf cart back. Today would be a quick mile. It was all the time I had.

When I started to run, I began to feel better. A lot of people run just for exercise, hating every minute of it. For me, though, it's a spiritual experience. I love the sand, the water, the sunshine and the companionship I get from Harry and Bess. After years of running, I'm able to get to the runner's high in about fifteen minutes and it carries me the remainder of the run. Sometimes, I have to consciously bring myself to stop.

By the time we returned to the house, huffing and puffing, I was sweating like an NBA player in the final two minutes. I jumped into the bay with Harry and Bess to cool off. This is the part they like the best because they get to submerge me and each other ten or twenty times before I'm completely exhausted and give up.

Our Labradors, Harry and Bess, are littermates, even though Harry's yellow and Bess is black. They were very cute puppies, obnoxious adolescents and now, the equivalent of twenty-something adults. They are a joy to be around and we love them both in place of children: We don't have to pay for college and we'd likely get arrested for putting kids in a cage. That, and being childless has made our marriage seem more like a long honeymoon. Until the Andrews's hearings, I reminded myself. But those hearings were over now. The realization made my heart sing.

The dogs and I got out of the salty water and rinsed off at the outdoor shower. I left them in their kennel to dry off while I trudged up the back stairs. Now, they would wait patiently until after my shower for their breakfast.

Even with the bruised lump on my forehead, everything about the morning was so blessedly normal, except that I still hadn't found George.

I started Cuban coffee before I headed to the shower. When I came out, dressed in purple and jade plaid crop pants and a jade golf shirt, not wanting my clothes to detract from the lovely purple color of the egg on my forehead, my coffee was ready.

Where could George have gone, so early in the morning? I had no idea. I glanced at my watch. No more time to wait. I called the dogs to eat, filled a travel cup with coffee, let myself out of the house and went down to Greta, my car. Unlike my husband, I could always count on Greta being exactly where I left her.

It was still early enough that dew on the St. Augustine grass and bright pink, red, purple, white and melon colored impatiens gave the morning a crystalline shimmer. As I drove Greta out from the circle in front of Minaret, the sun softly lightened the sky over the Port of Tampa and Harbour Island to the east.

Why would anyone live in Florida without a convertible? In a convertible, you experience all of the gloriousness Florida weather has to offer. I have discussed this, over wine of course, with a number of native Floridians. Sometimes they say they never had a desire for a convertible until they owned one, or rented one, or took a ride with a friend. Once exposed, they're all hooked.

But how could you not know that being outside, able to feel the warmth of Florida living, would be glorious?

Oh, convertibles can be noisy. The tops get worn and have to be replaced periodically. In the old days, they used to leak. But now the only real drawback is that you can't have rain gutters over the windows. Given the amount of rain we get in Florida in the summer, that can be a serious drawback for people who frequent drive-through windows.

But otherwise, is there any choice really between a stodgy old Rolls Royce and the least expensive convertible? Sport utility vehicles? Give me a break.

My spirits lifted with every minute we spent outside, as Greta and I headed across the Plant Key Bridge toward the Bayshore. The sun sparkled on Hillsborough Bay while two dolphins, swimming side by side, raced Greta and me the length of the bridge. They won. It was glorious. I've always loved mornings. It's just that George and I usually sleep through them.

The short drive from Plant Key to Great Oaks golf course took me east on Bayshore Boulevard and into the old Palma Ceia section of town where the large, plantation style clubhouse and a beautiful thirty-six-hole golf course was nestled in the center of South Tampa.

In another month, early morning golf would be pleasant. But now, in January, the temperature was just a little cool. Our tee time was seven forty-two. We would finish our eighteen holes before noon. We play a scramble, which means all four golfers hit the ball at every hole and then we choose the best ball.

In theory a scramble speeds up play and all teams achieve a good score. For a social event like this one, it was a good idea. But in reality, four golfers have to have a conference over every hole and the decisions that eventually get made are not always quick or conflict free.

The event was already going strong when I arrived and let the valet park my car. I went into the locker room to collect my shoes and met my friend and playing partner, Mitch Crosby, outside. Mitch and a few other golfers had gathered around waiting for General Andrews, the guest of honor, to give the opening speech.

According to the posted schedule, our group would be the fifth foursome off, after General Andrews's, our local State Attorney Drake's, Senator Warwick's and the Mayor's foursomes. I was glad two foursomes would be between us and Drake. He was one of the most obnoxiously ambitious men I'd ever met. Two foursomes ahead of us, we'd never have to make small talk with him.

We were standing around, trying to stay warm, when one of the waiting golfers said, "Where's George, Willa? I thought he'd come out for the opening. He's usually here."

Pride kept me from admitting that I had no idea where my usually solid, supportive husband had gone.

"Maybe he went jogging." I said the first thing that popped into my mind without thinking that George hates jogging and everyone knows it. Everybody laughed.

"Sure," one of the guys joked. "What's her name and how long has George been seeing her?"

They laughed again at my expense, while I squirmed. The teasing continued until someone raised a topic that turned the conversation and removed George's whereabouts from the spotlight, allowing my bright red face to settle back down to its normal pale pink tone.

Taking advantage of the reprieve, I spoke to my playing

partner. "I can't believe I agreed to team up with those two today, Mitch. What was I drinking when you got me to consent to this?" I asked him. I continued to sip the coffee I'd brought from home, which had finally cooled enough not to burn the hair off my tongue.

Mitch and I were playing today with Dr. Marilee Aymes, one of my personal favorites. The fourth member of our group, though, was Christian Grover, a local lawyer who causes me an everlasting stomachache, and everybody knows that, too.

"I thought maybe your consent had something to do with that pretty blue egg on your forehead. Like you were deranged or something," Mitch grinned. "What happened to you?"

"I had the misfortune to be near Tory Warwick's flying Waterford last night," I said, as I gently patted the lump. "And it's purple. Matches my shirt."

"Flying Waterford is a natural hazard around her, all right. I should have recognized the imprinted pattern. Lismore, isn't it?" Mitch gave me a glance filled with mock concern as he wiggled his eyebrows.

"Smart ass," I smiled.

We kept up like this as we checked our bags and cart, found our specially marked balls and prepared to tee off as soon as we were given permission. The other foursomes were milling around, too. The opening ceremony was already a half-hour late.

CHAPTER EIGHT

Tampa, Florida
Saturday 8:30 a.m.
January 22, 2000

FINALLY, SOMEONE APPROACHED THE microphone and said we'd begin without the opening remarks today because General Andrews hadn't yet arrived. They moved the general's foursome back in line and the second group hurried to tee off.

Rumors that General Andrews was with President Benson, who might be joining us, quickly buzzed through the waiting golfers. But by the time our foursome was set to start, neither General Andrews nor the President had arrived.

In two separate carts, we waited our turn at the first tee. Marilee Aymes, a sixty-something cardiologist here in town, sat with Grover. I could hear her lighting into him before we even got started.

Whatever bad karma had given me these two as playing partners, it was worse for both of them. Unlike oil and water, it didn't appear they could be mixed into suspension of hostilities, even for a good cause and a relatively short time.

"Grover, have you ever played with these clubs before?" Marilee chided him. "They look like something you bought off an infomercial advertised by Suzanne Somers."

"Just because I'm not a golfer, Dr. Aymes, doesn't mean I'm an idiot," he responded. "Who would buy golf clubs from Suzanne Somers? With her chest, there's no way I could get the same angle on the ball."

Mitch put his hand up over his mouth to cover his smile. I grinned openly. The day promised laughter, something I'd missed lately. This tournament might turn out even better than I'd hoped.

Up at the tee, Mitch hit his first drive of the day about 220 yards, long for him and a good start for the team. I went next, then Marilee and finally Grover.

We were required to take everyone's tee shot once each nine holes. I prayed Grover would be able to hit his ball more than fifty yards at least once. He went up to the tee, stood looking over the ball and the fairway and finally, finally, hit the damn thing about three feet.

Mitch and I stifled our groans, got back into our cart and started off to find his ball, stopping on the way to pick up mine. As we headed down the cart path, we heard Marilee saying, "That's just great, Grover. Maybe we should get you some breast implants if you think it would help."

"I didn't think it was bad for the first ball I've ever hit," he said with mock innocence.

"You mean you've never played golf before in your life?" Marilee, a scratch golfer, was appalled. She'd sooner dine with gators.

"Nope. And I wanted to play with the best, so I paid extra to get teamed up with you," he grinned again.

I think I heard growling from Marilee, but maybe it was the cart engine. Mitch laughed out loud.

A few times in the first six holes, I shared a cart with Marilee Aymes, attempting to smooth the open hostility between her and Grover. Marilee was unpredictable and fun, but many people found her an unsuitable companion. Which was one of the reasons I liked her, even if her behavior was often outrageous.

On the fourth fairway, our talk turned to General Andrews and his nomination. All of Tampa had been discussing nothing else for weeks.

Marilee was angry over Craig Hamilton's shooting. "These anti-abortion nuts are getting to be a real problem, Willa. I've cut down my volunteer work at the free abortion clinic in the projects to one day a month. It's so unsafe now," Marilee told me.

"You're a cardiologist. Why are you volunteering at the abortion clinic?"

Marilee's tough exterior exuded indifference, but I knew her better than many people. Volunteering at a clinic was exactly the kind of thing she often did, but abortion was definitely out of her area.

"Somebody's got to do it," she said. "I mostly do the counseling and help out with the medical stuff if there's no one else. Some of these patients are so poor they can't feed themselves and the kids they've already got. I sympathize with them."

"It's a tough issue. I don't think I'd ever be able to get an abortion and I thank God I've never needed one," I told her.

"Amen," she said, in the first vaguely religious comment I've ever heard her make.

We reached the seventh hole with Grover never having hit another ball as well as his first three-foot drive. Marilee's patience stretched to the breaking point. When the drink cart came around, we took a break for cold water and sodas. It was about ten o'clock in the morning, maybe.

Grover ordered two beers and Marilee ordered scotch.

Mitch and I struggled not to laugh.

Mary Rose Campbell, the pretty, young drink cart driver who doubles as the club's barmaid told us that General Andrews had never arrived. They'd tried calling him for the past two hours, but got the answering machine. Someone had been sent out to his home to find him.

"No one can figure it out. Why, General Andrews hasn't missed a Blue Coat in ten years. What do you think happened to him?" Mary Rose said in her whispery little voice. She bent over to give the guys a good view of her rump while she dug down in the ice chest looking for Grover's beer.

Whether to tweak Marilee or because he really is grossly rude, Grover punched Mitch conspiratorially in the arm and said, "Don't you want to order a beer, too, Mitch? Sure improves the scenery."

Before anyone else could react, Marilee hauled off and punched Grover right in the jaw, knocking him onto the grass.

Howling, he grabbed his face and shouted that he'd sue her for battery.

It was the second time in less than twenty-four hours that I'd seen a mature woman act like an immature child. My mouth fell open in amazement.

"Kiss my grits," she said. She jumped into their cart and sped off.

Mary Rose Campbell seemed to have a great deal more sympathy for Grover's sore jaw, so we left Grover with her and the drink cart.

Mitch and I rode all the way to the eighth tee, but we couldn't hold back any longer. The morning had turned into a comic farce that lightened all of our spirits probably even Grover's. We laughed so hard we were holding our sides and trying not to wet our pants.

Marilee returned quickly with my brother, Jason, in her cart. When they drove up, she said, "Here's my new partner."

Then, she walked right up to the tee and hit the ball over 280 yards.

Jason leaned over and said, *sotto voce* to Mitch and me, "She just swooped into the clubhouse and grabbed me. Is now a good time to tell her I've never played golf before?"

Mitch's turn was next and he gathered enough composure to hit the ball in the right direction and then join Marilee in her cart. I managed about 150 yards and Jason, who I think was kidding about never having played golf before, at least made contact with the ball. Marilee snorted when Jason's ball landed about fifty yards out and took off with Mitch toward her ball, which was clearly the farthest drive.

That left me with Jason and Jason with Mitch's clubs. What a day. And we had eleven holes to go. The purple egg on my head started to throb as I took the wheel and headed off down the cart path.

"Did General Andrews ever show up?" I asked Jason.

"No, and we're all pretty worried about it," he said. "He doesn't answer his telephone and no one has seen or heard from him. They sent someone out to his house, but Andrews lives all the way out at Tampa Green, so it will take awhile to get there."

"Does Warwick know of any reason Andrews wouldn't show up? It's not like him to skip an event he's been sponsoring for years." I was a little worried, but not overly so. "Andrews told me last night he'd be here."

Jason looked away from me and denied having any inside

information, which I took to mean that he knew something he wasn't at liberty to divulge.

I respected Jason's confidential capacity as counsel to the Senate Judiciary Committee, but Andrews's private sponsorship of a golf tournament shouldn't have been an issue in his confirmation. There was no reason for secrecy.

"Are they worried about a repeat of yesterday's shooting?" I pressed him.

Jason seemed to consider his answers carefully.

"I don't think so. The local cops wanted to give him police protection, but the general refused. He's refused all extraordinary security measures, even though we've told him it's standard procedure for any nominee." He shook his head in disbelief. "Andrews says a U.S. Army four-star general can take care of himself. It would be nice if he'd start doing it."

"What do you mean?"

"We've all counseled him on how to get his nomination approved. But he just won't cooperate. He makes it damned difficult for the party to support him, even if he was the President's choice." Jason sounded disgusted, whether for the nominee, the President or the process, I wasn't sure.

"Despite what you told Frank Bennett last night, does the party want to support the President on this one?" I asked him. During the hearings, it seemed to me there was little about the process that was supportive of the President—or anyone else—but particularly General Andrews.

Jason looked at me shrewdly. "What have you heard from George about that, Willa?"

The question startled me. George was very highly placed in Republican circles but his influence with Democrats was non-existent. George thinks all Democrats are ideologically incompetent to sit on the Supreme Court, as he'd made plain to everyone he'd spoken to during the past few weeks, often to my complete mortification.

"What would George know about the Democrats' strategy? He'll barely talk to your boss on the street and he threw him out of our house last night."

One of the many subjects George and I disagree on is politics.

George is on top of all the issues, fully cognizant of the nuances of each. He's the only man I know, besides maybe Frank Bennett, who can identify all 100 senators and most congressmen by sight.

I, on the other hand, used to be able to identify both Florida senators and Sonny Bono. Since Sonny died, I'm down to two.

Jason shrugged, maybe a little too casually. "I'm sure you're right. It's just that there are so many rumors floating around Washington and George knows everything that happens. I thought maybe he'd told you."

"Told me what?"

I was really getting exasperated. If this cloak and dagger is how all of Washington works, no wonder they never get anything done.

Jason pretended to consider the question, stalling until we got to the ball and he could get out of the cart near the others so he wouldn't have to answer. When he tried to get into Marilee's cart afterward, I made it impossible. Unless he wanted to acknowledge that he was trying to ditch me, which would tell me something, too.

"I'm not going to let this drop, Jason, so you might as well tell me now," I said with the courtroom sternness I reserve for lawyers about to spend the night in jail for contempt.

"You know, you've always been so supremely stubborn." He

said it fondly. I think. "How much do you know about the history of Supreme Court appointments?"

"Very little. Why?"

"It's fascinating, really. For instance, did you know that when Taft was President, he was promised a Supreme Court appointment by Teddy Roosevelt in exchange for political support?" Jason asked. "Then, Roosevelt didn't live up to the bargain, so Taft asked President Harding to appoint him Chief Justice and Harding did it."

"You're right, Jason. That's just fascinatingly irrelevant. What does that bit of history have to do with Andrews?"

Strategies that worked in my courtroom were less effective on the golf course, but I had no way to force Jason or any other private citizen to tell me anything.

As if to underline my impotence, he ignored my question and asked one of his own. "Do you know how the selection process works?"

"Not really."

"When a Supreme Court Justice resigns, retires or dies, the President asks his chief of staff for nominees. The chief works with the Attorney General and White House Counsel on a list of potential candidates."

Hoping this was going somewhere, I murmured encouragement.

He continued, "A tentative choice is made and then the Chief of Staff asks key party senators for their views. The President usually talks to the opposing party whip, to judge the opposition." He must have sensed I was chafing with impatience. "It is a highly political process."

I gave him a small grin along with a dose of sarcasm. "Tell me something I don't know."

"The point is that the normal process wasn't followed in Andrews's case. None of us knew about his nomination until it happened."

I must have looked puzzled still, so he spelled it out for me. "The senators are not happy about that. It discounts their power. And it means none of their favorites got a chance."

"So the contentiousness, the hostility, is some sort of playground squabble between the big boys over who's more important?" I asked, not bothering to hide my disgust. The only difference between men and boys is the price of their toys and the size of their battles.

Jason sighed. "Partly. But it's more than that."

He waited a couple of seconds, as if he hadn't already made up his mind how much to tell me. "The rumor is that the President appointed Andrews because of some secret deal between them. President Benson's part of the deal was just to make the appointment. Which he did."

Jason took my arm to draw my glance toward him, briefly, before he told me something I should have guessed long ago. "The President doesn't want this nomination confirmed. Andrews will be too unpredictable once he gets on the bench."

It made sense, in a politics-as-usual way. If President Benson didn't want Andrews confirmed, that explained why the members of his own party had felt free to show open hostility to Andrews instead of closing the ranks to protect him.

"And what about Warwick? Where does he fit into all this?" I asked.

"Exactly where you'd think," Jason said, sounding indignant now, as if I should know that Warwick was above all reproach. "He's furious with the President. But he can't show that on national television."

Almost like a cartoon light bulb going off in my head, I finally got it.

"So Warwick's joined forces with George and the Republicans to defeat the nomination?" My incredulity was plain.

"Politics makes strange bedfellows, Willa. You know that." Jason was resigned and tired of talking about it. "Are you happy now that you know the whole story?"

The throbbing purple egg on my forehead seemed to mock me, pounding home my naiveté. "I don't know if I'm happy or not. It sounds like politics at its worst to me. What possible reason could there be for the President to ignore the best interests of the country and appoint Andrews in some sort of horse trade?"

"That would depend on what the trade was, wouldn't it?"

Now Jason just sounded tired. I noticed deep circles under his eyes suggesting he'd had another sleepless night.

It didn't occur to me to wonder what he'd been doing all night. He was resigned to see this thing through, but he didn't like it. Nor did I.

The rubber chicken lunch, served on the patio, was all the more unappetizing because Senator Warwick delivered the keynote speech.

The mayor's foursome won the tacky and cheap blue sport coats that were the first prize, along with bragging rights for the next year. Our group finished ten over par; not a stellar score for a scramble and we had no hope of winning, even after we applied Grover's big handicap.

As I exited the locker room a few minutes after the final awards were handed out, I felt all of the jocular energy in the club had shifted to something much more somber. The few people who remained were gathered around in small groups. The buzz of conversation was quiet, but anxious. I looked around for someone who could tell me what had happened, but everyone I knew well enough to trust had already left.

I glanced up and saw the television in the bar area, usually tuned to a sporting event, running a cable news bulletin, but I couldn't hear what was being said over the din of the crowd.

Men had bowed their heads. They were speaking to each other, with worried frowns on their faces. I saw a couple of women near the service station, including the pretty bar maid, Mary Rose Campbell, crying.

"What is it?" I asked someone standing next to me. I touched his arm and felt alarmed, absorbing the impact of the unnamed disaster through my senses. "What's going on?"

A man I recognized as a part of the Mayor's winning foursome, still wearing the tacky blue coat that was his trophy just an hour or so before, turned his now ashen face toward me and said, "General Andrews was found dead about eleven-thirty this morning."

I rushed out to my car and turned on the radio, where I hoped to get accurate information that I could understand. The story was to the point, but contained enough detail to make me realize that some investigation had been done before the information was released:

Tampa's first Supreme Court nominee, General Albert Andrews, is dead. The general apparently committed suicide, despondent over the course his confirmation hearings had taken and the shooting of his long time secretary, Craig Hamilton, Thursday.

Police Chief Ben Hathaway announced just a few minutes ago: "It appears that General Andrews shot himself early this morning. His body was found in his fishing boat on the small lake in back of his Tampa Green home."

Of course, the general was upset over the turn the hearings had taken. But enough for a man who'd fought and survived three wars to kill himself? How could this be true?

Tears sprang to my eyes as I thought instantly about Deborah's hopeful face when I first saw her last night. She and Andy had seemed so happy together then, before he'd made such a spectacle of them all and she'd looked so stricken.

How must she feel now? Wouldn't a wife see this coming? Had she?

A tear made its way down my cheek and I brushed it away.

Judges don't cry, I reminded myself, even in private.

And how could I be crying for Andrews anyway? I hadn't even liked the man.

I pulled over to turn down one of the side streets off the Bayshore and sat for several minutes. Exhaustion settled in on top of the pain in my head, to say nothing of the pain in my heart, the exact source of which I still hadn't located.

I sat there a long time, trying to deal with the news and listening to the radio for more information.

Finally, the driver of a city garbage truck behind me laid on his horn, jarring me back to the present. The truck appeared huge in my rearview mirror.

He leaned his head out and shouted, "Hey, Lady! Get out of the way! Can't you see? I got to get those trash cans!"

I looked blankly in front of me and saw the trashcans plainly, for the first time. I pulled slowly back onto the road.

During the short drive home, I heard the Andrews suicide story repeated on three different stations. No one knew any more than what Chief Hathaway had said at the press conference. I didn't notice the scenery I passed the rest of the way.

At Minaret, I left Greta with the valet and went up the stairs two at a time, running on adrenaline. I burst into the living room calling for George. Harry and Bess came bounding toward me, but George was nowhere to be found in any of the ten rooms of our flat. Granted, I looked quickly. But I'm sure I would have found him if he was there: there just aren't that many places to hide.

I went back downstairs and into the Sunset Bar, where neither the bartender nor the waitress had seen George all day. I checked the kitchen, the dining rooms and the outdoor dining areas. There were a few late lunchers, but no George. Finally, I found Peter in the office tallying up the sales for the morning.

"Have you seen George?"

"Not today. I thought he was with you." I must have looked confused, because he followed up, "Not to play golf, of course. I just thought he had gone out to the club early this morning when you did. When I got here, his car was gone and so was yours."

Deflated and worried now, I walked slowly back to the Sunset Bar and sat at my favorite table overlooking the water where George and Jason and I sat last night. Being able to sit outside and watch both the sunrise and sunset is one of the best things about living on Plant Key. Now, I barely noticed the view.

Where could George have gone?

I reviewed my efforts to find him.

Unusual for him to be away early in the morning. He sleeps late every day because he's up so late at night. Being absent on Saturday for the lunch business was something he'd never done since he'd opened the restaurant. George thinks the owner needs to be visible, even though everyone loves Peter.

Ordered a Sapphire and tonic with lemon on the rocks, and sat thinking about where George could be, how Andy could possibly have committed suicide, and why.

An hour later, still no answers.

The drink made me sleepy. I'd looked everywhere and couldn't find George. There was nothing else I could do at the moment. I walked slowly through the restaurant, still looking around, then back upstairs.

When I got into our bedroom, the heavily lined, floral damask drapes were drawn. The room was dark and there was George, snoring as if he hadn't slept in weeks.

I was so relieved to find him, safely alive, that I didn't feel the tears on my face. I lay down on top of the sheets and, worn out, fell fast asleep, too.

CHAPTER NINE

Tampa, Florida
Saturday 5:30 p.m.
January 22, 2000

A FEW HOURS LATER, I awoke disoriented and foggy. I turned over to reach for George and he wasn't there.

Not again.

My eyes popped opened, immediately awake.

I hopped out of bed and walked into the hallway, slipping into my pink silk robe as I went toward the kitchen. George was seated at the table having coffee.

"Hello, sweetheart. How'd you sleep?"

Just like he hadn't been gone all day; without a word as to where he'd spent his time. Instead of focusing on how relieved I was to see his sleep-rumpled self in his green summer cotton bathrobe and white silk pajamas, I lost it.

Almost vibrating with relief, masquerading as tension land anger, I said, much too sharply, "Where the hell have you been?"

"What do you mean? I left you a note."

"Oh, really? Where'd you leave it, in the refrigerator?"

Sarcasm now, too. My relief sounded suspiciously like rage. It didn't seem to bother him, though.

"No," he said with exaggerated patience, like he was dealing with a mentally deficient person. He put his coffee cup down softly. "I left it on the table beside your pillow."

I whirled around and marched back into our bedroom, over to my side of our king-sized bed, and looked down at the pedestal table holding my reading glasses, an alarm clock, a small crystal lamp and, damn damn damn, a handwritten note on one of George's personal monogrammed cards propped up against the telephone.

In his strong, almost indecipherable scrawl, it said:

"Darling, Gone to breakfast. See you after the Blue Coat. Good luck. I love you."

I read it. Then I picked it up between my thumb and forefinger as if it was some sort of nasty laboratory specimen.

It was his paper, his writing. The note had been about eight inches from my face when I woke up both this morning and just now.

I'd missed it.

I'd gotten all upset for no reason.

I hate to eat crow. I just hate it.

I carried the note with me back into the kitchen where George was still calmly having his coffee and reading today's *New York Times*.

"Find it?" he asked, just a little too sweetly. I could almost see the canary feathers on his lips.

"I found it. I'd like to say I didn't find it, but it was there. Next time, how about leaving notes on the kitchen table where you know I'll be sure to look?" If I have to eat crow, I'm certainly not going to be gracious about it. "Let me share the paper."

Like Mark Twain, I, too, have been through some terrible things in my life, some of which actually happened.

We drank coffee and read the paper. For about half an hour, I pouted silently, feeling very put-upon, which is why it took so long for me to remember to ask George if he'd heard about Andrews's death.

I asked him just as he was sipping hot coffee and he almost choked.

"What? How? When?" He shouted when he'd quit coughing.

"I don't know exactly when. I heard it on the news on my way back from the club. Why don't we turn on the television? There's bound to be more information by now," I said, talking to his retreating back as he moved toward the television in the den.

By the time I joined him there, George had located the story on all of the all-news channels and flipped between them. Each stated that General Andrews had been found at home, an apparent suicide. Chief Hathaway's earlier statement repeated.

Nothing new except the very last sound bite: "A source close to the investigation told us the general left a suicide note, but we have not confirmed."

Rehash of Thursday's shooting of Craig Hamilton outside the Capitol building followed. Since Thursday, authorities had confirmed that the shooter had indeed been trying to kill General Andrews, the reporter said. The shooter's late night interview replayed. His face, eerily normal looking, appeared on the screen, while he explained his homicidal behavior in a calm and rational manner that chilled me to the bone.

"I expected him to come out of the car first. I'm sorry I hurt Mr. Hamilton. It was the general I was after. He has no right to kill unborn babies. No murderer will sit on the Supreme Court. Never."

George flipped quickly through channels, shaking his head, distraught. "What is this country coming to? Why is it that people think they can just kill someone they don't agree with? Why don't people trust the process?"

"Jason says the whole process is the problem," I told him.

"What?" He sounded startled.

I told him what Jason had said to me about Andrews's appointment: that it was the result of an under-the-table deal, some sort of Faustian bargain between the President and Andrews.

"That's true, Willa, but it's not unprecedented. And most people have no idea how behind-the-scenes politics in judicial appointments work anyway. I meant people should trust the confirmation process."

"Well," I said evenly, "that didn't seem to be going so well, either. Citizens were worried enough about the process to protest, picket and shoot at Andrews."

I shivered again as I glanced at the shooter's placid face, still on the television screen.

I told him what I'd heard the television analysts say when Margaret and I watched the last day of hearings in my chambers. "More than two thousand names of law school faculty members who spoke against Andrews were listed in the Congressional Record, even more than spoke against Bork when he was defeated."

George gave me a weary look. "I know," he said. "I've seen countless advertisements in the papers addressed to senators by citizens against Andrews."

Gently, I laid my hand on his back, helpless to make him feel better. "Sweetheart, the process wasn't working. People were protesting, but their voices seemed to remain unheeded. Every day in my courtroom I hear about tragedies like this. People just don't have unlimited patience to wait while the wheels of the process grind along so slowly. "

George hung his head, his arms resting on his thighs. "But Andrews should have known better. He should have waited. Supreme Court Justices aren't confirmed by sound bites. Even if he wasn't confirmed, there's no disgrace in that. There's a long history of nominees who weren't confirmed. More than twenty percent aren't. Not being confirmed is no reason to kill yourself."

He was blaming himself. Perhaps he should have expected something like this, but like me, he hadn't.

"Maybe Andy just didn't like his odds," I suggested. "Maybe he couldn't face defeat."

My suggestion didn't seem to make George feel better.

No further information about Andrews's death was to be had on any station. When the stories degenerated to the brawl in George's restaurant last night, with witnesses describing the verbal volleys between Warwick and Andrews, and George's more physical approach, George finally turned off the set and we sat together on the upholstered love seat in the quiet room, Harry and Bess lying near the door.

After a while, George turned toward me, took my hand and gazed steadily into my eyes. What he said next, his calm demeanor and lucid comments, gave me the same chill I'd felt when the shooter explained his motives.

"You know he didn't kill himself, don't you? There's no way Andy would have done that. Someone murdered him."

Fear sucked away my breath. "George, you don't know that. If they say it was suicide, they believe it."

He looked down and played with my wedding ring, twisting it

around on my left hand. "No. If they say it was suicide, they want the public to believe it. That doesn't mean it's true."

My heart pounded harder and I wanted to draw my hand away, make him stop talking about this. "Why would you think he didn't kill himself? You've barely talked to Andy in years."

"Because I know Andy and I know he would never, never kill himself." He dropped my cold hand, as if it was too hot to hold.

"Goddamn it!" he shouted.

Then, he threw the remote control across the room and stalked out while I stared after him, completely bewildered.

CHAPTER TEN

Tampa, Florida
Saturday 7:00 p.m.
January 22, 2000

I WALKED OVER AND picked up the remote from the floor. It's amazing how tough those things are, I thought. It didn't even crack.

I heard George slamming drawers in his dressing room and then leave by the front door.

He left? He just left?

I couldn't believe it. My legs dropped me down on the loveseat again.

Who was this man inhabiting George's body? My George never lost his control, but I had seen this stranger lose it twice in the last twenty-four hours.

George had put so much of himself into this fight, felt so strongly about it, spent so much energy and time on it. I had hardly seen him in the past few weeks and when he was home, he was so preoccupied that he either spoke of nothing else, or didn't speak at all.

But I know George didn't plan to win the battle by losing the general. For once, what he affectionately calls my Mighty Mouse routine, my desire to fix everything that comes my way whether people ask for my help or not, failed me. As much as I loved George, and wanted to help him, there wasn't anything I could do to fix this. I had no choice but to wait it out and hope that when the dust settled, George and I could find each other again.

The dogs didn't know what to do, either. Both of them came over and put their heads in my lap. I rubbed their ears as I tried to comfort us all.

After a while, when I finally acknowledged that George wasn't coming right back, I turned to my all purpose solution for whatever emotional disturbance ails me: my work.

Donned black jeans and a cream T-shirt and went into my study to wrestle with *Newton v. The Whitman Esquire Review* while I did what wives had done for centuries, what Deborah Andrews had done for decades: I waited for my husband to come home.

CHAPTER ELEVEN

THE NEWTON FILE HADN'T gotten any smaller since I'd left my briefcase next to Aunt Minnie's chair yesterday. I told myself that the only way to get started was to start, although it was hard to muster any enthusiasm for the project. Concentration was tough because I listened for George to return.

The case involved an obnoxious abuse of privacy by a newspaper that was, to my mind, better left to sink into the pit of sordid, unnoticed comment. This might have happened. Except that Nelson Newton had decided, literally, to make a federal case out of it.

Both parties involved in the case left a lot to be desired. The plaintiff, Nelson Newton, was a notorious local lawyer with political aspirations.

Politics as a motive for unsavory behavior seemed to be consuming my work life as well as my home life, I noted sourly.

The defendant, *The Whitman Esquire Review*, was a radical alternative scandal tabloid that, but for the First Amendment, would have been put out of business long ago by an outraged public interested in decency.

It was a mark of our decline as a society that Americans consumed the tabloid's salacious details with the same guilty pleasure that we devoured more than twenty quarts of ice cream every year.

Unlike when I practiced law and could choose my cases, as a judge I couldn't reject matters I found distasteful. This dispute, over the extremely radical practice of "outing," didn't belong in the public forum of my courtroom.

"Outing" was a nice name for the outrageous practice of printing true information disclosing sexual preferences that law-abiding citizens preferred to keep private.

Such information wasn't meant for public consumption, in my view.

I had trouble not only with what *The Review* chose to say, but also with their right to say it. Everyone was entitled to some privacy. And those involved should get to decide both whether their most personal secrets get shared and with whom.

That said, a trial was not a process designed to protect anyone's privacy. Trials are open to the public and frequently reported in the mainstream media. If *The Review* should not have printed the offending piece in the first place, as Newton claimed, airing the dispute in a public trial certainly wasn't going to put the cat back in the bag.

I picked up the last of six pleadings files looking for the final pre-trial order I had entered on the case outlining the parties' expectations for proofs at trial. Broadly speaking, this was a defamation case; count one alleged libel and slander, and count two alleged breach of the private facts tort, claiming obliquely that *The Review* had published private matter about Newton without his consent.

The case was in federal court because the parties were citizens of different states. Newton was a Florida citizen and *The Review* was incorporated and had its principal place of business in San Francisco.

The Review, Newton claimed, had wrongfully reprinted anonymous local gossip in a blind column labeled *About Town*. Newton alleged that everyone in his business circle knew the offending story was about him, causing him great personal harm.

What Newton didn't say was that the story would likely cost him votes if he ran for mayor, which, rumor was, he planned to do in the next election. Newton claimed that *The Review* had printed pure gossip with malice—that is, with reckless disregard for its truth or falsity—and that the story had harmed him to the tune of $25 million.

Usually, my work absorbed all of my attention. I served the judicial system and, thus, did something important to society. But tonight, the only thing important to me was George. Absently, I rubbed the purple lump on my head and tried to concentrate.

The Review denied any wrongdoing and stood by their story, which had appeared in the popular but gossipy "Mr. Tampa Knows Best" column. Truth, they said, was Mr. Tampa's absolute defense

The idea struck me as absurd, even if it might be legally correct. Sometimes truth was the most hurtful thing one could disclose about another, I knew.

Alternatively, *The Review* argued that it had printed the story without malice and was not liable because Mr. Newton is and has been a public figure.

Well, I wasn't so sure about that, but I had ruled earlier in the case that whether Newton was a public figure or not was for the jury to decide. Public figures, too, should be allowed a personal life.

Since trial court judges are not required to be without opinions, I had mine about the case and the practice of outing. Aside from the titillation factor, what possible difference could an individual's sexual orientation make to the public at large? Even if Nelson Newton was gay, which he denied, so what?

The world wouldn't stop. Being gay is not a crime. It wasn't even a problem with his marriage, since Newton wasn't married. Not now anyway. Wife number four left him just before the story appeared. Indeed, that was one of the facts cited in support of the truth of the story by the paper.

Thumbing through the stuffed file folders, I noticed two things that exacerbated my headache: the witness lists took up three single spaced pages and Newton was representing himself.

He might, as the old adage goes, have a fool for a client but what it meant to me was a longer than normal trial with many more opportunities for reversible error and a serious strain on my limited judicial resources.

I've had cases with Nelson Newton before. He can't say his name in less than twenty minutes. Just the thought of him representing himself through three pages of witnesses made me tired.

I pulled out the offending news story that became indelibly imprinted on my brain in the last few weeks and read it again.

What prominent Tampa lawyer lost wife number four and won't get married for a fifth time because he likes men better? Those in the know have seen him in the locker room with his hands where they shouldn't be. Shame on you, Mr. N., for staying in the closet. You should have the courage to be who you are.

The item contained few facts. I wasn't sure how *The Review* planned to prove the story was true and I wasn't really interested. Federal judges shouldn't become embroiled in personal privacy issues like this one.

The Review, a very radical gay paper, had been publishing a series of articles "outing" gays all over the country, and particularly on October 11, dubbed "National Coming Out Day." They employed stringers in each major market to add what they called "local color" to the stories.

"Mr. N" was only one of several items *The Review* had published along similar lines, but Newton was the only subject who had sued in my courtroom. If avoiding unfavorable publicity was Newton's true goal, making the case a media event in Tampa wasn't the way to do it.

Had Newton been a different sort of guy, I'd believe his motives pure. To educate the public, say, or to promote privacy rights, which I, for one, believed in.

But this was Nelson Newton—a publicity hound of long duration. He had a hidden agenda here. And I didn't like being used to foster it, whatever it was.

I was a public servant and Newton was a member of the public. Open access to the courts gave him the right to be in my courtroom for the small filing fee, a concept I normally supported; but cases like Newton's forced me to reexamine.

I've never been able to divorce my desire to serve the judicial system from the practical effects of its failures.

In this case, Newton had the right to sue, but he was manipulating the process for his own ends. When litigants did that, and it happened all too often, my patience barked at the end of a very short leash.

I glanced at my watch. It was getting late, but George hadn't returned.

Dragging my attention back to the file, I examined the exhibit lists, reviewed the trial briefs and then the proposed jury instructions submitted by both parties. Somewhere along the way, finally, I was able to lose myself in the work.

Before I knew it, I'd worked right through dinner and George had never come home.

I called down to the kitchen and ordered a late night snack to be sent upstairs, which is one of the great perks of living over a restaurant. While I waited, I turned on the news. Nothing new was reported on General Andrews's death or anything else of interest.

Following my meal, I soaked in my tub for a while, read a recent novel and then my eyelids became too heavy and I finally admitted to myself that I was too tired to wait anymore.

When I turned out my bedside lamp at about one o'clock, I closed my eyes and thought about George.

Why was he acting so strangely?

Worried about him, about us.

I could still visualize him on the first night we'd met, when George became the center of my world and changed my life forever.

I was just seventeen, a gawky, unsure freshman at the University of Michigan. He was a senior and, for some reason, became interested in me. We'd both attended a screening of *The Thin Man*, the old William Powell and Myrna Loy classic, shown on campus by the film society. In the days before videotaped movies were widely available, viewers had to wait to see their favorite stories, and this one was a rare treat.

I was consumed by the old movies I'd watched with Mom during the long weeks of her final illness. *The Thin Man* had been one of her favorites and experiencing it again made me feel closer to her. The story is a comedy that never failed to make me laugh and recall our happier times together.

George approached me after the film, asking if I'd like to get a coffee. Oddly, I wasn't nervous. George made me feel so comfortable and relaxed and, inexplicably, at the same time, my body fairly hummed with sexual tension. The feelings were delicious and I reveled in them. A sexy, good-looking man showing interest in me was, at that time, a new experience.

We discussed the movie for hours that night, and we identified more than forty films that we both loved. George looked so much like William Powell, well, I guess we just got caught up in the moment. He always claims he was smitten by love at first sight, but George never had to kiss the Blarney Stone to be full of charm.

Still, he'd rescued me from myself at a time when I badly needed rescuing. My mother had died the year before and I felt adrift trying to find my way in the world. George's arrival always seemed sent from heaven. Mom would have loved him, just as everyone else does.

Even then, I'd believed he was perfect for me. Of supreme importance to my teenaged self was that he was taller than I. At five feet eleven, I'd towered over most boys in high school. I walked around with my shoulders hunched to look shorter. Like a big-footed puppy, I hadn't grown into myself yet.

After that first night, we became inseparable. Going to the movies became one of the many passions we shared. George was then, and is now, an excellent lover. He's funny, intelligent, kind. He's always been my best friend. Since we met, I've never preferred the company of any other person as much as I loved being with my husband.

I had always enjoyed the fantasy of the two of us cocooned in ourselves, joined against the world outside. Until recently, that illusion had thrived.

Now, our marriage had turned into a fishbowl of thick, murky water that obscured my senses.

For the first time ever, I could feel the knots in my stomach as I worried about George and I was afraid for us.

George was a political player, but he'd gotten so invested in this battle. His recent behavior was completely different from his usually detached manner of dealing with life.

He'd spent long nights with the party chairman, working with Jason whenever possible. Even, I found out today, working closely with Senator Warwick, a man whose ideology and personality George detests. I'd heard him on the phone, many times late into the night, talking to all of the senators he knew personally, urging them to vote against Andrews.

Now, after everything that had happened, I actually suspected he'd attempted to meet with the President. This sounded farfetched, except that George knew President Benson. Politics is like any other world. If you stayed in it long enough, eventually everyone you knew in your younger days rises to positions of power and influence by processes of aging and attrition.

My scratchy eyes objected to one more waking moment. I closed them just to rest.

What I didn't understand was why defeating the Andrews confirmation mattered so much to George. He believed Andrews was not suited to the job, and we'd talked for hours about why. But a lot of people aren't suited to their work—like my boss the Chief Judge for instance—and it never seemed to bother George.

The strain had turned George into someone I didn't recognize. And maybe he felt a little guilty. If Andrews did kill himself, George would feel at least partly to blame because he'd tried so hard to defeat Andrews's nomination. George desperately wanted to win the fight against Andrews, but not at the cost of the man's life. Surely.

CHAPTER TWELVE

Tampa, Florida
Sunday 6:05 a.m.
January 23, 2000

THERE IS A SCIENTIFIC explanation for why time seems to pass more rapidly as we age. According to this theory, we humans measure time against our experience. The older we get, the more experiences we have and thus the shorter a year seems in comparison. Or ten years.

This is a great theory and it's probably even true, but it doesn't explain why time passes so slowly when you want terrible things to be over.

Awakened too early, groggy and heavy-eyed from lack of restful sleep. My mind had churned all night and I felt as if I hadn't slept at all.

Felt the weight of George's body on the bed next to mine. He'd come home some time during the night and was snoring soundly. I eased out of bed, thinking that if he got enough sleep, he might return to his old self today.

I stood there, looking at this man who, in many ways, had become a stranger to me. This guy looked like George, for the most part. He wore George's silk boxers just now, the ones I gave him for Valentine's Day with the red hearts on them. But he was obviously someone else. This man had been short-tempered and consumed by politics; he'd ignored his restaurant and our dogs; and he'd barely held a reasonable conversation with me, or anyone I knew, for several weeks.

My George is patient, kind, loving and full of that old concept: honor.

My George sleeps in pajamas.

I crept out into the kitchen and put on the coffee, whispering to Harry and Bess to be quiet as I let them out the back door and picked up the newspapers off the porch. We get three newspapers every day, the two local ones and *The Wall Street Journal*. On Sunday, we also subscribed to the *New York Times*.

By the time Harry and Bess got back, my coffee was done. Cuban, strong and sweet, my caffeine of choice. I took my papers and coffee mug, the green one George had given me that said *I Hate Mornings*, out to the veranda and sat at the table overlooking the bay, the dogs at my feet.

The sun was just starting to peek through the horizon again. Sunrises are truly glorious miracles even though I prefer to sleep through them. This morning, I tried to appreciate the pinks, oranges and blues in the sky. That's hard to do when your eyes are closed.

The headlines were much as I expected. ANDREWS COMMITS SUICIDE. Barring some terrorist airline hijacking, the death of General Albert Randall Andrews would be front-page news everywhere today.

Everything above the fold dealt with Andy's death and, for the first time, they had printed the note he left in his study before he went out to the boat to kill himself. The unwelcome tears that had seemed so near the surface for the past few days sprang to my eyes as I read the note. I told myself my vulnerability was due to exhaustion as I blinked the tears away, replaced my unusual sensitivity with stronger curiosity that felt more comfortable, and read the note again.

CHAPTER THIRTEEN

GOODBYE MY DARLING DEBORAH. Please take care of our children. Make sure they understand how much I've loved them all. I can't continue under such traitorous attacks, especially from friends and colleagues. I'd planned to serve my country once again as a Supreme Court Justice. Now, this Old Soldier's career is over.

All three papers carried essentially the same story on the front page, which had been picked up from the local papers by one of the wire services.

I read through the stories with the critical eye I normally reserved for legal briefs. General Andrews was found dead after suffering a gunshot wound to the head early yesterday morning. His body was discovered in the fishing boat that was tied to the dock behind his Lake Thonotosassa home. Andrews habitually fished each night, the report said, and his home was so remote from others that no one heard the gunshot.

The operating theory was that General Andrews had placed his revolver to his right temple, holding the gun in his right hand, and pulled the trigger.

Andrews was survived by a wife, two sons, one daughter, a son-in-law and no grandchildren.

The papers rehashed the low points of the recent confirmation hearings. They speculated that the contentious hearings and the potential vote against him were the reasons for the general's suicide.

Senator Warwick was quoted: "It is a tragedy that the Republic should repay him for his decades of service by publicly humiliating him to the point where he felt he had no choice but to take his own life."

There was more in this vein for about six column inches, which I dismissed as the worst sort of public grandstanding, particularly when I knew Warwick's real views on Andy's appointment. Honest politician. Now there's an oxymoron.

The local papers carried a number of stories and columns about Andy's contribution to the community, his charitable activities and his commitment to education. There was even a story on the sports page about yesterday's Blue Coat golf tournament. I was mildly amused to see that one of the teams had been disqualified, my group had come in fourth and our designated literacy program would get $2,500 prize money.

I'd refilled my coffee mug several times and the sun was moving quickly toward the yardarm, as the pirates who once sailed these waters are believed to have said, when George finally joined me in his bathrobe. He brought his own coffee—he detests mine—and rubbed his stubbled face across my cheek before he sat down across from me at the table.

While he was sleeping, I had decided to act like nothing untoward had happened between us, so I just said, "Good morning, sweetheart. Did you sleep well?"

"No, not really," was all he said in reply. He looked out on the water and appeared to be concentrating on some inner conflict, but he didn't say what it was and he didn't talk any more.

Determined to wait him out, to let him explain things to me when he was ready, in his own way, I went back into the house to make more coffee before I finished the papers.

When I came back with two carafes on a tray, one for him and one for me, George said, "Do we have anything planned for today? I'd really like to go out to see Deborah, if that's all right with you." He lowered his voice so that it was hard to hear him over the gentle lapping of the waves below. "I'd like you to come, too."

It was the first time George had asked me to do anything with him in quite awhile. I felt the grip of fear that I'd been unwilling to acknowledge begin to loosen. This was George, my beloved. He was coming back to me.

I reached over to kiss his rumpled self, holding his scratchy cheeks in both hands. He tasted just as he always had, and he returned my kiss as longingly. We've made it, I thought. We've gone through the dark place and come out on the other side.

"Of course, I'll go with you. But," I stopped, not quite sure how to word my thoughts delicately and unwilling to destroy the renewed warmth between us with bickering.

"What?" he asked me gently.

"We haven't really known Deborah for several years," I said, tentatively. I didn't need to remind him of the harsh words he'd said while throwing them out of the restaurant the last time we'd seen Andy alive.

George winced. "I'm sorry about that now. Andy and I were close once. I respected him then and I've always liked Deborah. I need to pay my respects." He spoke quietly, almost to himself. "You don't have to come along, but I'd like it if you would."

"Of course I'll go with you. It's the right thing to do, anyway. I'm not sure we'll be welcome?" I put a little lilt in my voice, to make it a question. He didn't respond. "But I suppose we just come back if we're not wanted."

He gave me a weak smile that pierced my heart one more time.

CHAPTER FOURTEEN

Tampa, Florida
Sunday 3:30 p.m.
January 23, 2000

LAKE THONOTOSASSA IS AN old community about fifteen miles east of downtown Tampa, out in the country. The Andrews's house was built on land leased to him by a local university in a sweetheart deal several years ago. It was a good public relations gesture to practically give the ten-acre estate to Andy when they were trying to get him to agree to become president of the university after he retired.

Andrews declined the presidency, but he kept the land. Rumor was that he paid a fair price for it when his memoirs were published last year.

We had to park George's silver Bentley about half a mile down the two-lane road and walk up to the house. Media vans were parked along the public road, as close to the driveway as they could get without actually trespassing.

As we approached the driveway, Frank Bennett, who seemed

to be everywhere these days, spotted us. With a photographer behind him and microphone in hand, he requested a statement he could broadcast on the evening news.

"I don't think this is the time, do you, Frank?" George asked him. "Besides, we don't know anything. We're here to pay our respects, that's all."

Frank looked at me beseechingly, but I backed George up on this one. I didn't feel overly friendly toward Frank after Friday night. There was no reason to make a bigger circus out of such a tragic event.

I don't believe the public has a right to intrude on grief, depriving loved ones of privacy they need when they've suffered the ultimate loss in death. Even when the deceased was a Four-Star General and a Supreme Court nominee.

But Frank wouldn't give up. His camera was rolling; he started talking. "Tell me this, Judge Carson. Do you believe General Andrews committed suicide?"

I opened my mouth to say that was a police matter when the gremlin inhabiting George's body resurfaced.

"No, Frank, she does not. That's unthinkable." The tenor of his voice was harsh, offensive. "General Andrews was a war hero and one of the bravest men alive. He would not kill himself." George turned to take my arm. "Now turn that damn thing off and have a little respect, will you?"

Frank didn't have time to close his gaping mouth before George turned us sharply and escorted me quickly through the gaggle and up the long driveway.

The Andrews's driveway was rough and uneven, but lined with orange and live oak trees. Spanish moss hung down from the branches and a dense blanket of kudzu covered most of the ground. Someone had cut the kudzu vine back on either side of the driveway to keep it from smothering the entire area, but any surface was fertile for the vine that strangles everything it touches. I stepped lively, imagining all the snakes that must be living under there.

We walked the length of the quarter mile distance, all the way up to the house, past limousines, army vehicles and every imaginable type of car and truck. That current status symbol of the middle-aged white American male, Harley Davidson, was also well represented. Who would ride a Hog to a condolence call?

Eventually, we reached the front door of the Andrews's Georgian-style home. George rang the bell and in less than thirty seconds, someone I didn't know managed to open the oversized oak door. The room teemed with people wedged as close together as brick pavers. We struggled to plow our way through. Whether we'd even be able to find Deborah, let alone speak with her, seemed doubtful.

The room and the whole house for that matter was filled with both familiar and unfamiliar faces. Some were dressed in various military uniforms, and others donned dark clothing to show respect for the dead and comfort the bereaved. From experience, I knew that the bereaved couldn't be comforted by anything a mourner wore, or anything one said, for that matter. Only the passage of time made such loss somewhat bearable.

We stood a little uncomfortably in the living room for a few minutes until George spotted Police Chief Ben Hathaway across the room, heading in our direction a little too purposefully for my comfort.

Ben is a big man and I always have the impression that he won't be able to stop his forward momentum in time to avoid walking right over whoever is in his way. That quality made the sea of mourners part for him as he pushed forward. Hathaway is not only tall, but heavy. Yet, he maneuvers like a ballerina. He's clever. And secretive.

Ben has been a cop too long to betray his true intentions, which made me even more wary of him.

"Hello, George," he said, extending his hand. "Willa," as he nodded toward me. "This certainly is a madhouse, isn't it?"

"I didn't expect to find so many people here. What's going on?" George asked him.

"Most everyone likes Deborah. People are shocked. It's hard to accept that the general killed himself." Ben was trying to speak softly. The trouble was that everyone in the room was speaking quietly, which created a low rumble over which truly quiet voices could not be heard.

"I'm certain he didn't." George said, with the same vehemence he'd used with Frank Bennett outside.

Ben looked at him curiously. "Why?"

"I knew Andy for twenty years. Served under him in the army, did you know that?"

"No, I guess I didn't." Ben said, a little cautiously.

George's army career isn't something he usually talks about. I was surprised he'd bring it up here.

He said, "Well, Andy would *never* have killed himself. He thrived on adversity. He thought suicide was the coward's way out. There's no way he did this to himself. No way."

I hadn't noticed Frank Bennett enter the house, but now he stood nearby, listening intently. Frank was a friend and a local celebrity, as Andy had been. We all knew him. He was entitled to pay his respects just like the rest of us.

But Frank wouldn't leave anything he overheard out of his professional life, either.

Ben's attention focused on George. A small crowd gathered.

Some had their backs turned, pretending they weren't eavesdropping on our conversation.

"Did you ever talk to him about it?" Ben asked.

"Yes, years ago. One of our mutual friends committed suicide; Andy wrote him off as cowardly."

"How's that?"

"Andy thought the man should have shown more courage in the face of adversity; that the issue was a small one and he should have been above it."

I glanced around uncomfortably. The crowd had grown larger and they'd become quiet, listening intently now, and not bothering with pretense.

"Anything else?" Ben asked George.

I didn't like his tone or the question. Not at all.

"Andy never believed any of the suicides reported in the media actually happened. He thought that Vince Foster was murdered, for example." There was a shocked murmur rippling through the surrounding crowd now.

I spied Deborah Andrews a few feet inside the house. I turned to George and took his arm.

"Will you excuse us, Ben? We need to pay our respects to Deborah." I started walking away, pulling George with me and the crowd of frankly curious onlookers parted for us to walk through. Deborah's back was turned to us; I leaned over to whisper to George. "You need to curb your views while we're here. It's not the time or the place."

He squeezed my arm gently to emphasize his agreement while people we didn't know continued to look at us, pretending not to stare.

CHAPTER FIFTEEN

DEBORAH ANDREWS HAD BEEN polite since birth.

I noticed, as I hadn't on Friday night, that her brown hair was streaked with gray and her blue eyes were faded. She'd added a few pounds over the years and she looked every nanosecond of her age, which I guessed to be about sixty-five.

Today, she wore a black silk dress with short sleeves, The obligatory pearl choker adorned her neck and small pearl earrings were clipped on her lobes. Deborah's only other jewelry was her wedding ring, the plain gold band Andy had put on her finger over thirty years before. The way arthritis had swollen her knuckles, she wouldn't have been able to get the ring off if she'd wanted to. Which, we all knew, she didn't.

Standing next to Deborah Andrews in the darkened living room of the large, unkempt, rambling house, was her daughter, Robbie. Nothing about Robbie resembled her mother, physically or temperamentally. Had that always been so?

Robbie glared at us with unconcealed malevolence that startled me into defensiveness. She was taller and about a hundred pounds heavier than Deborah, but nothing about Robbie was soft or compliant. Her hair was highlighted and cleverly styled. She wore chic glasses that made her round face appear even fuller than it was. She had three chins and each one of them seemed to be lifted in sharp defiance. Robbie held onto Deborah's arm as if Deborah would fall without the support, as if Deborah needed to be shielded from us.

When I'd known Deborah Andrews, she would never have needed support from Robbie. If anything, it had been the other way around; Robbie had been the flighty one.

Today, Robbie had cried off all her makeup—if she'd had any on to begin with—which was unfortunate. The uncharitable thought that sprang, unbidden, to mind was that Robbie had the kind of face that needed every bit of a makeup artist's skill. She stood there, as if she was lost and without any clue as to what had happened to her father, but she'd be damned if she'd let any of us get close to Deborah. Robbie seemed especially hostile to George and me, but I might have been projecting a little.

I remembered the chasm I'd fallen into when I lost my mother and, if Robbie had lowered her emotional armor just a tiny fraction, my empathy for her would have overwhelmed me. As it was, her attitude was jarring. I gripped George's arm a little tighter, trying to hold onto my lifeline.

Deborah, gracious as always, held out a hand to George, who took it, kissed her cheek and murmured something privately into her ear. I bent over to give Deborah a small hug, myself. She seemed to need the contact. Or maybe I did. The house smelled strongly like cats, but I didn't see one. Not that anything on the floor would have been visible in this crowd.

"Hello, George, Willa. It's so good of you to come. I wasn't sure you would." Deborah said quietly.

"I didn't think you'd have the nerve, after the way you behaved," Robbie said with more honesty. "If it wasn't for you, my father would still be alive."

Well, obviously I hadn't been projecting Robbie's hostility to us. All charitable thoughts I might have had for her situation immediately evaporated.

Deborah turned to her smoothly and patted Robbie's hand. "Robbie, dear, George was justified in protecting Willa. Your father would have done the same for me."

"That's not what I meant, and he knows it." She pointed her chin at George, defiantly. "He was the one who led the opposition to Daddy's nomination. Without him, Daddy would be on the Court by now. He'd have had no reason to kill himself."

Her spite was palpable. It oozed off her like lava flow, causing me to worry about a potential violent eruption.

"George did what he thought was right, Dear. We can't hold it against him now." Deborah, always generous of spirit and kind to others, was a woman who loved too much. Or maybe she displayed the kind of mannerly conduct that George's Aunt Minnie would have called breeding.

Robbie glared at us both, but kept further opinions to herself. She didn't allow us to talk with Deborah alone, though.

"We're very sorry about Andy, Deborah. Neither one of us can believe it," I said, in a serious bit of understatement.

Deborah's eyes glassed up and tears welled in her lower lids, threatening to spill onto her face where earlier tears had left tracks in her makeup.

"I can't believe it either, Willa. I've known Andy all my life.

We lived next door to one another from the time I was born. I don't know what my life will be without him." Her voice broke and I was afraid she'd break down completely.

Robbie, took over, thanked us for coming and said her mother should go lie down for a while. They headed off to one of the other areas of the house.

Offering condolences to Deborah had been more difficult than I'd imagined. After that, I needed a little time to myself, too. I left George in search of the bathroom.

Unfamiliar with the layout of the house, I blundered into what must have been the general's den. The room felt like an alien place to me, somewhere that I would never have been invited, where I didn't belong. It held the allure of the forbidden. Perhaps, I'd find a powder room here.

My nose wrinkled up almost involuntarily at the cat smell, which was close to overwhelming. Still, I didn't see a cat.

The room was dominated by a large wood desk and the brown leather armchair behind it. It was filled with army paraphernalia: flags, guns, plaques, framed certificates and photographs. Lots of photographs depicting Andrews with national and world leaders.

I wondered whether Andrews had written his memoirs here. The rooms where writers work had always fascinated me. I loved to read and I viewed the writing process as near magic. Someday, I planned to learn to write novels, but that day was far off in my future.

Andrews's memoirs had caused quite a stir when he published them a year or so ago. He'd kept extensive notes of his army experiences and he used those notes to write his autobiography. He was sharply criticized for taking official army documents and using army personnel for the project.

He used the U.S. Army as if it were his personal corporation, they said, acting like he was the CEO. He denied any wrongdoing, offered to return the documents and pay for the personnel. But the damage to his reputation had already been done.

Recalling the scandal, I realized it hadn't driven him to suicide, lending further support to George's disbelief of the official explanation for Andrews's death.

A dirty fireplace, a couch and two chairs fronted the massive desk. The weather would get quite cool out here in the country on winter nights. A fireplace would make the evenings cozy. There was a soft antique Iranian rug in front of the hearth and several other souvenirs of lifelong military travel.

A man's man lived here, the decor seemed to say. Nothing soft or feminine about any of the furnishings. I wondered if Deborah had felt excluded from most of her husband's life, and how she'd dealt with that.

To the left side of the desk, a door led to the outside of the house, which, when I thought about it, made sense. The general would have wanted to admit visitors for private meetings without disturbing his family.

Finally, I found what I'd been looking for. The head, for I'm sure General Andrews would never have called it the powder room, was just opposite the private entrance. It wasn't the cleanest bathroom I've ever been in, clearly the province of a man. I ducked in and took care of things.

As I was leaving the bathroom, careful to return the seat to its original up position, I heard two guests talking in the general's den. I waited a moment to avoid disturbing their privacy.

"Deborah said Andy was reading in here Friday night around eleven. They have separate bedrooms so she didn't know what time he went to bed," one of the men said.

The other guest, a woman, replied, "They'd been arguing and

she went to bed angry. How would you like to have to live with that?"

I've never been a comfortable eavesdropper. Thankfully they moved on, and I let myself out to the hallway before someone else came into the room.

I wandered around the house for a while, looking for George, and eventually stumbled into the large country-style kitchen that overlooked the small brown lake. Here, too, the house could have used a good cleaning and some maintenance. The cat smell was stronger because of the litter box in the corner. The lake and the dock behind the house were visible from the French doors.

The fishing boat in which Andrews died was tied to the dock. Yellow crime scene tape and a uniformed officer I didn't recognize posted there prevented curiosity seekers from walking out onto the dock or bothering the boat.

Not normally voyeuristic, I was drawn by the opportunity to view the crime scene.

I slipped out the back door and walked carefully across the yard, grateful for my flat shoes, scanning for snakes. I stopped in front of the officer, who had watched me make the journey from the house.

"This certainly is a beautiful lake, isn't it?" I asked him. I still didn't recognize the man at all, and he apparently didn't know me, either.

"Yes, ma'am," he said. "You gotta admire a man who can afford a place like this."

"Is that the boat where he died?"

"Yes, ma'am, it is."

"It sure is a mess, isn't it?" I tried to see out into the boat, which was about twenty feet from where we stood. It was full of blood and other things, hopefully remnants of successful fishing trips.

Without glancing back at the boat, he replied, "Yes, ma'am."

I was getting the picture that I wasn't going to learn any pertinent information from this officer, whether he knew me or not. Nothing ventured, nothing gained. So I asked him, "Do you think the general committed suicide?"

"I'm sure I don't know, ma'am."

"Is there anything at all you can tell me?" I asked him.

"Not if I want to keep my job, ma'am."

Because cases come to my courtroom long after the crime has been committed, there are very few crime scenes that I've actually witnessed firsthand, but I've seen hundreds of crime scene photographs. Maybe a picture is worth a thousand words, but a personal view gave me visceral information.

The quiet, for example. I heard nothing out here, even sounds from inside the house. And the cloying odors. The entire area smelled like dead fish and dank, rotting vegetation. What a nasty place to die. Pictures would never convey the frightening aura of solitude and danger I felt simply standing here.

This lake was private. There was no public access and no other visible houses around it. Like most dark lakes in Florida, I was sure there were alligators floating beneath the surface and snakes just around the water's edge.

The entire effect was eerie, like a horror movie, but more vivid. The short winter day was ending and I told myself that the cool breeze was responsible for the gooseflesh on my arms.

But if there were visible clues to a murder here, they weren't obvious to me.

I said goodbye to the officer, went back inside, found George and insisted that we leave. He was more than ready, so we writhed back through the television cameras and ignored Frank Bennett when he asked whether George would like to comment on Robbie

Andrews's accusations against him.

I could have spent the evening discussing everything thoroughly with George, because for the first time in a long time, he seemed willing to talk about it. But I thought we'd had enough for one day, there would be many long, leisurely hours to hash it all out, and our relationship would get back to normal.

Spending time in a house of mourning gave us both a desire to be alive, I guess. We went to bed together and made long, slow, quiet love, tainted with the understanding that Deborah Andrews's loss allowed me the opportunity to reclaim my beloved, although we were a long way from our previous relationship.

I hoped George and I had weathered a rough spot, and with Andrews's nomination permanently defeated by his cruel death, we'd now pick up the pieces and somehow resume our lives. I craved peaceful days, shared evenings, and passionate nights. Maybe, after a few weeks, a romantic vacation in Bermuda.

CHAPTER SIXTEEN

Tampa, Florida
Monday 7:00 a.m.
January 24, 2000

MONDAY MORNING, I IGNORED my continuing unease as I
ran the dogs, showered, dressed, picked up the *Newton* file, made
plans with George for dinner and scurried off down the back stairs
to the garage. Greta's top was still down from Saturday, and I
didn't bother to put it up. The wind can't hurt my very short hair,
and the morning was already turning into a fine Florida day.

Some federal judges use their law clerks as chauffeurs, but I
really enjoy my time with Greta. Some say Greta's too flashy for a
judge to drive. But if you're from Detroit like I am, cars are the
essence of life itself. How could I give up Greta just for a job?

I drove carefully but quickly down our version of Palm Beach's
Avenue of Palms, over the bridge off Plant Key away from Minaret
and turned east onto Bayshore Boulevard toward downtown Tampa.
The view was, as always, spectacular. Hillsborough Bay,
particularly along the Bayshore, is truly beautiful.

Not many years ago, the Hillsborough River, Hillsborough Bay and Tampa Bay were completely dead. After a massive cleanup campaign, fish, dolphins, rays and manatees are regularly spotted here. If a body of water can be reclaimed, a loving marriage can be reclaimed, too, I thought.

Greta and I passed the old mansions along the north side of the Bayshore, interspersed with the newer condominiums and a few commercial establishments, like the Colonnade Restaurant. It was closed this morning, but by lunchtime, it would be filled to capacity with the Old Tampa crowd, as well as the current crop of snowbirds who came every day to enjoy the spectacular view.

I followed Bayshore over the Platt Street Bridge toward the Convention Center. As I approached Davis Islands, then Harbour Island, and turned north on Florida, I passed what used to be called Landmark Tower and is now the SunTrust building.

A small cloud covered my emotions. One of my friends who'd worked in that building died this year. I hadn't thought of him for several months. The recent death of my friend had popped into my mind several times since Saturday. I tried to shake it off and reclaim my earlier hopefulness as I quickly passed the building, then a series of storefronts and Sacred Heart Church along the four-block stretch to the courthouse.

My office is one of the last ones housed in the old Federal Building, circa 1920. It is a beautiful old building with wood details way too expensive to duplicate today. In 1920, the Middle District of Florida was a much smaller place than it is now. The building is old, decrepit and much too small.

Which is why we have a new federal courthouse just down the street. Maybe, when the Chief Judge, the man we call CJ (who I'm sure hates me), is promoted or retires, I'll get to move to the new building with all the other judges. I took his parking spot the first day on the job and he's never forgiven me for the small trespass. Since then, I've done quite a few things he doesn't approve of. He has no real power over me, which irritates him even more.

I am the most junior judge on the local federal bench. In seniority, age and the CJ's affection, I have the least desirable location. I have no rank among my peers and receive no special privileges.

My courtroom and chambers are on the third floor, in the back. Getting there from the parking garage helps me keep my schoolgirl figure.

CHAPTER SEVENTEEN

Tampa, Florida
Monday 9:02 a.m.
January 24, 2000

FORTUNATELY, THE TRIP FROM Plant Key to the garage at
the old courthouse is a short one. I was able to park Greta, jog up
three flights of stairs, walk into my office, grab my robe and get
onto the bench only two minutes late. Not bad.

The parties, seated at their respective tables, looked very
subdued. The Whitman Esquire Review attorneys numbered six,
with two additional paralegals in the gallery. The president of the
paper was the client representative. The woman sitting next to him
was Mr. Tampa, the author of the offending piece of trash they
were all here to defend. I'm told the Ann Landers newspaper
advice column was once written by a man. I guess truth in media
doesn't extend to gender identification.

Boxes of exhibits and other papers were stowed behind the rail
that separates the gallery of visitors from the rest of us so as not to
be seen by the jury.

In what every trial lawyer would recognize as deliberate contrast, the plaintiff, Nelson Newton, sat by himself at the counsel table closest to the jury box. He had only one wrinkled, dirty, letter-sized manila folder on the desk in front of him. He was holding an ink pen that looked like he'd picked it up at a car rental desk.

Newton's somber navy blue suit, shiny from too many trips to the cleaners, could have come from J.C. Penney twenty years ago or the Salvation Army this morning. He wore a yellowed, dingy and frayed white oxford cloth shirt with a button-down collar. His red, white and blue striped tie had soaked up its share of spilled lunches.

Dressing for court is a little like selecting the right costumes for a play. The idea is to have credibility with the jury, to look like a person they can root for; one they'll want to win. A trial is a contest and there are winners and losers, as much as we try to pretend otherwise. The game is not decided on points. It's one roll of the dice when the case goes back to the jury room; you never know who's going to get lucky and who'll go home broke.

The last time he tried a case in front of me, Newton had worn this same outfit every day for three weeks. He'd told me it was his lucky suit. The jury gave his client two million dollars that time on what I'd have said was a loser before the verdict came in. "Counselors, any last minute issues before I bring in the jury venire?" Little butterflies danced in my stomach. After all these years, my performance anxiety had reduced to a manageable level, but it was still there. I wondered if Laurence Olivier or John Barrymore, great stage actors, had ever conquered stage fright.

Media types, if they were in attendance, were of the print variety. No cameras were allowed.

This was the part of the trial to which I had to pay very close attention. It was my job to guide us through the morass of potential reversible error that lurked around every question during jury selection.

Both lawyers said, simultaneously, "Ready, your honor," and I motioned the Court Security Officer to bring in the jury pool, the sixty men and women who had been waiting out in the hall for this moment.

I focused my attention totally on the process. My butterflies were still there, but I knew they'd calm down after the first half-hour. The trial had begun and my passion for my work lifted me into that place where time passes too quickly to measure.

Prospective jurors filed in, one at a time, and sat in the gallery. The clerk called out the numbers and names of each registered voter. The tension in the room rose to a level that resembled a high hum. As each name was called, the clerk directed the jurors to take one of the twelve seats in the jury box and then filled the six extra chairs the Court Security Officer had set up in front of the box.

One could take a bite out of the air in the courtroom at this stage. After a few days, a trial takes on a more relaxed feel. But in the beginning, the participants are uncomfortable and the jurors are mostly bewildered; the parties try like hell to select a jury that will be biased in their favor; everyone on both legal teams is tired and sleep deprived, worried about that one last thing they hadn't done in preparation.

That tension was like nothing else in the world: the trial lawyer's equivalent of an Olympic event. Ready, set, go. Sometimes, I really missed the entire experience, but after splashing the cold water of insight on my face, I always came to my senses.

This jury venire looked like all the rest. Mostly women, casually dressed. A few men, college aged students or retirees.

Each carrying something to read during the long waiting periods inherent in the experience. All were here either because they couldn't get out of jury service one more time or they didn't have anything else to do.

Resting my hands on the desk to keep them from shaking with stress, I began to ask the preliminary questions from a prepared list I use in every trial: Did anyone know the litigants or the lawyers; did they have personal knowledge of the facts; was there any reason they couldn't be fair? Stuff like that. Yes answers would get them released from service, for cause.

Then, unlike a lot of federal judges, I always turn the questioning over to the lawyers. After some earlier mistakes when I first took the bench, I'd learned not to let the lawyers get out of control, though. I limited their *voir dire*, or questioning of the prospective jurors, to one hour each. How they used that hour was up to them, but they got one hour, no more, no less, to determine how or if they wanted to use their preemptory challenges.

On television, two or three cases are tried in an hour. In real life, a trial is slow and tedious. Even the short ones. Jury selection alone could take several days for some cases. As a trial lawyer, I'd once tried a case for sixteen weeks. As a judge, I'd bend over backwards to keep that from happening.

The plaintiff, Newton, would begin every phase of the trial and was positioned closest to the jury box because he had the burden of proof. He stood up and slowly buttoned the middle button of his single-breasted jacket, fumbling a little on purpose, beginning with his first gesture to win the jury over to his view of the case.

Newton walked over to about the middle of the rail in front of the jury box and stood there, letting them get a good look at him.

He was short and overweight. What hair he had left was gray

and cut in a fringe around his spherical head. His eyebrows were gray, too, making his violet eyes more startling somehow.

Newton put on his best good ol' boy accent, even though he was educated at Harvard just like I was, and said, "How many of you all believe you're entitled to personal privacy regarding your own life, assuming you're not doing anythin' illegal and ain't hurtin' nobody?"

The jurors identified with him instantly. That connection was the one thing he had that couldn't be contrived. All good trial lawyers perfected the art, or they quickly accepted another line of work.

"Please raise your hand if you agree." Every hand went up. He looked at them all, one at a time, made eye contact and nodded slowly, confirming a silent contract with each one.

"Are any of you all public figures?" No one admitted it, if they were. "Does anyone know what a public figure is?" He said the word as if it rhymed with "jigger."

The bewilderment I saw on their faces surprised me. Hard to believe there was anyone left in America who didn't know what a public figure was.

The Andrews nomination had spawned countless hours of discussion by the media about the character assassination our law allows of public figures. Obviously, just because some people thought Supreme Court appointments were required viewing, that didn't mean everyone agreed.

One juror, a young man in the back row dressed in a Pewter Pride golf shirt, raised his hand. "A public figger like who?" he asked, "say one of the Bucs?" He meant one of the Tampa Bay Buccaneers football team. Everybody nodded, apparently in agreement that Bucs were public figures, since it was impossible to live in Tampa without being aware of the team.

"Yes, that's right," Newton nodded, too. "Does anyone here recognize me to be a celebrity or a politician?" All heads shook negatively. I suppressed a smile. That must have been a blow to his ego at the same time it supported his case.

Newton had never been modest. In fact, over the years his name had probably been in the paper at least as many times as any local football player. The walls of Newton's office were lined with the newspaper and magazine accounts of his trial successes. He'd been on television enough that some of the jurors might have seen him.

"Well, lemme ask y'all this," he started, and my antennae went up. I sat a little straighter. I'd developed a sixth sense about trials. I knew I was going to have trouble from the defense team by the posture of lead defense counsel.

Newton continued talking to the Bucs fan in the third row who had answered his last question. "Suppose your wife had an affair, Mr. Bates. Now, I'm not sayin' she did, because I don't know nothin' of the kind. But let's just s'pose she did, for the moment, all right?"

Mr. Bates looked unsure, but he agreed by nodding slightly. "Would you like it if *The Tampa Tribune* printed that information in the paper?"

"No!" Mr. Bates responded emphatically, and he looked quite indignant about it, too.

"If *The Tribune* printed that your wife had an affair and it wasn't true, do you think they should get away with that?" Newton put his hands in the pockets of his suit coat, which made his elbows stick out like chicken wings while he rocked forward on the balls of his feet.

"Certainly not!" Mr. Bates showed his indignation plainly.

"And if *The Tribune* did print such a thing, such a scandalous thing, do you think it would hurt you or your wife or your children in any way?" Newton asked.

"Your honor!" Defense counsel jumped to his feet, almost shouting his objection. "He is trying to prejudice this jury by asking questions that he knows do not represent the true facts in this case. He knows he is a public figure under the law and what was printed about him was absolutely true. He's trying to mislead this jury and taint the whole panel. I move for a mistrial."

Newton was guilty of all this, just as the defense attorney was posturing to undo the damage as early as he could.

Again, in deliberate contrast, Newton acted unperturbed. "Judge, I think it's for the jury to decide what the true facts are in this case. That's why we're here. And I'm entitled to explore their opinions. That's what *voir dire* is for, as counsel well knows. I oppose any motions for mistrial and," he stopped for a moment so that his point would be emphasized, "I promise to be polite and not interrupt defense counsel if he will stop interrupting me." The jury snickered. Newton was smooth and sure. He knew the game and he knew how to counter all the other side's moves. There is no substitute for experience in the local jurisdiction. The home-field advantage applied to the game of trial, just like any other high stakes game.

By now, my butterflies had relaxed and I was well into the rhythm of the trial. I overruled the objection, but instructed the jury that defense counsel was well within his rights to make it. I denied the motion for mistrial and instructed both counsel to make any such motions at the bench, out of the hearing of the jury, because I did not intend to have my trial interrupted by grandstanding.

It was familiar territory to all but the jurors. Like a drama in its hundredth performance, each of the actors recited the well-worn lines and like the untutored audience they were, the prospective jurors remained ignorant of the backstage tricks that made the performers successful.

Newton continued his *voir dire* in the same vein, raising the issues with the jurors and making *The Review* out to be a scandal sheet of the worst order. Which, of course, it was.

A couple of times I reminded him that this was not argument, but jury selection. Otherwise, I allowed him enough rope to hang himself.

The jury would remember Newton's *voir dire* and that the facts he portrayed didn't resemble what they heard in the trial. Whether they'd hold that against Newton during their deliberations or not was always the multi-million dollar question.

Newton finally ran out of time and yielded the floor to the blue-chip, silk-stocking law firm partner from New York who had been admitted to practice in my court specially to handle this case. Although the jury wouldn't be told, he wasn't a member of the Florida Bar, so he was burdened with the handicap of playing the game in an unfamiliar arena before he opened his mouth.

The man stood up to adjust himself before he began his *voir dire*. A new actor had entered the stage and the jurors paid attention.

He was about 6'2", with a full head of expertly coiffed and colored blonde hair, manicured nails and a medium-gray plaid suit that looked as expensive as it undoubtedly was. He wore brown shoes and the hose (for they were not mere socks) picked up the pale brown threads in the suit.

His brilliant white shirt had French cuffs with gold knot cufflinks just peeking out of the bottom of the sleeves of his suit. As he pulled down on first one cuff and then the other, straightening them just right as he flexed his shoulders, his clear nail polish reflected the glare of the fluorescent lights.

The tie was a yellow print knotted in a half Windsor and it hung straight down his flat stomach to just above the shiny gold monogrammed buckle of his brown alligator belt.

He looked the picture of what he was: an $850-an-hour hired gun. His name, he told us all, was "A. (for Archibald) Alexander Tremain, VI." When he announced himself to the jury, I noticed tittering in the back row, as I suppressed my own grin.

CHAPTER EIGHTEEN

Tampa, Florida
Monday 11:05 a.m.
January 24, 2000

TREMAIN STOOD IN THE same spot Newton had used to hold
the prospective jurors enthralled for the last hour and then he
turned to look at the remainder of the jury pool in the gallery
behind where Newton was now seated. To each group, Tremain
nodded his head slightly, but he didn't smile.

"I want each of you to know that today, if you are selected for
this jury, you will have the responsibility of deciding whether the
United States Constitution is something we all live by, or whether
it's not." He stopped and looked in turn at each of the eighteen
prospective jurors in front of him. At this rate, his hour for
questions would be up before he got any information at all.

"At the end of this trial, the jury that is selected here will be
asked whether the First Amendment still means anything in this
country, or whether true speech can be punished. Mr. Bates," he
picked out the juror who had seemed so sympathetic to Newton

earlier, "do you believe in the United States Constitution?"

"Yes, sir, I do." Mr. Bates gave the expected answer. Our voters are a pretty patriotic and conservative lot. Except for South Florida, which was populated primarily by liberal Democrats from the Northeastern United States, the rest of the state has had a strong, conservative Republican electorate for years. That dichotomy has gotten the state into trouble in national elections. But here in Tampa, it was best to remember the probable perspective of local jurors.

Someone had apparently clued Tremain in and he had taken the advice of trial specialists, attempting to condition the jurors early to laws they might find personally repugnant and excuse jurors who couldn't make the commitment.

"Do you believe that you have the right to say just about whatever you want in this country? Not the privilege, but the right?" He raised his voice when he said "right" and pounded a closed fist into his flat palm.

"I guess so, yeah. But I don't think you should hurt anybody by saying things that aren't true. That's not constitutional." Mr. Bates remembered Newton's hypothetical about his wife's adultery.

"You're right, Mr. Bates, you're absolutely right. If you knowingly say something that's not true, that shouldn't be protected by the Constitution most of the time. But what if it is true? Shouldn't you be able to say anything that's true and not be afraid of being sued?" Tremain pushed his advantage and his theory.

"Sure." Mr. Bates gave in. He was a true lawyer's nightmare. He wanted to be on the jury so badly that he'd agree with anything you asked him. The lawyers had no way of knowing which way he'd vote, so leaving him on the jury would be a wild card. The trial lawyer's equivalent of white-knuckle time.

There was nothing I could do about Bates. One of the parties would have to strike him or he'd remain with us through the course of the trial.

Tremain nodded approvingly, giving Mr. Bates a figurative gold star. Then he moved on. "I certainly hope none of you are gay or lesbian?"

There was an uncomfortable silence in the room. Some jurors shook their heads and looked from side to side, almost involuntarily, wondering where this was going. The statement of the case that was read to the jury at the beginning of the *voir dire* never mentioned what *The Review* had printed about Newton.

"If any of you eighteen potential jurors are gay or lesbian, please tell us now, because you must be excused from this jury," Tremain said firmly.

"Objection!" Newton shouted, jumping to his feet as I banged down my gavel and sternly admonished the defense attorney. The jurors chuckled self-consciously, looking around for raised hands. I asked to see both counsel in chambers and we left the courtroom for my smaller hearing room, each of the members of the defense team following behind Tremain the way goslings follow their mother.

I turned to defense counsel as we entered my chambers, "Just what exactly are you trying to do here? If this is standard *voir dire* in your part of the woods, I can tell you that's not the kind of question we routinely ask here in Tampa."

"Your honor, the issue of Mr. Newton's homosexuality will be at the heart of this trial. He denies it, but he has put the truth of the matter squarely before the court. I think my client is entitled to know whether any homosexuals are on that panel. They should not be sitting in judgment on the decision to publish this material. I want them all dismissed for cause." The rest of the defense team nodded on cue.

"Judge," Newton responded, all pretense of the country bumpkin magically erased. "Assuming some potential jurors are homosexuals, the defendant would not be entitled to excuse them on that basis alone. If he tried, it would be objectionable and possibly even illegal. That last question should be stricken and no others like it should be allowed in the rest of the *voir dire*."

Newton was hot and I didn't really blame him. But he had to have known Tremain's attack was coming. Like a lot of things, though, knowing and experiencing are vastly different.

"Do either of you have any law on this for me?" I looked at them both, sternly. They didn't, which made me suspect that the defense knew what the law was and it wasn't good for their side.

If Tremain had any support for his argument, he'd have been waving it in my face. In triplicate. Like so many issues that come up during any trial, I had to fly by the seat of my pants and hope for the best. That's what judicial discretion was most of the time: careful application of the sophisticated wild-ass-guess method.

"I don't know what the legal answer to the question is, but I found your question personally offensive, Mr. Tremain. On that basis, I will not allow any further questioning into the personal sexual habits of jurors." I turned the doorknob to return to the courtroom. "And if any more questions like that are asked in violation of my order, I will declare a mistrial. Understood?"

To his credit, Tremain didn't argue. His point had been made with the jury panel and we all knew it. Newton requested a curative instruction, which I agreed to give, but it wouldn't help. The cat couldn't be forced back into the bag.

I asked both lawyers whether they wanted a mistrial now, to start over. They declined.

We went back to the courtroom and finished up the jury selection without further incident. Not surprisingly, at the end,

Tremain used one of his peremptory challenges to dismiss Mr. Bates.

When I glanced at my watch, I was amazed that we'd reached the late afternoon. Absorbed in the problems of others, I'd managed to forget about General Andrews for a while. We'd made good progress today. Our jury was sworn and I'd adjourned until the next morning for opening statements.

As soon as the gavel came down, my personal world flooded back into my thoughts, bringing back the unease I'd gone to sleep with last night.

CHAPTER NINETEEN

Tampa, Florida
Monday 5:30 p.m.
January 24, 2000

KATE AUSTIN, MY MOTHER'S best friend and the woman who has been like a mother to me since Mom died when I was sixteen, lives in a bungalow on Oregon Avenue, four houses from the Bayshore. The house sits on an exposed corner lot and the kitchen looks out over the side street.

Both George and I worried about strangers being able to drive up and see Kate standing in the kitchen, but she said we watch too much television. She wouldn't even put blinds on the windows. She says she moved to Florida for sunlight, but we know she moved here for me.

I pulled into the driveway and walked up to the screened back door, calling her name as I approached. I didn't want to startle her, since I hadn't called to tell her to expect me.

Kate was in the backyard working on her newest project, an English garden. As always in her presence, total calm washed over me and I felt more relaxed than I had in days.

I should have come here before now. It's not easy for me to admit that the strength and competence I have as a judge when dealing with other people's problems doesn't always translate into taking care of myself. George had always understood that about me and been my advocate.

When I had to face the fact, I comforted myself with the old adage that the lawyer who represents himself has a fool for a client. In my case, that was certainly true. I could fight the fiercest battle for someone else, but for myself…

I watched Kate for a few minutes, still flexible enough to get down on her knees in her garden easily. Kate had been doing yoga for thirty years and she was still as flexible as any twenty-five year old. The yoga was part of Kate's New Age philosophy that seemed to serve her well at the same time that it annoyed my conservative husband.

Almost as if she knew I was there, Kate turned around and waved to me. Was she clairvoyant? She claimed to be. She said it was a skill anyone could develop. She did seem to be one step ahead of my emotions all the time, a trait that often annoyed me.

Kate put away her tools and suggested a glass of iced tea, the quintessential southern hospitality offering. We chatted about nothing in particular for a while in the kitchen as she washed up, poured the tea into tall glasses, added a sprig of mint and a slice of lime to each one.

Then she carried a small tray with the glasses and cookies she'd made using an old family recipe out to her patio. We sat, enjoying the companionable silence overlooking her wonderfully overgrown flowers.

Kate's garden is so wild and uncontrolled, like nothing else in my life. All the flowers are mixed together erratically, the colors both brilliant and subdued. Our gardens at Minaret are beautiful, too, but they're perfectly ordered, weeded, matched and wouldn't dare encroach on the brick paths or the grass. Kate's garden was creative and free, a reflection of Kate herself.

After a while, Kate said, "Dear, why don't you just ask me what you came to ask? The suspense is more than my heart can take on such a beautiful afternoon."

My connection to Kate is intense, almost as if she were my real mother. She can sense my moods and can usually tell when I'm troubled. She says it's because she's a channel for the universe and she trusts her intuition. That may be true, and it comforts me to think so.

Or, it may be that I rarely come by just to chat anymore, so that every time I come over it's because something is bothering me. That's George's theory, anyway.

Whatever the reason, whenever I'm in trouble, I go to Kate. She knows it and I think she likes it. Everyone wants to be needed.

Today, I wanted reassurance. I hoped George would return to normal. But what if he didn't?

"It's George," I said.

"George? Mr. Wonderful? Your knight in shining armor? That George?" She teased. Actually, Kate thinks more of George than I do, if that's possible. They are members of some kind of mutual admiration society that makes it useless to complain about one to the other.

"It's not funny, Kate. George has been acting very strangely and I just don't understand it. Now that this Andrews thing is behind us, I'm hoping he'll be better. But I'm worried." So I told her about his outburst at the restaurant and how he threw the Warwicks and Andrews out for good.

"Good for him." She sounded almost as indignant as George

had been. "It's about time Tory started acting her age instead of like a thwarted toddler. Throwing crystal glasses, indeed. Are you all right now?" She reached over and moved my hair away from the right side of my forehead so she could look at the lump, which was a lot smaller, but the bruise was still slightly visible.

"I'm fine. It's George I'm worried about. That night, I don't know what time he finally came upstairs. The next day, he was out and gone before I got up. He made up some story about breakfast, but that's not likely," I said, continuing my litany of grievances, afraid to express the extent of my worry.

"Maybe the man wants a little privacy, Willa. He stays right where you can find him ninety-nine percent of the time. Isn't he entitled to a little mystery? Once in a while?" Kate never accepted even the smallest criticism of George.

When we first married, she told me I should never tell her about arguments with my husband. She said that he and I loved each other, so we'd make up, but she would not be able to forgive him if he hurt me.

So, I rarely complained to her about George. But in truth, there'd seldom been much to complain about at all in the seventeen years we'd been married. George was near perfect as far as I was concerned. Until lately.

George wasn't a man of mystery at all. Never had been. But everyone was entitled to privacy. "Sure he is. But he could just say that. Why does he have to make something up that we both know is untrue?" As we discussed this, I became more upset, not less. "I'm not used to George lying to me."

"Okay. George is protective of you and occasionally wants a little privacy. What's so terrible?" She ate a cookie and offered the plate to me. I shook my head.

Then I told her about his temper tantrum at Deborah's house

with the reporters, his insistence that Andrews didn't commit suicide and how interested Chief Hathaway was in George's murder theory.

Kate seemed a little more concerned, now, but tried to reassure me. "Tell me what it is, exactly, that you're worrying about," she said. Solemnly. Seriously.

CHAPTER TWENTY

HESITANTLY, I TOLD HER. "I think George is in some kind of trouble."

Unlike the relief of turning on a light to expose the absence of the bogeyman in the closet, voicing my concern seemed to make it more real.

Kate reached over and patted my hand. "Willa, you love George and you don't want to lose him, which makes sense. You've just come from Deborah's home, a widow, and the possibility of losing your husband has foolishly captured your imagination."

"But it's not foolish, Kate. I feel it," I told her, voicing for the first time the truth. I did feel like I was losing George. I didn't want to be melodramatic about it, but he seemed to be slipping away from me and I didn't know how to hold onto him.

"You're imagining things. And you're worrying

unnecessarily," she said. I wanted to believe her. "Let me think about it and we can talk some more. But now that you've told me, don't you think about it anymore or that will just confuse the energy."

Kate poured another glass of tea and changed the subject, but I couldn't concentrate on what she said.

Unfortunately, I wasn't a child anymore. I couldn't just decide not to think about George and wish my concerns away.

When I was younger, Kate had a worry box. She would have me symbolically put my worries in the box and she would lock them in with a small gold key that she wore around her neck. I'd forget about my troubles and she would tell me that she'd given them to the Universe to handle.

What worked when I was sixteen didn't work as well at thirty-nine. But I was still willing to try it. At this point, I was willing to try anything. I felt that, on some level, my marriage was in trouble, and what made me so uneasy was that I didn't know, couldn't figure out exactly, what that trouble was.

When I arrived home, I learned that Kate's worry box had flown open and let my anxiety out.

CHAPTER TWENTY-ONE

Tampa, Florida
Monday 7:00 p.m.
January 24, 2000

GEORGE WAS WATCHING THE evening news rehash the General Andrews mess. When I turned my gaze to the television screen, a little "oh" escaped my lips when I saw George's image, his voice repeating what Frank Bennett described off camera as "Prominent Republican strategist George Carson's murder theory." Just the title set my teeth on edge, but I couldn't drag my gaze away.

Next, Frank cornered Police Chief Ben Hathaway. "Have you found any evidence to support a cause of death other than suicide?" he asked.

And Ben's reply: "I can't comment about an ongoing investigation beyond the official statement I've already given."

Frank returned to the camera, and concluded. "Chief Hathaway did not deny the possibility that General Andrews was murdered."

I sat down heavily beside George on the couch. "Why would Frank air such a thing?" I said, breathless.

George replied, too calmly, "Frank has a responsibility to tell the truth, Willa. Andy didn't commit suicide and we all know it. If Frank puts the real story on the air, the truth will come out, the killer will be found. Otherwise, Andy's suicide will just be another speculative story for years, like Marilyn Monroe."

He turned off the television and asked me if I wanted a drink. I wanted a dozen. He poured me a full glass of Sapphire and tonic.

Before I sipped the gin, I voiced my sober conclusion.

"Frank asked you if he could run the story before he did it, didn't he? That's the reason the story didn't play last night."

George was unperturbed. "Of course, he asked me. But I'm sure he would have aired the truth even if I'd objected. Frank is our friend, but not at the expense of his journalistic ethics."

I felt my alarm rise another notch. "You've always thought 'journalistic ethics' was an oxymoron. When did you get to be so supportive of the media?" Anxiety injected my tone with unwanted sarcasm, but George just turned and walked out into the night air. Whether he heard me or not, I didn't know.

I followed him out to the veranda and the dogs lumbered after us. We sat in our usual white wicker rockers. I took a big gulp of my gin and tonic and changed my approach. "George, don't you see? This story makes it look like you know something. Like you have some inside information." I took another swig, seeking an instant tranquilizer, but the comforting numbness didn't come.

"I do have inside information," George said quietly.

Not only was the gin not tranquilizing me, every nerve ending now buzzed throughout my body. Maybe this was the intuition or spirit guide Kate was always telling me I had. And maybe it was just years of experience as a lawyer and judge, but I knew, even before George explained it to me, that this was not good news.

"What inside information is that?" I squeaked out, past the lump in my throat.

"You'd better have a bigger drink. This will take awhile," he said. I didn't argue. I handed him my highball glass and waited until he returned with a tumbler. He'd refilled the ice, Sapphire and tonic. We were out of lemons at the small bar in the den, so he'd substituted a lime.

George sat in deep reverie for a while. Because I feared what he would tell me, I didn't rush him. I sipped my drink, watched the gentle lapping of the bay against our beach and concentrated on my breathing until I felt myself finally begin to relax.

Really, what could be so alarming?

As Kate had said just hours ago, this was George, after all. The man I'd been married to for seventeen years. I knew him better than he knew himself. What could he possibly tell me that would be so bad?

Finally, he began, in a quiet, slow way, as if he were telling a story around a campfire. "You know that before we met, I was in the army and I served under Andy overseas."

He seemed to need me to acknowledge this, so I said, "Hmmm." George's army career was exactly the kind of thing that made me love him as I did. He'd joined the army right after college, even though he didn't have to, because he thought it was the right thing to do.

George was always doing the right thing and he never had any trouble figuring out what the right thing was. Maybe it was his Lutheran upbringing, or that WASP noblesse oblige. Whatever it was, George navigated by a strong moral compass that was sometimes bewildering to me.

When we were dating, I thought dependable George wasn't

likely to throw too many curve balls at his wife and that was just what I wanted. After a lifetime of insecurity, my mother's death, Dad leaving me with Kate, feeling adrift and alone, George's brand of support and security was just what I'd craved.

Seventeen years later, I was still satisfied with it. The problem was, the shifting sands of George's life were changing both him and our relationship. The entire situation was baffling to me. I couldn't understand it, and I didn't want to.

George continued, "When I first met him, Andy was the best kind of officer the army could turn out. He was an honorable man who viewed his career as a calling. He insisted his men abide by the highest moral code he and the army could exact. There were so many examples of this during the time I served under him that I can't name them all, and I'm sure I've shared some of them with you before."

Again, an affirmative response seemed to be called for. "Hmmm," I said.

"Andy and I came to be friends. I didn't make the army my career, but he didn't hold my decision against me." George smiled a little. "We had a connection regardless of how infrequently we saw each other. Whenever we could, we'd meet for dinner or drinks, but the years put distance between us."

He paused again, sipped his Scotch this time, and added more firmly, "Until Andy was promoted to Colonel and stationed in Tampa not long after you and I moved here."

I remembered the time well. We were new in Tampa then and the Andrews family was one of the few we'd known. We saw Andy and Deborah and their children as frequently as Andy's busy travel schedule would allow.

That was when I'd come to like Deborah immensely, although she was drinking heavily, even then. She was a busy mother and I didn't see her often, so we finally lost touch.

Even in those days, Andy was a bit too much of a man's man for my taste and his views on women bordered on misogynistic. Mostly, in my presence, he simply behaved as if women didn't exist.

I remembered several social occasions where Andy stood tall and straight, quiet and polite while women in our circle talked. He wasn't listening and he rarely responded unless we asked him a direct question. It was more like he was waiting for the noise to stop.

When a quiet moment inevitably occurred, Andy would turn to one of the men and start a totally new conversation about something none of the women were the least bit interested in, such as the maintenance routine for the stealth bomber or something.

He wasn't exactly disrespectful, but he treated women as if they were flies buzzing around a picnic: Something that couldn't be helped and were best ignored.

Back then, both Andy and I had made allowances for each other because of my respect for Deborah and our mutual admiration for George, our common friend. But I never spent any time alone with him. The idea just wouldn't have occurred to either of us. We'd have had absolutely nothing to talk about.

George's voice brought me back to the present.

He continued, now, in that same far away, remembering kind of tone. "Derek Dickson was another officer, the third member of our triumvirate. Derek made his career with the army, but he served in a different unit from Andy and his career stalled out after he made Colonel."

My head had started to spin a little because of the gin and not having eaten anything since my tuna sandwich at lunch. I squinted my eyes and tried to pay attention.

George cleared his throat. "One day, we heard that Derek's boy, a young First Lieutenant, had committed suicide. Derek was crushed. The boy had gone to West Point. Derek had been so proud of his son."

He left to refill his glass, and he took his time about it, gathering his composure.

When he returned, I felt the chill he exuded. He'd become more remote, his emotions in check, determined to finish the distasteful story.

"I wanted to send a gift of some kind to Derek and go to the funeral. I wanted Andy to go with me."

"Did he?"

"He flatly refused. He said the boy was a coward who couldn't face his responsibilities and the army didn't need him."

George stopped a second or two, then finished. "He said the army didn't need Derek either because he'd obviously sired a deviant."

My breath drew in quickly, in shock and disgust.

George refused to look at me. "Andy, unbelievably to me, tried to arrange a posthumous dishonorable discharge for cowardice, but it couldn't be done. Andy and Derek quarreled about it."

Then he raised his eyes to mine and I could see how much it cost him to tell me this now, years later. In an even softer voice, so that I had to strain forward to hear him, George said, "Derek killed himself the next day."

Incredulity heightened my disgust. "That's despicable! I had no idea. Why would Andy do such a thing?"

To deliberately hurt a man and his family when he'd suffered the death of his child was gratuitously cruel beyond measure. I'd known Andy to be a single-minded military man back then, not a harsh, heartless monster.

And I knew George. He felt guilty. I sensed it in everything he told me, in everything he'd done these past few weeks to keep Andrews off the court.

"I couldn't fathom it, even then," he said quietly. "But it was obvious to me that the Andy I had known years before was not the man who literally ruined Derek's life."

"What happened between the two of you?" For I knew there was still more to this story.

"Andy and I fought about it and some pretty harsh words were said. Words I never regretted, even once," George's defiance reminded me of the principled man I was used to, and I was glad to see that man was still there, somewhere. "After that, I distanced myself from Andy and I guess he distanced himself from me, too." George stood up now, at the veranda's rail, looking out over the bay.

There was more. I waited.

"Over the years, you know, you hear things. I heard a lot of similar stories about Andy's lack of compassion. Even the way he treated his kids was overly rigid and controlling. He acted like they were his to command, too."

I hadn't said anything in quite a while. I didn't know what to say.

"I'm sorry," was the best I could manage.

George sipped his drink for a while, almost as if he was alone with his thoughts. But he wanted me to know now, to know what he'd kept to himself all these years.

He turned around to face me. "I finally came to believe that Andy was mentally unbalanced. As he rose further and further up the ladder, and eventually received his fourth star, I became truly alarmed."

George walked back into the den and returned with a light throw I used on the sofa sometimes. I blamed the evening chill that had settled on my shoulders for causing gooseflesh to rise on my arms. He placed the throw around me, snugging it up close, and cupped my cheek in his hand before he knelt down to look me in the eye.

"That's why I worked so hard to defeat his nomination. Why I couldn't let such a man sit on the highest policy-making court for the next generation." George looked directly at me, trying to communicate the intensity of his feelings. "There were so many good men in the army. And many more good candidates for the court. But Andy was unfit to serve. I knew it. President Benson and Sheldon Warwick knew it. I think even Andy knew it."

George continued to look at me intently. I realized it was important to him that I understand now, although he hadn't shared any of this with me before. I nodded. It was all the speech I could manage.

He took my silence for lack of comprehension. "But don't you see? Andy would never have given up on any fight. Fighting was how he solved all his problems. He would have seen this battle for the Supreme Court seat to the bitter end and he was too damn close to winning."

He stood up again and put both hands in his pockets. "A heart attack from the stress could have killed him or maybe some other lunatic with a better aim could have gotten him." His voice filled with strength and conviction. "But he would never, never have taken himself out of the game early and definitely not by suicide. Someone killed him. No one will ever convince me otherwise."

I drew the throw closer around my shoulders and tried to stop shaking.

The minutes passed as I struggled to get myself under control, to face one central question I couldn't answer: Was I more upset by the story itself or by the fact that I'd never heard it before?

CHAPTER TWENTY-TWO

I THOUGHT I KNEW everything there was to know about my husband. I'd believed we were soul mates in the way few couples are. I knew his favorite meals, vacation spots, what he liked to read, even the underwear he preferred.

I knew all these trivial details of George's life. How could I have had no clue about his failed relationship with Andrews, something so important? A serious personal friendship had exploded in a spectacular and awful way. Yet, George had kept it to himself.

What other things had he kept secret?

I shook that off. Or tried to.

Maybe our connection had just never been tested before, I hoped.

My most significant personal tragedy, the death of my mother, happened long before I met George.

Since we'd married, our lives had been pretty uneventful, upwardly mobile, middle class, white bread normal.

Like the lives of most of our friends.

George had been my lifeline to the world. He acted as my anchor, my sounding board. He was my protection and companionship. We lived in a special world. He cared for me and I cared for him. We shared everything.

Or so I'd thought.

If I found out he had other secrets, what would they do to our lives?

Could we live with such knowledge?

I really wasn't sure. And it was that lack of certainty that unnerved me. I needed to be sure of George, I wanted to be sure of him. Dammit, I had been sure.

Until lately, I had been dead certain I knew who and what my husband was.

My emotions careened uncontrollably from hysteria to catatonia. I felt alternately sad and angry, near tears and near rage.

Because I didn't know what to say or how to say it, I said nothing. I was so lost in my bewilderment, so focused on my personal feelings, that I didn't hear George leave the flat awhile later. He must have gone downstairs to work, I thought, to the extent I noticed at all.

By the time I found my way back to reality, it was dark out and getting colder. There were no lights on in the flat and the dogs were outside, howling to get in. In fact, that was the noise that roused me and made me realize that George wasn't there.

I stood on shaky legs and opened the door to let Harry and Bess run headlong into the room. After petting them for a while and giving them a few treats, I did what I always do when I need to control my emotions.

When I don't know what else to do, I work. I know I use work as an escape from life, a substitute for life. It's where I go to get away from everything that I can't cope with. I know it's not healthy, but it's better than other self-destructive methods of escaping the world. And it works.

I got comfortable in sweats and began to work on the Newton file in preparation for tomorrow's opening statements. In the den, I sat at the desk where Aunt Minnie had done her household accounts as a young bride. It was a partner's desk; one person could sit at either side and both could work in the middle.

At some point, hours later, noticing I was hungry, I called downstairs, asked George to send up whatever tonight's special was and join me for dinner. When he said he had already eaten, I realized it was after ten o'clock. I'd been working for over three hours and didn't remember a thing I'd read. I'd have to start over and try to concentrate this time. It would be a long night.

Making room on the desk for my dinner tray awhile later, I noticed the black leather book Kate had given me for Christmas last year sitting on the small table beside my favorite reading chair. It was embossed in the center with the words she'd said to me when she gave me the journal, "When your heart speaks, take good notes."

The pages of the book were blank. Kate insisted that keeping a journal would provide guidance and connection to my intuition. Every time I saw her, she asked me if I'd started to use it. She'd asked me today, in fact, but I had ignored the question.

Maybe now was a good time. If I wrote down some of these thoughts I was having about George, maybe I could at least leave them there on the page and pay attention to my work.

I wrote for over an hour, putting down all the things that had happened in the past three days and how I felt. I wrote long paragraphs describing how shaken I was over George's secret. And I wrote one short sentence about how stupid it was for him to tell Frank Bennett about it.

Finally, I approached the questions I feared most: If Andy didn't commit suicide, who killed him? And did George know the answer to that question?

My hand shook so badly that I couldn't read what I wrote next: what would the State Attorney do to George?

I slammed the journal closed and threw it on the floor. It landed face down in the corner under one of Aunt Minnie's twenty wing chairs that seemed to sprout full-blown in their ball-and-claw feet every time I had my head turned.

It would be a damn long time before I touched that thing again. Not only did writing in the journal not make me feel better, I'd come to a conclusion that everybody else must have reached yesterday. I'd never felt so stupid.

I left George a note, got my car keys and stomped off down the stairs, out into the cold air of the wee hours. Although I hadn't glanced at the clock, it had been hours since my dinner had been delivered.

Greta and I drove over to St. Pete beach. I had a long, long walk. I settled onto a towel on the beach and stared out into the endless dark horizon. And just as the sun was coming up over the horizon, drove home, got dressed and headed to the courthouse.

Nothing was resolved and I didn't feel any better and if either of those lawyers messed with me today, they'd be damn sorry they had.

I stopped at Cold Storage, my favorite Cuban coffee place, on the way to the office. Cold Storage lost its lease on Florida Avenue when the City sold the land to new development after the Ice Palace increased business over there. Now, it was located at the corner of Whiting and Tampa Street in a much bigger building.

Sometimes when restaurants move, they lose their ambiance. But Cold Storage managed to reproduce its graffiti on the walls, pictures of patrons and welcoming atmosphere in new, larger surroundings. I drank the heavenly mixture of sweet, strong Cuban coffee and scalded milk in the way an addict consumes heroin—I needed it.

When I arrived at the Courthouse, I saw the news vans in front and seized the new target for my anger. If the lawyers in my case were giving press conferences I'd throw them all in jail. I didn't want my cases tried in the media. The courtroom is where all evidence would be presented.

If I had to put a gag order on the participants to get the point across, that's what I would do. I'd done it before and if that big city lawyer didn't know it now, he'd know it in the next ten minutes, I fumed.

By the time I got up to my office, I'd worked myself into a fine snit and I was ready to take on everyone who crossed me. All of which I blamed on the caffeine in the Cuban coffee.

I pushed open the outer door to Margaret's office and stormed through without even so much as my customary good morning. I snatched my robe from the hook on the back of my door, put my arms through it and marched out into the courtroom, ready to vent my rage on the first person I saw.

Absolutely no one was there. I asked the Court Security Officer where the parties were and he said he didn't know. I glanced at the clock. Eight thirty-five, five minutes after we were set to start.

The ruckus from the hall was the flock of media I'd witnessed out front just a few minutes before. I turned to the Court Security Officer. "Please go out in the hall and tell both Mr. Newton and

Mr. Tremain that if they are not in here in five minutes, this case will be the first in history to have judgment entered against both parties." To his everlasting credit, he didn't laugh at me. "Tell the media they are, from this point forward, barred from the courtroom and do not let them in."

I couldn't keep the media out indefinitely, but I could do it for the next thirty minutes at least.

Until one of them went to the CJ and he entered an order allowing them back in which I knew he'd do the second they asked him, just to tweak me.

And because he'd be right.

"Yes, ma'am!" the officer said, on his way out as he said it. The court reporter gave me one of those, "What's with you?" looks, but I didn't care.

The relationship of the press to the law was an issue I'd always felt strongly about, but on no sleep and less patience, I would definitely have made good on my threat to give Mr. Newton the fifty million dollars he requested and to dismiss his case with prejudice at the same time. Let them figure that out in the Eleventh Circuit Court of Appeals.

Apparently, the officer got the point across, because both lawyers hurried into the courtroom and remained standing at their respective counsel tables while the officer kept everyone else out. I was still standing as well and we all looked foolish.

Getting myself under control, I gestured to the court reporter to begin taking down the proceedings, and managed to speak in an even tone instead of like a madwoman.

"Counselors, listen closely because I am only going to say this once and I expect no misunderstandings. This case is pending before the United States District Court for the Middle District of Florida. We spent the entire day yesterday selecting a jury. The case is not being tried to the media and the jury is not the public. From this point forward neither of you are to discuss this case with any member of the media, on or off the record, until the verdict is returned and the jurors are released. This order includes any conversations of any kind.

"If I so much as hear a rumor that you are talking to a friend over coffee who happens to be employed by one of the newspapers, I will enter a verdict against the offender in this case immediately. And I will award fees and costs in amounts I deem appropriate. Is that perfectly clear?"

"But, Your Honor—" Newton sputtered.

"Judge, you can't—" Tremain spit out simultaneously.

I cut them both off with a slam of my gavel.

"There will be no argument and no further discussion on this subject. I can't bar the media from the courtroom forever, but I can stop you from talking to them. It is completely within my discretion to do all that I've told you I will do." I turned to the officer and told him to bring in the jury in ten minutes. "Don't test me, gentlemen."

The system fails only because we let it. That wasn't going to happen in my courtroom, where I still had control. Not in this trial, and not in any other.

Despite my outward calm, I was still breathing hard. I felt my fists clenched at my sides and strained to release my fingers.

Both the lawyers were united against me now. That was perfectly fine with me. I was legally right here, they were behaving like jackasses, and I was tired of it all.

Besides that, at the moment I was spoiling for a good fight with somebody.

Too bad the CJ wasn't here right now.

CHAPTER TWENTY-THREE

Tampa, Florida
Tuesday 9:30 a.m.
January 25, 2000

ONE OF THE MOST exciting days of any trial is when the lawyers make their opening statements, a time I normally anticipated with some curiosity, if not joy. Openings are similar to the trailer for a movie: they give an overview of what's to come. It's the first time the jury, the judge and the other side all hear the whole story.

No matter how much a lawyer prepares for opening, she is never quite sure what the other side will say. Sometimes, what is disclosed in opening is a fact or a theory the other side had never considered.

The closer a lawyer gets to trial, the more he begins to believe his own case. A dangerous road to travel because it makes him believe he can see what's around the blind corners.

Newton v. The Whitman Esquire Review was one of those cases where both lawyers were going to be unpleasantly surprised.

Back in my chambers, while I waited for the lawyers to prepare, I attended to the thousand and three details that somehow just multiplied on my desk like rats in a laboratory. I've never had, nor do I want to have, any actual experience with rats. Pink telephone slips must be related to rats in some molecular way, though. What else could explain their proliferation?

There were two messages from the CJ. I gleefully put them at the bottom of the pile, and I began to handle the others. As usual, caught up in my work, I became unaware of the passing time.

Margaret buzzed me on the intercom. "Judge? It's getting late," she said.

The courtroom was full when I went in again, twenty minutes late. I vowed to work on this problem. I hated judges to be late when I practiced law. I'd been convinced it was a personal snub, that they just couldn't be bothered to be on time for the litigants who were, after all, their reason for being. Or that they thought their precious time was more important than ours.

Life was just one long, educational experience, wasn't it?

When the trial began again, I nodded to Nelson Newton who rose to his full five-feet-four, smoothed down his stained red tie, and sucked his protruding gut in enough to button the rumpled blue suit jacket, as he prepared to make his entrance.

I've seen Nelson at social functions and at George's restaurant. I know for a fact that he owns more than one suit and all fit him perfectly. He wore this outfit because he wanted to appear poor and needy, to make the jury feel sorry for him, particularly in comparison to Tremain's expensive tailoring. For the same reason he sat at counsel table alone and used the bare minimum of documents.

Continuing his personal mime game of 'me David, they Goliath,' Nelson picked up his one manila file folder and pulled out three wrinkled sheets of five-by-seven notepaper that probably came from the same car rental desk as his pen. He looked the sheets over, front and back, returned them to the folder, and stepped up to the podium.

Of course, he knew very well he couldn't see over the podium, but he wanted the jury to know. He turned and asked permission not to use it. I granted the request. He knew I would. He asks every trial, even though I don't require lawyers to use the podium and no permission is necessary. More elaborate play-acting. But Tremain hadn't seen it coming.

Before he ever said a word in his opening, Newton had the jury on his side. His disadvantages, albeit carefully orchestrated, were designed to make the jury think he was the underdog. Americans always root for the underdog. It may be genetic. Christians one, lions nothing.

I felt my mood lighten and hid my smile behind my hand as I pretended to cough. Once again, work engaged me, and I was able to forget about George and Andy and my collapsing marriage and murder for a while.

Nelson began without further preamble. "All of us were told growin' up that sticks 'n' stones would break our bones, but names would never hurt us. Our mamas didn't want us fightin' in the schoolyard, so they told us to just ignore kids who called us names." He had the jury nodding in agreement.

"But we knew then, just as we know now, that names do hurt us, don't they? Calling someone names can not only hurt their feelings, but hurt their business and their relationships with their family and friends."

The jury looked like parishioners in a tent revival, they were so attuned to Nelson by now.

"That's what this case is about. *The Whitman Esquire Review,* a newspaper printed out in San Francisco, called me a name." He emphasized San Francisco as if it was the very essence of hell, instead of a marvelous, cosmopolitan city.

"They don't know me and they don't know our town. But they called me a name anyway, and they printed it in the paper, and it's hurt me." He stopped here and looked hurt. The posture was so affected that it was hard not to laugh at him. Although the jurors weren't laughing. Some of them actually frowned toward Tremain and his client.

"They shouldn't have done that. I know you won't let 'em get away with it. I don't know about San Francisco," he stressed the word again, "but here in Tampa, we're decent folks and we've got standards. It's up to you all to let *The Whitman Esquire Review* know that. Thank ye."

Newton actually ducked his head when he finished and sat back down at his table.

The jury looked over at Tremain with interest. How could he hope to compete with Mom? They were still interested in the answer at this point, but it was a critical juncture for Tremain. For my part, I wondered whether that $850 an hour *The Review* was paying him would turn out to be worth it.

Tremain had a large, black three-ring binder in front of him on the table containing his trial notebook. It was filled to three-quarters' capacity, tabbed and organized with white, pink, blue and yellow paper in the different sections. It definitely conveyed the impression of preparedness. And maybe more than a little overkill.

He closed the binder and rose to give his opening without it. No crutches. Except for his slow, deliberate clothes-adjusting routine, which he performed only when the jury was in the room. What was the subliminal message? I found the habit annoying because it took him so long before he ever got started on anything.

Tremain had no trouble standing behind the podium; He towered above it. He gripped the sides with both hands, the better to give the jury a look at his plain gold wedding band, a piece of jewelry his opponent did not possess.

Tremain leaned into the podium, toward the jurors, but leaving both the podium and the rail between them so as not to invade their space. I wondered again which of the high-priced trial advocacy programs he'd graduated from. Many of his techniques bordered on textbook.

"First, I want to thank you for your service as jurors in this case. I know you are not the country bumpkins Mr. Newton makes you out to be, just as he isn't the bumpkin he pretends to be." He stopped here for effect, pretending to need a sip of water.

"I know you have busy lives and taking time out to help us is a hardship for you. I want you to know that we appreciate it." He nodded toward his client and his entourage at the defense table.

"But more than that, aside from going to the polls to cast your vote, serving as a juror is the most patriotic thing many of you will ever do. This is your chance to uphold the laws of the United States." He let his voice ring out like a presidential candidate accepting his party's nomination.

I felt impressed. The man had talent. And it was not a bad contrast, actually. Mom versus Patriotism. The sides were chosen and the battle joined.

CHAPTER TWENTY-FOUR

Tampa, Florida
Tuesday 1:30 p.m.
January 25, 2000

TREMAIN WENT ON ABOUT the constitutionality of free speech, the right to print what's true, newsworthiness and the legitimate concerns of the public, for about thirty minutes. By the time he finished, the jury would have had a hard time remembering anything Newton said. They were all puffed up with the importance of their job to the continued viability of the nation.

This trial promised to be more than a fair contest. A little hard to tell the Christians from the lions at this point, but I was still on Newton's side. I knew firsthand what it was like to have your life be the subject of everyone's morning coffee conversation and I didn't like it, either.

Newton's first witness was Mr. Tampa, herself. She was a youngish woman, about twenty-five, with purple-black hair and a small diamond in her pierced nose. She was dressed like a member of the cast of *The Rocky Horror Picture Show*, or a trashy lingerie catalogue model.

Mr. Tampa took the stand, raised her hand and swore to tell the truth, "Of course."

"Are you a man or a woman?" was Newton's first question.

"A woman."

"Were you born that way?"

"Of course."

"Then calling yourself Mr. Tampa is misleading to the public, isn't it?"

The jury snickered.

The questioning went on in this vein for a while, Newton trying to show that Mr. Tampa was a fraud and her column full of lies. We took a break after the direct, but Tremain would have some rehabilitating to do when we reconvened.

By the time we got to the lunch hour, I'd had as much grandstanding by both of these lawyers as I was willing to put up with. I told the jurors they could go home for the day and I told the lawyers that I would hear argument on their various evidentiary motions at two o'clock, before Newton put on his next witness tomorrow. Then I left the bench, seeking sanctuary, and maybe a nap, in my office.

When I got to my desk, Margaret had ordered my standard tuna sandwich for lunch and set it on my conference table with spring water and flatware. She'd put out my messages from the morning and a list of matters I should have handled that afternoon.

Right on top, she'd written a note that George had called three times this morning and said it was urgent. She'd underlined urgent three times, too. The little flutter in my stomach was hunger, I hoped. And I tried to dredge up a little anger, too, for protection.

For weeks George had acted like I didn't exist; last night he told me a terrible secret and then left the house; and now he wanted to talk, so it's urgent. My spine stiffened. I was busy. I had a full afternoon ahead and more calls to return than I could possibly finish before two o'clock. Calls I'd been ignoring while I worried about him. He could wait. I wasn't really ready for any more revelations just yet. Whatever he had to say would certainly keep until I got home.

Still in the mood for a good fight, I picked up the phone and dialed the CJ's extension. On the fourth ring, he picked up. "Chief Judge Richardson," he answered.

Normally, getting through to him was like trying to call directly to the President. CJ thought one of his privileges was to have his calls screened, even on his private line.

"CJ, it's Willa Carson returning your call." I refused to play the power game with him. "What can I do for you?"

"I'm reassigning you to preside over the asbestos cases," he told me without preamble. "You'll have three hundred new files on your docket next week."

"What?" I asked him, my voice loud enough to reach all the way over to that fancy new courthouse where he was hiding as he gave me this news. "I don't have time for that nonsense."

The asbestos cases were once again clogging the court dockets across the country. At one time, there were hundreds of thousands of them. After twenty years, we'd gotten them down to numbers in the mid-six-figure range. Still, they were an administrative nightmare and made trying to handle a court docket a little like trying to wade through unprocessed sewage.

"Sorry, Willa. It's your turn. Everyone else has taken a year or two of this and now, you're in the box."

I slammed down the phone, which I was sure simply made him happy to know that he'd gotten my attention one more time.

Then, after promising myself not to speak to the CJ again until hell froze over, I trudged back to the bench, moving slowly under the heavier load.

Just to prove that things can always get worse, at three o'clock, in the middle of Newton's argument that Tremain should not be able to put on witnesses who'd allegedly had homosexual affairs with Newton in the late seventies because such affairs were irrelevant to the truth of the assertion that Newton is gay, Margaret came out with a note and handed it up to me on the bench.

I flipped the note open and read it quickly. Then, I closed it again, rubbing my fingers along the crease. I told the lawyers I'd hear the remainder of the argument tomorrow, adjourned and slowly left the bench.

If I hadn't been so emotionally wired, if I hadn't stayed up all night, if CJ wasn't trying to bury me alive with work, I could have handled it. I know I could have.

As it was, I didn't start to shake uncontrollably until I was safely locked in my office.

CHAPTER TWENTY-FIVE

Tampa, Florida
Tuesday 3:15 p.m.
January 25, 2000

A COUPLE OF QUICK telephone calls to Tampa Chief of Police Ben Hathaway's office revealed what I needed to know.

"George was arrested for the murder of General Andrews and arraigned this morning, Willa," Hathaway said.

My heart skipped a couple of beats. "Do you know where he is now?" I couldn't bring myself to ask if George was at the Orient Road jail. That was one of the many places I'd never expected to find my husband.

Hathaway's tone expressed mild alarm to my practiced listening ear. "He was released after he made his own bail about an hour ago."

I breathed a little easier. Homicide suspects aren't usually allowed bail in Florida and George's release in a matter of hours was unusual as well as quick. I gathered some small comfort from that, although I had no idea why his release had been allowed.

My silence lasted a couple of beats too long. Hathaway's alarm notched up. "We told him not to leave the jurisdiction. Don't you know where he is?"

No, I wanted to scream. *I don't know where he is and I don't know what he's been doing and I'm not even sure who he is anymore.*

"Willa?" Hathaway said, a little more tension in his tone, "Do you know where George is or not? I convinced Drake to release him because I believed he wouldn't leave town. Were we wrong?"

I switched the receiver to my other hand before it slipped out of my sweaty palm. "No, of course not, Ben. I've been in trial. I just heard about all of this. I called you first. I'm sure he's at home."

Ben humphed, a sound that sort of escaped his lips too close to the phone, as if he'd been hit in his ample stomach. He spoke more quietly, but with more urgency, too. "If you find out he's gone, Willa, you'd better call me right away. We've known each other a long time. I'll be the only friend you've got if George makes Drake look like a fool for doing you a favor."

His words had the opposite effect from what I'm sure he intended. They calmed me immediately. I blew out the breath I hadn't realized I'd been holding.

State Attorney Michael Drake wouldn't have done me a favor on a bet. George either, for that matter. Drake hated us both.

If he'd agreed to release George, let him make bail, it was only for one reason: Drake didn't have enough evidence to indict.

At least, not yet.

The realization provided a thin flicker of light at the end of a very long, dark tunnel. But I could travel toward it. I could see a little bit, and maybe, just maybe, figure this thing out.

I put as much reassurance and calm in my voice as I could

muster. "Of course, Ben. I'll call you right away if I don't find George at home. But I'm sure he's there. Don't worry."

I picked up my miniscule purse and my electronic car key and slipped quickly out the back exit of my office.

CHAPTER TWENTY-SIX

Tampa, Florida
Tuesday 3:45 p.m.
January 25, 2000

FOR THE SECOND TIME today, a media hive swarmed, blocking my path, ready to sting. I managed to get through the blockade of reporters and television vans posted on the Bayshore near the entrance to Plant Key Bridge, but they filmed my progress.

Knowing they probably had long lens cameras focused on Minaret's front door, I had to sneak around to the back entrance of my own house.

The second I walked in the door, I heard the television playing in the den. George was home. A wave of hope flooded my body and I sat down heavily on a chair in relief.

George was watching the story of his arrest played out on national television. My gaze, too, was drawn to the pictures of a plainclothes detective I didn't know escorting George out of an unmarked car and into the Orient Road jail. At least, they hadn't put handcuffs on him.

Still, Drake must have tipped off the media that the arrest was coming. Drake never missed a media opportunity. Arresting George, a prominent businessman in the community and the husband of a U.S. District Court Judge would certainly qualify. Drake attempting to profit from our misery ratcheted up my anger a couple of notches.

"Are you so pleased with your celebrity that it wasn't enough for you to live it, you have to watch it all over again?" I sniped at George. He was here; Drake wasn't.

He patted the place on the sofa next to him and I vacillated between sitting down to watch and continuing with my outrage. I sat.

George put his arm around me and hugged me closer to him. He's always been able to see through me and he had to know I was scared. "I want to know how they justified arresting me. The police won't tell me anything, so I have to get my information the way the rest of America does. Watch with me and we'll talk when it's over."

Again today, Frank Bennett had the local report and it had been picked up by the networks. I resented that someone I had counted among my friends would capitalize on the complete disruption of my life. When we're down, I thought sourly, we learn exactly who are friends are, don't we.

Outside the Orient Road jail, Frank read his story well, looking straight into the camera. "George Carson, local restaurateur, surrendered himself to authorities today at his home on Plant Key in South Tampa."

I smiled at that. Our island is private property. At least the television cameras couldn't camp out here.

"Mr. Carson was charged with the murder of General A. Randall Andrews who died early Saturday morning from a gunshot wound to the head. Although initially reported as a suicide, the police quickly discovered that General Andrews was murdered. In the face of increasing pressure on the State Attorney Michael Drake from outraged citizens and prominent politicians, Mr. Carson was charged with first degree murder."

My lip curled. Prominent politicians. *Now we know who that is, don't we,* I thought.

"Police ballistics reports confirm that the murder weapon, a .38 caliber hand gun, used to kill General Andrews was registered to Mr. Carson. We have very little additional information about Mr. Carson's arrest, except that Police Chief Ben Hathaway told us Mr. Carson had means, motive and opportunity. In an unusual development for Florida courts, George Carson is now free on bond."

What followed were the inevitable interviews with Andy's family, his friends and anyone who would talk about George to the press. I was dismayed at the number of people who didn't really know us, but were willing to talk about us just for their fifteen minutes of fame. I made a mental note to cross every one of them off our Christmas card list.

They should have been more charitable toward George, who had never done anything dishonorable in his entire life. He was a pillar of this community, and this is how they repaid him. Altruism. Bah. Humbug.

When George began to rewind the digital recording he'd made on the story in preparation for replaying it again, I'd had enough. He'd turned off the phones, and the answering machine blinked like mad. I got up and unplugged the phone from the wall. With a glance back toward George, still immersed in Frank Bennett, I went into our room to lie down.

Later, I asked myself why I didn't talk to George. Or why he didn't explain things to me. But at the time, it was all just too much. I'd had no sleep the night before. Sleep deprivation is a form of torture and I wanted to believe that some of my emotionalism was attributable to sheer exhaustion.

The rest was fear.

I'd had enough experience with the feeling to recognize it for what it was: an all too healthy fear of abandonment.

If I couldn't deal with the world right now, at least I could escape it.

In less than five minutes, I'd fallen into a deep slumber. I slept through until the next morning, not waking even when George came to bed.

CHAPTER TWENTY-SEVEN

Tampa, Florida
Wednesday 8:00 a.m.
January 26, 2000

GEORGE HAD PUT ON the morning coffee and brought in the papers by the time I wandered out into the kitchen. Front-page news was his arrest yesterday.

Looking like he hadn't slept in three days, George sat at the kitchen table drinking coffee and eating a bagel. I filled my coffee mug and went to shower and get fortified for the day.

Tried not to think about the whole sorry mess until I was dressed in the professional suit of armor that gave me the judicial detachment I desperately needed.

Plugged the phone back in and called Margaret at home. I told her to advise the lawyers that we would begin with Plaintiff's first witness, as planned, tomorrow. She wanted me to take the week off.

The idea appealed to me, except that I couldn't imagine what I'd do with all of those empty hours. Work had always filled my life with purpose and importance. George had his politics and his restaurant. We lived separate lives together, and we liked it. We were more interesting to each other that way, almost like living with an exciting, mysterious partner instead of the rut many of our long-married friends had fallen into.

"No," I told Margaret, "don't reschedule anything on the calendar. I'll see you as planned." I heard the silence of her disapproval. "And Margaret?"

"Yes?"

"Don't allow anyone to call me at home unless they have a life and death emergency," I told her.

Like the one I was living in.

Then I squared my shoulders, took several balancing deep breaths and went into the kitchen to have a serious talk with my husband. The man I once believed I knew better than I know myself. The one who had been charged with murder.

George was still at the table, reading the papers, mainlining coffee. He looked wired. His eyes were bloodshot. Red veins not only in the whites but in the hazel irises as well; pupils dilated.

Deep wrinkles that weren't there last week had appeared between his nose and the corners of his mouth. I've heard stories of hair turning white overnight and never believed them. I looked anxiously for gray hair and didn't find any more than had been there last week visible on George's beloved head, but that was the only thing missing from making him look twenty years older than when I'd seen him last night.

All my defensiveness melted away.

This was George. The man I loved, whom I'd loved for years, who had taken care of me and supported me since we'd first met. George, the pillar and strength of my life.

I knew he wasn't a murderer and that was that.

Regardless of what Michael Drake said, no one would ever be able to prove something so patently false, I told myself, as if repeating the words would make them true.

I had no idea what was going on here, but I intended to get to the bottom of it and I intended to see George cleared.

God help anyone who stood in my way.

Gathering my strength of will, I said, "George," as I sat down across from him at the table. He looked up at me and then through me. He didn't appear to be listening at all. I reached over and touched his hand. "George. I need to talk to you. Okay?"

He said, "Sure. What do you want to talk about?"

CHAPTER TWENTY-EIGHT

Tampa, Florida
Wednesday 9:20 a.m.
January 26, 2000

FEAR URGED ME TO scream at him; my words were sharper than I intended. "I want to talk about how it is that I'm sitting across the table from a man charged with murder. I want to talk about how your gun got to be a murder weapon. I want to talk about what the hell is going on here."

The volume of my voice had jumped up of its own volition with every sentence until I felt I was almost shouting the last question, losing control. My precious control. I wasn't used to it and I didn't like it.

Tried again. Consciously lowered my voice. Slowed it down.

"George, please. I need to know what we plan to do."

He turned his vacant gaze toward mine. "What is there to do? I'll wait until Ben Hathaway finds out who killed Andy. The charges against me will be dismissed and forgotten."

He sounded as if we were discussing one of the dogs being

sick on a rug he didn't particularly like anyway. "In the meantime, I'll continue with my life the same as I always have."

In the reassuringly calm way he'd handled every crisis of our lives, he said, "What else would I do?"

But this was different. Literally life and death. If George was convicted of murder, he could get the death penalty. We kill murderers in Florida. All the time.

"You've been married to a lawyer in a family of lawyers for seventeen years and you can ask me that?" Too shrill. I'd tried to whip up some of that passion I'd seen him display when he was fighting against the Andrews nomination. He could be passionate in altruistic pursuits. How about in self-preservation? "We need to hire the best defense attorney we can find, for one thing."

The look he gave me was genuine surprise.

"What for?" He patted my hand. "Calm down, Mighty Mouse," he said, in his normally affectionate tone for the nickname he'd given me years ago. He thought it perfectly described my drive to help those who couldn't or wouldn't help themselves.

Yet he had never needed my help. Indeed, our relationship was exactly the opposite. George took care of us. He liked it that way; so did I.

"Willa, I don't expect these charges to go beyond the stage they already have. Ben Hathaway assured me that they are continuing their investigation. I feel certain he's being truthful with me." His matter-of-fact belief in the justness of the system colored his perceptions an unrealistic shade of secure. "And the man who killed Andy will be found and brought to justice. Don't worry."

I ran splayed fingers through my hair in frustration. I was quickly losing what little sanity I had left. People think I'm not patient. But I am. It's just that no one recognizes my patience when I'm exercising it.

As calmly as he'd spoken to me, I asked, "Has it ever occurred to you that what the police are looking for is more evidence that they have already arrested Andy's killer?"

For the first time, he appeared shocked. Alive. Attentive. Thank God. "Willa, are you saying that you think I killed Andy? Because if you're saying that, then we have a much more serious problem here than my arrest."

How could he have misunderstood me so completely?

"Of course I don't think you killed Andy," I said. "But think like Drake. What questions will he be asking?"

I listed the ones I could come up with quickly. "How did your gun get to the scene of the murder? And where were you at the time Andy was killed? You were so determined that Andy would never be confirmed as a Supreme Court Justice. Unless you knew Andy was going to die, how could you have been so certain?"

Now, George was truly angry. At me. He stood abruptly and knocked over his chair in the process. "You let me know when you figure it out, Willa. In the meantime, I'm getting dressed, packing my things and moving to the club."

He turned in the doorway for a parting shot. "I'm sure you don't want to be sleeping with an accused killer. And I don't want to sleep with a woman who's supposed to have complete faith in me. But doesn't."

He stalked out and I didn't go after him.

My head fell to the table as I considered his reaction.

Maybe some time apart was a good idea.

Maybe we both needed time to reflect.

This was the first serious test of our marriage. In seventeen years, we'd never had a disaster to weather together.

Could we do it?

I believed we could. I needed to believe we would. But was that enough?

He would calm down, come back to the kitchen, talk this all over, I thought.

But he didn't.

I heard the front door to our flat close as George walked through it, shutting me in. I went back to bed to close out the entire world.

CHAPTER TWENTY-NINE

THUNDERCLAPS JARRED ME AWAKE, dreams so fresh I saw them like a movie. I was sixteen again, spending the last year of my mother's life as her constant companion. She was telling me that she'd never leave me, as her life was slowly ending.

In the dream, I saw her after death experience, saw her spirit leave her body and move toward the light.

As she vanished, she said, "Be brave. Take care of George for me."

Then she was gone as the dogs jumped on the bed when the lightning and thunder started.

The dream left me badly shaken. I don't often dream of my mother and when I do, it always upsets me. This was a new dream and completely unlike the last moments of my mother's life.

In reality, mom died peacefully, when my back was turned. It was as if she'd waited until I wasn't looking to leave me. She'd struggled with breast cancer for several years and finally gave up long before I met George.

My almost forty-year-old brain understands why mom died. I try to believe that her spirit lives on with me. But the young girl I was then still feels the loss deeply. In emotional crises, I often dream of mom.

But I've learned things about fear. Fear is always with us, lurking around the corner, waiting to jump out and scare us when we're most vulnerable.

If you let it, fear moves into your head and takes over your life. The only thing to do with fear is to face it, deal with it, and dispose of it.

What I knew now was that I could choose to be afraid and wait for the worst to happen. Or I could take charge of my life. I've done it before. I could do it again. I'd need to exercise what Aunt Minnie called pluck. Fear would not overwhelm me.

Just then, the doorbell rang. Both dogs ran barking to the door. I wanted to ignore the caller, but I didn't. When I looked through the peephole, I saw Kate.

My resolve wavered. I invited her in, tempted to fall into her arms as she held me and let me cry. It was what I would have done as a girl, the solution that would be so much easier. Let Kate deal with it, retreat and wait for the worst to pass over.

Self-pity was near the surface, too. Emotions I hadn't known were buried in my psyche seemed to be bubbling up like the stench from the floor of Hillsborough Bay at low tide. What had I done? Why was everyone in my life leaving me? Where did George go? Would he come back? My heart was truly broken and I could have allowed Kate to mend it, as she'd done so many times before.

I did none of that, of course.

Judges don't cry.

Except at sad movies, and funerals, and weddings, when small children are injured or someone sings the National Anthem beautifully.

And when their hearts are broken.

Kate calmly asked me what the problem was. Clairvoyance again? Probably she'd seen the same news reports we had and knew how upset I would be.

"Am I the only person on the planet who believes being accused of murder is not the best way to live your life?" I said, sounding petulant to my own ears.

Kate's tone, as always, was gentle with me. "He's *accused* of murder, Willa, not convicted. There is a difference."

Defensiveness caused me to be impatient. Weapons launched, like Patriot missiles, unerringly hitting their target. "Of course there's a difference," I said. "But neither one is all that desirable, in my view."

Kate looked at me closely for a long time. "Have you started writing in the journal I gave you at Christmas?"

"For God's sake," I said, snidely. "My husband is accused of murder. Writing in a journal about my feelings on the subject is not going to change that."

Unperturbed, she said, "I was thinking you might try using it to figure out how to get yourself out of this mess you've made."

Something inside me snapped, then. For the first time in my life, I raised my voice to Kate.

"*I've* made? You think *I've* made this mess? Is it *my* gun that killed an army general? Am I the one that now has mug shots down at the police station? Was it *my* face on the evening news describing how it wasn't possible that Andy committed suicide? Are *my* whereabouts at the time of the murder unaccounted for?

Am *I* the one who's been making it plain to the entire world how I would never allow Andrews to sit on the court?"

Kate seemed unmoved by my outburst, but I couldn't stop myself. I just kept rolling on, letting out all the frustration even I hadn't realized was inside.

"Am I the one who told General Andrews that I'd kill him if he ever hurt my wife again the very night before he died?" I jumped up and turned to face her then. "You floor me, Kate. You really do."

When I'd vented my spleen, I didn't feel better and Kate didn't look the least upset.

She sat quietly for a long while, waiting for me to stop staring at her like a pit bull.

"Actually," she finally said, "I was thinking more of the mess you've made of your relationship with George and whether you are going to be able to repair the damage before the rift between you becomes the Grand Canyon."

I collapsed onto the chair. As ever, Kate put her finger right on the pulse of my anxiety. I could love George while he served his time in prison, but I didn't want to live without him and I wasn't interested in finding out whether I could.

"You know George didn't kill General Andrews. Why don't you prove that first, if that's what it takes to get your life back in order?" She gathered up her things and gave me a hug before letting herself out of the flat. "I suggest, though, that you might use your journal to work on your priorities."

She left because she thought I had some serious soul searching to do. I was too stubborn to do it, though. Her comments had just made me more upset with George.

How could he put us in this situation? If he ever came back, I might throw him out for this.

Now there's the Old Willa, I thought, a grin finding its way onto my lips. That scared, trembling female was someone else. Someone I didn't have any intention of spending any more time with.

My husband was not a killer. I knew it, and soon, everyone else would know it, too. But what game was he playing?

CHAPTER THIRTY

Tampa, Florida
Thursday 8:00 a.m.
January 27, 2000

THE NEXT MORNING, I was in the shower when the telephone rang. Thinking it might be George, I nearly killed myself sliding from the shower to the handset in the bathroom. By the time I picked up, the machine had already kicked on.

"George? Is that you?" I said, over the tape.

"No, Willa. It's Frank Bennett. Isn't George there with you?"

Shit! Why didn't I screen the call? Now what? It would make a bigger impression on Frank if I hung up than if I tried to give him some explanation that he would, hopefully, accept.

I said, "No, Frank. He went out for some bagels and he's not back yet. I thought he might have forgotten something. What can I do for you?"

Frank accepted my explanation without comment, but he'd be more watchful from this point forward. George had to come home today, or it would look like we'd split up over his arrest. Which, of course, was what we'd done.

But it wouldn't help in the court of public opinion, which I didn't give one whit about except that it would matter to Drake, the State Attorney. I crossed my fingers, hoping discretion would rule Frank on this issue until I could get George to see my point and come home. We have three guest rooms, if he wanted to keep pouting.

"Do you want to comment on the latest information we've gotten on the Andrews killing? It concerns George." Business as usual with Frank.

Simultaneously wanting to know and dreading the answer, I asked, "What information have you got?"

"Robbie Andrews is giving interviews. She claims George met with Senator Warwick and the President the night her father was killed and finalized their plan to defeat his confirmation."

Standing wet and naked in the bathroom, I almost convinced myself I was cold and that's why my hand, holding the phone, was shaking.

Hearing nothing from me, Frank went on, "Robbie says George was intent on defeating her father's confirmation. She said George had allowed himself to be used as the front man by her father's political enemies."

Now I was very cold, but that wasn't what caused me to tremble.

Frank concluded, "Robbie said George killed Andy because George and his friends were losing the confirmation fight and George couldn't stand the public disgrace of that loss. She claims George's entire personality was tied up in his stature with his chosen political party and losing the confirmation meant he'd lose that stature, too." Still hearing nothing from me, he finished, "Would you or George care to respond to that?"

I slammed down the phone.

Frank would report my non-response as a "no comment," and it was just as well. If I'd offered my comments, they would have done both me and George more harm than good.

Feeling, in every sinew of my lawyer's body, that the best defense is always a strong offense, I tried to work up some righteous anger.

Talking to myself, I said out loud, "What business does Robbie Andrews have trying to put another nail in George's coffin? And what the hell was George doing the night Andy was killed?" I was on a roll now, so I kept giving myself the pep talk. "A secret meeting with the President of the United States? Come on! How likely is that?"

Of course, I wanted to kick myself for ruining George's alibi. I had only myself to blame for the fact that everyone in Tampa knew George hadn't been home with me in the early morning hours when Andrews was killed, anyway. Why did I say that he'd gone jogging to all those people at the Blue Coat? It was information I couldn't have been compelled to disclose because of the marital privilege, if I'd kept my mouth shut.

But, at the time, I'd thought there was no harm in it. I realized after George's arrest that what I hadn't known last Saturday morning might very well hurt us both now.

"Come on, Willa," I said to my reflection in the mirror as I ran the blow dryer. "George didn't commit murder."

But one of the others he'd been with could have done it. Presidential aides have done worse and lived to tell about it. I could name a few who are still in prison.

Trying not to get distracted from the plan I'd made for myself sometime during the night, I dried my hair, applied minimal makeup and dressed in jeans and a long-sleeved, cotton shirt.

On my way out the door, I slipped on the flat shoes I hadn't worn since our condolence visit to Deborah, then drove Greta over to the club and entered the dining room, prepared to face the lion in his den.

CHAPTER THIRTY-ONE

Tampa, Florida
Thursday 9:00 a.m.
January 27, 2000

JUST AS I'D HOPED, George was seated, fully dressed, having breakfast with the *Wall Street Journal.*

The relief I felt to find him there, right where he should be, in the first place I looked, was palpable. He looked so perfect this morning. He'd rested well. He was shaved, dressed as he always is, and eating his usual breakfast. George's steady behavior was comforting. Predictability isn't always a bad thing.

"Good morning, George," I said, loud enough to get his attention away from the financial pages. Mindful that the wait staff was no doubt watching and unsure of his reaction, I didn't go over and kiss him. But I certainly wanted to.

He lowered the paper and smiled at me. My heart melted. He folded the paper, stood up, gave me a kiss. "Good morning, sweetheart. Breakfast?" He held the chair so I could join him across the table for two. "I tried to call you last night for dinner, but apparently you weren't home."

He said this without an ounce of accusation in his voice and once again I accepted how much bigger a person he is than I am.

"I was home. I saw the machine blinking, but I thought it was just reporters, so I didn't pick up the messages." I settled into my chair, placed the napkin on my lap, and accepted a cup of coffee. "I did try to call you around seven for the same reason," I said, inviting him to explain his whereabouts.

He didn't.

"I'm sorry I missed you," he said. I heard genuine regret.

The waiter came by to take my order. I asked for a three egg ham and cheese omelet with toast, orange juice and coffee. George raised an eyebrow. Usually, my breakfast consists of coffee with cream. George is the big breakfast man.

"I didn't have dinner last night; I'm famished," I explained to him. I wanted to keep on the right track, not get off into any kind of bickering. I came here to convince him to come home and I focused on that goal.

So I asked him about the stock market, always good for a half hour's friendly conversation. Since George left the bank, he's paid more attention to his investing. He says it's the perfect occupation: very lucrative, you're your own boss, and you can do it in your pajamas.

I've tried to follow his stock tips, but I don't devote enough attention to it. He's always twenty-five to thirty percent up at the end of the year and I lag around ten percent. Not that we're competitive about it. Much.

We discussed his recent stock moves through breakfast and when the waiter had removed the dishes and freshened our coffee, George waited for me to come to the point in my own good time.

Surprisingly, I found it hard to begin. I'd never been in this position before and I wasn't used to apologizing.

"George, I'm sorry we fought yesterday," I told him. Insufficient as an apology for what had happened, but true. "I'd like you to come home."

Again, he raised his eyebrow at me, in a gesture so like Harry, our Labrador, I almost laughed.

"I'd like to come home, Willa, but I just don't think I should," he told me.

My heart sank. I had hoped he'd reviewed the situation and come to the same conclusions I had.

"Don't look so crestfallen," he said. "It's not that I don't want to come home."

He placed his hand over mine on the table and continued sincerely. "It's just not good for you to have me there at the moment."

He'd thought this through, maybe even rehearsed his speech. "The spillover publicity won't be good for your career and you're edgy and nervous about my arrest."

I pulled my hand away and put it back in my lap.

"Think about how the CJ will use this against you, if he can," he continued. "It'll be better for you if we live apart until this is over." He sounded so calm, so reasonable, so stupid.

As with many other discussions we've had in the past seventeen years, he wouldn't be persuaded to change his mind. No matter how wrong he was. He'd decided to do this for me, whether I wanted him to or not.

His actions reminded me of that old story about the young couple who wanted to give each other a meaningful present. Each of them gave up the one thing the other loved best to get something neither cared about.

"I'm sure you believe you're doing the right thing. And I won't tell you it's easy for me to see you on the news and in the papers and have everyone we know willing to believe you're a murderer," my voice caught on the unfairness of those accusations.

"Thanks for your concern, Darling," he said dryly.

I felt chagrined and I might have even blushed.

"You know what I mean," I faltered and lowered my voice. "Have you considered how bad it looks for you to have moved out of our house? People will think that I believe you killed him and that's why you left. They'll think I have no faith in your innocence."

I was distraught and almost pleading by this point. I knew how juries viewed a faithful wife and how they viewed an unsupportive one. Regardless of how George and I became separated, State Attorney Drake would feel more confident of winning if he could convince the jury that George's wife had deserted him.

But he remained undeterred. Like trying to push a determined elephant. I leaned forward, trying to make him feel how wrong he was, how much I was right about this. "They'll think that if your wife won't support you and stand by you through this crisis, I must know that you've done something wrong. Don't you see? If you don't come home," I said, blinking furiously, "People will convict you before you're even indicted."

The course of public opinion has never mattered to George. He feels his true friends will stand by him, will know his true character.

As for the rest of the world, George just doesn't care what they think. For himself, anyway.

On my behalf, he was ready to choose pistols at twenty paces over the smallest perceived slight.

In this instance, I knew, public opinion mattered. Maybe it always does.

We discussed the situation for a while longer but he wouldn't budge.

"I can't move back to our flat, Willa," he said, as his final word on the matter. "Not until this whole issue is resolved. I just won't put you in that position."

"Regardless of how I feel about it?"

"Regardless of how you feel about it," he parroted. "This is my decision to make, Willa. I'm doing what I think is right."

George has a lot more faith in the judicial system than I do, because he doesn't see all the times when it fails. He did not expect to be indicted or convicted. He wasn't even considering the ramifications to himself or to me, and he would not turn from his course.

He believed he was protecting me by leaving me until justice prevailed and he could return home, vindicated. Seventeen years of experience in this marriage convinced me that he'd stay the course, no matter how it hurt both of us. He thought his decision was the right thing to do.

Men can be so stubborn.

Awareness forced me back into the chair and kept me silent in the face of his determination. Now, I understood that if George was convicted of murder, he would divorce me. He didn't realize divorce was an option right now because he didn't think he could be convicted. But I knew otherwise. Unless something dramatic and unexpected happened, he would likely be convicted.

And George would never allow me to be tied to a husband in prison.

Now that I realized fully what was at stake, our life together, and George's very existence, I knew what I had to do. I was a good lawyer once. Maybe even had the makings of a great lawyer, then. I'd won many cases during my career, but never one so important to me.

So I stopped trying to convince him to return home and steered the conversation instead to the evidence against George. Since no human can be in two places at once, I started with the biggest question.

"George, I have absolute faith in you. You know that. But Drake obviously doesn't. Let's just tell him where you were when Andy was killed, he can check it out, and this will all be over." I took his hand across the table.

"It's not that easy, sweetheart."

"Why not?"

"Because I gave my word. I said I would not disclose that information."

"Even to me?"

George looked right into my eyes and gave my hand a little squeeze. "All these years, you've never wanted to get involved in politics. Now that you're on the bench, you're supposed to be politically independent. I won't compromise that and I won't let you compromise it." His stubbornness might kill us both. "You've kept many professional secrets from me and I've respected that. You have to respect my decision. I gave my word."

Holding down my anger at his pig-headed single-mindedness now, I accused, "So it was something to do with the confirmation." He said nothing. "All right, then. How did your gun get to be a murder weapon? Maybe if we know that, Drake will still let you go. It's the only real evidence they have against you."

"I don't know. I'd tell you if I did." I must have looked skeptical because he said, "Really. I would. I haven't seen that gun for a while."

"Well, where was it the last time you saw it?"

He let go my hand, sat back in his chair, and said, "On that, I'm still checking."

Exasperated now, I cross-examined him, the long-buried skill surfaced. "You don't remember?"

"I'm not prepared to discuss that just yet," he said.

The food I'd eaten with such relish now sat like lead in my stomach. I could keep confronting him, but his will was stronger than mine.

I'd lost too many arguments with him in the past. I knew not to start up about something so important when he held way more information than I did.

So I gave it up for now and turned our conversation to other things, trying to end on a pleasant note. I had other battles to fight and I would need his help later.

What I knew that George refused to accept was that Drake had a deadline. He needed to find enough evidence to present George's case to a grand jury for indictment, and, as a practical matter, he had to do it within the next three weeks. After that, we could insist on an Adversary Preliminary Hearing where testimony is taken and evidence presented and the judge determines whether there is sufficient evidence to indict George.

But Drake would move quickly. He had momentum now and he'd want to take advantage of it.

I felt as if I had a bomb with a fairly short fuse strapped to my back. Drake's deadline was now our deadline. We had less than three weeks to convince Drake that he could never try George for murder and win. Could we do it?

CHAPTER THIRTY-TWO

Tampa, Florida
Thursday 9:30 a.m.
January 27, 2000

BACK IN MY CHAMBERS, before I took the bench, I got out my *Florida Bar Journal* directory issue and looked up Florida's best criminal defense attorney, Olivia Holmes. Olivia could be the poster child for the idea that names determine destiny. Could it be mere happenstance that she bore a feminized version of the moniker of one of the greatest American jurists of all time, Oliver Wendell Holmes?

I knew that she lived in Miami, but Olivia also had offices in Tampa, Orlando, Gainesville, Jacksonville and Tallahassee. Today, I reached her in the Tampa office, on the third try. I made an appointment to meet with her at Minaret early afternoon.

I put down the receiver slowly, wondering if I'd done the right thing. Olivia Holmes had never tried a case in my courtroom, which wasn't surprising since there just aren't that many female trial lawyers in Florida, let alone that many doing federal criminal trial work.

Besides that, it takes an iron will and a strong level of self-confidence to hold a man's freedom in your hands and know his life depends on your skill and judgment. Not many lawyers have the stomach for it. I don't.

Olivia and I had had a distant professional association over the years. We hadn't been friends, partly because neither George nor I could agree with Olivia's politics.

A criminal defense attorney usually justifies the work of putting criminals back on the street by believing she's serving the judicial system. Some go so far as to claim that it's an honor to do so. They believe the prosecution must always prove its case, or lose. They believe they are guarding basic constitutional rights that must, at all costs, be guarded.

Criminal defense lawyers believe that drivel about how it's better to let a thousand guilty men go free than to jail one man who is innocent. I've seen too many families and victims of the guilty defendants who go free. For them, philosophy rings hollow.

All of that stuff sounds good in theory. The problem is that theory and reality are so far apart. These days, a truly innocent man is rarely, if ever, brought to trial.

It's hard enough to get the guilty ones arrested, tried and convicted. If they are arrested, they usually plea bargain. If they go to trial, they're usually guilty. And when the defense attorney puts them back on the street, they commit another crime and we do the dance again. The recidivism rate is astronomical and the justice system is losing ground every day.

A criminal defense attorney is necessary, but not heroic. They aren't crusaders or protectors of the American way.

At least, I hadn't thought so before. Like so many people

before me, as soon as I needed a good criminal lawyer to defend my husband on a bogus charge, I bent my principles.

It's the age-old problem of being an American lawyer: we know the difference between right and wrong and good and evil but we also see the similarities.

I was counting on the system's frailties to help George, not to hurt him. I hoped to avoid an indictment and prevent a trial. I wanted a lawyer who had beat Drake many times before.

Once Drake had his ego on the line by going to the grand jury and indicting George, there would be no way to avoid a trial.

I absolutely believed George was not guilty of murder, but his chances of winning at trial against a determined prosecutor were slim, indeed. Drake had the advantage of the full force of government resources, solid forensic evidence, a high-profile victim, a well-known defendant, and Robbie Andrews had provided the public with a strong motive.

I knew George would never kill because of an assault to his ego, but jurors would believe it. Men have killed for less. If we got to the point of trial, we'd need Olivia Holmes and a team of horses to pull George out of the muck.

CHAPTER THIRTY-THREE

Tampa, Florida
Thursday 10:00 a.m.
January 27, 2000

WHEN THE NEWTON TRIAL resumed, it seemed more trivial to me than ever and I was barely aware of it.

My thoughts returned to George again and again as Newton began his case in chief by calling his expert witness to the stand. There would be no surprises, since the famous psychiatrist, a specialist in treating criminal psycho-sexual disorders, had been previously deposed and had fully explained his opinions.

Listening with only half my brain, I heard the expert testify that Mr. Newton's sexual preference, whatever it was, was a private fact that had been publicly disclosed. He said disclosing Mr. Newton's sex life was offensive and objectionable to all reasonable people of ordinary sensibilities and could not be of any legitimate concern to the public.

Further, he said, unless Mr. Newton admitted he was a homosexual, which he most certainly had not, labeling a person "homosexual" without his consent denies a basic human right: the right to self-identity.

Most of it was above the jury's head, steeped in history and philosophy. The short of it was, though, that personal relationships are private matters and ought to stay that way. Most of us in the room agreed with that, except, presumably, Mr. Tampa herself. And her employer.

When Tremain rose for his cross, he covered truth, justice and the American way again. He questioned the expert about hypocrisy, lying and misleading others. He covered the social necessity to eradicate AIDS, which kills indiscriminately, and the courageous coming out of gay celebrities like Rock Hudson, Chastity Bono, Richard Chamberlain and Ellen DeGeneres.

Finally, in rapid succession, he asked, "Sir, are you married?"

"Yes, I am."

"How long have you been married?"

"Twenty-five years."

"Do you have children?"

"Yes. I've got three adult children, two girls and a boy."

"Are you heterosexual?"

"Absolutely."

"Did you mind telling us these things about yourself, sir?"

"Of course not."

Tremain turned around and looked at the jury pointedly. "You don't consider these facts about your life private?"

We couldn't hear the answer over the laughter in the gallery and the jury box, but the court reporter got it down. He'd said, "I do consider my life to be none of your business."

The rest of the trial day was spent on one witness after another who provided testimony I found impossible to follow. My attention wandered. I was grateful when we finally recessed at 1:30 and I could get to more important work: George's defense.

CHAPTER THIRTY-FOUR

Tampa, Florida
Thursday 1:45 p.m.
January 27, 2000

I FOUGHT MY WAY through the reporters posted at the entrance to the Plant Key bridge and reached Minaret after Olivia Holmes arrived. Was it unreasonable of me to think she'd be driving something a little less conspicuous than the bright red Ferrari parked in our driveway?

"Olivia," I said, shaking her hand. She followed me around to the back stairs and up to our flat.

I hadn't asked George for his permission to hire a lawyer, but I hoped I'd be able to talk him into it if Olivia would take the case.

Defense attorneys had called the house almost non-stop since George's arrest, offering to work for the free publicity of the trial and the subsequent book and movie deal. After all, a Supreme Court nominee had never been murdered before.

This was the case of a defense lawyer's lifetime. Those who wanted to be George's lawyer knew they didn't have to win. Just having their names in the paper was all that mattered.

But, by reputation I knew that Olivia was particular and she liked not only to be asked, but persuaded.

Olivia Holmes built her stellar career by defending high-profile defendants in political crime cases. When the senator's mistress was killed, the congressman's son was arrested for dealing drugs, the mayor's wife was charged with vehicular manslaughter for driving under the influence, Olivia got them off. Sometimes with a plea bargain, sometimes with a little back room dealing, sometimes with a spectacular trial, but Olivia's clients never went to prison.

Early in her career, she'd represented anyone who would hire her. These days, Olivia's clients had to be innocent. At least that was the rumor.

I figured she'd want the case because defending George could add to her reputation and not spoil her record.

"Please join me in the den," I told her.

Olivia accepted iced tea and we settled ourselves. "First, Willa, let me say right off the bat that if you've called me here to ask me to defend George, I accept. If you hadn't called me, I'd have called you."

I schooled my features not to reflect my surprise. "I don't have to beg?" The tales of Olivia's refusals to represent the accused were legendary.

She laughed. "I love those stories. They make it possible for me to charge my exorbitant fees. After the client begs long enough, if I say yes, he's willing to offer me his firstborn child."

"You're joking, surely."

"Actually, no, I'm not. You'd be surprised how many unwanted children there are in the world," her tone was serious now. "But some of what you've heard is true. I do have plenty of work. More than I want. And I'm sad to say that there are always more criminals than good lawyers to defend them. So I do turn a lot of work down."

She stopped for a quick sip. "I'm swamped right now, actually, and it will be hard for me to handle this case." She settled into the chair, perched on the edge so that her feet would touch the ground. "Although I'm hoping there won't be much work to do for very long, I'm sure you realize that the evidence against George looks damning. But I'm sure George didn't kill General Andrews. We have someone else to thank for that."

I felt a little better, for a second. Until she added, "As soon as I find out who did it, I'll probably volunteer to defend him, too."

Her last words startled me. She hadn't meant them facetiously.

I leaned forward. "Olivia, this is very serious business to us." I stopped a second for effect. I wanted her to understand me clearly. "Neither one of us has ever been in a situation like this and we want it over with as quickly as possible. In fact, I'm so angry with Ben Hathaway that I could personally strangle him without any hesitation. I can't believe he'd accuse George!"

Either Hathaway or Drake could have made the decision to arrest George. If Drake was calling the shots, Hathaway would have had no choice but to comply. At the moment, I didn't know which of them was driving this situation, but I intended to find out.

Olivia folded her tiny hands in her lap. She wore rings on three fingers of each hand, but not on either ring finger. "Of course it's not a joke, Willa, and I'm not joking. I am more than willing to defend George." She ticked her reasons off, one finger at a time. "First, because I feel sure he's innocent. Which is not to say that he won't be convicted, you know. In fact, unless things change dramatically, I'd say Drake is feeling pretty sure he has a winning case here."

I must have looked as alarmed as I felt, because she softened her tone and continued, "Unlike a lot of criminal-defense attorneys, I've gotten to the stage in life that I don't have to defend the guilty ones anymore. Everyone knows my clients are not guilty, and my reputation will help you with public opinion."

"What's the second thing?" I asked her, once I could find my voice again.

"I do believe that General Andrews was the worst possible candidate for the Supreme Court," she said, as if Andrews's death was an acceptable solution to that knotty problem. "So, yes, I'll take the job if you and George want me. And I'm proud to do it."

I digested this, taking her measure as she spoke. My gut told me she was sincere.

My gut had been wrong before.

I said, "Well, you should know that I certainly believe there's no one who will do a better job than you. But there are a couple of problems."

"No kidding," she replied, dryly.

I hesitated a moment to show my displeasure at her levity and she noticed. "George doesn't think he needs a lawyer, let alone the best we can get. Obviously, I disagree."

"George has always struck me, at least by reputation, as someone who had more sense," she said, while she reached into her pocket and pulled out a cookie. "But I'm not accustomed to forcing my services on someone who doesn't want them," she said as she ate the head off a piece of Mickey Mouse shortbread.

The sight of the cookie caught me off guard, reminded me of George's teasing, calling me Mighty Mouse. I felt the emptiness in our flat, felt his absence. It took me a second to regain my composure.

I spoke more sternly than I intended, "I think I can persuade

George that he needs not just a lawyer, but you in particular. I just wasn't going to try to talk him into it until I found out whether you were interested. Please leave that part to me."

Still munching on the cookie, she said, "All right, I can live with that. What other problems do we have?"

She popped the last of the cookie in her mouth, brushing the crumbs off her fingers with a damp napkin.

I told her, straight up. "According to the news reports, there's a lot of evidence against George, and he refuses to explain any of it. He seems to think that the truth will set him free and someone else will find out what the truth is."

She grinned. "Although many Americans would feel the same way, that idea is absurdly naïve for a man with his political savvy."

Unnerved again by her matter-of-fact acceptance of the trouble George and I were in, I cleared my throat before I said, "Yes. Well, I hope you'll be able to convince him that it's in his best interest to help himself."

Husbands have a tendency to ignore their wives' advice. Sometimes an independent expert can present the same arguments and be more persuasive. George had plainly rejected my opinion this morning. Maybe Olivia would have better luck.

Olivia considered the implications. It's almost impossible to defend an uncooperative client. If she knew the case would never go to trial, it wouldn't matter. But if she actually had to make an opening statement, cross examine witnesses and mount a successful defense, not having George's cooperation would make the task daunting, if not downright impossible.

Finally, she said, "Well, you're experienced. You know what the risks are. Why don't we wait and see if we can persuade him. If we can't, I'll have a talk with Drake and see where they're going with this. If it looks like it's going to be the whole shebang, then George will have to decide whether he wants to trade his gourmet cuisine for prison slop. I'm a great lawyer, but I'm not a miracle worker."

Modesty didn't seem to be one of her faults. Nor could she be accused of being coy. Success does strange things to a tiny woman.

"What else?" she asked me, seeming to know that while I'd already delivered some seriously bad news, there was more to come.

I considered just telling her my plans. I'd practiced saying the words. I am personally investigating the murder. And I will control the defense. No arguments. I even looked in the mirror, to see if I could look her right in the eye and say such an outrageous thing.

When it came time to deliver the lines, I couldn't do it.

Instead, I told her, "We just need to be aggressive. We've got to stop this freight train as soon as possible."

She seemed to realize that I hadn't told her everything but didn't push.

She said nothing for what seemed like several minutes. I imagined I could see the wheels going around in her head, testing the pieces of the case and trying to figure out what I wasn't saying.

If I told her I was going to investigate the murder on my own because I didn't believe anyone else could possibly free George, it would be more than enough to cause her to turn down the case. The idea was, for any lawyer we might hire, unethical.

No lawyer would stand for it, wouldn't even believe a judge would suggest such a course. Interference in the progress of the investigation, making the spouse a potential witness when her testimony could otherwise be protected by the marital privilege, second guessing by the client. Enough to make even a bad lawyer run, not walk, in the opposite direction.

I wouldn't have allowed me to investigate the murder, even informally, if I had been in her shoes.

But I was in my shoes and I would leave nothing to chance. Making sure that George came home to me, safe and whole and as soon as possible, might have been the most important thing I'd ever done in my adult life.

I couldn't trust anyone else to do it better.

Kate believes the Universe handles all the details; I know that it doesn't.

Finally, Olivia drained the last of her tea and asked if we could take a walk down on the beach. To my mind, we hadn't gotten all the issues resolved yet.

"I think we need to get to know each other a little bit before we make a commitment, don't you? Let's have a talk," she said.

Like everything else she'd done, it was unconventional. But then, the situation was unconventional, too.

I led her down the back stairs and let Harry and Bess out ahead of us. We walked around the island, away from the house and, hopefully, any reporters who might be out there with telephoto lenses.

Olivia is as unusually short as I am unusually tall. Standing together, we must have looked like the female version of Mutt and Jeff. Her impeccably tailored suit reminded me of the fancy lawyer trying his case in my courtroom, but hers must have been custom-made. Nowhere could she buy such beautiful suits in size zero.

Finding shoes must have been even more impossible. Her feet were smaller than my hands. Standing next to her made me feel freakishly large and gawky. I moved away a few paces, hoping for perspective.

CHAPTER THIRTY-FIVE

Tampa, Florida
Thursday 2:35 p.m.
January 27, 2000

OLIVIA KICKED OFF HER four-inch heels and left them on the beach, walking just out of the water line where her feet only got wet when a larger wave came up, which was rare. There's no such thing as surf in Tampa, except during storms.

We walked quite a while in silence, occupied by our own thoughts.

Eventually, still looking straight ahead as she put one foot in front of the other, Olivia said, "My parents were so happy when my brother, Thomas, was born. They'd waited over ten years for a boy and they feared they'd never have him."

The topic came out of the blue and I had no idea where she was going with it, so I just said "hmmm."

Olivia continued, "Not that they weren't happy with me, but my dad wanted a boy."

Still puzzled, I said, "Not an unusual desire."

"No, it wasn't. We lived on a plantation in Louisiana at the time," she said. "The old farm place. Been in the family for generations, but the taxes and maintenance were making it impossible to keep."

Every time she paused, I felt like I needed to respond, but I didn't know what to say. "That's happened a lot, I understand," was the best I could muster. It seemed lame, even to me.

"Dad was about to sell the old home place when Mom got pregnant. He was so sure there'd be a boy to inherit, he waited." She stopped again, but I kept quiet this time. "The struggle to keep the place going nearly killed Dad, but he knew his son would want to live there."

I wondered what the point of this story was, but this was a chance to practice learning to trust Olivia a little bit. I simply waited during the silence, as we continued to walk.

She continued after a time. "Thomas was a wonderful child. I loved him as if he'd been my very own present from God. To my parents, he was a miracle."

"Was he?" I asked her. "A miracle?"

"Well, unlike some kids who get that kind of adulation early in life, Thomas wasn't wild or spoiled really. He loved everyone and everything." Her voice had taken on an almost dreamlike quality now. "He was a gentle soul who really could have been the model for Margaret Mitchell's Ashley Wilkes, you know?" she said, referring to the rather spineless character in *Gone With The Wind*.

I laughed out loud at that. "Ashley Wilkes has captured the hearts of generations of women. I can't imagine why, though. I always liked Rhett Butler better."

She laughed, then, too. "Well, Rhett was a take-charge, get-it-done sort of fellow. I probably liked him the best, too."

Then, she returned to seriousness. "The point is that Thomas never should have been in the army. But he joined because generations of Holmeses had served in the army and he was steeped in tradition, the family heritage and so on."

I nodded again.

"So, he joined up. Actually, he got into West Point and he came out an officer. A second lieutenant." She reached into her pocket and retrieved her car key.

When she handed it to me, I saw that she carried her brother's dog tag. It was like so many army id tags I'd seen over the years, but it was worn and bent. She'd been carrying it around a long time.

I handed the key and the tag back to her.

She walked in silence for a while, then bent down and picked up a pretty good size conch shell that had washed up since this morning.

She took up her story again. "Anyway, Thomas was just starting his career. He served under General A. Randall Andrews." Ah, I thought, beginning to see where this was going. Some personal reason made her willing to defend George. That was an unexpected blessing; a personal agenda might make her easier to control, later, when she figured out that I was investigating behind her back.

She stopped then, unexpectedly. "Thomas died. There aren't many American casualties in peacetime, but Thomas was one of them."

The information shocked me. I wasn't expecting it. But then, this entire encounter had been completely out of the ordinary. "I'm sorry," I told her. "How did it happen?"

Olivia threw the conch shell, then, so hard that it hit a live oak tree and shattered. "General Andrews killed him, that's how it happened." If you've ever tried to break a conch shell, you know how much force it takes. She had a lot of strength for a little woman. Something to keep in mind.

I tried to reason with her. "In the military, these things happen, Olivia. Tough decisions have to be made. You can't just blame General Andrews for your brother's death because he was the commanding officer at the time." Maybe she was mentally unbalanced. Maybe I'd made the wrong choice.

She turned then, and looked at me steadily. "You misunderstand me. General Andrews literally shot Thomas. Andrews killed my brother." Her tone was quiet and firm; her look challenging me to disagree with her. "The official version is much different, of course. But that's what happened."

I nodded and said nothing while I gathered my wits. What could I say? You're crazy? There's no way such a thing could happen? "How do you know all of this, Olivia?"

She watched me a bit longer, more intently. "Someday, when we have more time, I'll tell you."

I could have asked for more details, but I didn't think she'd elaborate. Besides, I didn't need to know her motives. All I wanted was for her to help George.

Then, maybe satisfied that I accepted her story, Olivia turned to continue her walk.

We were about halfway around the island by now. I could no longer see downtown from where we stood; we'd reached the northernmost point of Plant Key and started around the other side. She took almost three steps to every one of mine, but she didn't seem to rush.

"Not long after Thomas died, Dad sold the plantation. Then he and Mom just seemed to give up." She continued her story in pieces and I stopped trying to respond every time she took a break.

"They're in a nursing home, their room a shrine to Thomas. Both of them live completely in the past. There's nothing that can be done. They're in kind of a living death brought on by grief."

She stopped walking again, and turned to face me. "I owe the man who killed General Andrews quite a lot. I want him to get the best defense possible." She wasn't tall enough to look me in the eye, but she turned up her chin and tried. "If George killed Andrews, I want him to go free, just like General Andrews never answered for killing Thomas."

By now, I found her account bewildering. What motivates people is never what I think obvious.

She finished her thought. "If George didn't kill Andrews, I don't want him convicted just because the public wants to paint this as the murder of an American war hero." She almost spat out the last few words.

I didn't know what to say. I walked on toward Minaret and Olivia came along. She was still silent, giving me a chance to digest what she'd told me, I guess.

But I wasn't thinking about her story.

What I thought about were the strengths and weaknesses of having someone with such an emotional stake in George's future at the helm of his defense. Retaining Olivia might be as bad as doing the job myself.

But, Olivia's personal vendetta would make her more malleable as we went along, and I intended to be sure George never went to trial. I needed the aura of innocence around George that Olivia's reputation would give him, and there was no one else who could supply that protection.

Right at that moment, I felt confident that I could control her, at least long enough to accomplish my goals.

"I see why you want the job," I said. It was a good time to test the waters, a little. "But I will be doing whatever I think is necessary to prove George did not kill Andy."

I'm not sure she understood me. Maybe she thought I meant I would do whatever the wife of a criminal defendant normally does.

"If you can't live with that, you'll have to wait and volunteer to represent the real killer, when he's charged."

She nodded her agreement, then stated her own conditions.

"I won't take a fee for my work right now," she said. "You can make a donation to the Thomas A. Holmes Foundation for the value of my services. I'll be a volunteer. You can't fire a volunteer."

We both laughed at that, even though I caught the veiled threat that she would be on the case whether I wanted her there or not.

Maybe we did understand each other, because that was exactly the message I'd delivered to her.

We returned to the point where she'd left her shoes. She bent down to pick them up and shake out the sand. She forced her bare feet into the pumps. Then I walked her back to her car.

"One more thing, Willa."

"Yes?" I was cautious now.

"I won't let you surrender Andrews's killer to Chief Hathaway. Andrews got what was coming to him. I don't intend to see anyone punished for it."

She got into her Ferrari and sped off over the bridge, leaving me to wonder if she wasn't the one who had killed Andy.

She was certainly capable of it.

Revenge is an excellent motive for murder, especially since she believed a heinous wrong had been dealt her by one truly evil man.

As I watched her car make its way across our bridge, I realized that I might not care whether she'd done it, and that bothered me more than knowing there was a real chance that she had.

CHAPTER THIRTY-SIX

Tampa, Florida
Thursday 3:20 p.m.
January 27, 2000

I CLIMBED UNDER THE wing chair and retrieved the journal I'd thrown there in a fit of pique. Not, as Kate suggested, to dialogue with my inner self. If I was going to investigate murder, I needed an easy way to keep track of what I did, to keep the details straight and quickly available. Something I could carry with me.

From long experience I knew there were few people I could rely on in the world. George and Kate.

And me.

I am always more confident when I control my own life. I could do things quickly, and make sure they stayed done.

I see the hidden relationships others don't see. Many, many times I've received a file of seemingly unrelated facts and put the puzzle pieces together when others before me had failed. I'd never needed to use that skill on us, but now was certainly the time.

Job One: get George out of trouble and get our lives back on track. Soon.

We were playing beat the clock, now. Under Florida criminal procedure, a person can be held up to ninety days without a formal indictment. George's unusual release on bond didn't alter that rule. Still, after twenty-one days, we could demand that Drake produce his evidence. That meant I had a narrow window of opportunity to convince State Attorney Drake not to indict George. No time to waste.

I grabbed a *Café con Leche* and my journal and began to list everything I knew so far about General Andrews, Olivia Holmes and George's recent activities. My thoughts developed slowly and appeared on blue and white, unlined, recycled paper.

Without George to talk to, I carried on a conversation with myself in writing. But some gremlin, or maybe what Kate would call my spirit, was talking back. It was energizing, in a strange way. Is this what it felt like to be schizophrenic? Is the only difference between me and them that my voices don't talk in my head, but rather write in my penmanship, in my journal pages, in response to my questions?

After a while, I realized I was out of facts and merely musing.

Everybody has enemies. As peaceful as I am, there are at least a few people who cross the street to avoid me. On any given day, the CJ and I might actually come to blows. And Michael Drake would gleefully lock George in a cell and throw away the key.

Everybody loves somebody sometime, but no one is loved by everyone all the time.

Thomas Holmes's family couldn't be the only personal enemies General Andrews had made in the past sixty-five years.

The list of Andrews's enemies had to be a long one, even if I discounted all of the faceless, nameless multitudes that attended

Andrews's confirmation hearings. Those people were the best and most desirable choices for Andrews's killer because I didn't know any of them.

But what if there were countless others, too? Some of whom I did know?

One way to get George out of this mess was to find other likely suspects, creating reasonable doubt of George's guilt and assuring he'd never be convicted.

Drake, being the political animal he was, would not want to fail. No certain conviction would mean no indictment. That was my goal. I put a dark blue box around it.

But how to get there?

If I could look at the police file, find out what they had, where they'd been, then I'd know what to do next.

It would have been helpful to discuss this with Olivia. But as long as she was on my list of suspects, I couldn't really do that. Besides, she'd tell me to leave the investigating to her and the police, something I would not do.

For a few minutes, I considered using Frank Bennett. He'd have a lot of information to share. But working with him would be like trying to ride a tiger. He'd want the story, and he'd want to air it as soon as the news happened.

Maybe I could make a deal with him that wouldn't come back to bite me. It was a decision I couldn't make yet, but I'd think about it.

I looked at the plan I'd so carefully thought out and written down in the past few hours. Some revisions were in order and I made them.

Then I left for Ben Hathaway's office. He'd be there. The man had no life.

CHAPTER THIRTY-SEVEN

Tampa, Florida
Thursday 6:05 p.m.
January 27, 2000

BEN, WHO HAD BEEN sort of a friend of mine until he'd arrested my husband, was at his desk when his secretary ushered me into his messy office. You'd think the Tampa Chief of Police would have better quarters. His office was in the exceedingly ugly blue building on Madison and Franklin, right in the heart of downtown Tampa, where the Tampa Police Department had moved a couple of years ago. Local reporters called it the Cop Shop.

As I entered, Ben stood and came around the desk to greet me. I tried not to physically recoil and sat down before he got the chance to touch me, making it awkward for both of us. He nodded and leaned against his desk.

"What can I do for you, Willa?" He asked me gently, sounding like the friend I once believed he was.

"I'll come right to the point, Chief." His eyebrows went up a little at my tone. He crossed his arms over his chest. His pure physical bulk was foreboding, and the power he now held over George's life was more intimidating. I began to feel sorry, just a little, for some of Tampa's more sensitive criminals, if that's not an oxymoron.

I drew in my breath and phrased my outrageous opening request as a demand. "I want to see your file on the Andrews murder investigation."

Ben stood up a little straighter and walked back around to his chair, putting as much official distance between us as the cramped quarters would allow. "I'd like to help you. You know George is one of my favorite people. But I can't break the rules, even for George. Or for you."

"I'm not asking you to break the rules, Ben. I'm only asking you to bend them. You know we'll get the file eventually."

We both knew that once George was indicted, Drake would be required to turn over anything that's exculpatory.

I said, "The evidence against George was on the six o'clock news. So where's the harm?"

This last part came out a little more sarcastically than I'd intended. It still pissed me off that Ben Hathaway had come to our home to get George instead of allowing him to come downtown for questioning. It was one of the many things I'd never forgive him for, when this was all over.

But I couldn't let that influence me now.

"That may be," he said. "But whether or not to release the file is not my call. That one will be made by Drake, when and if it comes to that." He gave me the official line. "This office doesn't open its investigative files to the families of accused murderers. And the Florida Supreme Court will back me up on that."

I returned his steely look. Ben Hathaway and I had played the power game before. Usually, he only asserted the power he had. He played strictly and professionally by the rules, which wasn't hard to do because the rules and the resources were stacked in his favor.

For every task there's the easy way and the hard way. The easy way is, well, easier, but the hard way works just as well.

"You could give me the file if you wanted to, Ben. It's within your discretion," I reminded him. "We'll get it eventually anyway. There's no harm in your handing it over to me now."

He gazed at me with an expression I interpreted as consideration, which encouraged me to continue.

"Ben, how much of your department's resources are directed at finding General Andrews's killer? Not yesterday, or two days ago, but right now?"

"As much as we need to devote to it." He sounded a little defensive.

"In other words, nothing. Am I right? You think you have a suspect in custody, arraigned and turned over to Drake's office." I tried, unsuccessfully, to control my belligerence. "You have other crimes to solve and you don't have that much manpower."

I looked him straight in the eye now, showing him that we both knew the score.

"You're not even looking for the real killer, are you?"

Ben looked down at his big paws clasped on the government-issue imitation walnut desk. His ears grew more than a little crimson at their tips.

When he raised his head, he answered me slowly, as if addressing someone with poor hearing or less than full mental acuity. Or, maybe, as if he were being watched through the glass walls that surrounded us and his voice were being broadcast directly to his supervisors.

"We don't need to look for the general's killer. We found him. We arrested him." Quietly, he finished, "If you want to see the file, ask Drake."

I stood to leave. "Chief, you and I both know that George Carson did not kill General Andrews. If Drake wants to take George to trial for this, he certainly can. But if he does, he'll lose."

Next, I delivered the truth he tried to ignore. "And Drake will take you down with him. You'll be the laughingstock not only of Tampa, but the entire country."

I turned toward the door. "Everyone is watching this, Ben. Everyone."

"What do you want me to do, Willa? My hands are tied. Drake wanted a quick arrest. He got one. George is on the wrong side of Drake's ambition." He held his hands out, palms up, to demonstrate his point. "They've done battle before and it's Drake's turn to hold the winning cards. It's out of my hands."

Now that he'd been softened up, he was ready to hear my real proposal. "I want you to let me look at the file. I'll make you an offer, just once, right now."

I waited until he nodded, almost involuntarily. "Here it is: You let me look at the file, help me unofficially and I'll tell you first when I've figured out who killed Andrews."

His eyes widened but he didn't laugh. He considered my proposal seriously because he knew me, and he knew how determined I can be.

Still, I sensed he was about to refuse again. "I intend to prove that George did not kill Andrews. When I succeed, Ben, you know how foolish you'll look? No one will trust you to run your department. You know what a small town Tampa is. You might have to move."

Watched him thinking it through.

Eventually, he would realize he had nothing to lose and everything to gain by helping me. I was promising not to embarrass him, not to let the situation get out of control if George wasn't Andrews's killer. He wanted to believe me.

To give him a little credit, Ben Hathaway does like George. He likes me, too, for that matter. He wanted the killer to be someone else, but he had no reason to believe he'd arrested the wrong man.

Unlike me, Ben was not his own boss. Someone higher up called the shots and that someone wanted a quick solution to this incredibly thorny issue. Bringing down a powerful member of the opposite political party was, for Drake, a bonus that would give him the career boost he'd been seeking for years.

Ben looked past me through the glass partition on the top of his wall, and shook his head, negative. "I can't do it, Willa. I'm sorry. If President Benson himself asked me, I'd have to say no. I want to help you. But you can't just march in here, let God and everybody see you, and demand special treatment. I've got no discretion in this. The answer is no."

He did look sorry. He looked like a sorry S.O.B.

I tortured him with my best venomous stare. No impact.

"Ben, you disappoint me. I thought you had some integrity. I'd never have believed you'd be part of a plan to ruin my husband just for politics," I told him sorrowfully. Before I walked out, I said, "If you change your mind and develop some backbone, you know where to find me."

The doorknob turned in my hand and the door was forced open, making me lose my footing. I'd been facing Ben, turned away from the door. When I glanced back, I looked right into a hard brown glare from Michael Drake, State Attorney.

Drake was tall and wrinkled. His face resembled a Shar-Pei but his temperament was strictly Rottweiler. Drake had gotten where he was by tenacity and deference to those who could put him in office and keep him there. He was a party puppet, and everyone around here knew it. Michael Drake was motivated by one thing, and one thing only: shameless self-promotion.

"Hello, Judge Carson," he said to me, without an ounce of warmth.

The man was repulsive. Standing toe to toe, his eyes revealed the naked ambition that propelled him, a consuming fire that would burn everyone in his path.

"Michael," I said, refusing to give him the respect of his title or turn away from his searing gaze.

He stared me down a few moments longer with no effect before he gave up and turned to Hathaway.

"Why are you in closed session with the wife of an accused killer, Ben?"

Although there might have been legitimate reasons for me to be here, Drake made it sound like I was illegally or unethically in cahoots with Ben Hathaway.

The accusation stung, more so because I had, in fact, come here to ask Ben to do me a favor. I could feel the uncontrollable flush of embarrassment as it crept up my neck and into my cheeks.

But Ben's eyes narrowed and his nostrils flared. A different flush warmed his face, an angry one. Ben had refused my request for the file, not because he wanted to, but because he'd done Drake's bidding. Now, he was being falsely and openly accused of treachery. Drake's fire would burn Hathaway, and me, too, if that's what it took to move Drake ahead.

Drake had intentionally left the door open and Ben's outer office was stuffed with eavesdroppers. The exchange would be common gossip before the next hour had passed. Ben was seething; he clutched his fists by his side.

I cursed myself for coming here. Although I'd never thought I'd run into Drake at this hour, in retrospect, it had been a foolish risk.

Ben said nothing in answer to Drake's question, but the tension in the room jumped up several notches. No biting retort sprung to my lips.

I gathered all of my judicial dignity and left the junkyard dogs to fight among themselves. All eyes in Ben's outer office were on me as I exited the room. Walking down the hallway, waiting for the elevator, I heard Ben's office door slam closed and the two men shouting at each other, until the elevator doors closed behind me.

But I'd learned something.

Hathaway and Drake didn't agree on George's arrest. Otherwise, Drake wouldn't have accused Ben in front of me and other witnesses. Now, I knew that Ben had been leaning toward my point of view even before I arrived in his office. He could be persuaded to help us. It was a valuable piece of information. But was it enough?

CHAPTER THIRTY-EIGHT

Tampa, Florida
Thursday 6:25 p.m.
January 27, 2000

WHEN THE DOORBELL RANG, I looked through the peephole to see Ben Hathaway standing there. With a briefcase.

I wasn't totally surprised. After Drake's open disrespect, and attempts to embarrass Ben in front of his subordinates, I'd expected Ben to rebel and stop supporting Drake, who wasn't grateful for it. That's what I'd have done. Ben and I had been allies before, even friends. Neither of us had any great love for Drake. Never underestimate the male ego.

Ben couldn't openly support us against Drake, but he didn't have to. All I needed was a little head start by getting a look at the file a few days early. Anyone who assumed George had killed Andrews, which was just what Drake claimed to believe, would realize that sharing the investigative file with us now instead of three weeks from now would not change the truth and should have been no big deal. Ben wasn't taking any real risk here. Either

Drake believed in his evidence or he didn't. I knew Ben would come to the same conclusion. Eventually.

If I could show the public what a total jerk Michael Drake actually was, so much the better. I let Ben in.

"Okay," he said, holding up his thumb and forefinger on his right hand. "But I have two conditions of my own. One, you keep me up to date as you go along." He folded the forefinger down.

"No problem." I lied; he knew it.

"Two," he held up his thumb. "You tell me who you think killed Andrews and I'll arrest him. None of your elaborate confession schemes."

I must not have looked properly agreeable.

He said, "I mean it, Willa. I don't want you or George getting killed over this."

I reached for the briefcase, and he pulled it away from my grasp.

He tried once more to persuade me. "This guy murdered a decorated army general, for God's sake. General Andrews was more than able to defend himself. Have you thought about that? If you cross him, the killer won't let you live just because you're a judge."

I nodded; he wasn't impressed. "I'm serious here, Willa. If you think arresting the wrong guy will get me run out of town on a rail, think what Drake will do to me if I let you and George get killed by the same perp."

I waited until he offered the briefcase to me, asking nicely, "Do it for me. Please."

Only because I was beginning to worry that he'd change his mind again, I agreed. Realistically, it was the sleeves out of my vest anyway. What was I going to do with a cold-blooded killer who would shoot Andrews in the head and then just walk away? I had no interest in being a hero.

All I wanted was my husband's life back.

Ben came fully into the room then, making his way to the only chair that would hold his bulk. I settled across from him, the briefcase close to my side, my hand gripped around the handle in case he changed his mind and tried to take it back from me.

"Let me tell you a couple of things first," he said. "The full autopsy report isn't done yet."

"Okay."

That wasn't unusual. Even an expedited full autopsy report still takes several days.

"The science crew in this case was two of my best technicians. These guys know what they're doing," Ben told me.

The crew's job was to locate, identify, preserve and remove for analysis, all substances that might be clues to solving any crime that occurred.

Ben said, "These two criminalists work together all the time. They're good guys. They have a routine they've developed that's very thorough."

That didn't mean they'd found everything, just that they'd likely be good witnesses, able to describe in meticulous detail everything they found and how they found it. If they'd found anything to incriminate George, they'd be able to get it into evidence easily. Half the cases a criminal defendant wins are won because evidence against him is excluded.

Ben's point was that evidence wouldn't be excluded in George's case, and he waited a few moments for his message to sink in.

"Another thing I might as well tell you," he said. "We knew, almost immediately after we found the body, that Andrews was murdered."

I thought back to the Saturday afternoon of the Blue Coat, when I'd listened to Hathaway's report on the radio.

"Why did you say it was a suicide, then?" I asked, a couple of beats before I could answer my own question. "Drake's idea, right?"

Ben nodded. "Drake thought it would give us some time to find the killer, if he felt secure enough to hang around."

My ire bubbled up. "So Drake thinks George is stupid, too? If George killed Andrews, why would he go around telling everyone he was sure Andrews had been murdered, and play right into Drake's hands?"

It was one thing to think George was a killer, but quite another to think George was a stupid killer. Drake was a jerk.

Ben chose not to respond to that. He rose and made his way toward the door. "I'm going downstairs for a late dinner. I'll be back in two hours." He gestured toward the briefcase. "I'll pick it up after."

George always said people would do the right thing if you gave them a chance.

"I'll keep it right here until you're finished," I said, but I couldn't find it in my heart to smile at him.

Before Ben left, he gave me two more rules: no copies; and never tell a living soul he'd done this.

I thanked him and he left me to my work. He wasn't really doing anything wrong by helping me. I couldn't force him to give me the file, but he could release it voluntarily. Still, Drake wouldn't like it, which made it a big risk.

I took the briefcase into the den and opened it. The official police file, labeled People v. George Carson, was nothing more than a five-inch Redweld jammed full of papers. A note on the top that said the file was scheduled to go the prosecutor's office shortly, which meant Drake hadn't seen it all yet. Timing is everything.

I reached into Aunt Minnie's desk drawer and pulled out my headset. It would be faster if I dictated what I found as I went along.

My legal training had not deserted me. I'd already set up my own shadow file. Organization is the key to a lawyer's life. Legal documents multiply like rabbits in the dark. They're worse than rats and telephone pink slips.

As I'd done hundreds of times as a lawyer, I reviewed the file. Like most legal work, it was slow, tedious, and solitary.

First, I went through and dictated a list of the file's contents. Things have a way of disappearing from police files once they're turned over to the prosecutor. I'd had a number of experiences like that as a lawyer. Since I'd been on the bench, lost evidence happened in my cases more often than I'd like to admit.

I'm not big on conspiracy theories. I don't believe that AIDS was deliberately transmitted to the gay population by the CIA as a test of biological warfare; the Government introduced drugs to the black community; or the defense department is concealing aliens in Roswell, New Mexico. I don't even believe that President Kennedy was killed by a conspiracy of his political enemies.

But I know that things legitimately get lost and overzealous lawyers sometimes fail to look hard to find them when they pull out all the stops to win a case.

Which was what Drake would be doing here.

Competitiveness, the desire to win at all costs, is alive and well in America, and it pervades our entire culture, not just professional sports.

When I went through the file the first time, I saw a normal homicide investigation file. If anything, the file was maybe a little more complete than usual.

I flipped quickly through the initial report of the first officers on the scene: crime scene photographs, autopsy photographs, toxicology report. A few interview notes with members of the victim's family, George, friends, colleagues. Inventory of Andrews's pockets where they'd found the suicide note, the boat. Pictures of the gun, ballistics report.

When I'd finished the list, I returned to the beginning and went through more slowly, wishing technology had developed to the point where I could scan everything. Someday.

CHAPTER THIRTY-NINE

Tampa, Florida
Thursday 6:55 p.m.
January 27, 2000

THE HOMICIDE SQUAD AND the medical examiner's office
had been called at the same time. Regardless of the cause, where a
death is unattended or a death certificate cannot be issued by a
competent physician, someone from the medical examiner's office
has to examine the body to estimate the time and probable cause of
death. Nothing unusual about that.

The photographs of the scene weren't too gruesome. Mostly
they were pictures of Andrews slumped over in the boat. The
photos were taken from every angle, though, and revealed that
he'd slumped due to the hole in the side of his head.

The fingerprint reports listed fingerprints appearing on almost
every flat surface. Most of them belonged to members of the
Andrews family and Andrews himself. A few were unaccounted
for, so far. George had been fingerprinted when he was arrested,
but none of these prints were his. That was a break.

They'd bagged the gun and taken samples of the bloodstains.

Physical evidence was limited, but what existed had been gathered, photographed and sent to the various laboratories for analysis.

Except for the body, of course, which had been sent for autopsy by the medical examiner.

There would be no DNA to match at this crime scene. The killer left no bodily fluids. If skin cells or hairs were left behind, they'd been blown away by the wind.

Around the Andrews's backyard, investigators found nothing remarkable. No footprints or car tracks that the killer might have left. But it's pretty dry here in January and the ground would have been hard, resisting imprints of any kind.

Butterflies, which felt more like disgusting squirming maggots, returned to my stomach when I read the next page into my microphone.

The gun found on the bottom of the boat was a snub-nosed .38 caliber Colt revolver, serial number Y327141, which had five shells in the cylinder, one having been fired. I had to stop a second and swallow hard before I could continue: "Registered to George Carson."

The police officer at the scene picked up the gun by sliding a pen through the trigger guard. This meant that no one obliterated valuable data by sticking something down the barrel.

Ben's earlier warning about the admissibility of evidence against George reverberated in my mind and the maggots in my stomach thrashed about. I forced my attention back to the file.

The officer's report claimed he had smelled the fresh odor of burned gunpowder when he smelled the gun barrel, suggesting that the gun was recently fired. Fingerprints on the barrel, the cylinder and several of the shells belong to George Carson, I read.

At this point, the maggots caused my stomach to revolt. I yanked off the headset and stood up; paced quickly, taking deep breaths. Snagged a bottle of water from the fridge and swallowed about half of it to tamp down the bile.

Glancing at my watch, I saw that Ben's two-hour dinner was half over. No time to fool around. Reluctantly, I took my seat and replaced the headset.

"Gunshot residue tests revealed no indication that Andy had recently fired a gun with either hand," I dictated. "In a true suicide, a negative result might mean the victim had on rubber gloves, or held the gun in a plastic baggie, or maybe even that no residue escaped. But since Andrews appears to have died instantly, those possibilities are unlikely."

The only legitimate conclusion was that the gun was fired by someone else.

One bullet had been removed from Andrews's skull, a .38 caliber. Again, modern technology was working against George, because the ballistics tests confirmed the gun found at the scene was the murder weapon.

Using an interesting technique I hadn't seen before, the criminalists had used a length of string to trace the angle at which the bullet had entered Andrews's skull. While it wasn't exact, they did place the approximate spot the gun was held when it was fired: outside the boat, on the dock.

The faint powder burns on Andrews's head indicated that the shooter must have been about three feet away from him. Burns would have been stronger if he'd shot himself.

As Ben had told me, no reasonable doubt existed: Andrews was murdered. And Drake had known it from the outset.

"Liar," I said under my breath, felt better.

Drake lied about the suicide. Maybe he'd lied about other evidence, too.

Now that I had everything dictated, I had less than half an hour left to go through the file a third time, more carefully, my figurative magnifying glass over each piece of paper.

I started with the interview notes. The interview with George was either the shortest suspect interview in history or there was another set of notes somewhere. These notes contained only George's assertion that he had no idea how his gun ended up at Andrews's house and that he'd been at a breakfast meeting the morning of the murder.

Thanks to me, everyone knew that George had not been home. But he'd refused to say where he was in response to police questioning, too.

"What was George doing that was so important he'd keep the secret rather than exonerate himself by providing an alibi?" I heard myself dictate into the section of the document I'd labeled *Open questions*.

If I knew that one thing, I could end the whole mess. George couldn't have been in two places at once. Damn George's honor. Whoever he was with that night certainly didn't feel bound to help George. It was like him to keep his word, even when others didn't. But this was the time for self-preservation.

As for George not knowing how his gun ended up in Andrews's boat, I took that to be true. And I had made a note earlier in my journal to follow up that issue with him. Beginning where he'd last seen the gun might help me find out who'd used it to kill Andrews.

The interview notes didn't say anything about George's answer to those questions, if they'd been asked. These notes were incomplete. Another issue for the *Open questions* list.

The interview with General Andrews's daughter, Robbie, was a little longer. Her alibi for the time of the murder was that she was working. Too bad, I thought, uncharitably. I didn't like Robbie and she clearly despised both George and me. It would have been such a tidy package if Robbie had killed her father and framed George for the murder. Too tidy, unfortunately.

Still, Robbie worked at home. Her alibi had been verified when Robbie had shown the investigator the online therapy column she'd been working on at the time. I made a note of that, and to follow up with a few questions of my own. That is, if Robbie Andrews would talk to me.

She had also told the police that George had been plotting with Senator Warwick and President Benson to defeat her father's nomination. She said George would stop at nothing to keep Andrews off the bench.

This was obviously where Drake got the idea that George would have a motive for murder, but it seemed pretty weak to me. That motive would fit every protester at the Capitol last week, including the shooter who had tried to kill Andrews while I watched the episode on live television in my chambers.

The other interviews had been even longer than Robbie's. The police had interviewed John Williamson, Robbie's husband, Deborah Andrews and both of the general's sons. They'd also interviewed Senator Warwick and my brother, Jason.

And that was all the interview notes in the file, although I was sure there would have been further interviews done.

The only consistent thing about them was that they all had provided confirmed alibis and George had not. The detectives had tried to meticulously rule out all of the other potential suspects with a personal motive located here in Tampa.

In a high-profile murder like this one, other law enforcement agencies were no doubt assisting with the investigation. The protestors would be located and ruled out, one at a time. Craig Hamilton's shooter would be thoroughly questioned. Even if he'd acted alone, he might have like-minded colleagues.

The investigation could be secretly continuing, even if Ben Hathaway didn't know about it. At least, I hoped so.

As I dictated into my headset, I noticed a few other things, but I was just trying to get it all down. There would be time for analysis later.

I listed the coroner's conclusion on manner of death: "homicide, inconsistent with suicide." Next, I simply dictated his evidentiary support for this conclusion: The angle of entry of the bullet into the temple was inconsistent with a self-inflicted gunshot; no powder burns on the general's temple, suggesting the gunshot was fired from some distance rather than with the gun placed on the side of his head as a suicide would do.

Exactly two hours later, hoarse from dictating and emotionally exhausted, I finished. I put the file back into Ben's briefcase and returned to the living room just as he knocked on the door again.

"No wonder people don't trust the government, Ben," I told him as I handed the briefcase over to him. "They lie."

He stood immediately inside the door, away from the line of sight of any inquisitive diners down below. "Only when we need to. Remember, Drake isn't out too far on a limb here."

Ben ticked off the evidence Drake had used to support George's arrest. "George has no alibi; his gun complete with his fingerprints was the murder weapon; George made it plain to one and all that he would make sure Andrews never sat on the Supreme Court. Add to that his fight with Andrews downstairs the night of the murder. It's a set of facts that will definitely support an indictment, Willa. George is in trouble. You'll need a miracle to get him out of this. You might want to suggest he consider a plea."

The maggots thrashed viciously; I put a hand to my stomach.

"Drake will need a lot more for a conviction," I argued.

Ben looked at me as if I'd just landed from Mars. "Drake's office is still investigating," Ben said, as he left.

I closed the door; my body slumped heavily against it as I realized anew just how much trouble we'd landed in and we'd need a miracle to get out.

CHAPTER FORTY

AFTER HATHAWAY LEFT, I prepared for a late dinner with George. There was much I needed to discuss with him. He had some explaining to do and I was determined to get him to do it.

I'd ordered the chef's specialty, Rack of Lamb Julius Caesar, cherry vinaigrette salad with Gorgonzola cheese, broiled tomatoes and a baguette. For dessert, we'd have George's favorite: *crème brûlée*, served warm in a cereal bowl, with raspberries and blueberries on the bottom. I'd scheduled the food to arrive at nine o'clock.

My queasy stomach had begun to recover as I chose from the menu. When I looked at my watch, I saw that I had about thirty minutes before George arrived.

I took a long, scented bath, opened a bottle of Cabernet and tried to relax, to stay in the present and not catastrophize. I was determined to discuss matters with George, but I wanted to keep our relationship on the same easy plane it had been this morning.

This, too, would pass, I hoped. When it did, I wanted our lives to return to the way they had been—to the extent that was possible.

I dressed carefully. I put on my black lace bra and matching black bikini panties. A cream silk shirt George liked topped a knee length dark green silk skirt that I left unbuttoned up the front to well above my knee. You could see the bra through the shirt, which was the effect I wanted.

I'd had a pedicure before all this madness started, so I put on open sandals. I slipped on my diamond stud earrings and the diamond pendant George gave me for my last birthday along with my slim platinum wedding band.

Light makeup, just enough to accentuate my eyes and a little bronzer on the cheekbones. A rosy copper lipstick completed the look. I was sure George would approve.

I went out to the curio on the wall in the living room that contains my Herend zoo. The animals had been Aunt Minnie's. I think she'd had a Hungarian admirer at one time. He'd given her a beautiful set of Queen Victoria china and the whimsical porcelain figurines painted in the technically difficult fishnet pattern.

Based on the number of animals Aunt Minnie had in her collection, the relationship must have lasted for a while. Aunt Minnie named each animal and recorded those names in the inventory we received when George inherited the house.

Aunt Minnie's zoo was now mine and George added to the collection. Whenever a particularly special opportunity arose, he ordered an unusual piece from Lucy Zahran in Los Angeles to give me. All of Aunt Minnie's pieces, and mine, are one of a kind.

I picked up Otto, the magical raspberry unicorn. I closed my eyes and made a wish, rubbing his pointed gold horn with my finger. Aunt Minnie told me once that Otto had the power to make wishes come true. Would mine?

I iced a bucket of Champagne and set out the special champagne glasses we'd bought when we spent a month in Paris for our tenth anniversary. We'd had such fabulous sex there. My cheeks warmed at the memory. George would get the hint.

As I finished my preparations, I heard him knock on the door promptly on time. So old fashioned, George acted like the invited guest he was.

George smiled slowly and with appreciation when I responded to his knock. "Please come in, Sweetheart. You do live here, after all."

"Indeed, I do. Any chance I can get a warm greeting from the hostess?" He put his arms around me and gave me one of those kisses that took my breath away. How could I be so passionate about a man I'd loved for more than twenty years? It wasn't something I could analyze, it just was. That passion was doubly precious to me tonight, when I realized how close I was to losing George, the love of my life.

When I couldn't stand up any longer, we went directly to the bedroom, leaving dead generals and criminal lawyers and ballistics reports where they belonged in another world.

Quite awhile later, I was lounging in our bed wearing the cream silk shirt and nothing else. George poured the last of our Champagne. I vaguely remembered hearing the waiter bring our food about an hour earlier, and I was, all of a sudden, famished.

"George, darling," I said, snuggling a little closer to his chest and running my hands over the curly black hairs that grew there, "Aren't you hungry? I ordered a fabulous meal. I think it's in a heated cart out on the landing."

"I'm starving, actually. Why don't we go see what you've

got," he said, kissing me one last time, causing me to forget the food for a good long while.

Eventually, we put on our robes and he brought the still-warm meal into the dining room where I had set the table with Aunt Minnie's linens, china, silver and crystal. I'd had flowers sent up earlier in the day.

During dinner we talked about the things we always talk about: our friends, our neighbors, what happened with him today, what I did. Of course, my report of my day was a significantly abridged version. Time enough for that later.

When we reached the point for coffee, we moved out into the cool night, still wearing our robes, and enjoyed the stars. The full moon shone on the sparkling dark water like a shiny mirror reflecting the sky. Under other circumstances, this would have been one of the most romantic nights we'd spent in a long time.

As it was, I was acutely aware of the rest of my agenda. Finally, seeing no way to gracefully bridge the gap, I just asked him what was on my mind.

CHAPTER FORTY-ONE

Tampa, Florida
Thursday 11:35 p.m.
January 27, 2000

"GEORGE, I TALKED TO Ben Hathaway today," I started
tentatively.

"Did you now?"

He didn't seem too upset so far, so I plunged on. "Yes. He
said his department has stopped investigating Andrews's murder.
Seems Drake feels they're better off with the provable case they
have now than an un-provable one if they start fooling around with
it." I'd prepared for an explosion, but, thankfully, it didn't come.

With the moon, we didn't need lights, so I'd flipped off the
switch before we came outside. I sipped my coffee and glanced
over at George, who was thoughtfully quiet for a while before he
responded to me. "I know you're worried about me, Willa. Truly,
I'm worried, too. I recognize that political expediency is
occasionally served at the expense of justice. But I believe in
Ben and that the truth will be told, either at the trial or sometime

before they actually execute me." He smiled wanly at his weak joke.

I was grateful for the night that hid the tears that sprang to my eyes. I couldn't accept that my sweet, thoughtful, loving husband would ever be subjected to such a fate. I just couldn't accept it. Ever. "Look—" I took a deep breath and put a hand on his arm. "I hired you a lawyer today. Olivia Holmes."

Softly, but I could hear the edge in it, George said, "What makes you think you have the right to hire a lawyer for me?"

George is the one who takes care of us. He doesn't like anyone to forget that. Sometimes he takes this knight in shining armor thing a little too far, whether he recognized it or not. "Obviously, it's subject to your approval. But, you have to have someone. With your assets, the court isn't going to appoint you a lawyer, you can't represent yourself and I sure can't do it," I told him. "Besides, I thought you'd like her. She has the reputation for being the best there is."

George respects my legal talent, so he asked, "Why do you think she's the right choice?"

"Because she has a reputation for representing only innocent defendants, for one thing. I didn't think you'd want a lawyer who's known for getting the bad guys off."

"True," he said. I could hear the smile in his voice now. "I prefer to look like what we are. It's a good message for the media, too, I suppose."

I was encouraged by his tone and his words. He'd started to think strategically, which was a big step from his philosophical rage of innocence. George is good on strategy. I had often discussed strategy and tactics with him when I practiced law. He was really good at the conservative, majority, middle-America approach.

"Yes, it is. No one except Olivia seems to be picking up on the fact that you are not a killer. Maybe our friends will even start to get the idea," I said, bitterness creeping uninvited into my tone.

George set his cup down, reached over and took my hand. "You mustn't judge them too harshly, Willa. Before the hearings uncovered his ideology, Andrews was well-loved around here. People are outraged at his death. I haven't offered any excuses for myself. And you saw how incriminating the evidence is." He stopped a second. "What are they supposed to think?"

"You're being a lot more forgiving than I'm willing to be with them all." Normally, I try not to give a fig for what people think about me. Judges usually aren't too popular, since we're supposed to make the hard decisions. I'd accepted that as part of the job. But, I do want people to think the best of George. He deserves it.

Besides that, Michael Drake lived and died by public opinion. He was an elected official and he wanted to move up the ladder, where even more people would need to vote for him. If public opinion was on George's side, it would be that much harder for Drake to stay the course against us.

George squeezed my hand and then let it go. The cool night air surrounded my palm once his warmth retreated. "Let's wait and see how it turns out. I have gotten quite a few supportive calls, actually."

I felt a little better, encouraged. "Really? From whom?"

"All of your family. Your Dad. Kate, Jason, Mark and even a wire from Carly in France, for starters." He listed Kate and all of her children. "Everyone in the restaurant. Senator Warwick. President Benson, although that has to be kept quiet." He shot me a warning glance. "The President can't be supporting Andrews's accused murderer. How would it look?"

That got my back up again. "Since when have you cared how

President Benson looks? He's not exactly a personal friend. Or your favorite politician." I wasn't to be appeased. As far as I was concerned, this lack of faith in George from the rest of our friends was inexcusable.

If it's in times of trouble when you find out who your true friends are, then it didn't seem like we had as many as I'd thought a few days ago. Nobody knows you when you're down and out. Except we weren't out. Down maybe, but definitely not out.

We finished our coffee in companionable silence. When I could put it off no longer, I sprung my idea, just the way I'd rehearsed it. "George, between the two of us, we're definitely smarter than the average bear, wouldn't you say?"

Again, that dry smile. "That is at least one of our conceits."

I smiled, too. "Yes, but true anyway. We can figure this out. We have to figure it out. We're the only ones who want to." I knew I sounded a little desperate, but I'd seen the police file. George hadn't.

There would be no investigation of other local suspects if we didn't do it. Drake's cold, steady gaze had told me everything I needed to know on that score. He was planning to prove George killed Andrews and ride that publicity to his next promotion. Maybe all the way to the Governor's mansion. At least, that's how he saw it.

I was not willing to sit around and wait for the real murderer to take credit. If Andrews had been killed by some crazy group with an anti-Andrews agenda, they'd have claimed credit already.

No, the murderer was someone who wanted to remain anonymous, who would be more than happy to let George take the blame.

"I wouldn't say we're the only ones who want to find the killer, although we're certainly the ones with the most serious interest." His tone sounded almost academic and I began to lose my carefully cultivated calm. Another argument was not what I wanted, so I put a lid on my impatience.

But I needed to get into the particulars or we'd just end up where we were before.

"Seriously, then, I can think of several people who might want to murder Andrews. All those special interest groups who were attending the hearings: the right-to-life crowd already tried once and failed, the gay-rights groups were very vocal and angry, all of the non-Caucasian races he offended, not to mention the feminists and the Republicans." I ticked them all off on my fingers, each with individual members who were capable, ready, willing and able.

Now, he lectured me. "That's the trouble with free speech. When you exercise it, people automatically assume you're going to act violently to establish your points."

I ignored the invitation to discuss philosophy. "But a lot of people do use free speech to incite violence. You know that as well as I do and there was a good example in Craig Hamilton's shooting. That man was an easily led ideologue, an instrument of destruction." An involuntary shiver made my last words trail off.

I told myself it was the chilled air that reached my bones as I wrapped the silk robe closer around me and tried to warm up.

George loved a spirited debate and he took this as an invitation. "But what about the concept of free will? Do you really believe that people can be coerced to behave in ways that are repugnant to them?" he asked.

"Do you really believe they can't?"

He looked at me then, with a puzzled expression. "Yes, actually. I think everyone makes his own life and is in control of his own destiny." He must have noticed the gooseflesh on my legs.

He rose and took me by the hand, leading me back inside where it was warmer. "We all have the ability to choose whether to do an immoral or illegal act. The choices we make define us."

I followed him docilely back into the warmth, but not into this quagmire of philosophy over reality. "You sound like you've been talking to Kate. But I'm not interested in discussing esoteric concepts. I want to consider possible murder suspects. It seems to me we've got to include every member of Andy's family and," I said, remembering Olivia's story about her brother, "every soldier Andrews ever came in contact with, as well as his close friends and acquaintances."

"Is that all? Should be a snap to wrap this up by morning." He smiled his indulgence of my plan.

"You have any better ideas?" I challenged.

"No. But I will have in the morning. Now is not the time to panic, Mighty Mouse. You don't always have to save the day. Let me sleep on it." He sat his glass down, kissed the top of my head, and went into the bedroom. I took the glasses into the kitchen. I'd do the dishes later, as a sort of meditation. I looked forward to an occupation for my hands while my mind worked on more knotty problems.

When I came out of the kitchen, George was in the den, fully dressed. I was stunned. How could he think of going back to the Club to sleep after everything we'd gone through tonight?

"Where are you going?" I asked him. "I have a lot to talk to you about yet. We have to examine the evidence. Figure this out. You can't just leave."

He walked over and held me. "Everything I said this morning still goes, Sweetheart."

He kissed me again, long and lovingly this time.

When we parted, he said, "I need to stay away from here until this gets resolved. I'll be in the restaurant, like always. Drake will notice I'm behaving normally, if that worries you. But I intend to keep suspicion away from you."

When I started to protest, he put his index finger over my lips. "It's no use trying to argue me out of this. You got me to agree to Olivia and to investigating this murder ourselves. Count this as a successful use of your feminine wiles and get some sleep."

He moved his finger, gave me another kiss and walked out.

CHAPTER FORTY-TWO

Tampa, Florida
Friday 8:35 a.m.
January 28, 2000

THE TRIAL DAY, WHICH after today I had limited to four
mornings a week, continued to be substantially less mesmerizing
than my private life. As CJ promised, another three hundred cases
had been added to my load. My docket clerk badgered me to get
them on the calendar.

I had very little time to investigate Andrews's murder, but
there was no chance I'd stop. I could live without this job. I could
return to private practice or take an in-house counsel job. But I
couldn't live without George and I wasn't willing to let Drake take
George away from me.

Too many things on my mind; staying focused on the Newton
trial was increasingly difficult.

Fortunately the case was a jury trial, so I didn't need to pay strict
attention to everything that happened. The jury would decide the
facts and I only needed to make evidentiary rulings as they came up.

We were still hearing Newton's case in chief. Moving right along, but shortened trial days meant little accomplished.

There was no way Newton could keep the fact that he'd been married four times from the jury. The information was contained in *The Review* story he was suing over. He'd tried to take the sting out of his marital history on *voir dire* by choosing jurors who had been married more than once, but Tampa is still a pretty conservative place. Divorce is common, but not desirable.

Instead of relying on the marital privilege to exclude spousal communications, today Newton planned to call the most recent of his four ex-wives to the stand. His strategy escaped me. Maybe he was trying to show that since he'd been involved in at least four heterosexual relationships, he couldn't possibly be gay. Like the jurors, I'd just have to wait and see.

"What's your name, ma'am?" Newton asked his first witness.

"Jennifer Newton," said the fourth former Mrs. Nelson Newton.

She looked like a young Tampa matron on her way to church: fresh, neat, not overly showy. Nervous. She held a tissue in her small hands, twisting it so tightly that her knuckles whitened. I thought she looked like she could use a tranquilizer. The entire jury already felt sorry for her.

"Do you know me?" Newton asked her, with a smile and a wink to the jury. Several of them smiled back.

"Yes. We were married for five years," she managed to answer, in a small, trembling voice. Without the microphone on the witness stand, no one would have heard her.

"Do we have any children?" he asked, turning around to look at his youngest son, sitting with his other four sons in the first row of the galley behind his chair.

"Yes. Nelson, Junior. He's seven."

"Now, Jennifer," he said gently, "I'm sorry to have to ask you this, honey, but please tell the jury why we divorced."

I remembered the divorce and it hadn't been friendly. He must have muscled her to get her here at all. I was as curious as everyone else as to what she would say.

She looked down at her hands and then out toward her son. Her eyes filled up, making them look even more like doe eyes than before.

"You know the answer to that, Nelson. You fell in love with another woman."

And then she did start to cry. Not quietly, either. Great noisy sobs. Newton said he had no further questions and we took a recess so she could pull herself together for cross.

Nelson had managed to pull the jury's heartstrings and establish that he had been a husband and was a father. He'd also proved he was unfaithful to this young, attractive wife. Would the jury think those facts proved he wasn't gay?

When we returned, after Tremain got up and got himself adjusted, he said he would have to ask Mrs. Newton some embarrassing questions that he didn't think children should hear. He asked me to have Mr. Newton's children removed from the courtroom and offered to have one of his paralegals stay with them out in the hall.

I granted the request and when the boys were safely out of earshot, Tremain began his cross examination.

"Mrs. Newton, how many times was Mr. Newton married before he married you?"

"Three."

"Was Mr. Newton married when the two of you started your affair?"

"Yes."

"And, was Mr. Newton having an affair when the two of you were married?"

"Yes." She looked like she might start to bawl again, but Tremain waited until she blotted the tears from her eyes. "Mrs. Newton, how tall are you?"

"Five seven."

"And how much do you weigh?"

"About a hundred and ten."

"Have you always worn your hair short like that?"

A tentative hand reached up and patted her ultra-short hairstyle similar to mine.

"Nelson asked me to cut it short and I just did it for him." She cupped her hand around the nape of her neck where the hair dipped to a point.

"Now, Ma'am, I'm sorry to have to get personal with you and I certainly don't mean to be offensive. You understand that, don't you?"

Her chin began to quiver again, but she said, "Yes," in a tiny, little voice. She returned to twisting the now soggy tissue.

"Ma'am, after you became pregnant with your son, did your husband ever make love to you again?"

This started her to bawling again in earnest. She never answered.

Tremain looked at her pointedly for a few moments and then said, "Please let the record reflect that the witness burst into tears and was unable to answer the question."

Since the court reporter takes down every word said in the courtroom, his words were automatically recorded. He'd repeated the request for emphasis, in case the jury missed the point.

Then, he turned and went back to counsel table and sat down. From there, Tremain said he didn't have any more questions and I let the fourth Mrs. Newton go. We could hear her caterwauling in the hall all the way to the elevator.

The jury frowned at Tremain. Jennifer Newton had no doubt reminded them of their daughters and granddaughters. I doubted Tremain's theory had reached any of the jurors.

Newton called his third wife to the stand. She was sworn and seated.

Belinda Newton Phillips was a physical copy of Jennifer Newton, but more flamboyantly so. She dressed to make a statement. About ten years older than Jennifer and a hundred years more sophisticated. This woman probably hadn't cried since the doctor spanked her at birth. I, for one, was relieved that we'd be spared the waterworks this time.

"Tell us your name, please." Nelson, too, was less solicitous of her.

"Belinda Johnson Newton Phillips," she said, making sure the jury heard the full import of her impressive Tampa pedigree. Both the Johnsons and the Phillipses were long-time, wealthy citrus families. Every juror was probably familiar with the names.

"Mrs. Phillips, tell the jury how you know me."

"Unfortunately, when I was young and rebellious, we were married for a short time." Her *hauteur* was off-putting.

"It's obvious you don't like me, Mrs. Phillips. Tell the jury why you've come here to testify today on my behalf."

"Because, to my everlasting regret, I allowed you to father one of my children." She smiled at another fair-haired boy who, even though he was very obese, bore an obvious familial relationship to Nelson and herself. "I don't want Johnson's life tarnished any more than it has to be by the fact that you're his father. There is no question in my mind that you are not gay. That's all I came here to say."

Newton quit while he had a chance of being ahead, and sat down.

Tremain rose to face the fierce third Mrs. Newton. "How do you do, Mrs. Phillips?"

"I'm fine," she said, leaving no doubt in anyone's mind that she'd like to give Tremain a sound thrashing, either for making her appearance on behalf of Newton necessary, or for embarrassing her son by making a public spectacle of his father. Hard to tell which.

"Mrs. Phillips, I take it Mr. Newton wasn't much of a husband to you?"

"That's right."

"How long were you married?"

"Two years."

"And why did you divorce?"

She looked at Tremain, then at Newton and finally, at her son. "Because Nelson didn't love me. He never had. And I deserved someone who loved me. So, I left him."

"Nothing further."

We all waited while Mrs. Phillips and Johnson left the room together. She exited as regally as she had entered and left behind uncontested testimony that Nelson Newton was not gay. It was the first time the statement had been made on the record in the trial and I wondered just exactly how Tremain would rebut it.

Only contested questions of fact would go to the jury. If, at the end of the trial, the only evidence on Newton's sexual preference was the third Mrs. Newton's testimony, I'd be obligated to direct a verdict for the plaintiff. Meaning Newton would win and Tremain would lose. I didn't expect Tremain to let that happen.

Newton next called the second Mrs. Newton, and I was beginning to question his sanity if not his trial tactics. The last two witnesses proved he lived with women and fathered children, but they also shed doubt on his sexual preferences and made him look like a cad. He had to prove *The Review* had published a false statement about him, and he'd made some progress. In his shoes, I'd have stopped while I was ahead. But he had a foolish plan and he intended to follow it, regardless of what happened.

That, I understood. I was doing the same thing, wasn't I?

CHAPTER FORTY-THREE

Tampa, Florida
Friday 1:00 p.m.
January 28, 2000

MRS. ALICE NEWTON WAS closer to Newton's age, but she, too, was a physical duplicate body type to the third and fourth Mrs. Newtons. That is, her physique was more that of a young man than a mature woman. She was tastefully attired, but not expensively so. She wore gloves and a hat. She was probably a sustaining member of the junior league, active in her church and a member of the Tampa Garden Club. She looked the part.

Just as he had with his other two exes, Newton began by asking her how they were acquainted. By now, we all knew what was coming. "I was once your wife," she said, with precision, and more than a little embarrassment.

"How many children did we have together, Alice?"

"Two boys, Matthew and Samuel," and she smiled for the first time at her two sons. Both were short and had facial features more resembling Newton himself.

"How long were we married?"

"Seven years."

"And why did we divorce?"

She looked thoughtful, and this was the first time I appreciated the true motives Newton had for keeping his sons in the courtroom. She didn't want to hurt her children, any more than the third and fourth Mrs. Newtons had. But this woman seemed genuinely at peace with her past.

"Mrs. Newton, please tell the jury why we divorced."

"I was young," she said. "I got lonely. I didn't understand why you had to work all the time. And I wanted you to spend more time with your sons. Divorcing was a foolish thing for me to have done and I've regretted it for years."

Newton wiped a crocodile tear from his eye and thanked the witness. Before he sat down, he went over to his sons and touched each of them on the shoulder. Alice Newton sat straight and tall in the witness box.

Tremain said "No questions, your Honor," from his seat, so we were spared the peacock routine this time.

Newton declined to call the first Mrs., thank you God, and that concluded the day's trial events. I couldn't help thinking that Newton had made progress today and Tremain needed to have at least one or two rabbits in his hat.

CHAPTER FORTY-FOUR

Tampa, Florida
Friday 1:05 p.m.
January 28, 2000

AFTER TRIAL RECESSED FOR the day, I planned to interview the general's daughter, Robbie Andrews. But before I did, I went back to the ancient computer in my chambers and signed on to the Internet.

Robbie Andrews is a licensed psychologist. A few years ago, she started a revolutionary online therapy service, which I planned to check out.

The same people who had been writing to newspaper columnists for free advice seemed willing to pay money to write to an online therapist. Anonymous psychotherapy is a concept that would have Freud turning in his grave, but I had heard Robbie lecture about how popular online therapy was and how it really delivered a valuable service to those who would not seek therapy if they had to reveal their identities in public.

What I suspected she meant was that her clients could receive online therapy without making an appointment with a therapist or payment by their employer-sponsored health insurance plan.

Anyway, I'd never looked for Robbie's Internet column because I'd never been interested. Now I was. She'd told Ben Hathaway that she was working at the time her father was killed and she used her online therapy business to prove it. To test her alibi, I needed to understand her business.

The police file interview notes said Robbie had offered Ben a look at her computer logs to prove she had been engaged in a therapy session on Saturday at five-thirty in the morning, the estimated time her father was killed. Exact times of death are impossible to establish without an eyewitness, but the police were going with the estimate. An electronic alibi. What next?

To be fair, the session she'd claimed to be involved in had lasted the conventional fifty minutes, twenty minutes before and after the murder. How convenient.

Robbie wasn't the only one with an alibi for the exact time of the murder. I just wanted to investigate someone other than George and it was easy to start with my computer. If I could find a way to discredit her alibi, then Drake would have to consider her a viable suspect. Especially if her false alibi was disclosed to Frank Bennett, the reporter.

"Live by the press, die by the press, Drake," I said.

Robbie's online service was called Ask Dr. Andrews. I'd heard her say it was a blatant attempt to appear at the beginning of the advertising alphabet, but savvy marketing skills are no crime. Without them, all businesses would die.

It took me several minutes to find the site. I marveled once again that anyone could find anything on the information super-highway. There are millions of web sites and the search engines are far from perfect. Nevertheless, after a few tries, I found

Robbie's site and several other therapy services, too. I decided to browse the others first, to gain familiarity with this odd concept.

Some of the services were exactly like the Ann Landers or Dear Abby newspaper columns. They were open to the public and consisted of a letter of general interest followed by a no nonsense piece of advice. Easy answers are often the best, but hardest to implement. Without continuous support, these services wouldn't be very helpful.

Kate would disagree. She's told me many times that a difference in perception creates a shift in reality. Perhaps, for their clients, these services provided such a useful shift.

Another type of online therapy was a fee-for-service arrangement where the client wrote a confidential, encrypted problem of two hundred words or less and waited twenty-four to forty-eight hours for a two hundred word response. The client paid a flat fee by credit card, in advance, and was then guaranteed a timely reply. I guessed that these sites must have assigned some kind of automatic date code when the questions were submitted and when the responses were returned.

These services were confidential, unless you could decrypt them, which I couldn't do. Typical problems were probably those for which the type of service was advertised. Management concerns, workers compensation issues and substance abuse claims seemed to be the gamut of choices. Each service advertised a specialist for every need on staff.

I'd had no idea there were so many Internet psychotherapy choices. Maybe Kate should go online. Her particular brand of journal therapy wouldn't be out of place and might even be very lucrative. I wondered if insurance companies would pay for it.

Ask Dr. Andrews seemed to be a combination of the other types of services. She had a regular advice column that was new every day. The site also offered personal advice through an encrypted service.

Like the other sites, Ask Dr. Andrews described the free services offered, as well as payment arrangements for those services Robbie charged for. Ask Dr. Andrews appeared to be unique because the confidential personal sessions were designed to be continuous therapy, much like the conventional type.

She even offered real time sessions, which must have been done through some kind of instant messaging technology. At the courthouse, we had silent big brother technology installed on our computers that recorded all instant message sessions to prevent unauthorized uses.

Robbie's site would have something similar. Otherwise, she'd violate the medical record statutes that required psychologists and other medical providers to keep contemporaneous records of medical treatment.

Yet, I'd seen no reference in the police file to hard-copy confirmation of any instant messaging session at the time of General Andrews's murder. I added this to my list of unanswered questions.

Robbie's web page actually had a clever design and I wondered if Robbie had done it herself or if she'd had a professional designer. Not that it mattered, except the professionalism of the site suggested she was serious about the business.

Robbie's credentials were prominently displayed, including her licensure in Colorado and Florida and her length of experience: fifteen years. She was the "pioneer" in the field and "devoted herself exclusively" to online therapy.

After my brief virtual tour of her competitors, I now breezed quickly through the sample questions and responses from the therapist, and a list of the types of common problems for which Robbie provided therapy.

Unlike the other services, she was willing to accept patients with depression, anxiety, relationship problems, sexual orientation issues and antisocial behavior.

The whole idea was a little scary, really. How could Dr. Andrews possibly evaluate antisocial behavior if she couldn't see the client? The liability issues must be tough to overcome. Maybe she'd been sued over this, but if so, I hadn't heard about it, and it's impossible to keep a secret in Tampa. I made a note to check for lawsuits against Robbie Andrews.

I looked at Dr. Andrews's columns for the past few weeks.

They contained the usual human hassles that could be found in the agony columns of most newspapers. The letters disguised the names of the supplicants and reflected cute, anonymous signatures such as Torn in Temple Terrace or Curious Caretaker.

There were more than a few letters about cheating spouses, wedding etiquette in the age of divorce and multiple families, and so on. The column had a search feature that would allow readers to search for common questions. Just for something to look for, I typed in suicide.

Quite a few letters came up. Most were from anguished family and friends of suicides. Teenaged boys seemed to have killed themselves more than other groups. The smallest group of suicides were children under the age of ten, thank God.

Almost universally, the survivors of suicide were deeply troubled over why they hadn't anticipated the suicide. Dr. Andrews's advice was along the lines of forgiving themselves and recognizing that the suicide was brought on by mental health problems like anxiety and depression. Robbie wrote often that once someone determined to kill himself, prevention was almost impossible. I wondered if such platitudes, though true, comforted the survivors.

One of the letters was a little more unusual. The writer asked whether he should feel guilty about killing his boss and making it appear to be a suicide. He'd done it years before and had gotten away with the murder. Now that the writer suffered from a fatal illness, he wanted to confess his crime to "get right with God."

Dr. Andrews advised him that long kept secrets should go with him to his grave and he should ask forgiveness when he arrived wherever he was going. Since the death was so many years ago, she said, it would serve no purpose to bring it back up to the family now.

My advice would have been different. The family should be told that their loved one hadn't killed himself, in my view. But I wasn't a licensed psychologist.

I checked the date on this letter and Dr. Andrews's response. She'd written the column more than three weeks before her father was murdered.

Could the man's letter have prompted Robbie Andrews to kill her father? At least I could prove she knew it was feasible to murder someone, create the appearance of suicide, and get away with it. I printed the column and folded it into my journal.

As I was about to log off the site, another idea occurred to me. Robbie's service required a credit card to access the encryption software before submitting to online therapy.

I made a note to figure out a way around this and also to ask Olivia whether we could subpoena the files Robbie had been working on the morning of the murder. Robbie's files would likely be protected by the psychotherapist/patient privilege, but we might be able to get them if we agreed to allow her to redact the names of the clients.

It took me a few minutes to decide what I wanted to say. My letter was somewhat true and I kept it short:

Dear Dr. Andrews,
My husband has been accused of a crime he didn't commit.
This is causing a huge problem in my marriage. What should I do?
Faithful Wife

I jotted down the date and time that I hit the send button. And I saved the letter in a special file.

I'd check for the answer tomorrow, see how long it took her to respond. Then, I'd know just how long she'd been aware of the suicide/murder letter. The knowledge might not help me, but it was an easy thing to do and seemed to carry little to no risk.

Then, I logged off, stuffed my journal into my tote bag, picked up my keys and my tiny purse and left to visit Dr. Andrews, face to face.

CHAPTER FORTY-FIVE

Tampa, Florida
Friday 2:15 p.m.
January 28, 2000

ROBBIE ANDREWS AND JOHN Williamson lived in the section of South Tampa called New Suburb Beautiful. It was not as new or as tony as Beach Park, but the residents were mostly upper middle class professionals in John and Robbie's age group, early thirties.

Young children played in the yards in numbers large enough to justify calling this a baby boomlet haven. It was a neighborhood Kate would thrive in and I would never consider.

I consulted my notes from the police file for the Andrews/Williamson address and pulled up in front of an out-of-place, Midwestern-looking, ranch-style house.

The house resembled a red brick shoebox turned long ways on the lot. It had white trim and black shutters on either side of each window. A two-car garage at one end opened onto a driveway that went straight in from the street. The garage door was closed.

The police file interview notes said Dr. Andrews worked at home every weekday from five o'clock in the morning until at least six in the evening. Her absence might prove she'd lied to Ben Hathaway. If Robbie wasn't home when she was supposed to be today, maybe she wasn't here the Saturday morning her father died, either.

Alas, when I rang the bell, an attractive, young Latino woman with dark, curly hair dressed in jeans and an Outback Bowl jersey that hung below her knees, answered the door.

"Hi. I'm Willa Carson. Is Dr. Andrews home?" I tried friendly. I'd counted on the element of surprise to get Robbie to talk to me.

The woman did let me inside the front door. So far, so good. But only so far.

"Dr. Andrews is working with a patient right now. She's booked until six o'clock. Would you like to make an appointment?"

"I'll just stop by some other time. It's a social call, really."

I tried to look around and past this gorgeous gargoyle at the gate, but I couldn't see much. The house was one of the older ones in the area and it lacked the vaulted ceilings and open feel of the newer Florida ranch-style homes built in and around Tampa.

The consuming silence proved that online therapy is quiet. No one could know for sure if Robbie was working or not.

"Well, Dr. Andrews is booked every weekday until six and Saturday mornings with standing appointments. I can tell her you called and have her call you, if you'd like," Gorgeous Gargoyle said.

It would probably be awkward for me to tell her I wanted to startle Robbie into talking to me. When all else fails, try the truth. Most of it.

"I wanted to surprise her. I'll just come back later. Please don't spoil the surprise."

The woman got into the spirit of the supposed spontaneity. "Oh. Okay. Sure. Just come back around six-thirty. She'll be here then."

It's a wonder there aren't more home invasions, I thought. People will tell you almost anything if you look friendly and harmless. I thanked her and left with smiles and waves. Then, I walked out to Greta like a disappointed sorority sister unable to share the secret handshake with an old college chum after all these years.

Planning my return.

That much was true.

CHAPTER FORTY-SIX

Tampa, Florida
Friday 3:30 p.m.
January 28, 2000

GEORGE HAD CONSENTED TO meet with Olivia Holmes. We all gathered at Minaret. After pleasantries were exchanged and George gave his tacit approval of her, Olivia took charge of the meeting.

She began with the few things she'd learned.

"Drake wanted to arrest George in front of the television reporters, but Ben Hathaway refused," she said.

I tamped down my ire at Drake and kept quiet.

"Your prompt release on a mere $100,000 cash bond was primarily a professional courtesy from the sitting judge toward Willa, one of his colleagues on the bench," she looked over at me, then at George. "That George is a prominent citizen was also a factor. And Drake didn't object after George surrendered his passport."

"Really?" I asked, somewhat surprised.

Olivia shrugged. "If Michael Drake turns out to be wrong, they'll all have enough egg on their faces politically without looking like uncivilized jerks, too."

I swallowed my retort and George merely said "hmmph."

Olivia seemed pensive for a couple of seconds, and then continued. "The next step is for George to be formally indicted. Capital murder can only be charged by grand jury indictment in Florida."

George smiled a little at this. "There, just as I thought. No grand jury will indict me and this will all be over."

She shook her head, negative. "While it is theoretically possible that the grand jury won't return an indictment, it's almost sure to happen."

"Why?" he asked, indignant now.

"If Drake wants an indictment, they'll give him one. He could indict a baboon, if he wanted to," she told him, revealing one of the many hard truths of the process.

I said nothing. I hadn't told Olivia about the police file and I didn't mention it now. George would flip a gasket if he knew I'd already stuck my nose into this business and Olivia's reaction would be only slightly more ballistic.

From reading the file, I'd concluded that the probable cause they'd used to support his arrest was the usual triad: means, opportunity, and motive. Drake thought George's desire to keep Andy off the bench would be enough to support the indictment. While we theoretically had twenty-one days before Drake had to convene the grand jury, I expected him to do so quickly, while public outrage was still on his side.

George's mouth fell open. "Do you mean to say that he can railroad me?"

Olivia looked chagrinned while she answered his question,

one she must have answered at least a hundred times. "Don't you watch television?"

George was not amused. In truth, neither was I. It's amazing how your sense of humor vanishes when your life is threatened by forces over which you have no control.

"As a practical matter, Drake isn't going to take a case to trial that he can't win. I've known Drake for most of my life. He's tried over 250 capital murder cases and he's won every single one of them," she said.

George whistled under his breath and Olivia nodded. "It's an impressive record, but all it means is that he pleads out the cases he can't prove. If he has an agenda, it's to keep his winning streak intact so he can someday run for Governor."

George's response was automatic, "Over my dead body will that ignoramus be Governor."

I relaxed a little, because that was exactly what I'd have expected him to say.

Olivia was not amused. "Careful, George. That kind of comment is one of the things that landed you in this mess."

He looked over at me pointedly, smug, as if to say he was right all along and we were being overly dramatic. "Drake can't convict me. I didn't kill Andrews. We shouldn't worry about the indictment because he won't take my case to trial if he can't win. Just as I thought."

Olivia didn't let him off the hook so easily. "Not exactly. If Drake thinks he can get a conviction on this case, he *will* go for it. This has been front page, lead story on every available media. You are not a sympathetic defendant. The victim was prominent. It's the kind of case that can make or break a prosecutor's entire career. He doesn't want egg on his face, but he's not going to just go away, either. All he wants is victory. He'll do whatever he can to make that happen. Underestimating him is a mistake."

Here, she placed another of what I recognized now as her strategic pauses. "Believing he won't get a conviction is the only reason Drake might not try. He hates to lose. And he won't lose this case."

While George thought this through, she added, "And don't forget, the decision may not be solely Drake's. Everybody's got a boss. He has people he reports to. He's up for re-election next year."

I understood exactly what she meant, and so did George.

Winning a big case against George, a prominent member of the other party, for the cold-blooded murder of a Democratic leader would assure Drake another four-year term as State Attorney and maybe even set him up for the Governor's mansion, or more powerful, national political office. Those career goals were exactly what Michael Drake was after and everyone who knew anything about him was aware of his single-minded obsession with power.

Olivia continued, "Make no mistake. This kind of opportunity rarely comes along. Drake and the mayor and everyone else will all want to get the greatest possible mileage out of it."

George let out a long breath and asked, "So, how long will all these shenanigans take? I have a restaurant to run, a life to live here."

His impatience with what he viewed as the ridiculousness of all this was obvious, even to Olivia.

She leaned forward, crossed her wrists, "Both of you need to understand something. This is a long process. I don't know when you'll be indicted. It could be as much as another two weeks." When George started to sputter, she held up her hand for him to wait. "But I think Drake will move quickly to indict. After that, you'll be arraigned and then we can begin the formal discovery process."

Olivia delivered the bad news, straight up. "It will take at least nine months to get this case to trial, and we'll be working like crazy between now and then to be ready."

George exploded. "Nine months!" he shouted as he jumped to his feet. "I'm not going to be consumed by Drake for nine months! This is outrageous!"

He paced our small den like a caged beast. Which is exactly what he had become. Used to roaming around at will, moving in powerful circles, George would not flourish while being watched under a microscope.

Olivia explained things patiently, but firmly and without any particular optimism. "Yes, George, it is outrageous. But there is not one thing you can do to rush it."

She began gathering her documents and stuffing them back into her file. "What we have to do is to try to end the process long before trial. We have to persuade Drake that they've got the wrong man. Our best shot is to do that before the indictment," she said, echoing my own thoughts two days ago.

It made me feel a little sick that the conclusions I'd reached on my own were valid; I'd have preferred to be wrong.

George digested Olivia's comments for a little while, and then said, "What if we can't persuade him? Drake is not my number one fan." He looked over at me then. "Or Willa's."

Olivia nodded. "Then we'll just have to keep trying."

She stood up to leave, and when the two of them were side by side, George looked like a giant. "You're in trouble. We might be able to get you out of this mess with an airtight alibi."

She looked at him pointedly, but he said nothing. "Just as I thought. I'll do the best I can. I'm hopeful that this will all be put behind you eventually and you'll be able to go on with your lives. No promises."

Lest we took comfort from her prediction, Olivia was quick to add, "But it won't happen quickly and it won't be painless. You two are just going to have to suck it up and show the world what you're made of."

George and I walked her toward the door.

She delivered final instructions. "The last time I checked, you both had responsibilities. Keep going. Behave as normally as possible. Let me do my job and," this last part was directed at me, "stay out of the way."

George and I talked briefly after she left. I tried not to let him see how totally befuddled I was. Not over the process. I was all too familiar with that. No, what upset me was the sheer absurdity of it all.

How could this possibly have happened? I am a good person. A public servant. My husband is as honest, kind, and traditional as any man anywhere.

The idea that we were involved in murder was a very, very bad joke. Right?

CHAPTER FORTY-SEVEN

Tampa, Florida
Friday 5:30 p.m.
January 28, 2000

THE TAMPA GUN CLUB and Shooting Range was about fifteen miles from downtown, out on Tampa's all-purpose commercial highway, Dale Mabry, named after a popular local son. The club was quite a distance from Plant Key and it took me over forty minutes to travel ten miles in the early afternoon traffic.

George had learned to enjoy shooting handguns during his army days. He said shooting released tension and sharpened his reaction times. When we lived in Detroit, where the weak are killed and eaten, he used to keep guns in the house. No matter how much I insisted that I would never, ever use one to shoot an intruder or anyone else, George remained confident that I would if I had no choice. So far, neither opinion had been tested.

Years ago, George kept handguns around the restaurant, just because, he said, "you never know." Our home was open to the public and at least once a week or so, some diner wandered up toward the flat, out of curiosity, to look at the house. We'd never, knock on wood, had any kind of trouble with George's guns. Until now.

Greta and I continued north on Dale Mabry, where homogeneity flourished. If it's true that every American lives within three miles of a McDonald's restaurant, metro Tampa is beating the national averages soundly.

I passed franchise after franchise, home improvement, furniture and discount stores, hotels and motels gathered near the airport, and the relative newcomer's book superstores with coffee shops and live entertainment, that had become the gathering places for Tampans after dark.

These days, every city in America contained the same. It was hard to distinguish Los Angeles from Boston anymore. Nervous travelers who once felt uncomfortable leaving home, concerned about bad food and worse sleeping conditions, now worry needlessly. Whatever they have back on the farm, we have everywhere. But for me, all the individualism of the country's regions has been destroyed. There seemed to be no reason to leave home.

Eventually, I passed most of our driveway-to-driveway civilization and ended up on the very north end of Dale Mabry Highway. The gun club was on the right. I turned in.

Maybe there wasn't a lot of money in running a gun club because the driveway wasn't paved and neither was the parking lot. Dry and dusty now, the lot must have been a river of mud every summer afternoon when the skies opened up and flooded everything without copious manmade drainage.

Fortunately, I wore washable clothes and hadn't put Greta's top down this morning. When I got out of the car, a cloud of dust settled over us. A small breeze moved the dust imperceptibly.

About ten similarly dusty vehicles, mostly old, beat-up trucks, resided in the parking lot. I couldn't really visualize George's Bentley parked out here. I walked the few yards to the door holding my breath.

The inside lighting was dim and the noise deafening. Unlike other gun ranges George had dragged me to over the years, this one did not have a soundproof wall between the shooting area and the front door. Here, I looked through clear glass to an area where the shooters were standing. They all wore ear-muffs. I tried lifting my palms to cover each ear, but that only improved the situation marginally.

At the counter, a middle-aged, overweight man with a shaved head and a day's growth of beard stood, also wearing ear protection. I walked over and introduced myself. He didn't move. I touched his arm and he glanced up, apparently used to being touched to get his attention.

The guy looked me over and gestured to a door at one side of the counter. I went through it into what must have been a soundproof room. He followed me in and closed out the noise with the door. The quiet was startling.

Now, I stood in a soundproof room where various shooting equipment and ammunition were sold, with a gun nut I'd never met and no one knew where I was. I'm generally not given to paranoia, but this situation made me wildly uncomfortable. I decided to take care of my business and get out of there as quickly as I could.

"Can I help you?" He asked me again.

I held out my hand. "I'm George Carson's wife, Willa."

He took my hand in one big, hairy paw and covered it with his other paw. On one hairy forearm was tattooed: *Semper Fi*. He looked so sorrowful, and held my hand so gently, I was ashamed of my earlier paranoia.

"I am truly sorry about George, Mrs. Carson. He is one fine man. I just can't believe he killed General Andrews." He spoke slowly and clearly, still holding onto my hand. As if I might be hysterical and he needed to talk me down off a high building before I jumped. "If there's anything I can do for George, you just let me know, okay?"

Maybe I'm not as good at hiding my feelings as I think. Or maybe he talked to all the little ladies this way. At least the ones who might be married to murderers.

I cleared my throat and tried to extract my hand from the warm, moist grip that swallowed it. "Actually, uh, what did you say your name was?"

"Curly, ma'am." I tried again to pull my hand away, but he kept a tight hold on it.

"Um, Curly. Of course. George has mentioned you. It's nice to meet you." George had never said anything about this man to me in my life, but I wanted to get my hand back. I pulled gently. No luck.

"It's nice to meet you, too, ma'am," he said, sorrow for George and me practically seeping from his pores.

Yes. Well. Let's get to the point.

CHAPTER FORTY-EIGHT

"CURLY, I NEED TO see George's locker and pick up some things. Is that okay with you?"

I gave my hand another little tug, just to see if I could dislodge it. He tightened up. It was like playing with Chinese handcuffs. The more I tried to pull my hand away, the tighter his hold became.

"Sure it is, ma'am. But you need a key to get into George's locker. Did you bring one?"

"I guess I just thought you'd have a key. You do have one, don't you Curly?" I wasn't batting my eyelashes and blushing, honestly.

He hesitated a few seconds, looking at me with more curiosity than hostility. If George had guns in his locker, which I suspected he did, Curly had to be wondering what I wanted them for.

"Do you want to shoot, Miz Carson?" He asked me, his head

tilted sideways in a gesture that reminded me of our dogs when they didn't quite understand my instructions. "I don't know if I can let you do that without Mr. Carson's permission."

Shoot? A gun? Me? I felt my head shaking back and forth, almost involuntarily. I tried to put him at ease. "I just need to look for the shooting log George keeps, Curly. I know he keeps track of when he shoots and how well he does. And he keeps an inventory of his guns. I want to look at that."

And I wasn't pleading, either. If my tone was a little less confrontational than the one I use in the courtroom with recalcitrant litigants, it was purely expedience.

Curly thought about it, at glacial speed. It wasn't smart to underestimate your opponent, but Curly was either dim-witted or foxy and slow on purpose.

I bet on the former. "You can come with me and watch what I look at, if you want," I suggested, as if he wouldn't have thought of that on his own.

I wanted to rifle through George's locker by myself, but if the only way I could get Curly the Giant here to let me do that was with his supervision, that would be better than no look at all.

About a month later, Curly finally nodded his head and released my hand, which now felt curiously cold and lightweight after its imprisonment in the damp recesses of his grip. He told me to follow him and we went back out into the noise where conversation was, thankfully, impossible. Curly picked up his keys and walked through another door, into the locker room, while I followed.

Apparently you don't have to shower and change clothes to use a shooting range, because there was only one room filled with lockers and nothing else.

The lockers were numbered and stacked in sets of two, one on the top and one on the bottom, with a long bench separating them horizontally. Lockers abutted each other in rows covering every wall of the room. Two or three rows of back-to-back lockers rested, freestanding, in the middle of the room. The noise was a little less earsplitting in here, but multiple gunshots continued, like closely set fireworks on the Fourth of July.

Curly led me toward the back wall of the locker room. There were men and women standing around the lockers. I didn't recognize any of them and they didn't recognize me. And to be honest, I wasn't looking too closely. The last thing I wanted was to see someone I knew.

When we got to George's locker, I almost laughed out loud. The locker number was 007. Did George imagine himself as some sort of James Bond? Reliable, sturdy, predictable George? Did he have a Walter Mitty life? Or was this just a joke?

Curly opened the locker for me, and stepped aside to let me see. Hanging on the hooks on either side of the locker were two sets of ear protectors that resembled the ones Curly now wore around his neck like a choker.

I breathed a sigh of relief when I found the spiral notebook containing George's shooting log on the bottom shelf. Either Michael Drake didn't know enough about George's habits to have obtained a search warrant for the locker, or he simply hadn't gotten to this point in his investigation yet.

Under the log was a single sheet of plastic laminated paper containing a list of his guns with serial and license numbers neatly printed. The licenses themselves, I knew, were kept in our safe deposit box.

I picked up the log book and flipped back through the last few entries.

George is a man of habits and rituals. Maybe all humans are.

His habit here was to shoot each gun in the order it was listed on the inventory. The log reflected that he'd come to shoot at irregular dates and times, which was a little unusual, and not enlightening.

But then I noticed that he had been here every Wednesday morning for more than two years. And on Wednesdays, he shot the snub nosed .38, the gun that killed General Andrews.

The log also reflected that George sometimes lent his guns to other people. His blocky printing listed the borrowers' names, most of whom I recognized, but some of them were strangers to me.

Curly cleared his throat. "Um, Miz Carson, are you about finished here? This is kinda unusual, you know?" He seemed to be a little impatient with me, now. Perhaps he was having second thoughts about letting me in here.

Actually, I found that comforting, in an odd way. If Curly didn't want to let George's wife into his locker, maybe he kept other unauthorized people away. That wouldn't be a good thing for George's defense, but it made me feel safer to know that just anyone couldn't walk in here and steal a murder weapon.

Quickly, I counted the number of guns listed on the inventory. Seven. Then, I looked at the boxes stored inside the locker. Seven.

I counted again.

How could that be?

I flipped through the log, checking to see whether George had, for some reason, listed more guns in another location. I didn't find any such list.

Long ago, I learned that I think best in pictures, so I closed my eyes and visualized George removing the .38 and using it. In my mental movie, he cleaned the gun thoroughly when he was finished as I knew was his habit. When he'd cleaned the gun, he returned it the purple velvet bag and then the black, clearly labeled box.

The box sitting right there, in plain sight, on the shelf in front of me. Stacked neatly with all the other boxes. All seven of them. I felt like shouting *Eureka!* but that would have drawn more attention than I wanted. I reached up and lifted the box slightly, without bringing it out of the locker. I was right. The box was empty.

George, my ritualistic, practical husband, would never, ever, have taken the gun away from here without the box. And without the box, the gun would have been so much easier to conceal. Another question arose now: how did the gun and the box get separated?

Glancing up, I noticed Curly watching me, shifting from foot to foot. Sometime this century, he might decide I shouldn't have had access to George's locker at all. There were other people in the locker room and none had seemed to recognize me yet.

"Curly, does George have more than one locker?"

The puzzled look on his face was almost comical. "No, ma'am. This is the only one. Why?"

Ignoring the question, I counted once more. I pulled out a disposable camera and took a picture of the locker, inside and out. If Curly wanted to know why I did so, he didn't ask.

Then, I told him, "I'm going to take George's log and inventory with me." I stuffed the documents into my tote bag before he could protest. Without making the mistake of offering to shake hands in farewell, I said, "Thanks for your help," turned around and headed out of the locker room.

"You're welcome, Miz Carson," he said to my retreating back as I beat feet with the log and the inventory in the bag under my arm.

CHAPTER FORTY-NINE

OUT IN THE PARKING lot, seated in the car, engine running and air conditioning on, I pulled George's gun log and inventory out of my tote bag and began to study them. My journal and digital recorder were also in the bag, but I was too impatient to dictate.

I pulled out my checkbook, which had a tiny, unreadable pocket calendar going back two years and forward three more. I'd left my reading glasses at the office and I couldn't read the miniscule numbers on the calendar in the darkened interior of the car. I fished out the small, flat flashlight I'd been carrying in my purse the past couple of years. Even with the light, I could barely make out the calendar's markings.

Squinting at the tiny print, I saw my quick observation inside had been right. George had recorded a regular schedule of Wednesday morning shooting in his log for the past three years.

Aside from Wednesdays, his shooting schedule was irregular.

Some days, he shot in the morning, some days in the afternoon. Some weeks he shot two or three times, and some weeks, only on Wednesday.

The really interesting thing was that on Wednesdays, he always shot the .38, the murder weapon. But I noticed that he sometimes shot it on other days of the week as well.

If someone wanted to steal George's .38 without his knowledge, the best time to do it would be Wednesday afternoon. That way, they might have kept the gun for about a week before he planned to shoot it again. Maybe he wouldn't miss the gun during the week. The thief couldn't be sure, but it was as close to a reasonable bet as he could make.

The Andrews murder took place on a Saturday, so the gun thief could easily have gone undetected.

Of course, the thief would have to get past Curly, but surely another member or guest of a member could have done so, using the right amount of guile and speed. Curly was by far the most physically intimidating person I'd come across, but his reflexes and movements were slow and, I suspected, he was not a Rhodes scholar, although appearances are often deceiving.

Someone could have gotten past him. After all, I'd just walked out with the log after taking photographs.

And someone had definitely removed the gun from George's locker and the club.

That fact couldn't be denied.

Looking back at the inventory, I confirmed that George had seven guns listed. He'd bought the .38, the inventory reflected, about five years ago.

Once I found the .38 on the list, I compared the inventory to the gun log. George's meticulous rituals were evident again. He shot the guns in order, from the top of the inventory to the bottom.

If someone had wanted to predict which gun George was likely to shoot next, that would have been fairly easy to do.

After staring at them for a while, I realized neither the log nor the inventory reflected whether each gun was in the locker at any particular time. That is, George didn't have the equivalent of a library card to document when each gun was removed or returned.

My methodical husband would have had no need for such a system. George always keeps track of his possessions. He never loses anything. It's quite annoying, really.

But in this instance, I knew that if George's guns were taken out of the locker, he would have been the one to take them. And he'd know exactly where each one was.

Unless it was stolen, and his response to my questions about his gun led me to believe that George felt otherwise.

Drake assumed George took the .38 out to Andrews's house and killed him with it. I would never believe that happened. So the question was still: how did George's gun get into the hands of the killer?

Three hard, rapid knocks on the window inches from my face sounded like gunshots.

I jumped and whipped my face around to see Curly standing outside my door.

My hand flew to my pounding heart as I tossed the log onto the passenger side floor and gave thanks for Greta's automatic door lock feature. I felt like he'd startled three years off my life.

When I'd calmed down a second or two, I realized he was talking to me, through the closed window.

"Miz Carson? Miz Carson?" He held up his right hand, showing me my disposable camera. "You left this inside."

I pulled the button to lower Greta's driver side window. Then, I reached out and snatched the camera with my left hand. "Thanks,

Curly," I said, pressing the button to automatically raise the window again before I moved the gear shift into reverse and waved goodbye, leaving him staring after me.

CHAPTER FIFTY

Tampa, Florida
Friday 6:45 p.m.
January 28, 2000

IN THE AFTERNOON DALE Mabry traffic, even though most of
it was headed out of the city in the opposite direction, it took me
too long to reach South Tampa. I finally made it to Robbie
Andrews's house, but it was later than I'd wanted to be.

God watches over fools and children, because as I rounded the
corner onto Jetton Street, I saw Gorgeous Gargoyle get into her
Honda and pull out of the driveway. Mercifully, she went the other
way. I didn't think she'd noticed me.

I made a mental note of the time she left. If I wanted to
surprise Robbie Andrews again, I would make it a point to come
by after her assistant had gone for the day. All I wanted was to
confirm her alibi for myself. It seemed weak to me. And she was
just a little too quick to point the finger at George. But then,
maybe I was just engaging in denial and wishful thinking.

Which started me to thinking about when Gorgeous Gargoyle

might arrive for work in the morning. Maybe ten? So how could she know when Robbie's online therapy sessions began?

I pulled into Robbie's driveway and parked Greta in the middle, blocking both sides. Halfway up the front walk, I heard the automatic door opener lifting the heavy double garage door. I returned to the driveway just in time to see Robbie entering her car inside the garage.

"Hello, Robbie," I said as I approached.

For a woman who worked at home on a computer where no one could see her, Robbie certainly was well dressed. When I work at home, I favor cotton shorts and T-shirts. Not Robbie.

Except that she was larger than three runway models, Robbie could have come straight from the fashion houses of Paris.

She wore a trendy haircut, great makeup and flowing caftan type clothes, all suggested her clothing budget exceeded her huge size. Spiked heels caused her to appear taller than five-feet-three. And she had beautifully manicured hands and feet.

Robbie held her purse straps near her shoulder with one hand and her keys in the other. Slung over her back was one of those fashionable and pricey bags that everyone in Tampa seemed to carry since the new International Mall opened. The bag looked like an open horse feeder, what the designers call a bucket bag. I stayed far enough away from her that she couldn't hit me with it. That thing would pack quite a wallop, I imagined.

Looking at her, it occurred to me again why advertising works. The newspaper is full of bad news while advertising sells hope, possibilities, potential. We want to believe. Advertising, like multiple marriages, was the triumph of hope over experience.

Robbie bought it all. She tried to hide her size by covering it in expensive packaging, probably hoping people would focus on the wrapper and not the contents.

"Willa, I really have an appointment and I don't have time to deal with you right now." She snapped at me, nastier than she had been at her mother's house a few days ago.

Holding onto my patience, I ran my hand through my short hair, which had been blowing around since I'd left the Gun Club and stopped to put Greta's top down. I hadn't replaced my lipstick and my clothes looked like I'd been walking around in a dusty parking lot. Which, of course, I had. I felt tired, grimy and not really up to doing battle with Robbie Andrews.

"I only need a few minutes. Since you can't get out unless I move my car, why don't you just talk to me and get it over with."

The war of her emotions was plain on her face. First anger, then outrage, and finally, resignation. But she didn't have to be nice about it.

"All right. What do you want?" She emphasized the want, managing to put as much derision in the word as possible.

What I really wanted was to scream at her, and maybe hit her a couple of times, too. But I didn't think that was a good idea. I really had very few options. If Robbie didn't talk with me voluntarily, I had no legal right to force her. It's not like I owned a badge.

I tried reason first. "I need to talk to you and I don't think either one of us wants to discuss this in the driveway. Why don't we go inside? I won't keep you long."

Without another word, Robbie walked right past me and up to the front door, digging deep into the bucket bag for her keys. When she got to the door, opened it and stepped inside, she turned around and snapped, "Come on then. Let's get this over with. I have to be somewhere else in fifteen minutes."

I hustled to get through the door before it slammed in my face.

Robbie continued walking through the house and into the

dining room where she remained standing and didn't offer me a seat. I followed quickly after her, but I noticed the beautiful antique furnishings in the house. Many of them would have suited perfectly at Minaret.

"What do you want?" she said again, emphasizing each word and stressing the last one as she had before.

Maybe she could have been more disagreeable. I didn't know her that well. She acted like a spoiled child. Perhaps in her world, people talked to each other like that. In my world, we didn't.

Her behavior made me really want to beat the snot out of her, and the feeling surprised me. I'd never been in a physical fight in my life. I realized it was a good thing I didn't carry a gun. At this moment, I might have been tempted to threaten her with it.

I pulled up some much needed strength from somewhere, instead, and made myself respond to her churlishness with calm reason. "Robbie, you must want to know who killed your father. That's what I want, too." I spoke politely to her, but she wasn't fazed.

As rudely as before, she said, "George has been arrested already, in case you've forgotten. I'm interested in putting this behind me and going on with my life. And I don't want you pestering my mother, either." She stopped for a second and gave me another of her scowls. "Now if there's nothing else, you're making me very late."

Oh, the hell with it. "Look, Robbie," I said, more firmly, as I pulled out an antique oak dining chair and sat down, "neither one of us is going anywhere until I get the answers I came for. Now, you can sit down and talk to me for about ten minutes and then I'll leave. Or you can keep up your routine and we can stay here until all Florida freezes over."

Maybe it wasn't my best moment. But I had very little choice.

I had no legal right to press her, and we both knew it. Either I had to motivate her to talk to me, or I'd go away empty handed. George had too much at stake for me to give up so easily.

She waited several seconds, apparently concluding she'd have to throw me out bodily if she wanted to get rid of me before I was good and ready to go. She sat down, folded her hands on the table, and in what I can only assume was the best manner Dr. Andrews the psychologist could muster for badly behaved patients, she snarled, "What is it you'd like to know?"

I resisted the urge to slap her, but I had to sit on my hands to do it. My patience was exhausted by the situation and her histrionics. I deliberately asked her something personal. "Tell me about your relationship with your father."

She bristled again, raising her hackles, whatever hackles are. "My relationship with my father wasn't any different when George killed him than it was years ago when you and he were friends, Willa." Her voice broke just a little, I thought, but I might have imagined it. "He detested me. He had no use for girls or women. You know that." She started to rise. "Is that it?"

"Not quite. How did you feel about him?" I watched her closely. She actually started to get a little blinky, like she had some feelings under that armadillo exterior she dressed in Chanel.

She steadied her chin and returned to her armor of belligerence. "I loved my father because he was my Dad just like any girl loves her daddy. But I didn't like him very much. I didn't know him well enough to like him. He saw to that. He wasn't much of a father, really. Not to me, anyway."

Robbie stopped for a few seconds, and then, as if she'd made a decision, she added, "You'd have to ask my brothers how he was to them. I'm sure he loved them very much when we were all younger."

She said the words with such bitterness that I involuntarily recoiled. There was something more there, something under the surface that didn't make sense.

Her reaction to her father's misogynistic view of women was understandable maybe, but her comments about his relationship with her brothers was unnecessarily poisonous. "And how about his relationship with your husband? Did they get along?" I almost whispered the question, trying not to antagonize her further.

Her eyes widened, then she pursed her lips and pressed them together so that hard white lines formed at the corners. "Yes. My husband and my father got along. They got along as well as anyone could." She paused, then added, "Which is to say they could be in the same room without getting into a fist fight, something George couldn't manage."

Biting my tongue to avoid the sharp retort that bubbled up from somewhere south of civility, I said, "Only one more thing, Robbie. How about your parents? I know for a long time, there was a lot of trouble between them. How was their relationship just before he died?"

I struggled to sound friendly and sympathetic. From long experience, I knew that I could get more from a hostile witness with sympathy than by badgering.

Like everything else I'd tried, it didn't work. Robbie stood up, picked up her purse and turned toward the door. "This interview is over. If you want to sit in my dining room until Chief Hathaway gets here to escort you out, feel free. But if you don't leave in the next ten seconds, I'm calling the police."

And to emphasize her threat, she dug into the bucket bag and pulled out one of the things she kept in there in addition to the kitchen sink—her cell phone. She must have bumped her house alarm button in the process because the alarm started its loud, shrill screaming as she dialed 911.

Unwilling to be intimidated, I continued to sit and look steadily at her while she dialed. When the operator answered, Robbie said, "I'd like to report an intruder in my house. I know her name. Would you like me to tell you on this recorded line?" She looked at me meaningfully.

I could barely hear her over the noise of the house alarm. But, she'd effectively called my bluff. It wouldn't be good for me to be named as an intruder in a recorded 911 call by Robbie Andrews when my husband was out on bail after being charged with murdering her father. Those 911 calls are all taped and I'd heard the tapes played back in murder trials. The evidence was always riveting to the jury.

A siren wailed somewhere in the distance, growing louder. It couldn't have been dispatched in response to her call, not that quickly.

The siren's noise level increased, now combined with the house alarm. I could barely hear myself thinking, She could shoot me and no one would hear the gun go off.

Even if the siren I'd heard hadn't been sent in response to Robbie's call, it could easily be diverted here.

"Judge Willa Carson is her name," Robbie said. "I'm afraid of her. Her husband killed General Andrews, my father, last week. Please send a car to my house. Now."

I could only hope that the 911 operator couldn't hear her either. Before Robbie had a chance to repeat what she'd said, I snatched her phone out of her hand and hung up. I handed it back to her and then I left. Slowly.

Seated in my car, I told myself leaving the house instead of wrestling Robbie to the ground was the wisest thing to do.

Otherwise, I might have been arrested for assault. I gripped my hands into balled fists so tightly that my short trimmed nails bit into my palms.

No wonder her father hated her, I thought rather uncharitably. There's not much there to like. Nature or nurture, though?

Robbie hadn't figured out how to rise above her upbringing and make a success of her life, that much was obvious. No one who is happy with themselves could be so blatantly superficial and so miserable to everyone else.

On my way home I began to feel sorry for her husband, John Williamson.

CHAPTER FIFTY-ONE

BY THE TIME I got home, ran the dogs, spent some time with a Bombay Sapphire and tonic over ice with lemon and a good Partagas, I felt a little more charitable toward Robbie, but not much.

I logged onto the Internet to check my letter to Ask Dr. Andrews. My letter wasn't in Robbie's column for today. She'd responded to a couple of questions about personality conflicts at work (grow up and get along), three problems with teenage rebellion (this, too, shall pass) and a question of infidelity (nobody's perfect, forgive and forget).

All were interesting and much more colorful than my newspaper's Dear Abby column, but seemed irrelevant to George's case. Since I still hadn't figured out a way to use the encrypted service, I logged off.

Engaged in quiet but heated conversation, George and my

brother, Jason, didn't notice my approach. They were seated in the dining room at George's place and probably had consumed more than one cocktail each. I was only about an hour late.

George said, "He shouldn't have done it. I don't care what his reasons were. It was not called for. The vote was going the way he wanted it. He was just trying to manipulate the process."

Jason was just as hot. "The whole process is about manipulation, and you know it. Andrews came by Warwick's office to lobby for a yes vote. I heard he went to every one of the senators on the committee with the same plea. You can't blame Benson for playing the same game."

"But the President was trying to torpedo his own nominee," George responded.

"Good evening gentlemen," I said.

Still glaring at each other, Jason stood up and gave me a quick hug and a kiss. George stood, too, held my chair and kissed me briefly. How gallant.

I pasted a smile on my face and kept my voice very quiet. "Don't look now, but you are beginning to draw attention from the crowd. I don't know what you were discussing, but unless you want everyone in the room to witness it, you should keep your voices down."

George poured me a glass of wine and Jason steered the conversation to his mother. We all talked affectionately about Kate for a while. After we ordered appetizers, I took advantage of the lull in conversation. "What were you two talking about when I came in?"

"Just politics. Nothing you'd be interested in," George said.

I smiled sweetly. "It sounded interesting to me. Did I hear Jason say that Andrews visited every one of the senators on the judiciary committee the day before he died?"

CHAPTER FIFTY-TWO

Tampa, Florida
Friday 9:30 p.m.
January 28, 2000

BOTH MEN LOOKED UNCOMFORTABLE, but Jason was the one who answered me. "It's not something we're supposed to talk about, now that he's dead. But what he did is not that unusual. It's been done before."

"I didn't realize the vote on a Supreme Court nominee was a popularity contest," I said.

"It's not. But it is politics as usual. The senators take the Supreme Court appointments very seriously because of how long the justices serve and the impact they have on the country. No one wants to vote yes on a man they know nothing about," Jason explained.

The political process seemed like one big bartering game to me. George was the politico in our family, and I was glad to leave it that way. But it occurred to me that any of the senators Andrews talked to the day before he died could have killed him. Who knows what was said between them? Andrews didn't seem to be able to get along with anyone. Should I add another one hundred names to my list of potential murderers?

I pondered this silently while George and Jason attempted to change the subject to the recent coup attempts in Cuba. When, not whether, Cuba would once again be open for American travel is a constant topic of conversation in Florida.

Tampa's cigar business, started and continued by Cuban immigrants, was already in full swing by the time Castro came to power. Still, Tampa's Cuban community has a lot of emotional attachment to Cuba and many say they are planning to return as soon as they're allowed to do so. At least to visit family and friends, if not to emigrate permanently.

Most Floridians believe Cuba will again be a tourist Mecca and hot vacation spot some day. The sentimental motive is a strong one, but many Cuban expats and other businessmen just want to be in on the ground floor of what they think will be a money-making operation. Key West has been planning for the increased cruise ship trade for years.

Reopening Cuba is a hot political topic, too. Senator Warwick and Jason were both very involved in lobbying for change. Jason and George could argue the merits of this issue for hours. But I wasn't as interested in Cuba as I was in General Andrews.

When I could get a word in, I asked them what else they'd been discussing when I walked into dinner. The way they looked at each other, I could tell I wasn't supposed to have overheard this bit of information, which, of course, made it more interesting to me.

"It's not something I can discuss, Willa. Strictly cone-of-silence stuff," Jason said.

I didn't buy that for a minute. "You were discussing it with

George. If it's so secret, why does George know about it?"

George looked up desperately for our waiter and flagged him over. We all ordered dessert and coffee.

I refused to be distracted. "Look. I'm not going to drop this. If you don't tell me about it now, I'll call Sheldon Warwick myself in the morning and ask him."

George was the one who responded. He said quietly, but with more firmness than I usually accept from him, "Just leave it alone. Please. Let's have our coffee in peace."

The more they wanted to keep the information from me, the more I felt it was important to my investigation. Which, of course, neither of them knew a thing about. "I'm not going to make a scene. But I am going to find out what's going on here. After we have our coffee we can go upstairs and talk about it. Or I'll find out some other way. You two can decide while I go powder my nose."

When I got back to the table, our key lime pie had been served. *Café con leche* for me and the wimpier decaffeinated Colombian for the men. We ate and drank in relative camaraderie, finishing our after dinner liqueur.

When we'd finished, I resumed my crusade. "Well," I said, "What's it to be? The word straight from you two tonight, or I start calling Senate Judiciary Committee members tomorrow?" I rose to leave the table. As I'd expected, they followed me out of the dining room and up to the flat.

When we got settled in our den, neither one of them had broached the subject, so I prodded them again. One last time. "What were you two talking about at the dinner table before I came in tonight?"

Jason fielded my questions. The choice was curious. Jason had more of a professional obligation to keep his secrets than George did because Jason was a senate employee, aide to Warwick and on the Democrats' side. "You know the confirmation hearings weren't going well, right?"

"Well for whom, is the relevant question," I said.

Jason ignored my sarcasm. "Senator Warwick was against the Andrews nomination from the start. Like George, Sheldon knew Andrews personally and didn't think Andy had the judicial temperament necessary for a Supreme Court judge."

George said nothing and I kept silent as well.

Jason cleared his throat. "Well, Warwick tried to convince President Benson to withdraw the nomination. Warwick knew Andrews was strong-willed and opinionated and, even if he had otherwise been qualified, that Andrews could never do the right thing politically to get confirmed." Jason looked directly at me. "Warwick knew the nomination would be a disaster."

"Andrews had been around politics a long time," George picked up the explanation now. "He'd made a lot of enemies among the people who knew him. No one was looking forward to standing behind the party's man."

Jason fidgeted, rubbing his hands together, as if to warm them, but it was seventy degrees tonight and he had on a tropical weight wool jacket and tie. He wasn't cold.

He cleared his throat again. "It was a very real political dilemma for Warwick and all the other Democrats. No one wanted to openly oppose the Presidential choice, but none of them wanted to or could vote for Andrews in good conscience. Warwick, as the chairman of the committee and one of the most senior Democrats on the Hill, was on the spot. The younger guys looked to him to figure out a way to finesse this."

George intervened. "And Warwick, for his part, had no intention of losing his seat over this nomination the way Illinois

Senator Alan Dixon lost his over the Judge Thomas vote."

For the first time, I was confused. "What do you mean? Thomas was confirmed." My lack of political savvy was a handicap in this maze of relationships and back room dealing.

Jason stood, put both hands in his pockets, and paced the room. "Thomas was a controversial nominee. Some people were unhappy with the way the hearings went and the way the vote came down. Politicians paid the price with their jobs. No one wanted to be in that position over Andrews. It was a bad spot for all of them."

George said. "They felt it was their leader, President Benson, who put them all on the hot seat. Nobody liked it."

"And that's where George came in," Jason said. "Warwick gave a statement to the press. He said that the committee had been criticized in recent years for being 'too supine and deferential' to the President in the Kennedy and Souter nominations. Warwick said that under his stewardship, the Judiciary Committee would take a more active role. He said there was no presumption in favor of confirmation.

George picked up the tale. "Benson and Andrews were outraged. It was a plain power play. Warwick said, in effect, that he was the reigning Democrat, not the President. And certainly not Andrews."

Jason sat down again, making an apology for his boss. "Washington is all about power. Nobody gives you power. You just take it."

I was beginning to see the problem. Warwick, the Democratic senior senator from Florida, was taking on the lame duck Democratic President in his second term. The President couldn't be re-elected, but the Senator could. In recent years, the political types have felt that control of Congress is more important than control of the Presidency. Longer terms of office and lack of term limits was one of the reasons why.

I'd thought I wanted to know all of this, but my desire was based mainly on their refusal to tell me about it. So far, I found the explanation a big yawn. And I had other things to worry about.

"This is all very interesting, in a political science kind of way," I told them both. "But what does any of it have to do with George?"

George answered this time for himself. "The Republicans never wanted Andrews. We were shocked when he was selected. We wanted to defeat him and Warwick was willing to help us do that. For once, Warwick and I were both on the same side. Jason works for Warwick. We were discussing the issues." He said it like a Packers fan would be interested in the 1997 Super Bowl game where the Packers won for the first time in over twenty years.

And I could buy that. The battle over Andrews's confirmation had been intense, but I hadn't realized Warwick had put all his political clout on the line. If Andrews was confirmed, and Warwick lost this fight, Warwick's career would be finished. The Democrats would replace him as party leader. He would go out in disgrace.

So Warwick had a personal stake in defeating Andrews's confirmation, too. George probably viewed this as a gift of Trojan proportions. George was on the verge of winning a round against the Democrats with the Andrews nomination. And, I could tell by just looking at him, he'd loved it.

Jason was still focused. George, more savvy in the conversation game, could sense my waning interest and would have let it go. Jason, the lawyer, was honed in on the question. He foolishly brought it up again himself.

"Benson feared that Warwick's behind-the-scenes opposition,

supported by George's efforts, was making a difference." Jason stopped, took a deep breath, and just spit it out. "So, to save face, Benson sent an emissary to each member of the party the Friday night after the committee hearings closed. The evening Andy died. The President's man said Benson had recently learned that the army had received sexual harassment complaints about Andrews."

"What?" I asked.

He ignored me. "Although the complaints had been fully investigated and were unfounded, neither Andrews nor the President wanted them revealed."

"What?" I asked again, feeling shocked and amazed, but titillated just the same.

Jason continued to ignore me, and finished up. "Andrews couldn't withdraw, but the senators could vote no on the nomination, with no hard feelings."

George added, "In fact, the President said he wished they would vote 'no,' to avoid political and personal embarrassment for everyone."

I was completely dumfounded now. "He let them all off the hook? Gave up his leverage? Why?"

This was not politics as I knew it was played in every arena, from the condominium board to the school board to Capitol Hill. George frowned at Jason and Jason, finally noticing how far he'd gone, must have realized that he'd revealed too much.

"I don't know why he did it. I'm not his advisor," Jason snapped.

George explained, "That's what we were discussing when you came in. Benson could have withdrawn the nomination when he saw Andrews wasn't going to be confirmed. But he chose to sabotage Andrews instead. It was a damn sneaky move."

And if General Andrews knew about it, the news might have

caused him to kill himself. Maybe his death was a highly creative suicide after all, for which George could easily be framed. I could imagine Andrews getting a charge out of making George pay for ruining his appointment. That motive made more sense to me than the one Robbie had cooked up for George.

But, George would have a motive for murder only if Andrews's nomination stayed on the table. When Andrews was rejected, George's motive would disappear.

If this piece of information got out, George could be off the hook. Things were looking up.

Besides, I thought, it might have been a political *faux pas* if Benson's treachery came to light after the vote, but it could be spun to the President's favor. Benson could simply have said that he'd received new information about Andrews, information that changed his mind about nominating Andrews. He'd look foolish for not having known about the sexual harassment complaints before he nominated Andrews, but that was an oversight he would be forgiven for, especially since he attempted to correct the problem before Andrews was actually seated on the court.

Benson had a reputation as a crafty politician. I suspected he'd sent the emissary fully expecting his effort to become public at some point.

George and Jason began their argument again. I tuned it out, waiting until the feel of the noise suggested that I could tastefully throw Jason out for the night. That point came about twenty minutes later.

I heard Jason say, "You and I are never going to agree on this, and it's getting late. I need to go."

He was still in a huff, but the result was what I wanted.

"I'm sorry you have to leave, Jason, but it is getting late," I said, much to Jason's surprise and George's, too, for that matter. I stood up and Jason had no real alternative but to do the same. I ushered him out with a hug and a promise to see him later in the week.

George would have followed Jason out, but I asked him to wait awhile. "I really need to be going, Darling. It's been a long day," he said.

"Just a short night cap first?" I suggested.

We took our liqueur over to the couch. "You know," I told him, "maybe Andy found out about Benson's actions." George said nothing.

I watched him through half closed eyelids. "If he found out, he could have been so upset that he killed himself, George. Maybe this really was a suicide." I suggested it softly. "People are always surprised by a suicide." I repeated what I'd read in Robbie Andrews's online column, "And we never want to believe it was inevitable."

"I can see why you think that's possible," George said, "but I don't think it happened that way. You know the physical evidence doesn't support the suicide theory. And so far, no one thinks Andy found out Benson betrayed him."

I heard the smile in his voice as he said, "Nice try, though. It would have been an easier answer than having me on trial for murder." He leaned over and kissed the top of my head. "I need to get going, sweetheart. It's late, and I need my beauty sleep." He got up to leave.

I grabbed his sleeve and got down to business.

CHAPTER FIFTY-THREE

"BEFORE YOU GO, I want us to talk about your gun. The murder weapon. I went out to the gun club, and the box is still in your locker. Why was your gun out of its box? How did it get removed from the club? And who took it?"

He'd drained his glass and leaned over to kiss me before he stood up again to leave. "Not now, Willa. It's too late to get into all that." He glanced quickly at his watch. "I've already discussed it with Olivia, anyway. Talk to her about it, or we can go over it later."

He leaned toward me and held me for one of those kisses that still take my breath away. When we eventually pulled apart, he said, "Trust me, it's not the link from the gun club we need to worry about. Goodnight."

Resisting the childish urge to stamp my foot in frustration, I locked up and went to bed with quite a lot on my mind for my subconscious to work out.

Kate swears that your mind solves your problems overnight if you just remember to program the questions before you go to sleep. I sure had a lot of questions to be considered. If I woke up with the answers tomorrow, no one would be happier than I.

CHAPTER FIFTY-FOUR

Tampa, Florida
Saturday 8:30 a.m.
January 29, 2000

PERHAPS I HAD SOME fabulous dreams that night, but when I awakened, I couldn't remember any of them. The sunlight was streaming into the open window, the air quite chilly. I stretched my arms out in either direction, there being no reason to avoid taking up the whole bed since I was the only one in it. Again.

I let the dogs go out by themselves. The hell with it. I probably wasn't going to be running any marathons any time soon, anyway. Sometimes resistance sidetracks me just like everyone else. Besides, I wanted my coffee and I wanted it now.

After a quick shower, I grabbed a to-go cup, picked up my tote bag with my investigative tools in it, and headed down to Greta. Traffic willing, I'd be out to Thonotosassa in less than thirty minutes. We pulled out over Plant Key Bridge and turned east on the Bayshore.

Multi-tasking, I picked up my cell phone and tackled the Olivia problem. George told me last night that they'd been having meetings and conversations that I didn't know about. He'd told her about the gun. I was out of the loop and I didn't like it. I'd never have hired the woman if I'd known she was going to be uncontrollable. I left messages for her at all her offices, her car and her home. That I couldn't find her made me even more uneasy. Who knows what she was out there doing that I didn't know about.

Greta and I drove along the Bayshore beside the five-mile continuous sidewalk, where once there had been a shoreline. In a gentler era, where grand waterfront estates once stood, high-rise condominiums now blocked the view. *The Tampa Tribune* reported that three hundred new luxury condominiums were slated to be built with a Bayshore address. It was this kind of progress that made me happy to live on Plant Key. Owning our little island means we decide what gets built there.

I passed one of Tampa's newest high-rise condominiums. I hadn't been in the building, but the pictures I'd seen in the sales literature made it look like a reasonable abode for super-rich dudes like Donald Trump or Bill Gates.

Housing was still a relative bargain in most of the areas around Tampa. Retirees come here to live in very nice (and some not so nice) mobile home parks. Young families and empty nesters settled in Brandon and other suburbs where a nice house could still be had for affordable prices.

But people moving to Tampa from more expensive housing markets, like the northeast or northwest, could apparently afford the newest luxury high-rises or the just as pricey golf communities north of town.

The traffic puttered along, moving well below the posted forty-mile-per-hour speed limit, and my impatience didn't hustle them along at all. Avoiding collisions with tourists who were driving erratically, stopping before they entered the expressway, turning left from the far right-hand lane, or doing forty miles an hour in a seventy-mile-per-hour zone, was one of the challenges of the winter season.

My favorite bumper sticker around here reads: "Someday I'm going to retire, move to Michigan and drive slow."

Once I reached the expressway, my attention focused on staying alive through the perpetual road construction. Was there a highway in America that wasn't being repaired? I-4 had been disrupted by construction for all the years I'd lived in Tampa. Drivers must keep their wits about them to avoid getting killed by out of control eighteen-wheelers and sightseeing tourists.

When I arrived, I was able to park near Deborah Andrews's house this time. The house had once been grand, but it had changed, gotten older along with the rest of us. Apparently, no one here loved gardening and the lawn service didn't do the world's best job. All the plants were overgrown and out of control.

The normally delicate liriope resembled the larger, more robust philodendron. Tropical plants overcrowded every section of the walkway and grew tall enough to cover the windows. The lawn looked well-trimmed, but it had bare brown patches all over it, as if it was diseased and no one had bothered to plug it.

Nothing had been painted in much too long. The door hinges and hardware were rusted. The place seemed abandoned, unoccupied. An army man is often away from home, but Deborah had been living here for years, waiting for her husband to come back from wherever he'd been posted. Whatever she did to keep herself busy didn't include house maintenance or gardening.

I rang the bell and eventually I heard someone shuffling toward the door, and talking. "Elizabeth, Judy, Caesar, get out of the way so I can open the door."

The knob turned. I heard no lock being opened. The house was out in the country, but someone had come onto this property and murdered Deborah's husband just a few days before. I would have had four locks, an alarm system and an armed guard installed by now, if I'd stayed here at all. It was curious that Deborah had done none of that.

Deborah opened the door wide, displaying no concern for the axe murderer who could have been standing there.

"Hello, Willa. Come on in," she said, as she bent down and scooped up a long-haired cat. "Elizabeth, look who's here. It's Willa Carson. You remember Willa, don't you, Judy?" This last was directed at another cat, standing near the door, off to the left.

I pushed the screen door open and it squeaked loudly enough on the rusty hinges that Deborah might not have needed an alarm after all. I stepped around Judy and two other cats, moving quickly to keep them from running out the door as I entered. "I don't remember you, Judy," I said, trying not to sound judgmental about the cats' behavior, or their smell, which had been noticeable the last time I was here and was now overwhelming.

"You like cats, don't you?" Deborah asked, as she walked farther toward the interior, in the same way she might have asked if I liked oxygen.

The house was dark and cool inside. Even without my small flashlight to illuminate the gloom, I noticed at least six other cats lying on the floor tile.

The litter boxes were out of sight, but definitely not well tended. The odor of ammonia from cat urine activated my gag reflex. I popped a piece of gum in my mouth and tried not to breathe.

"Sure, I love cats. George is allergic, though. What are their names?" I said, to be friendly.

"This one," she said, stroking the cat she still held in her arms, "is Elizabeth Montgomery. Kind of looks like her, don't you think? I always thought Liz had green cat eyes. Kind of like yours."

Beautiful green cat eyes, George would have added, if he'd been here.

His absence ambushed me again. I felt the prickly sensation behind my eyes and quickly focused on something else.

Deborah prattled on. "Here is Judy Garland and that's Caesar Romero." She pointed to each cat as she introduced them to me. "The others are Betty Grable, Jimmy Stewart and that old one over there is George Burns. I've had him forever."

I reached down to pick up Jimmy Stewart. Like his namesake, he was long and skinny and easy-going. He purred immediately, and I carried him along while I followed Deborah into the living room where cats sat on every available cushion.

"Marilyn Monroe," Deborah said to another white cat, "move over and let Willa sit down."

Marilyn showed no such signs of life, so I gently pushed her aside and sat down. White cat hair would be all over my navy wool slacks.

My hostess continued talking. "I collected the cats when all the children left home."

"How did you ever come up with names for all of them?" I asked as I put Jimmy Stewart down on the floor. He didn't go anywhere, just lounged at my feet. Marilyn Monroe jumped up to replace him in my lap. Swell, I thought. Now there would be long white cat hair on my thighs as well as my rump. I'd look like a sweater.

Deborah explained her methods of cat naming, in a long prattling paragraph that left no opening for me to respond. "I was in Key West with Andy once and we visited Hemingway House. Hemingway loved cats. He had six-toed ones. They've kept descendants of his cats on the grounds and named them after movie stars. Andy thought that idea was so stupid, but I liked it. He didn't like my cats anyway, so I just picked names for mine the same way. None of my friends have six toes, though." She held up one of the cat's feet to demonstrate.

She stopped a moment to breathe and then continued. "They're so much better company than people, don't you think?" She hugged Elizabeth and Judy at the same time.

Marilyn simultaneously kneaded my leg with her front paws and purred in my lap. I don't know if she was better company than people, but the kneading was comforting.

She put Judy down and Caesar Romero jumped up in her lap. Elizabeth Montgomery moved over for him to sit down. He was polite about it.

Deborah began another of her monologues, which allowed me time to examine the cluttered, unkempt room. The same lack of maintenance that was evident outside carried through to the interior. "My friend gave me George Burns when Andy went off to the Middle East the first time. I was so lonesome here then. He'd been traveling on short trips for years, but he hadn't been on assignment away from home since the children left."

She continued talking, but my attention wandered. The cobwebs in every corner were barely visible in the gloom. Dust balls flew over the tile floor, propelled by small breezes from an open window somewhere. Tabletops were marked with paw prints and long cat hair blanketed the upholstery.

"Willa?"

I gave her a quizzical look. I came here because I thought either Deborah or the house would tell me something about

Andy's death. Now, I wondered whether I'd wasted my time.

She repeated, "I said we could film an epic here with all the talent we have now, right?

She was kidding. I think. She didn't really seem to be talking to me at all. She seemed to know who I was, but she was distracted, unfocused.

Drinking? The last I'd heard, Deborah had entered a high-priced clinic and sobered up. Perhaps she'd had a relapse. God knows, she had been through enough stress lately to bring one on.

But I didn't smell the acrid odor of metabolized alcohol. Then again, there was hardly anything I could smell except cats.

"Deborah," I said gently, "I'm very sorry about Andy's death. I wanted you to know that."

She turned her blue eyes to me then, and looked squarely into my face for several moments before blinking slowly, like one of her cats. Then she smiled. Conversationally, she said, "I know you are, Willa. Just like I know George didn't kill Andy. George is a good man."

Given her daughter's behavior, I'd worried that Deborah would be as nasty as Robbie had been.

I shouldn't have worried. Deborah was so forgiving. That was probably what made her such a doormat to her husband and children all the years I'd known her.

"You must miss Andy," I suggested, removing Marilyn Monroe from my lap and attempting to deposit her onto the floor. A mistake. As soon as Marilyn got down, Cary Grant jumped up.

I gave up and accepted a cat as a part of my suit. At least Cary Grant was black and his hair wouldn't be as obvious on my slacks.

"Miss Andy? Not really. I hadn't spent any time with him in years." She said this lazily, without rancor. Maybe she was taking tranquilizers. Her affect was so flattened, her response time so delayed, that she must have been taking something.

I gently pulled all ten of Cary Grant's claws out of my left thigh, and he just as gently hooked them back in my right thigh, making holes through which my patience was leaking out.

I stood up and walked around the room. Curiously, there were no photographs of Andy or Deborah anywhere. There was one formal portrait of their three children hanging over the fireplace. The portrait was several years old.

"I guess I thought you two had been together more since you became empty nesters, but Andy's job probably took him away quite a bit," I said.

"Andy had been away quite a bit, as you put it, all of our lives. When the children left home, that reduced the number of excuses he had to make." Deborah stood up now, too. "Would you like a cup of tea?"

As an excuse to get away from the fur lap robes, I accepted. We walked into the kitchen, Deborah still carrying Caesar Romero. A trail of cats followed behind me. How many were there? I'd stopped counting at twenty.

In the dark kitchen there were six chairs, none of them empty. I remained standing.

Looking out the windows, I saw that the boat in which Andy died was still tied up at the dock. I'd thought it would have been impounded and removed by the crime scene investigators.

But this was a break for me. I'd walk down there after I'd finished with Deborah.

I returned to the living room, where I retrieved the tote bag containing my camera and slung it over my shoulder.

CHAPTER FIFTY-FIVE

WHEN I ENTERED THE kitchen, Deborah had managed to fill the teakettle. I watched as she opened the cupboard. Another cat perched on top of the plates stored on the cabinet's bottom shelf.

"Dean Martin," Deborah chided, "I've been looking for you."

She petted his head, but didn't ask him to move, then removed two lovely antique china cups and saucers of different patterns.

She left the cabinet door open. So he could see us, I guess. Deborah walked around the kitchen collecting the tea things as well as a box of what the English call biscuits and I call crackers. She set them all on a beautiful old silver tray with a silver tea service.

All this she accomplished with one hand, while still holding one or another of the cats. Cats occupied every available space, every cabinet she opened, every flat surface I could see.

Finally, Deborah finished the tea service and was forced to put the cat down to carry the tray. "Shall we go out onto the patio? It's lovely out this morning in the garden."

After I had moved Robert Mitchum off the chair I wanted and Deborah had convinced Grace Kelly to let us put the tray down on the coffee table she was sunning herself from, I quickly picked up my cup and held it in my lap.

Robert Mitchum eyed me from the floor right by my feet. It was a little difficult to maneuver the cup and plate, eat the stale crackers and keep an eye on Robert Mitchum while investigating murder. I realized the absurdity of the situation, but I didn't know what to do about it.

"Haven't you been lonely out here by yourself all these years, Deborah?" I asked her.

I felt more than a little ashamed that I hadn't kept in touch with her. One can never have too many friends and I'd always liked Deborah. She badly needed a human friend.

A wave of shame washed over me then, as it always does when I know my behavior would have disappointed my mother. I could do better. Most of the time, I try. It's irrational, at my age, to feel I'm disappointing a mother who died half my lifetime ago, but the emotion was visceral now.

Deborah allowed a smile to light up her face. "Not really. I have all my cats to keep me company, and you can see it's hard to get lonely with them around."

Then, the smile drifted away. "Besides, I've felt like a widow for years. In my heart, I buried him a long time ago."

Completely nonplussed, I blurted out the first thing that popped into my mind. "Do you mean you've been having an affair?"

She laughed. "Only with Cary Grant and Robert Mitchum here." Then, she sobered quickly. "Sex has never meant that much to me, or to Andy. It's never been worth it."

I didn't understand her meaning. "Worth what?"

Instead of answering me, she asked a question of her own. "Did I ever tell you how I got Andy to marry me?"

Without thinking, I almost asked her the question I'd had since the day Craig Hamilton was shot: why she'd wanted Andy to marry her and whether she'd been glad he did, but I just shook my head.

She looked dreamy, as if she was remembering her childhood's happier times. "I was the lonely little girl next door. Andy never paid me any attention at all, but I was in love with him from the time I was five years old. My own parents were dead. I was always at Andy's house and his parents became very dear to me." I itched to find my recorder in my tote bag, but I didn't want to interrupt her.

"Albert, Andy's dad, was my special favorite. He was disabled, you know, in World War II. He operated an old country store at the crossroads of nowhere and back, and I helped him out after school. When he didn't have any customers, he'd tell me stories about our town, the war, and Andy. How he loved his son!"

She offered more weak tea and stale biscuits. I took both, just to keep Robert Mitchum off me. The real Mitchum hadn't had as much trouble with women, I'm sure.

"Anyway, I was determined to marry Andy and to have Albert for my dad, too. When Andy graduated from college, we had a big party back at the house. Andy had been in ROTC and was going into the army with a commission two weeks later."

She stopped her tale for a while.

When I thought I'd have to ask her to continue, she said, "I got Andy drunk and seduced him. When I turned up pregnant, he had no choice but to marry me."

Deborah turned her bright, empty smile toward me. She

looked so fragile, a small woman, left alone too soon, living in seclusion with only her cats to console her. Sympathy smothered my pluck. There were plenty of tragedies in this story. Too many.

When I said nothing further, Deborah told me bravely, understanding, perhaps, that she was not the only casualty of her marriage, "I always felt sorry for Robbie. Andy wanted a boy desperately. He was so disappointed when Robbie was born. He never got over it."

What could I have said to that? Might I have said that Robbie was a vicious woman who could more than take care of herself? I couldn't bring myself to do so. "Well," I told her instead, "it sounds like Andy participated in the seduction, too. It wasn't totally your fault."

Deborah's eyes widened and her mouth formed a little O of surprise. "Actually, he didn't. Even when he was drunk, he didn't seem interested at all."

Then, flatly, as if the past was old, uninteresting history, "And after that, we only made love because Andy wanted sons."

I was appalled. Deborah was one of the most gracious, pleasant women I'd ever met. Many men must have wanted her. It was such a waste that she'd never been loved, except by her cats.

She took a deep breath then, and petted the cat on her lap in what might have been real contentment. "So you see, Willa, I didn't really miss him all that much. He was just someone else to wait on. And he treated all of us as if we were privates. We were allowed to do only what he ordered us to do. Andy was a very unhappy man and when he was around, he made the rest of us unhappy, too. It was a relief when he left, actually. Now that he's never coming back, I can't say I'm sorry."

She'd bowed her head and I couldn't see her face clearly. Was she rationalizing her empty life? Or was this the truth?

When George and I came to this house the day after Andy died, Deborah had played the part of the bereaved wife so beautifully. But then, she'd played the part of the army wife perfectly all those years, too. You never knew a marriage until you'd lived in it.

"It was worse for the children, though," she said, without being prompted.

"Why?"

She looked straight at me now, candid, sharp. "Because I chose Andy. I chose my life. They had nothing to say about it. These happy babies, growing up with a father who hated them. I've never forgiven myself for that."

"Surely you're exaggerating," I know I sounded shocked to her, because I sounded that way to myself.

She shook her head back and forth.

"Unfortunately, I'm not. It took years of alcoholism followed by more years of therapy for me to deal with it all. The children never enjoyed the escape of booze. It's ironic," she said with a quirky little smile in the corner of her mouth. "Andy wanted to be a family man because he thought he needed it to get promoted. You can't be a single general, you know. But he didn't want a family. And now, none of his children are sorry he's dead. Sad, isn't it?"

She didn't sound sad. She sounded kind of satisfied, actually. Like she'd won, in the end.

Her tone made it easier for me to ask her about Andy's death. She didn't seem quite so vulnerable at the moment. "We both know George didn't kill Andy. But, who did?"

People seldom ask direct questions. Even media interviewers. Unlike cops, normal people never just come out and ask: Did you do it? It's surprising what you could learn when you asked questions directly.

As if she was discussing strangers, Deborah replied, "It's hard to say. There are so many possibilities." She'd given me the impression that all three of her children might have murdered their father, and she didn't try to correct that impression.

Based on my experience so far, I thought Robbie, at least, was capable of murder. And after this interview, I had to accept that Deborah would have had reason to kill her husband, too. She was the one who was here, in the house with him the night he died. Had we all simply overlooked the most obvious suspect?

"Were you here the morning he died? Did you hear or see anything that might help me?"

"Yes, I was here. Sound asleep. I was in my room, with the windows closed, the curtains drawn. I'd taken a Valium before I went to bed." She shuddered. "That dinner at George's restaurant was so dreadful, I wanted to be swallowed up in sleep. I actually prayed to die in the night, just so I wouldn't have to face you or anyone else ever again." Now, a little anger crept into her tone. "Andy was always doing that to me."

"Doing what?"

The anger grew stronger. "Embarrassing me in public. Not caring how I felt. He never cared how other people felt. He just did whatever he wanted."

"You didn't kill him, did you Deborah?" I laughed a little, like I was making a joke. Some joke.

She didn't deny it right away. She took more tea, and another stale cracker onto her plate, not looking at me. I waited for her answer, sensing that something was going on here that I didn't quite understand and wasn't sure I wanted to.

Finally, she said, "No. I didn't kill him. Not that I hadn't thought about it. But if George did kill Andy?" she put a little uplift at the end of the sentence. "Thank him for me, will you?"

I felt disoriented, as if I'd been conversing with a multiple personality. I didn't know what to say.

She changed the subject back to her cats and I'd had enough of that. I stood up, as if to leave, but I asked her, "Do you mind if I take a look around outside? I'll stop back to say good-bye."

"Be careful of the gators," she said, as she carried the tea tray back into the house.

CHAPTER FIFTY-SIX

Tampa, Florida
Saturday 12:30 p.m.
January 29, 2000

THE BACK YARD WAS as overgrown as the front. Kudzu vines covered everything, including the trunks of the trees. The foliage grew so thick overhead as to completely block out the sunlight. Somehow, the yard seemed more sinister today than it had when I was here the last time. Maybe because now there was no cop with a gun standing at the entrance to the old dock.

I made my way carefully through the dank vegetation, each footfall meticulously planned. I wiggled my toes, thankful for my closed, flat shoes, and kept my gaze to the ground, watching for snakes.

Poisonous cottonmouths were most likely around the water. Unlike rattlers, cottonmouths were quiet, they snuck up on you, and their venom could kill a grown adult. I'd been told that cottonmouths were often confused with harmless water snakes, but my goal had always been never to get close enough to tell them apart.

Diamondback rattlesnakes were plentiful around here, too. They can strike up to four feet. I saw one on the golf course not too long ago and refused to get out of the cart for the rest of the game.

Torn between watching for alligators that might be hanging out in the brown tinted water and keeping my gaze fixed on the kudzu that covered what was once the lawn, I stepped slowly, conquering my fear, although I wanted to run straight to the dock and get off the damned kudzu. But one misstep could cause me to fall. And if there was anything I really didn't want to do right at that moment, it was lie down on the tangled mess.

I was almost to the water's edge when a tree branch as thick as my forearm slithered across my path. I screamed out loud and jumped back ten feet. The snake coiled up then and I could see the large lump in the middle of its thick body, distorting the characteristic diamond patterns clearly visible on its sleek skin.

He hissed at me and that was all I needed to run a wide circle around him and jump onto the dock, struggling not to fall into the brackish water. Maybe because he'd so recently fed on a field mouse or something (I prayed his meal hadn't been one of Deborah's cats), the diamondback let me go.

I watched him uncoil and slither on, disappearing into the kudzu at the edge of the orange grove.

When my pounding heart had settled down to twice its regular thumping rate, I found the courage to make my way along the rickety boards of the weathered, old fishing dock. But I swept my gaze from side to side, watching for alligators and cottonmouths.

Unlike cats, which are somewhat territorial and may stay fairly close to their chosen home, snakes and alligators cohabited and moved about freely. Both liked to kill small animals, including small humans. And they could do serious bodily harm to large humans like me, too.

Again, I realized that no one knew where I was. I hadn't told George or Olivia. And I doubted that Deborah even remembered I was out here. It wasn't likely my cell phone would work here, either. Even if I could manage to haul it out of my tote bag in time to call anyone for help. What in the world had I been thinking?

If a diamondback struck me, or an alligator attacked, I could die, and no one would know.

That was when the uncontrollable shaking started.

I also realized that Andy had to have been either the bravest man I'd ever known, or the dumbest. The story was that he came out here every morning, before daylight, to go bass fishing because the fish liked to feed then and might be lured onto his hook. Each day, he traversed that godforsaken kudzu snake haven in the semi-darkness, made his way to where I was standing now, and then into that small boat, just to go fishing?

Now that I'd reached the dock, I wanted to finish up the job I came for quickly and get the hell out of here.

CHAPTER FIFTY-SEVEN

Tampa, Florida
Saturday 12:45 p.m.
January 29, 2000

THE OLD DOCK WAS in disrepair, too, just like the rest of the place. The boards were slimy with green fungi. I put each foot down purposefully, testing the strength of the rotted boards, one at a time. The length of the dock was about thirty feet, but it felt like walking a very long gangplank.

I reached the spot where Andy's fishing boat was tied up about a hundred years after I'd wanted to get there. When I turned to see how far I'd come, I noticed the big bull gator sunning himself on the shoreline, inches away from the dock's entrance. He opened his mouth wide enough to let me see his powerful teeth and then closed it, smiling at me. As if to say, "Just wait. I'll catch you on the return."

For some reason, that did it. Whatever courage I possessed found its way back into my body. I squared my shoulders and got a hold of myself. That old gator was more afraid of me than I was of him. So what if more than three hundred of the damn things had attacked humans in the last fifty years? No gator had killed a human in a long time. I wouldn't be the first.

With judicial detachment, I stood now and looked down at the fishing boat. I reached into my tote bag, grabbed the disposable camera, and took some pictures. The first one was of the gator. If he killed me, I wanted to leave something so he could be identified.

The second that thought arose, I started to laugh. And then I forced myself to stop. I told myself it wasn't hysteria.

The aluminum fishing boat was about twelve feet long. It had an old Johnson outboard motor on it, twenty-five horsepower, according to the writing on the side. The little boat would scoot along with the motor opened up. The motor had been white once, but now it was covered with the same green slime as the rest of the boat.

Everything in the boat had an unused quality to it. There was an old, red tackle box, and a couple of fishing rods with open-faced reels attached. I saw a boat cushion that probably doubled as the required life preserver. A few coffee-stained Styrofoam cups rolled around in the bottom along with several inches of dirty water.

Based on the police photographs and the crime scene investigators' reports, the killer had stood on the dock, about where I was standing now. I held the disposable camera up and took a couple of pictures. In the shady daylight, I doubted the pictures would develop into anything useable.

At the time he died, Andrews was sitting in the only seat the boat possessed, the blue and white one from which he could steer by holding the protruding tiller of the small motor. My pictures of the empty seat weren't as gruesome as the pictures of Andrews, slumped over, with the hole in his head, that I'd seen in the police file.

I saw no blood anywhere on the boat or the seat cushion. Except for the remains of fishing trips past, and the black fingerprint powder that would cover everything until the next hard rain, the boat was like a hundred others used by fishermen everywhere.

What had I hoped to find here? I didn't know. But whatever it was, the only thing I'd discovered was the eerie dark and the musty, dank smell of rotting vegetation and dead fish. That and the level of nerve or stupidity it took for the killer to follow Andrews out here after midnight.

I dropped the camera back into my tote bag and turned to face the bull gator. With careful steps, I returned along the dock, toward the shoreline and stared him in the eye.

He didn't move. I glanced up to see whether I thought I could jump far enough from the slimy dock without falling to be out of his running range. Fat bull gators can run faster on their squatty legs than tall federal court judges. But he might lie there for hours and I was not going to wait.

I looked out onto the kudzu. The diamondback had moved on, but other snakes might be enjoying the welcoming environment. Indecision kept me in place another few moments until a rat ran right across my foot and caused me to scream.

The bull gator opened his mouth and the rat ran right into his waiting jaws. I knew the old gator had planned for that rat to be me.

Before I thought another second about it and lost my nerve, I stepped quickly off the dock, onto the kudzu and away from the gator.

Then I ran.

I didn't stop until I made it back to the Andrews's kitchen door and found myself pounding on it, shouting.

"Deborah! Deborah! Let me in!" Adrenalin coursed through my body.

She'd been standing there, watching me through the window, the whole time.

CHAPTER FIFTY-EIGHT

I DIDN'T WANT TO come back here, ever again.

But I couldn't leave. Not yet.

After I'd calmed down, forgotten a little bit of exactly how scared I'd been, and wrestled with the cats for a comfortable chair, I dredged up what was left of my courage.

"Did you see or hear anything at all the night Andy died that might help me? I love my husband."

Despite my best intentions, I heard my voice break a little. "And I don't want to visit him in prison for the rest of his life."

She studied me closely for several minutes. Maybe she was weighing her thoughts, deciding what she would tell me and what she'd keep secret. Or maybe she was floating in some kind of drug-induced haze. I couldn't tell anymore. And worse, I wasn't sure I cared.

I thought about marital privilege again. For weeks now, I'd

felt shut out of George's life, cast aside while he focused his entire reputation on something he believed was essential to the country and the lives of everyone who lived here.

As a result, I didn't know things I should know.

Basic things.

Like where he'd been on the night Andrews was killed and how his gun had come to be a murder weapon.

Was my husband innocent of murder? If George told me that he had killed Andrews, would I shield him? And if he was innocent of murder, but guilty of other crimes, then what? Would I invoke the privilege, if called to the stand to testify? Would George prevent me from doing that?

I wanted to know the rules of this crazy game George seemed to be playing with our lives. To me, it felt like Russian roulette.

The privilege, in this instance, was meant to shield George, not me. He could prohibit me from testifying against him. But it would be easier for him if I just didn't know the truth. Was that the real reason he wasn't communicating with me?

I shoved these unwelcome thoughts aside and refocused on Deborah.

In a court of law, she couldn't be forced to tell me many of the things she'd already divulged, and if Andy had been alive, he'd have tried to keep her quiet.

But the goal of the privilege was to encourage communication between husband and wife. Even when Andy was alive, these two hadn't communicated very well.

Like my husband, at least recently, Andy had kept his wife uninformed about his activities. Whatever Deborah might know, surely there was no harm in her telling me now. Unless she'd killed her husband.

Finally, Deborah's internal battle (between discretion and dishonesty? I wondered) ended.

"When Andy got the Supreme Court nomination, he thought he needed to pretend he still had a marriage a while. It's a lifetime appointment, but he had to get confirmed first. He knew he might not get there."

She shook her head, whether at his foolishness or the country's, I couldn't tell. "So, he started staying home more. He moved into the guest room, which is attached to his den. He could come and go through the outside entrance there. I rarely saw him, but he did get mail here."

She stopped talking for a long time.

Was I supposed to know something about the mail delivery? I couldn't think what it might be.

She began to clean up the kitchen, still struggling with herself. After a while, I realized she wouldn't continue unless I prodded her, so I said, "What kind of mail did he get?"

"Just the usual things at first. Magazines, bills, junk mail."

"And then, something else?" I prompted after another long pause.

"Yes." She picked up a hand towel and turned to face me, still standing in front of the sink where she'd been washing the cups and saucers. "Three or four plain business envelopes with no return address. At first I thought they were some type of advertising gimmick."

"But they weren't?"

"No." Still she hesitated. And then, seemed to make up her mind. "One day I did something I've never done before in my life. I listened to the messages on Andy's machine."

She lowered her face into the towel. Bright crimson flushed up her neck. I could barely understand her muffled words. "I was sure he had a lover and I'd find out why he never wanted me. Or maybe I just wanted my suspicions confirmed. I'm not even sure anymore."

"What did you hear?"

"A woman said: Stay away or you'll die." The words seemed frightening, but her tone reflected relief. "I wanted to have my fears confirmed. It does a terrible thing to your self-esteem to be sexually ignored for thirty-five years."

Tears slowly made their way down her face, leaking from the outside corner of each eye. No tantrums or hysterics. Silent tracks flowed down and dropped off her cheeks onto her shirt, making dark blue circles in the cotton. She seemed not to notice them.

I couldn't imagine actually hoping my husband was having an affair. The irony of trying to apply the marital privilege to Deborah and Andy was that they had no marriage at all. I felt a voyeur to the pain that no one had previously witnessed.

"Did you talk about the message with Andy?"

She squared her shoulders; voice firm. "I erased the message, and I didn't listen to any others. If more calls came, I'm sure they were all in the same vein."

"Did you tell the police about this, Deborah?"

She shook her head. "I'm telling you only because of George. I can't stand the humiliation of the world finding out about it."

She placed a soft hand on my arm. "Please use the information in your search for Andy's killer if you must. But don't tell anyone our true story. Please."

She pled with me, seeking something I couldn't promise.

On the way back to Tampa, I dictated today's events into my digital recorder. I recorded her remarks about Andy receiving threatening phone calls, but my opinion was that either she'd fabricated the entire story or the calls had come from one of the many faceless protesters I'd seen on television during the confirmation hearings.

People who sent anonymous notes and made threatening phone calls were usually cowards, not murderers.

Deborah had given me quite a bit to think about.

And I felt she knew more than she told me.

So I dictated, "Did she kill Andy herself?"

And my next thought, "Or does she suspect one of her children?"

That could be the only thing that would make her refuse to divulge the rest of what she knew, given everything else she'd told me.

Deborah wouldn't accuse anyone of murder, mostly because she didn't really care that her husband was dead. In some ways, she'd seemed relieved.

But if she suspected one of her children of killing Andy, she'd never say so. In her mind, they'd done her a favor.

I'd gone to Deborah's house to find information that would help me persuade Michael Drake not to seek an indictment against George. The trip had been fruitless.

But I was forced to think about all the violent women that surrounded the Andrews murder: Tory Warwick, Olivia Holmes, Robbie Andrews, and now maybe Deborah Andrews as well.

I tried to reach Olivia several times. She didn't answer any of the numbers she'd given me.

As I turned off the exit and made my way to the courthouse, I gave up attempting to talk with her personally. I left a message, asking Olivia to meet me in my office this afternoon, and I went there to wait.

CHAPTER FIFTY-NINE

Tampa, Florida
Saturday 3:30 p.m.
January 29, 2000

AGAIN, I LOGGED ONTO the Internet. Robbie's column was addictive. I'd been reading it every day since I'd first found it in the same way that I often turned to Dear Abby in the daily paper.

Robbie's opinions were harshly worded. Not much compassion there. Like father, like daughter on the compassion gene, anyway.

One mystery was why people contacted her at all, but her supplicants seemed to have an insatiable desire for public humiliation.

Today's topics were consistent with the pattern I'd noticed: three or six letters on three basic topics, career advice (don't sleep with your boss, no matter what), child rearing (kids need discipline and parents need a life) and advice to the lovelorn (forget happily ever after).

Not long after I began reading Robbie's column, the security guard buzzed me.

"Olivia Holmes is here to see you, Judge."

I hadn't told anyone that we'd hired Olivia. Judges meeting with lawyers was nothing unusual.

"Send her up," I said.

My gaze fell upon a note from Margaret that I hadn't seen before. It was not welcome news. *Asbestos files transferred; scheduled for serial status conferences, ten a day for the next thirty days. M.*

The CJ could assign me these cases. Administrative matters were his bailiwick. And there wasn't a damn thing I could do about it.

"Swell," I said, tossing the note into the trash on my way to greet Olivia at the door to my chambers.

She carried a yellow leather briefcase that would have cost me a month's salary. Federal judges made a decent living, but nothing like successful lawyers in private practice. We didn't take the job for the money.

Again, Olivia was dressed as the female version of the successful businessman. I wondered why that armor was so necessary to some women, particularly the diminutive ones.

She struggled to be taken seriously. She was less than five feet tall and well under a hundred pounds, not to mention beautiful. She looked like a hand-painted china doll. Perhaps the accoutrements of success added stature in a way that compensated for lack of physical size in a culture where size matters and bigger is better.

I invited Olivia to sit down, my tone icy. Some ground rules had to be established. I was grateful for Olivia's help, but we were paying more for her expertise than the price of a luxury car.

Beyond that, this was our life, our case, and I was married to the client. As the minister said at our wedding, the two of us were one.

Standing on the platform that my predecessor had installed to raise his desk up above those mere mortals on the floor, I towered over Olivia by almost two feet. She had to tilt her head up to look at me the same way one might look at the stars at night.

"Olivia," I said.

If she felt intimidated, she didn't act like it.

"Willa," she responded, just as professionally.

"Please sit down," I motioned her to one of the frightful green client chairs opposite my desk and returned to the over-sized black leather desk chair, another holdover from my predecessor. The chair and the platform had the effect of making me an imposing presence, a posture I'd exploited more than once.

"I don't want you calling me here and leaving messages with my secretary. My desk is not private. I have law clerks, the Court Security Officer, court reporters, my staff. Any of them can come in here and look at what's in plain view. If you need to talk to me, leave your name and number only on my private line. I'll call you back when I can." I said this firmly, and watched her bristle.

Clearly, she was used to much more deference than I was showing her. I thought she might actually resign, and it took awhile for her to decide how she wanted to handle it.

"Of course," she finally said, defiantly. "I thought you wanted people to know I was representing your husband."

"The fact of your representation is something I don't mind disclosing, but that's all. What else gets disclosed, and when, is our decision, not yours," I said.

"All right, Willa."

Her tone said she wasn't used to taking orders. Often, a criminal defense attorney is so much better informed than her client that she makes most of the decisions in a case. Olivia accepted my insistence that she wasn't in charge here, but she didn't like it.

Surly now, she said, "But you should know that two people can keep a secret only if one of them is dead."

Something about the way she said it sent a chill up my spine, and I shivered involuntarily.

"There's something else," I said.

Her face scrunched up with annoyance. "What's the problem? If you've got something to say, why don't you just say it, so we can get to work?"

"Alright, Olivia, I will," I said, bluntly. "I did not give you permission to talk to George about his gun and I was amazed to learn from him that you had. I don't want you to do it again."

Her eyes narrowed and a crease appeared between her brows.

She said, "You're suggesting that I'm supposed to defend George for capital murder and never talk with him except with your permission? That's a little unconventional, isn't it?"

Her face lit up as if she'd just figured something out. Her tone softened. "There's no need for you to be jealous. George may be the last faithful husband in North America."

How absurd.

CHAPTER SIXTY

Tampa, Florida
Saturday 4:30 p.m.
January 29, 2000

I FELT MY ANGER flare and struggled to keep control in the face of such impertinence.

"I am not jealous," I told her. "And, no, it is not unconventional to insist that someone who works for me do what I want them to do."

I emphasized my next statement, "I'm not suggesting that you should never speak with George, only that you do it when I'm present or I've agreed to it."

Olivia didn't respond right away. Instead, she went over to the water carafe on the small server in the corner and poured herself a glass of water. She returned to her chair.

She said, "Willa, we need to get something clear here. I accepted this case because I wanted to. I don't need the work. And you are not my client. George is. You know that."

She lightened her tone. "When you're charged with murder,

maybe you can call the shots. Now, if you and George want to fire me, then that's your choice. But that won't make me stop working on this case and it won't keep George from talking to me if he wants to do so." Paused to sip her water. "Why don't you think about it a minute. I need to go down the hall."

Set down her glass and walked out. On me.

No one had ever left my chambers without my consent.

I was flabbergasted. Flummoxed. Outfoxed.

And maybe some more "f" words, but I couldn't think of any that were repeatable.

Because, of course, she was right. George was the client, I was just the wife.

Even if he wasn't Olivia's client, he could talk with whomever he pleased. Something he'd amply demonstrated over the past few weeks, which was the main reason we were in this mess to begin with.

I had no leverage.

I'd chosen Olivia because I'd thought we shared a common goal that would make her easy for me to control. I could replace her, but the next lawyer would likely be worse.

When she returned, sporting freshened lipstick, we were both calmer.

A response was due from me, so I said, "You're right, of course. I apologize. This is very, very upsetting to me and I was shocked when George told me last night that you had been there to interview him and asked him about his gun."

Graceful in victory, she said, "We have a lot of work ahead of us, Willa, and we'll get further if we work together. It's pretty obvious that you and George are not communicating that well right now. He has taken care of you for seventeen years and he isn't about to stop doing that because you've decided it's time for you to take care of him," she lectured me. "So why don't you let me handle George professionally. Until we get this figured out?"

If I wanted George to get out of this mess, I'd have to let Olivia do her job. I didn't like it, but I really had no choice. "The least you can do is to keep me informed of what you're doing and your progress. So we don't duplicate effort."

"And you can do the same for me." She gazed at me pointedly. Olivia might look like a diminutive doll, but she was one hard woman. If I hadn't understood that before, I did now.

"Let's work together, shall we?" I asked her, and stuck out my hand. She took it and we shook on our new arrangement. Time would tell whether it would work any longer than the last one.

"You first," I said.

She smiled; judges rarely give in gracefully.

"Can we move to your conference room?" She said as she walked through the connecting door without waiting for my consent.

She put her briefcase on my conference table and extracted a light green pasteboard file with a flexible side that expanded to hold the papers she carried in it. From the size of the file, it looked like she'd been doing more than just talking to George without my knowledge.

"I've interviewed several witnesses and what I've learned has shed a lot of light on what went on the night before the murder."

I grabbed one of the ubiquitous yellow legal pads stacked on the conference table and picked up my pen to take notes. "In what way?"

"Well, after Tory Warwick beaned you with the crystal and George told everyone to leave, the Warwicks had a doozy of a fight on the way home. I interviewed both Tory and Sheldon separately and they told me essentially the same details." She flipped through her notes and gave me the highlights. "When they got back to their house in Hyde Park, about a five-minute drive from Minaret, Tory went up to bed and passed out. Sheldon claims he stayed in the rest of the night and then went to bed. But there's no one who can support that."

She had put on a pair of reading glasses and now read from the shorthand notes she'd made with black ink from a fountain pen on a white legal pad.

I admire anyone who can take readable shorthand. I've wished more than once that I could do it. Usually because I'd like to take better notes myself.

But right now, my inability to decipher shorthand thwarted my excellent skill at reading upside down.

"Since Andy was killed in the early morning, does it matter whether the Warwicks can prove their whereabouts the evening before?"

"Let me finish. The next morning, Tory claims to have slept until eleven. Alone. And Sheldon claims to have gotten up and gone directly to the Blue Coat golf tournament. Again, neither one of them can support the other." She looked at me over the tops of her half-glasses and held up two of her tiny, be-ringed fingers. "Both of the Warwicks had motive and opportunity. Of course, there's still the problem with the gun."

"Yes," I said, "Let me fill you in on that."

I told her about my trip to the gun club and what I'd figured out from George's logs.

"I could have saved you some time there," Olivia responded. "It's good you did the foot work so that we can prove the facts if we have to, but I asked George about it."

"So did I. He wouldn't tell me." I was peeved and she ignored it.

"Actually, George's explanation is quite simple, as most truthful explanations are." She read from her notes again. "He shot the gun every Wednesday at the gun club, as you discovered. The last time he shot it, Peter, George's maître d', was with him. George had to leave, but Peter wanted to stay longer and keep shooting, so George left the gun with Peter, who took it with him when he left the club that day."

She looked up at me. "For a lot of scheduling reasons that don't matter here, Peter never gave the gun back."

The explanation actually made perfect sense. Peter and George often shot together. Peter, too, had been in the military and liked to shoot handguns. George is not only fond of Peter, but Peter is very responsible. George would view loaning the gun to Peter as a friendly gesture, no more.

Also explained why George didn't tell anyone what he'd done with his gun. He wouldn't want Peter to be bothered.

"So how did the gun get from Peter to the killer?" I asked her.

Olivia tapped the fountain pen on one of her front teeth, a thoughtful expression on her face. "I don't know that yet. I haven't been able to interview Peter privately. But I will and I'd appreciate it if you'd let me do it my way. In other words, don't ask him yourself just now, all right?"

I nodded, and she continued. "George wants Peter shielded. Peter has talked with George about this and George says Peter's answer to the question is simple, too. But I told George I wanted to hear it from Peter directly and I don't want him to repeat it to you first."

She must have seen my resistance to her idea, because she said, "If you won't agree to this, Willa, I'll stop reporting to you right now. I won't have you interfering where I think I can do better. It's my call. You decide right now whether you'll be working with me or not."

What choice did I have? I agreed.

But if Peter just happened to tell me, or if I could get George to tell me first, that wouldn't violate my word to Olivia at all.

When I was in private practice, I was a very creative lawyer.

I told Olivia about my interview with Robbie Andrews, but I skipped the part about Robbie calling 911 while I was there. I also reported my work with the Ask Dr. Andrews column. Olivia took lengthy and skilled shorthand notes I couldn't read right side up.

When I finished reporting on my progress, I asked her if she'd done anything else.

"I've done a lot of things, actually. But what I think you'll be most interested in is my interview with Robbie Andrews's husband, John Williamson." With this, she smiled in a self-satisfied way that made me want to slap her and hug her at the same time.

John had been with the Andrews family at George's the night of Andy's murder and would probably have a good idea about what happened afterward. I should have interviewed him, but I hadn't thought of it.

I used to watch that old television series where the detective kept going back to his suspects, asking questions again and again. I thought, as the audience was probably meant to think, *Why can't this guy just ask everything at one time?*

Because you just can't think of everything all at one time, that's why. No matter how clever you are.

"Ok. You're very good and I'm sorry I got mad at you. What did John Williamson have to say?" We smiled at each other then, friends again, storm over.

"Jack's a very interesting guy," she said, using his nickname. "I'd never met him until now and I caught him at his office unexpectedly, otherwise I doubt he'd have consented to talk to me." She looked satisfied with herself again, even though I couldn't imagine very many men declining any request from Olivia for long. Not only was she beautiful and so petite that men would believe she was helpless and in need of assistance, but she was persistent. Jack Williamson never had a chance.

She read from her notes. "He said there was one hell of a row among the Andrews clan after George threw them all out of the restaurant, too. They started arguing before they left the dining room and continued into the parking lot. As luck would have it, they'd all ridden over together in a limousine, so they were able to keep up the fighting until the car dropped Jack and Robbie off in New Suburb Beautiful."

"What was the fight about?"

"That's the interesting part. It seems Deborah Andrews is a long-time alcoholic. Did you know that?" she asked me.

"I knew Deborah has had some problems over the years. Hers has not been an easy life," I told her.

"Right. Well, she's in a twelve-step program now and she was at the point where she was supposed to forgive everyone and ask forgiveness in return. So she scheduled the birthday dinner for Andrews, strong-armed the kids into coming, and set it all up as a surprise to him. Apparently he was surprised, but not too thrilled, so there was quite a bit of tension before the fight in the restaurant."

"I can believe that. From what I've seen, that family was a tinderbox waiting for a small spark anyway."

"Right again. The fight was one of those really nasty ones that dredges up old grudges and involves a lot of screaming." She skipped a few lines of her notes. "Jack said by the time he and Robbie got out of the car, she was in a fit of rage and crying. Of course that meant their part of the fight didn't end, either."

Having had a small taste of Robbie Andrews's ire myself, I could believe that. She had been vicious to me. I believed she wouldn't quit until she'd drawn blood from her husband.

Olivia continued. "The best part, for our purposes, is that these two went to bed separately and mad, too. And they woke up separately with no one to confirm what they did the rest of the night or in the morning."

I realized that Olivia was collecting evidence, attempting to create reasonable doubt as to whether George had committed the crime, in the hope that we could take it to Drake, the State Attorney, and persuade him to drop the charges before going to the grand jury for an indictment.

It seemed to me Olivia had now identified eight other people with motive and opportunity to shoot General Andrews besides George. And I hadn't told her about my visit to Deborah Andrews yet. Things were looking up.

Olivia opened her briefcase and took out a couple of sheets of paper, handing them to me over the table.

"What's this?" I asked her as I began to scan the closely typed pages. I needed my reading glasses.

She saved me the trouble. "It's the autopsy report on General Andrews. I got it from Ben Hathaway this morning when I went over there to discuss the case."

I'd found my reading glasses by this time and started to read quickly down the first page. The autopsy was unremarkable, except for the damage to the brain and the skull done by the bullet. Andrews exhibited the expected levels of deterioration of a human body in his age and socio-economic circumstances. The cause of death was pretty obvious.

The time of death wasn't quite so easy. The report considered *rigor mortis* (the rigidity that comes and goes shortly after death), *livor mortis* (the discoloration of the skin caused by the settling of the red cells of the blood due to gravity) and *algor mortis*, (the gradual cooling of the body).

Andrews was still in full rigor when they found him. That meant he'd been dead at least two hours and less than forty-eight.

Of course, we'd known he'd been dead less than two days because we'd seen him the night before. Sometimes, science was not the only answer. Which is a good thing for all us non-scientific types.

Blood had settled in Andrews's feet and buttocks, the report said, which was consistent with his sitting position. Again, the *livor mortis* pointed to the time of death as being at least two hours earlier.

Andrews's body temperature, measured at the scene, was low enough that the medical examiner felt confident he'd been dead at least six hours when they found him.

All of which is a convoluted way of saying that Andrews died well before time for the Blue Coat Golf Tournament. Knew that, too.

Reading through to the bottom of the first page, I didn't learn anything I hadn't known before. I became impatient with Olivia's drama. She probably sensed my feelings, but said nothing.

I flipped to the second page. Much of this I'd already learned from the police file, except the notation in the third paragraph where it said that the bullet, once they removed it from Andrews's head, had tiny strands of gray wool fabric embedded in the tip, possibly from a jacket or heavy sweater.

The conclusion was that the bullet had passed though a wool jacket or sweater on its way to Andrews's head. Find the fabric and whoever was wearing it was the killer.

There were probably only about twenty or thirty million people in America who owned at least one gray wool jacket or sweater. This was progress?

CHAPTER SIXTY-ONE

Tampa, Florida
Saturday 5:05 p.m.
January 29, 2000

BUT, THE GRAY FIBER was something we hadn't had before.

I grudgingly gave her the praise she was due. "Well, Olivia, I guess you do have a right to be pleased with yourself. You've gotten some real evidence for us to work with."

"There's a problem with it, though. The fiber itself is not that helpful, but it does tell us that we should be looking for a gray wool jacket or sweater. Like most businessmen, I assume George has several gray wool jackets?" She asked me, with a natural arch to both eyebrows that any woman would admire.

I was preoccupied with the report. "The curious thing is why Ben Hathaway hasn't asked to see any of them," I said.

"Ah, yes. That is the curious thing." She waited like a comedienne to deliver the punch line. "And why do you think that is?"

I finally looked up at her, giving her the full attention she craved. "Why?"

"Because they're afraid they won't find it." She was almost rubbing her hands with glee, like an Oz munchkin after a delicious sparerib dinner. "I asked Ben Hathaway if he planned to request a search warrant for George's closet. What do you think he said?"

"I give up."

"He said, maybe later. Then I asked him if he wanted me to look first. He said he'd appreciate that."

"I don't get it. Why do you want to do his job for him?"

"Think about it, Willa. If we look for a gray wool jacket with a hole in it and we find it, I have an ethical obligation to turn it over to the police. So do you. Otherwise, we'd be obstructing justice. Hathaway wins." She stopped a second or two. "But if we don't find it, he doesn't have to report a negative result after obtaining a search warrant, and his prime suspect is still his prime suspect. Hathaway wins."

She laid it out for me as if she was explaining the strategy behind a major league playoff.

"I understand all of that, Olivia. What I don't understand is why we would want to help Drake keep George under suspicion of murder for a second longer than necessary. You're supposed to be representing us, remember? If Drake looks like a fool, that's just fine by me."

I could have denied her the permission she needed, but she wasn't the only good strategist in the room.

Grabbed up my purse and said to Olivia, "Let's go search my husband's closets."

CHAPTER SIXTY-TWO

Tampa, Florida
Saturday 5:45 p.m.
January 29, 2000

WE TOOK SEPARATE CARS back to Plant Key and I was definitely not practicing my mindfulness during the drive. I was trying to decide whether to disclose to Olivia that George had moved out.

She probably wouldn't be able to tell just by looking at his closets, because he'd only taken a few things with him when he'd moved to the club. But the point of looking at his jackets was not to find an incriminating one. To do that, we'd have to look at them all, and some were at the Club with George.

For some reason, there were no media vans parked at the entrance to the Plant Key Bridge. Maybe we were catching a break.

I arrived at Minaret just moments before Olivia and we both parked in valet at the entrance. After I let us into the flat and got Harry and Bess calmed down and out the back door, we approached George's dressing room.

When we remodeled Aunt Minnie's house, we took one of the bedrooms and made it into two dressing rooms with walk-in closets: His and Mine.

George's closet was meticulous. His suits hung the same way you'd find suits displayed at a clothing store. Each suit on a wooden hanger and all facing in the same direction, colors grouped together, followed by sports coats.

Shirts were boxed and neatly stacked in cubbyholes. Ties hung on racks between the suits and shirts.

Casual clothes were separated by a row of drawers for underwear, hose, and the carefully pressed and stacked monogrammed linen handkerchiefs George carried every day.

Just standing in his closet, smelling his Old Spice scent on everything, bothered me. The closet was so George. I missed his steady presence.

"Knock yourself out," I said. "I'll make us a cold drink."

I left her in George's closet so I wouldn't give anything away while watching.

Olivia believed George didn't shoot Andrews and there would be no hole in any of his gray jackets to find. But George would never have left such evidence in his closet.

I assumed Olivia had already thought this through, but I wasn't going to help her with it. I knew things about George that no other human would know. While I might have to work through my own doubts, I would never disclose anything that would help Drake's case.

Olivia came out of the closet empty handed about ten minutes later. Smiling and shaking her head, amused by George's closet or by what she didn't find there.

"George is a real gem, you know," she said. "That closet is a wonder to behold. Because the curiosity is killing you, I'll just tell you that I didn't find any holes in any of his nine gray jackets."

I didn't argue with her, but it felt good to realize she didn't know everything.

Olivia followed me out to the veranda, sat in George's chair, and waited while I lit my Partagas.

"Now what?" I asked her.

"Now, I'll tell Ben Hathaway I've looked for a gray wool jacket with a hole in it and found nothing. He won't get a search warrant. You'll be spared the inconvenience and insult of a search. Believe me, after the police searched that closet, it wouldn't look anything like it does now."

Olivia reached into her pocket, removed and ate three shortbread wafers shaped like Mickey Mouse. She ate the ears off first, just like the child she resembled in size. She didn't offer me one. This was the third time I'd seen her do this. A blood sugar thing? She offered no explanation; I refused to ask.

We talked about the contents of the police file for a while. Both of us had seen it before, except for the autopsy report we'd gotten today. Much of the evidence didn't really point to anything, except for the gun.

I showed her the gun logs and inventory George kept, which provided written documentation that corroborated his story about when he last shot the murder weapon, although not that he had loaned it to Peter, as he'd told Olivia.

I kept almost nothing from her. It was a relief to let someone else share the load, even though I wasn't sure her small shoulders could handle the burden. I trusted her. What else could I have done?

Olivia was right that George would continue to believe his duty was to protect my office and me from scandal. But judges have been involved in all sorts of behavior that was much worse than being married to a man accused of murder.

One of my colleagues on the state court bench had defeated an impeachment attempt after being accused of pointing a gun at a law clerk and threatening to blow his head off.

And while I was practicing law in Detroit, a judge was accused of taking bribes for fixing traffic tickets, an offense clearly depicted on a video tape "sting." He was tried and acquitted and returned to the bench.

While we judges aspire to the heights of human potential, the fact is that judges are people, too. Like military generals. We are far from perfect.

So George was being overly protective. As usual. His desire to take care of me was something I often appreciated, but right now, his self-defined honor code was a block depriving our investigative team of some of its best potential strategic thinking.

We needed him. It was that simple and I planned to make him see that tonight.

CHAPTER SIXTY-THREE

Tampa, Florida
Saturday 7:00 p.m.
January 29, 2000

GEORGE ARRIVED CARRYING A small box beautifully wrapped with a big pink bow. He was casually dressed in his usual Florida uniform of well-pressed khaki slacks, a teal golf shirt and highly polished, brown woven loafers. No socks.

When he held and kissed me, he smelled wonderfully like the combination of Irish Spring soap and Old Spice deodorant he uses. I held him a little too close, a little too long. I really missed him and I was very glad he had come home tonight, at least for a while. I couldn't even think about the possibility that he might go to prison and be gone from me forever. The idea was impossible.

We both laughed when Harry and Bess jumped up between us, breaking us apart, as if to say, "Hey, what about us?"

They jumped, wagged their tails, ran in circles, acted like they hadn't seen him in years. I watched as George rolled around on the floor with them while I mixed drinks and opened my gift.

The present was a retired Herend wild goose in purple fishnet to add to Aunt Minnie's zoo. The goose—or gander, as it were—looked angry. He had his head extended and his mouth open, as if he was chasing away a fierce enemy.

The purple color is only available for special trunk shows and there hadn't been one in Tampa for a couple of years. When I asked him where he got it, he just winked and said, "I've got my sources."

Over the years, George has learned that the smaller the box, the more successful the present.

Remember Pavlov: reward behavior you want repeated.

I put the goose up on the mantel out of the reach of wagging tails and thanked him properly.

That took about twenty minutes and really messed up my lipstick.

We spent the evening the way we would have before all this craziness began. We dined on food from George's restaurant, consumed a bottle of red wine, and discussed affairs of the day.

After dinner, over liqueur and coffee in the den, I said, "Olivia has uncovered suspects who had stronger motives to kill Andrews than the one Drake thinks you have. We need to analyze the evidence and figure out what to do."

George sat his drink down on Aunt Minnie's highly polished mahogany table. On a coaster, of course. "Honey, listen to me. I have been talking with Olivia pretty regularly. I know what she's found."

He seemed amused. George simply refused to deal with anything he didn't want to deal with. His arrest fell into that category.

He said, "I don't want to spend the limited time we have together talking about this. I know it will all get resolved and it will be fine. Have a little faith."

In a cartoon, steam would have been coming out of my ears.

I tamped down my annoyance, knowing another argument would get us nowhere.

"Well at least tell me what Peter did with your gun. Do you know how the gun ended up at the Andrews's house?"

Apparently, I'd pushed too hard. His tone was no longer gentle. "Peter didn't do anything with the gun, Willa. He didn't give it to anyone and he didn't kill Andy with it. Let it go."

Then, he got up and walked out the door, just that fast.

"When this is over," I fumed to the empty room, "I will kill George myself."

I jumped up and paced around the flat, waving the glass of liqueur. "What is wrong with him? Doesn't he understand how serious this is?"

I wasn't overreacting. That had been made only too plain to me today during my conversations with Olivia.

George was smarter than the average criminal. Whatever he'd done, George was engaged in a battle of wits now with Michael Drake. George thought he was smarter than Drake, and I could only hope he was right.

I continued ranting in this fashion for quite a while until I ran out of steam.

After that, I was left alone with another night of furious journaling, unanswered questions and too much room in our bed.

CHAPTER SIXTY-FOUR

Tampa, Florida
Sunday 7:00 a.m.
January 30, 2000

THE MORNING PROMISED TO be another Chamber of
Commerce day, the kind that we used on all the promotional
videos. High, light clouds decorated a clear blue sky while a gentle
breeze rustled the palm trees. The kind of day when the locals
wore long pants and long sleeves, and the tourists went to the
beach and turned blue from the chill. The forecast called for a high
of seventy-six, and a twenty percent chance of rain. In contrast, the
high in Detroit was to be twenty-seven degrees.

Have I mentioned lately how much I love living in Florida?

Trying to restore some normalcy to my days through sheer
routine, while at the same time seeking an epiphany in the case, I
ran along the Bayshore today instead of around the island. Perhaps
the methodical pounding, in slightly different scenery, would jar
my brain and produce some fabulous insight that would end the
insanity that had become our lives. I could hope.

The days of an endorphin-producing run on the Bayshore were limited by threatening progress, the kind that was filling the land with high-rise condominiums and traffic. As I ran, the weather changed. The wind became stronger and managed to whip up a few choppy waves on the shallow water. The water now looked gray and stormy, but there were no raindrops imminent. I saw the Big Bend Power Station in the distance and was reminded of how long it had been since I'd gone to see the manatees that gathered there.

I wanted a long run to clear my head and the mindless repetition of putting one foot in front of the other soon allowed me to notice my surroundings.

Two men passed each other, running in different directions. Each raised a high five to the other.

"What's up, stud?" The westbound runner shouted.

"How ya doin', cool?" The eastbound one cried back.

Neither looked stud-like nor cool to me.

Bodies of every shape, size, and description populated the sidewalk, clothed in outfits similarly interesting. Handkerchiefs around shaved heads, striped shirts with plaid shorts on males; females in full war paint, dressed as if they were making a glamorous workout video. The number of infants sleeping in jogging strollers being pushed by adults on roller blades was surpassed only by middle-aged men jogging with headphones.

In short, I saw a typical day on the Bayshore, and felt a little better knowing that the world was still operating normally, at least in some spheres.

By the time I completed my morning routine, my plan was formed and I got to work.

Jason was staying with his mother, Kate, while he was in town. I called Kate's house and he answered the phone. Luck was on my side.

"Hello, Jason. How are you today?"

Almost as if the feeling traveled through the phone line, I could sense his wariness. After the recent revelations he'd made concerning his work for Senator Warwick on Andrews's confirmation hearings, I'd wondered more than once how well we understood each other anymore.

When I was growing up in his household, Jason was already off to college. He came home on weekends, but he had little time for a younger sister.

Still, the bond had always been there, and I thought I still felt it; did he?

"I'm fine, Willa," he said, impatience evident in his tone. Maybe busy with something he considered essential; resented my interruption. "Kate's not here right now. Can I tell her you called?"

So I skipped the pleasantries. "I need about thirty minutes of your time."

Confirming my hunch, he said, "Can't do it today, unfortunately. How about tomorrow?"

"I'll be there in ten minutes," I told him, and hung up the phone.

He might not stick around to talk to me, but I'd cross that bridge when and if we came to it.

CHAPTER SIXTY-FIVE

Tampa, Florida
Sunday 10:30 a.m.
January 30, 2000

IN LESS THAN TEN minutes, I pulled around the corner of Kate's house on Oregon Avenue. The driveway faces Watrous Avenue and provides a straight shot into the double garage. As I had at Robbie Andrews's house, I blocked both exits.

I hurried up, opened the unlocked screen door, and walked in. Unlike Kate, Jason the city boy, would have locked the door if he'd ducked out.

I walked through the small house and found him sitting at the desk in the television room that Kate uses to do her household bookkeeping. He looked a little foolish sitting there, I thought, among Kate's New Age paraphernalia. Surrounded by the moon and stars mobile and the Tarot chart, he held the telephone receiver up to his ear, listening. I could hear Sheldon Warwick's voice through the receiver from where I was standing across the room.

Jason gestured me to sit down and turned back to his call. "I know, Sheldon. There isn't much I can do about it right now. The local police are investigating, they've made an arrest, the ball's in their court."

He waited for Senator Warwick to finish talking, then said, "It's not an army matter. The general was retired and the murder was not on army property. This is a civilian investigation."

More silence on his end, as Jason shook his head and held up his hand, cupped so that the four fingers were on the top and his thumb on the bottom. He opened and closed his top and bottom phalanges, a gesture meant to explain that Warwick was simply yakking on and on. Instead, it reminded me of yesterday's bull gator.

"You have a lot more influence in the civilian world than I do. Why don't you use some of it if you want to know what's going on?" Jason didn't sound too deferential to his boss, now. Maybe their nerves were fraying just a little under pressure, too.

Jason signed off shortly after that by promising to meet with Warwick later today.

Then, he turned to me and said, in the same exasperated tone, "Now what can I do for you?"

Resisting the urge to snap back, I counted to twenty, while he continued to look at me and I studied him, trying to figure out a better conversation starter.

Jason had his shoes off. He'd donned well-worn jeans and a faded, once red T-shirt with *I Survived The Honolulu Marathon* emblazoned on the front in now-cracked purple letters.

"Did you?" I asked him.

"Did I what?"

"Survive the Honolulu marathon?"

He smiled and gave up his pout. "No. But I survived the girl I was dating at the time who did. She gave me the shirt and I refused to give it back when she left me."

"Sort of like the one who gets dumped keeps the ring?"

He laughed. "Something like that."

And the ice was broken. I, for one, was glad.

I hate personal conflict in my life. I deal with conflict in my professional capacity every day of the year. I didn't want it anywhere near my personal life. To avoid conflict, I usually tried to stay above the fray, ignoring my base emotions.

But I'd been plunged directly into this cauldron of intrigue and when George left home, I felt adrift without my anchor. This was totally new territory for me.

I'd been floundering around, trying to figure out how to keep my marriage together and rescue my husband, too. All I'd accomplished so far was allowing the time for bold action to pass, as the clock marched inexorably toward Drake's deadline.

I needed help, and I was finally ready to ask for it.

"Ok," he said, "what is it?"

This question was one I'd carefully rehearsed. "I need to know why the President appointed Andrews to the Supreme Court. It doesn't make any sense to me. There are hundreds, if not thousands, of qualified jurists he could have chosen. Andrews never even practiced law. He was a hothead who was used to giving orders that other people followed. I doubt he could even write a well-reasoned legal opinion. President Benson had to know that. So, what gives?"

"Everybody on the Hill is asking the same question and has been ever since this all started," he said, deflecting.

Sheldon Warwick had been Jason's boss for ten years. They were friends. Warwick is the chairman of the Judiciary Committee, the reigning Democrat on the Hill and a personal friend of both the president and the general. Common sense said

Jason knew the answer to my question. I was sure of it.

"You're more of a politician than I gave you credit for."

"What do you mean?"

"Don't tell me Warwick doesn't know and don't tell me he didn't discuss it with you."

"Assuming that's true, I can't breach Warwick's confidence." Taking a little pity on me, I guess, he said, "If you want to know, you'll have to ask Warwick yourself."

"So, he does know."

Jason laughed ruefully, shaking his head in defeat. "Look, Willa, I love you. I love George. But I can't tell you anything."

"Come on, Jason. We're talking about George's life here." I was pleading now, and he knew it.

He considered for a long time. How much loyalty did he have, and to whom? Hard facts make hard choices.

He said, "I can't tell you what I know without permission from Warwick, which I'll ask him for." I'd already started to object, but he talked right over me. "In the meantime, I'll give you a hint that will point you in the right direction if you won't tell anyone where you got it."

He was asking me now to trust him. Did I? What choice did I have? But, not knowing the full picture, I couldn't put on such a tight straightjacket.

"If I have to disclose what you say, I'll tell you first," I counter-offered.

After thinking about it some more, he finally nodded. "Fair enough, I guess, if you don't get me fired. If this thing blows up, I'll be without a job anyway."

He waited a couple of beats, as if he might change his mind, then he said, "So, here's your hint. Ask George's lawyer what happened to her brother."

Now, I was totally confused. What could Olivia's brother have to do with Andrews's appointment? She'd told me she believed Andrews killed her brother. At the time, I thought she was being overly dramatic. She obviously had no proof of her claim. If she had, she'd have had Andrews prosecuted when her brother died. And anyway, all of that happened years ago.

I couldn't see the connection. "Are you trying to jerk me around here? Because I really don't have the time to go off chasing wild theories. George is less than two weeks away from being indicted for murder."

My voice caught a little. "You haven't forgotten that, have you?"

He seemed to step back in the face of my outrage. "Just ask Olivia," he said.

"Olivia already told me. She took George's case because she thinks Andrews killed her brother and she wants revenge. So what?"

"No, Willa," Jason said softly, taking my hand and looking me squarely in the eye. "So *why*?"

He got up and walked into the bedroom. When he came out, he was holding a slim file folder. He handed it to me without another word.

Thomas Edward Holmes, deceased, it said on the label.

"What's this?"

"The final report on his death."

CHAPTER SIXTY-SIX

Tampa, Florida
Sunday 1:30 p.m.
January 30, 2000

GRETA AND I HEADED toward downtown where the Andrews twins, David and Donald, were staying at the Harbour Island Hotel. Greta's top was down when we drove over the Harbour Island Bridge. The sweet perfume of jasmine filled the air. Paradise definitely smells better than the rust belt.

I parked Greta myself in the underground garage and walked up the stairs to the entrance to the hotel. Florida waterfront hotels locate the lobby and registration desk on the second floor. You had to go up an escalator to get your bags to the front desk.

The system was so inconvenient that it must have increased tips to porters by at least fifty percent. But that's not the reason for it. The real reason is hurricanes.

If Tampa experienced a hurricane, something that hadn't happened here since the 1920s, Harbour Island would be underwater. The Hotel's second-floor reception desk, where all the computer equipment was located, was an attempt to prevent flood damage from the tidal surge that follows the big blow.

I'm not afraid of hurricanes. As natural disasters go, hurricanes are best because modern weather equipment detects them long before they hit land. Tornadoes and earthquakes are unexpected; floods last longer and do more damage; and snow storms are simply unacceptable. Hurricanes have killed fewer people than any other type of major weather disaster.

If a hurricane hit Tampa, we'd be in the first level of evacuation because, like Harbour Island, Plant Key lies below sea level.

But then, we might get a new house out of the insurance company.

At the front desk, I asked for David or Donald Andrews. David said he'd meet me in the lounge on the outside deck in ten minutes. Shortly after the waitress delivered my Perrier with lime, David had reached my table.

He sat down in the chair next to me, the one that faced the water. Somehow, he didn't strike me as the kind of guy I wanted to hug. In fact, I was so wary of the Andrews clan by now, I didn't even want to shake hands with him.

David had always been the serious one. He was a shy and quiet teenager the last time I'd had a conversation with him. The intervening years didn't seem to have changed his approach to conversation any. The only small talk was of the "nice to see you again" type that takes about thirty seconds. Then, he waited for me to say something.

I started in a direction that I was fairly sure he wouldn't have anticipated. "Did you know Thomas Holmes?"

His eyebrows shot up. Good. I'd surprised him. "Sure. I knew Thomas. He was a couple of classes ahead of me at West Point. Why?"

"Do you know how he died?"

Seemingly without guile, he said "Killed in a training accident. On maneuvers, somebody had live ammunition in their gun. It was investigated. No one was ever charged. I don't think they could find the gun that shot him."

It interested me that David knew the contents of the slim file that Jason had given me. The folder contained Thomas's death certificate. Killed by a single gunshot wound to the heart, it said. Age at death was twenty-eight. Manner of death was accidental.

Also in the folder was the final report of the investigation reflecting that Thomas had been shot during a training maneuver. Did David know that the murder weapon was conclusively identified as a handgun issued to Thomas himself, although the verdict on his death was not suicide? General Andrews's name appeared nowhere on the paperwork. There was no mention in the report of who found Thomas's body or where he'd been discovered. The documents looked official enough to be the official cover-up version Olivia had mentioned. I'd thought of about fifty questions to ask in the past thirty minutes.

Now David asked a question of his own. "Why? That was a long time ago."

"Was your dad there at the time?" His eyes widened and he looked at me with an inquiry that hadn't been there before.

"Yes," he said slowly. "Andy was there. But he wasn't in the field with Thomas. Why do you ask?"

I'd tried to figure out how Olivia's version of Thomas's death could be true, and the plausibility of her theory completely escaped me. I just couldn't see how Andrews might have killed Thomas and gotten away with it. And the paperwork certainly didn't support her idea. "But couldn't he have put the live ammunition in one of the guns, maybe?"

David shook his head. "I don't see how. How could the general know where Thomas would be, who would be in a position to kill him and what gun he would have? I don't think that's possible," he concluded. Then he added, "I'm willing to believe a lot of bad things about my father, but I don't see how he could have killed Thomas Holmes."

I let him think about it for a while. Then I said, "Let me put it this way. If the general had wanted to have Thomas Holmes killed in that training exercise, could he have arranged it?"

He considered the question. "I suppose so," he said, thoughtfully drawing out each word. "A four-star general can arrange just about anything." He leaned back and folded his hands over his flat stomach. "Hell, I don't know. Maybe he did do it. But why would he bother?"

That was another good question, the one Jason had posed and suggested I should answer. "David, you said Thomas was at West Point with you. How well did you know him?"

"Pretty well. I knew President Benson's son, Charles, too. We hung out together. My brother, Donald, and Sheldon Warwick's son," he answered me frankly. "Those were the early days of the Benson Presidency. We'd get invited to the White House. It was all pretty cool, really, for army kids."

This came out of left field for me. "Charles Benson and Shelley Warwick were in the army?" I had never heard this before.

"Shelley was. Charles just hung out with us. It's kind of hard for the President's kid to find friends, you know."

I thought about the presidential children I'd heard of over the years. All of them had seemed to experience a difficult adolescence. Living in the White House fishbowl was not easy, even for adults. For kids, it had to be equal parts excitement and prison.

I drew my attention back to David's story. "Charles was kind of a behavior problem even before his dad got elected. After they got into the White House, the general told me Charles became quite a handful." He took a break and looked across the water at the convention center, where the winter boat show was in full swing. "As a favor to the President, Senator Warwick and Dad arranged for Charles to hang out with us when we had the time. That's all."

Charles Benson, Shelley Warwick, Thomas Holmes and both of General Andrews's sons were friends, hung out together at the White House. And Charles Benson was a juvenile delinquent. I was getting warmer. The little hairs on the back of my neck were tingling.

"Are you and Charles Benson still friends?" I asked him.

He gave a quick, negative shake of his head again. "Something happened with Thomas and Charles. The general said we couldn't hang with either of them anymore."

"What about Shelly Warwick?"

"Shelley was a little older than us. He'd left West Point already." With a little grin, David added, "Charles was kind of a pain anyway, always getting into stuff and then we'd get into serious trouble for it. It wasn't worth it."

"What do you mean it wasn't worth it?"

He grinned now, applying adult insight to adolescent behavior. "Our Dad was a general, but Charles's Dad was the President. We had more clout with regular army guys, you know?"

I got it. The general's sons, the Senator's son, and Thomas Holmes, the son of generations of West Point graduates before him, had high status among their peers, but Charles Benson, the President's kid, was a notch or two up the ladder. None of the other boys would have been friends with Charles in the normal course of Washington hierarchy. Which meant that being friends with Charles would diminish the status of the other boys in Charles's presence, so they'd rather be the big fish in their own West Point pond than the minnows in the White House pool.

"How about Thomas?" I asked. "Did he mind being banished from Charles' company?"

As if he'd never considered the question before, David said "Actually, he did, now that you mention it. Thomas really liked Charles, you know? Shelley, Donald and I were just being his friends because the general said we had to. But Thomas and Charles were really close."

"How close were they?" The little hairs on the back of my neck were fairly vibrating now. Maybe it was the power of Jason's suggestion, but I felt I was finally getting somewhere.

"Inseparable in some ways, I guess," David told me. "Thomas was really pissed when the 'hands off' order came down from the general. Thomas said he wasn't going to do it. He said the army couldn't order him to abandon his friends; the general's reach didn't go that far."

"What happened?"

CHAPTER SIXTY-SEVEN

Tampa, Florida
Sunday 1:45 p.m.
January 30, 2000

"THE NEXT WEEK, THOMAS got orders to maneuvers in Korea. He was killed there a few months later. I never saw him again." David said this as if he was putting the pieces together in his mind.

"Was your father in Korea at the same time?" I asked.

He answered me slowly, "I think so," drawing the words out.

From the expressions that passed over his face, I could almost see the gears meshing, see him adding two plus two and coming up with what I had come to believe was the only possible four.

"Still think Andy didn't kill Thomas?" I asked him.

This time, he didn't bother to argue. He asked, "But why? It doesn't make sense."

He sat up a little straighter in the chair, mused aloud, "Andy was capable of killing. He'd done it a lot in Vietnam and other places." He stared out over the water again, thinking, trying to put it together.

When he spoke again, his tone was distracted, as if he was pondering the vagaries of human existence. "But why kill Thomas? He'd already sent Thomas half way around the world to separate him from Charles. That would have been enough, even for Andy. It was the army way."

I now considered seriously, for the first time, that Olivia could have been right. General Andrews might actually have killed Thomas Holmes, directly or indirectly, and it was something Jason must have known.

I realized I might never figure out exactly how Andrews had killed Thomas, but Jason thought the real issue was *why*.

Did David Andrews know the answer?

People who claim that they just know what to say when the time comes to say it infuriate me. I've never been able to do that. I usually plan out most important conversations in my head well in advance. Some of the dialogue I actually get to use.

Right now, my logic and imagination had failed me. So I used the direct approach, my usual fallback.

I leaned in to David and looked directly at him, resisting the urge to delay so that something more appropriate might occur to me.

"I guess you've heard that George has been charged with murdering your dad."

He actually smiled. Not a happy smile. Just one of those lines of the mouth that turn up on one side to let me know he found the statement mildly amusing. He nodded, but he didn't say anything.

"George didn't kill the general." I said, with as much conviction as I felt in my heart, which was considerable.

He nodded.

"You knew that?"

"Sure."

"How did you know?"

He studied me for a while, and I thought he was going to ignore my question.

But he answered. "George has too much to lose."

Then, maybe feeling a little sorry for our situation, he broadened the grin on his face and offered something he must have viewed as close to a joke. "Besides, he would've had to take a number and stand in line for the privilege."

"What do you mean?"

He straightened himself in the chair, put his forearms on the small round glass table between us and leaned toward me, like he didn't want to be overheard, even though we were the only ones on the patio. As if he was about to tell me a secret, but his whispered tone was farcical and exaggerated.

"Maybe you didn't know this, but Andy wasn't a very nice guy. He had a lot of enemies. It's not really a surprise that someone killed him, is it? Isn't it more of a surprise that someone didn't do it years ago?"

He waggled his eyebrows as if trying to clue me in that I should find his statements hilariously funny.

But I didn't find him funny at all.

The situation was tragic, for everyone. His behavior was odd, inappropriate.

I remained sincere, ignoring his attempt at comedy, and responded to his words. "I know he had a lot of public enemies, but I don't think any of them would have taken the trouble to try to make his murder look like a suicide. What I'm interested in are his private enemies."

His weird humor continued, as if he was sharing some blazing insight with a comic audience. "Most homicides are committed by family members or someone close to the victim, right?"

"You think someone in your family killed Andy?"

"I think all of us would have had good reason to. If incentive, motive, and opportunity count for anything, it makes sense, don't you agree?"

David's continuing sarcasm began to grate on my last nerve.

I said, "Yes. I do. But you know much more about the family than I do. Why don't you fill me in?"

His humor switched abruptly to anger.

"Dad," he emphasized the word with such vindictiveness that small droplets of spit hit me in the face. I struggled not to recoil from his fierceness. His hands gripped his highball glass so tightly I thought he might crush it. Now I realized that this wasn't his first drink of the morning. Many drinkers get quieter when intoxicated, and David was speaking in unnaturally quiet but angry tones now. Just how much in control was he?

"Dad loved all of us. Especially me and Donald."

He emphasized "especially" in a vicious way, like he was giving me a clue, trying to communicate something without saying anything specific.

Now, his tone changed abruptly again, to mock innocence: "Why would we want to kill Dad?"

He looked directly at me, almost challenging me to understand. Maybe he'd been thinking about this for some time. Perhaps he'd decided to tell someone and I just happened to be in the wrong place at the wrong time.

Or maybe he was out of control, drunk, or something else I hadn't figured out yet.

I leaned back and took a look at him again, resisting the urge to wipe his spittle off my face. David Andrews was tall, lean, strong and good looking. He'd been so since he was about nine or ten years old. He and his brother were as different from his sister in body type as they were in temperament, goals and life achievements. Neither of the brothers had ever married. Nor were they now in any kind of long-term relationships.

Sometimes, I'm quicker to catch on than others. This one took me another few seconds. "Are you saying Andy abused you?"

He raised his eyebrows again, in that mocking way, as if to say, so you finally get it.

Then, he answered my question. "Not sexually. He did manage to draw the line there. But psychologically. Emotionally. Yes. Every day." He drained his glass and gestured to the waitress for another. "Our lives were pure emotional torture. He was so happy that we were just like him. He just loved us so much, see? He'd punish us because he loved us, he said. He'd threaten us, freeze us out, keep his nose in every second of our personal lives because he loved us, you know?"

The vulnerable boy David had been was nowhere to be found in the angry man sitting across the table from me. His face worked around his memories and took on a nasty frown. He stood up abruptly, knocking over his plastic chair, then strode over to the rail and leaned both forearms on it, as he faced the water.

I followed him warily. I'd thought him one of his mother's harmless cats, but now I realized I'd opened the cage door and let an unpredictable tiger out.

David's father had been an extremely violent man and probably a murderer, if Olivia Holmes was right about what happened to her brother. Usually, the fruit doesn't fall far from the tree.

Not at all confident of what David might do next, I glanced around and saw no other people on the patio with us. If I needed help, I realized that a loud scream would reach the tourists across the harbor at the boat show.

Boldly, I joined David at the rail, but I stood aside, keeping my gaze firmly on his body language, leaving enough room to get away fast, should it come to that.

When the waitress brought him another drink, he took a big gulp, for fortification, maybe. Then he turned to face me. "I think now that he was trying to change us, to force us to be different. Straight. If such a thing was possible, he would have succeeded in changing us. I think he hated us and what we were. We *definitely* hated him. We would have done *anything* to get him off our backs."

When he saw that I finally understood, he seemed to calm down a little. He returned to his chair and relaxed into it, extending his legs out in front of him and crossing them at the ankles.

David sunned himself. He closed his eyes and dropped his head back, slouching further in the chair.

My mind twirled possibilities; each forced attention back to him. Eventually, he began to speak, without changing his position in any way. His voice was low and I had to strain to hear him.

He said, "Andy figured out we needed changing when we were about ten. When we were just figuring ourselves out. When we needed him the most."

David didn't say so, but that must have been about the time when he and Donald began to realize they were gay. It would have been a confusing time for them. An overbearing father, an alcoholic mother. The situation was no less difficult because it was a common one. What a horrible time the two young boys must have had trying to grow up.

"Dad spent all his free time raising us up right. Sexual

orientation is nature, not nurture. But Andy was on us all the time to be different. To change. Mom saw what we were and how he treated us. So did Robbie. They did nothing to help." David didn't seem to have any emotion left.

He drank and recited the story as if it had all happened to someone else. "Guilt, I think. That was when Mom really started drinking heavy and Robbie just started getting heavy. She was a pretty girl before that, you know? But it was weird that she just got so jealous of us. We would have happily traded places with her."

The waitress came by with another highball for him. I wondered how he'd be able to walk to his room. He was already pie-eyed.

He said, "The only break we got was when he was away. We prayed he would go. As soon as we could get away to military school, we left. No matter how hard it would be for us there, it was the only place he'd release us to attend. We were out of our home like a shot. And we rarely came back."

"Why'd you come back now? To celebrate his birthday?" Seemed far-fetched at this point.

That's what John Williamson, Robbie's husband, had told Olivia. That Deborah had gathered the family together to celebrate the end of the confirmation hearings and her husband's birthday. Given the level of hatred I'd witnessed in David just now, I didn't think he was all that into making his father happy.

He sighed. "You get older. You try to forgive and forget. You recognize that he has no power over you anymore. You know that you are what you were born to be. Your other family members have to be forgiven, too."

He looked at me again and drained his glass once more. "Anger eats you up, you know? It destroys your life. You try to get past it."

He set the glass down and looked around for the waitress to order another.

"Did you? Get past it?"

"Before he died, you mean?"

"Yes."

"I tried. I was in therapy for years. So was Donald. We finally figured out that Dad was more unhappy with himself in those days than unhappy with us. We were the scapegoats, not the cause of his problems. I think we've both managed to go on with our lives. But, as you no doubt noticed, the anger is still there."

David's story was heartbreaking. I thought about the little boy he'd been and the bitter man he'd become. In some ways, it was a good thing the general was dead. Alive, he'd have a lot to answer for.

"It was such a betrayal, you know?" he said now, still trying to figure things out. "We wanted to be like him. We were him. He was off protecting the country, for God's sake, and he couldn't take care of his own family."

For some reason, the venom was no longer apparent in his words. His sorrow was harder to witness.

I turned my gaze away from the naked pain in his face. "Did you kill him, David?"

I wanted him to say yes. I would have forgiven him if he'd killed Andy. Even Michael Drake, as ambitious as he was, would accept a plea to reduced charges, when he knew the whole story. David as his father's killer would have tied everything up with a neat bow. And I was weary of the whole sad situation.

But it was not to be.

"I'm sorry to say I didn't," David told me. "I wanted to kill him, God knows. I tried to make myself do it." He waited a beat or two. "The bond was still there, somehow. No matter how much I hated him for the way he'd treated me and Donald, our whole family, he was still my father."

David raised his now watery blue gaze to meet mine. "My biggest struggle has been not to become him. If I'd killed him, I'd be exactly what he was."

David waved to the waitress for another refill. His tolerance for alcohol showed me that he was following in his mother's footsteps, another sad part of this family story playing out with predicable certainty.

"Some days, I wish I'd killed him, Willa. But I didn't. And Donald didn't either. God forgive us." Just like his mother, silent tears began to slowly slide out of his eyes and down his face.

Anger had propelled me here, made me ask David these questions. I'd wanted to clear George's name and now I felt that I'd destroyed David's defenses to do so.

I wasn't very proud of myself right at the moment, but I didn't know what else I could have done, either.

What I'd learned were secrets I didn't want to know. Everything David told me supplied each member of the Andrews family with motive for murder. I'd achieved my objective, but at what cost?

I reached over and touched David's arm, thanked him for helping me, and took my leave. I paid the bar bill on the way out and asked the waitress not to disturb him for a while.

Then, I made my way back to Greta with a heavy heart.

CHAPTER SIXTY-EIGHT

IT WAS TIME TO compare notes and to find out whatever I could about Olivia's brother. I now believed General Andrews killed Thomas Holmes, but I still didn't know why. Jason said that Thomas Holmes was connected to Andrews's Supreme Court nomination. I had to find out how.

I dialed Olivia's number on my cell phone before I started my car. She answered her private line on the third ring. First, I told her about my conversation with David Andrews. She asked a few questions, but not many. I started the car and continued talking to her.

When I'd found my way back to the Bayshore, heading home, I asked her if Thomas was gay.

A lawyer gets very close to her clients when they go through the crucible of trial together. Trial is an intense and unique experience. Maybe that's why I'd begun to trust Olivia. Trusting doesn't come easily to me. Trust means a loss of objectivity. I invest too much of myself when I trust and then it's too hard to extricate myself from a relationship gone south.

Now, I worried that I'd made a mistake in trusting Olivia. After my interviews with Jason and David Andrews, I realized that Olivia's motives for murdering Andy were as strong, or stronger, than many others. What real evidence did I have that she hadn't done it? Just her word. Was that enough?

"Olivia? Did you hear me? I need to know whether Thomas was gay." I thought the question impertinent, and I was sure she did, too.

But a pattern had begun to emerge that disturbed me. General Andrews was a man of secrets and they seemed to be consuming him in the days before he died. His views against gays in the military had been extensively reported during his confirmation hearings. David said he was brutal to his own sons because they were gay.

The general didn't have his sons discharged from the army. He could have. Was he showing compassion? Or had he run into resistance for such a course before?

If Thomas Holmes was gay, that might explain what Olivia had described as General Andrews's enmity toward her brother. How would Andrews have treated gay soldiers in the days before military policy required acceptance of them? Based on what David said, I imagined the general must have made Thomas Holmes's life a living hell.

When Thomas Holmes served in the army, simply being homosexual would have been a dangerous matter. The widely debated but relatively recent policy, referred to as "Don't Ask/Don't Tell", provides that homosexuals can serve in the U.S. military, but requires that they keep their sexual orientation to themselves and do not engage in homosexual acts while in the service.

Failing to observe either criterion can result in an immediate, albeit honorable, discharge.

Like so many compromises, this one between gay-rights advocates and those flatly opposed to gays in the military, was unsatisfactory to both sides. The military and everyone around the issue was uncomfortable with the policy. It solved nothing and gave everyone something to complain about.

Many people felt the "don't ask/don't tell" policy violated the First Amendment. At least one federal judge had held the policy unconstitutional. And the policy was particularly ironic because the U.S. military's job was to uphold the Constitution, which protected free speech.

Opponents pointed out that the bigger problem was attempting to control behavior. Behavior problems between heterosexual males and females have caused a number of scandals in the modern military. Accepting homosexuals, opponents said, was akin to putting nude heterosexuals together in communal showers. In other words, the argument was that the soldiers wouldn't be able to control themselves.

There had been homosexuals in the military for generations, and often, others who served with them were aware of their sexual orientation, whether they were openly gay or not. But hate crimes ran rampant in the civilian world. No matter what the army's policies were, hate crimes would still occur there, too.

I now believed Thomas was murdered by General Andrews and Thomas being gay seemed the most likely reason.

Olivia answered my question. "I don't know if he was or not. Thomas was actually quite homophobic. Men hit on him all the time. It made him furious." She sounded thoughtful, as if she was trying the idea on to see whether it fit. "I always wondered about how fiercely he reacted. When guys hit on me, a simple no is usually sufficient."

As she spoke, Olivia sounded as if the idea of Thomas being gay had never occurred to her before. Could she have been that out of touch with him? Or was my idea way off base?

"What did Thomas do?"

"He'd blow a gasket. I saw it happen several times."

My theory sounded more and more likely to me as she talked. She seemed to be describing classic gay panic, an argument sometimes used to defend crimes resulting from over-reactive violence by the target of unwanted sexual advances. It was a self-defense excuse that relied on an irrational and unfounded assumption: that because one was gay, he or she would force sex on unwilling partners.

"Anything else?"

"Just one other thing," Olivia said slowly. "After Thomas died, several male friends came to the funeral that I thought were probably gay." She waited a couple of beats. "At the time, I wondered if he'd lived a secret life all those years, but I dismissed it."

I wanted to comfort her, but I didn't know exactly what to say. "You'll probably never know, and I'm not sure it matters," I told her.

"My parents need to believe in Thomas as the all-American hero, killed in the line of duty as an honorable soldier," she said. "I guess after I couldn't get President Benson to help me prosecute Andrews, I decided to just leave my parents with their illusions."

Now was the time to try out the rest of my theory, the one that made a little more sense than assuming General Andrews was a cold-blooded murderer.

"But what if Thomas was gay, and having an affair? He could have been court-martialed, couldn't he?" I pressed her, and her anger flared immediately.

CHAPTER SIXTY-NINE

Tampa, Florida
Sunday 3:30 p.m.
January 30, 2000

"I DON'T SEE WHAT that could possibly have to do with anything. Why don't you just leave it alone?" She snapped at me, and I was tempted to let it go. I guess the notion of Thomas leading a secret life was okay as a theory, but once I suggested an actual affair, that was too much for Olivia.

Something so painful might mean nothing now.

Or it might mean everything.

Jason had set me on this path for a reason, even if I didn't yet understand what that reason was.

"Don't you see, Olivia?" I asked her, as gently as I could. "If Thomas was having a homosexual affair, it might explain his death."

"How so?"

"Maybe Thomas approached someone else for sex and the general accidentally killed him. Maybe Thomas died because of General Andrews's gay panic."

She already believed Andrews had killed her brother. I handed her a plausible motive. My theory made sense, even if it could never be proved.

"How is this related to George's situation?" she finally asked me, deflated. "George isn't gay, or a soldier. Why would it matter to George if Andrews killed Thomas because of any hypothetical homosexual experiences?"

"It wouldn't matter to George, because he didn't kill Andrews. What we have to do is to find out who it did matter to," I explained patiently.

"Why would anyone kill Andrews over the situation with Thomas?"

Besides you? I thought.

"Or maybe Thomas being gay, if he was, had nothing to do with Andy having him killed," Olivia said.

"True. But then, why kill Thomas? We're back to that," I said.

CHAPTER SEVENTY

Tampa, Florida
Sunday 3:50 p.m.
January 30, 2000

BACK AT MINARET, ENSCONCED in my den, Olivia and I discussed every angle of the Andrews murder and George's case for a couple of hours. The list of suspects covered more than three pages of my journal.

Exhausted and dismayed, I asked, "Are we helping George with all of this, Olivia?"

"I think so. Drake stopped investigating once he arrested George. The number of possible killers Drake didn't rule out should be more than enough to establish reasonable doubt at the trial," she said.

"But what we want is to get the charges dismissed without an indictment." I deplored the whining tone of my voice.

"Drake, even though he was an Andrews supporter and is a staunch Democrat, won't want to take this to trial and lose," Olivia reminded me.

"But time is short. When are you going to try to convince Drake to look at other alternatives?"

Olivia looked down at her hands. I saw the lines crease her tiny brow. I recognized the frown that preceded bad news.

"Drake convened the grand jury today," she said.

Her words felt like a hard punch to my gut; they knocked the pluck right out of me.

Intellectually, I'd been expecting this. Drake couldn't be trusted. He had the advantage and he'd press it, hard.

But I guess I wasn't as prepared as I thought.

Olivia said, "Drake will move quickly. Tomorrow or the next day, he'll get his indictment."

I felt like a falling rocket, rushing down through the atmosphere too quickly, with no way to stop before I smashed into pieces that disintegrated before they hit the earth.

She touched my arm. "Willa, there's no middle ground. Either Drake drops the charges before that indictment is returned or George will be going to trial."

I knew George would never plead guilty. To anything.

I wanted to be alone, to curl up like one of Deborah Andrews's cats and sink into the oblivion of alcohol or sleep or both.

My breathing was ragged and I could find no words to speak.

Olivia touched me again. "Willa. You've got to pay attention. We've got work to do here and we're running out of time. Once Drake gets his indictment, he'll pick George up in a New York minute. There will be officers at your door in the next couple of days."

She opened her notepad and pretended to review her shorthand. Nothing at all passed between us for quite a while. Then, she began to tell me about her activities since we'd last met.

I missed the first few items. They just didn't seem important. All I could visualize was George behind bars.

"Willa!" Olivia fairly shouted at me and finally, I heard her. "I said, I interviewed Peter about George's gun."

My eyes blinked a few times and her words seemed to make it through the viscous soup of my brain.

"Peter brought George's gun to Minaret because he didn't have a locker at the gun club and he had no key to George's locker," Olivia read from her notes. "In a rush when he got back here, Peter quickly stashed the unloaded gun in the top drawer of the old sideboard in the foyer, meaning to return it to George the same day. George didn't come back to Minaret, for some reason, and Peter forgot about the gun. Then, with George being gone so much and Peter being busy when George was around, Peter just never thought about the gun when he had time to give it back."

The cold, icy edges of my heart thawed slightly. Peter was like one of the family. He'd told me himself that he was overwhelmed with remorse when George's gun turned out to be a murder weapon.

"Peter offered to quit right on the spot," Olivia said, "but, of course, George told him just to wait and see."

George had instructed Olivia not to share the information with the police and I agreed. For now. But we couldn't wait long. Drake was like a Doberman, snapping at our heels. He was ready to kill George, first with the indictment and then with the death penalty.

The thought began to fuel my anger. And anger was a good thing. Warmer, more welcome.

I'd been too civilized. Too soft. No more. I would handle this with George and Peter once we had George out of trouble. Without Peter's carelessness, none of this mess would be happening.

And I was through playing Nancy Drew. It was time for some bold moves and I was ready to make them. I hated Michael Drake in that moment. And the hatred moved me onward.

"Is there anything we can do about this grand jury?" I knew the basic answers already, but I needed a different perspective.

She considered my question, then said, "George could testify. He could tell them where he was the night of the murder and how his gun came to be a murder weapon."

Right. Just as I'd thought. Nothing we could do.

Olivia cleared her throat now, bringing my attention back to her. "One more thing."

"What?"

"Drake convened the grand jury today because he got the final finger print report on Andrews's study back from the lab."

The ice moved again inside my veins, freezing my heart and hardening my resolve. I waited.

She said, "George's fingerprints were in Andrews's study. Drake thinks George left them there the night of the murder."

CHAPTER SEVENTY-ONE

I HEARD THE HARD pounding on the front door of our flat from
the den where I sat in my sweatpants and T-shirt, working on
George's case. I'd already scrubbed off my makeup and my hair
stuck up in every direction. The dark circles under my eyes
resembled the color of eggplant and my sallow complexion could
have scared small children. Harry and Bess ran toward the door,
barking all the way.

A half-eaten apple was wedged in my mouth while I typed.
Glancing at the small clock on the computer screen, I noticed that
Olivia had been gone only about thirty minutes. She'd probably
forgotten something.

Removing the apple, I called out, "Just a second," loud
enough to be heard over their raucous noise as I maneuvered
myself around the desk and toward the front door in my bare
feet. A few more hard knocks followed, and more barking, so I

guessed Olivia couldn't hear me.

"Keep your pants on." I hurried the last few steps, stuck the apple back in my mouth, bent down to shush the dogs and grabbed their collars to keep them from running out, turned the lock, and quickly flung the door open.

My gaze, tilted down to meet Olivia's, instead fell upon the shiny silver monogrammed belt buckle lying flat on State Attorney Michael Drake's trim waist.

A sharp intake of my breath as I forced my gaze up to meet his eyes brought a cynical sneer to his thin lips.

There were two uniformed police officers standing behind him, guns drawn, pointing at Harry and Bess, who were still barking as if they'd seen the devil himself.

A perky female junior Assistant State Attorney stood at Drake's side, holding something in her long fingers, which were tipped with bright red acrylic nails.

"How did you get up here? This is private property," I told him, around the apple, trying to restrain two ninety-pound Labradors determined to get away from me.

"Good evening, Judge Carson," Drake said, with relish.

The officers were set in their three-point stance, guns pointed at my children, who were barking as if they'd like to eat the entire quartet. I was tempted to let them.

Bending over, I let go of their collars and put my leg across their chests, then my entire body in front of them.

"Back up! Back!"

I managed to get Harry and Bess to move enough to allow me to step through the threshold and close the door behind me, keeping the dogs inside and a solid oak barrier between them and the guns.

When I straightened up to my full height, removed the apple

from my mouth and wiped the drool off my chin, I stared Drake straight into his satisfied little eyes.

"What do you want?" I asked him, not making any attempt at small talk.

Drake nodded to the perky young female who handed me a folded piece of paper.

"Feel free to read the warrant before you let us in, if you'd like," he told me.

With nowhere else to stash it, I had to put the apple back in my mouth again while I opened the warrant, feeling like a complete fool.

While I read the document, Drake turned to the perky assistant and placed a too-familiar hand on her shoulder.

In an exaggeratedly friendly tone, he said, "See, I told you, Barbara. Judges are the same as everyone else. They relax at home in their sweatpants, just like you do."

He addressed me next. "Ms. Shading here has this idea that because you're a federal judge, you're somehow more special than mere mortals. She thinks you and your husband would never, ever do anything illegal." His tone took a harder edge. "But I assured her that you're not any different from the rest of us. Thank you for helping me prove it."

The young woman, Barbara Shading, looked down at her professional pumps. I recognized her now as a recent presenter at our local bar association lunch.

Drake's reputation for sleeping with his assistants suggested he was trying to make points with this one. But based on her presentation, she'd seemed wiser than other women Drake had impressed over the years.

Besides, I'd heard she had a high-powered boyfriend already.

If Drake sought to seduce Barbara Shading by demonstrating

his power over me, I took some pleasure in knowing that he'd underestimated her.

Ignoring Drake as best I could, I read the warrant. They were here to collect George's gun logs. The ones I'd removed from the gun club. So much for Curly's discretion.

I groaned when I saw that the warrant was signed by one of the Hillsborough County judges who disliked me because he'd been denied my seat on the federal bench.

The warrant gave Drake the right to enter the premises to search and seize the gun logs. But there was no way I was going to let that happen.

Once they came inside, they could seize anything else they found "in plain sight" during the course of the search. Because this was legal harassment, pure and simple, I knew they would stretch the plain sight concept as far as they could go. The flat would be a mess when they left and who knew what they'd take.

My thoughts flew to my journal and the Thomas Holmes file that Jason had given me. Both were lying in plain sight on my desk. Not to mention the pictures I'd taken at the Andrews house.

No way would I allow Drake a chance to seize any of it.

Besides that, Michael Drake had never been in my home and he wasn't coming in now, not if I could help it.

After stalling as long as possible by reviewing the warrant thoroughly, I sighed.

"Drake, your warrant seems valid. You're entitled to the logs. I'll give them to you," I told him, not friendly.

He sneered at me again. "We can come in and get them ourselves."

Drake knew as well as I did that this turf war was one I wouldn't want to lose. Nor did he want to lose face in front of Ms. Shading. We engaged in a silent battle of wills.

Harry and Bess continued barking on the other side of the door. Although the police officers had put their guns down, they remained willing to shoot, if need be. Harry and Bess just wanted to play; they wouldn't hurt Michael Drake, no matter how much I'd love them to chew him up and spit him into Hillsborough Bay.

But no one else knew that.

I let the barking speak for me for a few moments.

"I don't think my dogs would actually bite you or your colleagues," I left that thought hanging for a few seconds. "But I can't promise you that. And then what? One of you could get hurt. And these officers seem willing to shoot. You don't want me to sue you for harming my dogs, do you?"

Drake seemed temporarily nonplussed. Thwarted for the moment, he considered what to do next.

Ms. Shading interjected, "We don't really need to go inside if she gives us the logs, do we?"

Apparently still hoping to get her into bed, Drake wavered. It was the brief opening I needed.

"I'll bring the logs to you," I told him, as I turned the doorknob, quickly slipped back inside, and flipped the lock.

A few seconds later, Harry and Bess continued to bark their heads off playing this fabulous new game, and Drake began pounding on the door again.

"Judge Carson, open this door! Judge Carson, we have a warrant! Judge Carson!"

I hurried into the den, snagged the gun logs off the wing chair where I'd tossed them earlier, dropped the apple into the wastebasket and hot-footed it out to the door again. Between Drake's knuckles rapping forcefully enough to make the hardware rattle, I opened the door and slipped back out into the hallway, pulling the door closed behind me.

"Here," I said, breathing hard as I thrust the logs into Barbara Shading's hand. "This is what you came for."

Drake glared at me and I glared back.

I said, "Now get out."

He hadn't served the warrant before he'd entered onto our private island and walked, bold as brass, into Minaret. When he'd continued up the spiral staircase and made it all the way to my front door, there was no chance he'd thought he was standing on public property. He'd be in trouble over this whole incident, if I chose to make a big deal out of it.

I watched him consider his very limited options before Ms. Shading turned to him and suggested that they get back to work.

I'd embarrassed Michael Drake in front of two police officers and a woman subordinate. We both knew he wouldn't let me get away with that.

He glared at me with barely controlled hostility and said, "Until we meet again."

Until they'd exited the restaurant, I blocked our front door. The action made me feel brave, but really my legs were too rubbery to move.

CHAPTER SEVENTY-TWO

Tampa, Florida
Sunday 7:00 p.m.
January 30, 2000

MY RELATIONSHIP WITH SHELDON Warwick was purely superficial. He was one of Florida's two senators long before George and I moved here. He'd had to support my nomination as a U.S. District Court Judge and to steer me through the confirmation process, which he had done smoothly and expeditiously.

We traveled in the same social circles and had a number of common friends. His wife, Tory, is a casual friend of Kate's. And, of course, they ate at George's from time to time when they were in town.

Otherwise, I seldom had any dealings with either of the Warwicks. I didn't even know they had a son until David Andrews told me.

So I didn't know them well enough to arrive at their Bayshore mansion unannounced. They probably wouldn't have invited me in, had I attempted to do such a thing. But my visit from Drake, following so closely after Olivia's news that he'd convened the grand jury, made me realize I was running out of time. For expediency, and for no other reason, I called first.

I reached Tory, the Senator's wife. After she apologized about two dozen times for beaning me with the crystal when last we'd met, she said sure, I could come by for a drink before they went out to the symphony this evening.

When I arrived, the maid escorted me into the drawing room where Senator Warwick stood, holding a two-onion martini, dressed in his tuxedo, waiting for his wife to come downstairs. He offered me a drink and I declined. He didn't invite me to sit down, so we stood by the bar and talked like two guests at a cocktail party.

"Senator," I began, controlling myself by sheer force of will.

"Call me Sheldon."

"Sheldon," I started over, "I want to talk to you about General Andrews."

"That's not a subject I'm prepared to discuss with you, Willa. Not now or ever. Choose something else," he said. Firmly, but without belligerence. The voice of a man in control. One who gets his way. Always.

"Unfortunately, Sheldon," I emphasized his name, too, "short of throwing me out, and since your wife knows I'm here you'll have to explain that to her, you'll need to answer me." I was not going to be bullied by Sheldon Warwick. Not anymore. "Drake just left my house and he is presenting evidence to the grand jury. We don't have time to fool around."

To my way of thinking, Warwick had more to do with George's arrest than anyone else. He'd gotten George involved in some secret plan to thwart a sitting U.S. President. In some countries, that alone would have been treason.

"And if you throw me out, I'll find another, more public way to talk to you. Maybe you'd like to do this in front of my good friend, Frank Bennett?"

I was quite sure Sheldon Warwick would never want to respond to my questions about General Andrews on local television. But it wasn't an empty threat. I would involve the media now, if I had to. I had little to lose.

Warwick's eyes narrowed into small slits as he judged my sincerity.

"So, it'd be easier for both of us if we just did this now," I told him.

Warwick drained his martini glass and poured himself another, without changing the onions. I forged ahead. "I want to know why President Benson appointed General Andrews to the Supreme Court."

"Maybe he thought Andy was the best man for the job."

"We both know that's not true. It had something to do with Thomas Holmes." I waited a couple of beats, "And his murder." I watched Warwick closely. He'd played political poker for a long time. His facial expressions gave nothing away.

Instead of focusing on my use of the word murder instead of death, Warwick took a different tack.

"Who is Thomas Holmes?" he asked me.

I shook my head. "Won't work, Sheldon. You knew Thomas Holmes because he was at West Point with your son. You also know how and why he died and that President Benson wanted it all kept quiet."

Much of this I was just guessing. But I had to push somebody's hot buttons, and soon.

"My wife will be here any minute." He looked toward the staircase and called up, "Victoria, Willa's here and we've got to get going. Come on down, dear."

"Nice try, Senator. Now you've got about three minutes to tell me what I want to know. Because otherwise, when I leave here, I'm going straight to Frank Bennett, tell him what I know so far, and let him run with it."

He thought about it for a little while. We heard Tory yell down that she'd be with us shortly. He wanted to call my bluff, I knew. But what would he do?

CHAPTER SEVENTY-THREE

Tampa, Florida
Sunday 7:10 p.m.
January 30, 2000

FINALLY, WARWICK SEEMED RESIGNED to my tenacity. He answered my question quickly without fanfare.

"Thomas Holmes was a cocaine addict. He supplied Charles Benson with drugs and tried to lead him into addiction, which Charles was resisting, but Thomas kept pushing."

He drained the martini and plopped both onions into his mouth. "When the President told Thomas to leave Charles alone and never sell Charles drugs again, Thomas refused on both counts. President Benson discussed it with me and I suggested he ask General Andrews to arrange for Thomas's transfer overseas. Thomas could have been court marshaled for drug use, but that would have been devastating for Thomas."

"Not to mention the bad publicity for Charles and the President," I said.

He shrugged in response.

I hadn't known about the drugs. In fact, I'd thought Thomas was gay and he'd tried to seduce Charles. My theory was that Andrews had killed Thomas out of gay panic. So, I was wrong.

But the rest of the story was pretty much what I'd figured. "And how did Thomas Holmes get killed, Senator?"

"That really was just an accident. Olivia thinks Andrews killed her brother, but that is nonsense. Thomas was taking target practice in Korea, where he was posted, and he ended up fatally wounded. He was alone at the time, and no one found him until it was too late to save his life, unfortunately. There was a full inquiry into Thomas's death at the time. A stupid accident. That's all it was. I told Jason to give you the report. Didn't you read it?"

I should have known. Jason wouldn't have gone out on a limb to give me that file without his boss's permission.

The realization pissed me off. So I pushed his buttons a little harder.

"I don't believe you. I think Andrews killed Thomas or had him killed. And I think you and President Benson knew about it. Maybe you were both involved in it."

His eyes narrowed as he returned my steady gaze.

"I don't care what you think, actually," he said, as calmly as if he was discussing the weather. "And before you go to Frank Bennett, you might keep in mind that there are laws against such outrageous defamation, even of public figures."

Tory Warwick picked that moment to walk into the room.

"Hello, Willa dear," she said as she gave me a small southern hug and kissed her husband on the cheek.

"Tory, you've taken so long to get ready that we're going to have to go or they won't seat us," he said. "Willa, I'm sorry we have to rush. It's been a pleasure."

He called the maid to show me out and I was on the front

porch with the door closed behind me before I knew what happened.

I'd just been non-ceremonially dumped like a stinking, over-ripe melon.

CHAPTER SEVENTY-FOUR

SENSORY OVERLOAD. I NEEDED space, to drive with the wind rushing at me, blow the cobwebs out of my thinking and to take a really long walk along the sand. I wanted to hear the Gulf pounding in big waves, noise to silence my confusion and help me find the missing pieces of the puzzle that was General Andrews's murder.

My Detroit origins must have returned to me on a primordial level, because driving fast comforted me, always had. That didn't explain the hypnotic pleasure I got from experiencing pounding waves on the sand, which I assumed was even more basic to human evolution.

I left Warwick's house and sped over Gandy Boulevard and across the Gandy Bridge as quickly as I dared. This drive used to be fairly quick, but in the last few years Gandy has become almost as progress-choked as Dale Mabry. And progress means traffic.

It might have taken me less than fifteen minutes to make it onto I-275 south. I wasn't really checking the time. I opened up Greta's engine on the interstate and when I looked down at the speedometer again, it registered more than a hundred miles an hour. I backed off a little.

The freeway wasn't crowded and I could weave in and out of legally poky vehicles.

In no time, I was driving toward St. Pete Beach and Treasure Island.

The speed and the wind didn't blow away all the ugliness I'd heard today. It was dancing around in my head when I parked the car, put two quarters in the perpetually ravenous meter, picked up my journal and walked toward the water.

There were a lot of condos in this area, but I was mostly oblivious to the other people on the beach. It was a little cold for bathing suits, but there were a number of tourists lying on the sand, turning blue.

It amazed me when tourists simply did what they came here for, regardless of the weather. Vacations were like that, I guess. This was the time they intended to spend at the beach and, by God, they were going back with a tan, even if it meant enduring hypothermia to get it.

I don't remember what I thought about while I walked, but when I became conscious again, I found myself near Sunset Beach. One of Kate's bridge club friends has a condo here, and I was walking at the water's edge in front of her condo complex when she spotted me.

I wasn't surprised. It's nearly impossible to go anywhere without running into someone I know. We say Tampa is the big city with a small town feel, and this was one of the reasons why. People from bigger, more impersonal places like Miami, Chicago, or Los Angeles didn't understand this about Tampa, but it's true. Everyone knows everyone here.

It's foolhardy to assume one can behave badly without being noticed. The local joke was that if you wanted to have an affair, you had to go out of town.

Dottie was only about twenty feet ahead of me when I finally saw her. She came toward me, waving a handkerchief, calling my name. I couldn't focus on her small talk, but my "ums" didn't seem to deter her. Dottie could talk for thirty minutes to a wrong number. I'd seen her do it.

Finally, she took my monosyllabic responses for disinterest, but misinterpreted the cause. Dottie was what Kate called a little ditzy. It's true she was not a genius, and she was more involved in her bridge club than world events, but Dottie was a sweet soul and I often thought the world could have used more like her. There was not a mean or ugly bone in her body. If she wasn't so flighty, I'd have been able to tolerate her in larger doses, some other time.

"Are you and George getting along all right, dear?" she asked, putting her arm around my waist and walking along with me.

"What?"

"I said are you having trouble with George?"

"Oh. No." I must have sounded less than grateful for her sympathy.

She drew away from me slightly. "Aren't you upset about his arrest?"

"Not really."

And I wasn't, not at that moment anyway. I wasn't even thinking about George.

I was thinking about Andy, Deborah, Robbie, David and Donald, and how pathetic they were.

I was thinking about how horrible growing up in that household must have been and whether that would've been enough to make one of them kill their patriarch. How difficult to be homosexual, trying to serve in the old army. Maybe the new army, too. And how much harder General Andrews had probably made it.

I thought, too, about Olivia and Thomas and his parents and the sad tale of their lives. Thomas's premature death that had destroyed his parents' world. Whether Thomas's death had truly been accidental or not, he'd been shipped over to Korea because of his drug use and having crossed the son of the President, if Sheldon Warwick was telling me the truth. Would knowing any of that make their lives easier? I thought not.

I'd tried to fit the puzzle pieces of the Andrews murder together and figure out how and why he'd died. George, for the first time since the day Craig Hamilton was shot, was not uppermost in my mind. Before I caught myself, I almost asked Dottie: George who?

The shock made me realize that the whole sordid story needed a fresh eye. Maybe Dottie wasn't the best sounding board, but she couldn't have been any worse than the pounding surf.

I made up some hypothetical reason for bringing it up. And I didn't tell her the real names of the players. I tried to sound like I needed help with one of my cases.

But I'd long ago lost my objectivity. I felt I was looking too hard, and in the wrong places.

Dottie listened politely to my rambling account as we strolled together along the beach, the breaking waves a gentle accompaniment to our words. She nodded and glanced my way occasionally, but it seemed as if most of what I told her sailed right over her head.

Then she said something that, maybe because I was so close to it, just had never occurred to me before.

"So you mean the father was gay?"

I stopped in my tracks, but Dottie kept walking. After a few steps, she must have realized I wasn't next to her anymore. She turned around and looked at me. Clearly, she thought I'd lost my mind.

"What did you say?"

"I just asked if the father was gay. We get a lot of gays here on the beach you know. There's a large gay community in Tampa. They're all so nice to us. In fact, you know that general who was killed a few weeks ago? He was gay. He came here once with his boyfriend. He tried to disguise himself in some pretty crazy outfits," she smiled at the memory. "Of course, we didn't recognize him at the time. Not until later when we saw him on TV."

I reached out and grabbed Dottie by the arm, turning her to face me. "General Andrews came here with men?"

It was hard to believe anyone who knew anything about Tampa would assume he could flaunt an affair so close to home going unrecognized.

Of course, out of uniform, before he was in the national spotlight as the Supreme Court nominee, maybe he could have gotten away with it. Once.

"Not men, sweetie. A boyfriend. Cute one, too. My neighbor across the hall, he'd sometimes let men use his place."

"Dottie, what did the general's boyfriend look like?"

"Tall, dark and handsome, of course. Rugged looking. But he had this cute little widow's peak in the front," she gestured with her thumb and forefinger near her hairline. "You just never know," she said sweetly, patting my arm.

"How many times did they come here together?"

"Goodness, Willa, I don't know. I don't spy on my

neighbors." Spying on her neighbors was exactly what she did.

"Of course not. I thought you might have heard something, that's all."

"Why, Willa! I'm surprised at you. With all your troubles, I wouldn't think you'd want to be gossiping about someone else." She scolded me.

I remained silent and a few seconds later, she relented. "Well, maybe this will just take your mind off your troubles for today."

She patted my arm again. "Now let's see. I guess I saw them here together a couple of times or so since my neighbor went back to New York for the summer. He's a snowbird, you know. A decorator. He decorated one of the Kennedy's apartments. Actually, I think it was that sweet Caroline and her husband."

I thought I might scream if she didn't get to the point. At least, the point I was interested in. But I didn't want to frighten her or underline the level of my interest, so I simply asked, "Is that right?"

"Um hm. Anyway, I think the general first came to stay when Jeffrey left. And it seems to me that he was here, on and off, for most of the summer. In and out, I mean. Actually, I was about to report him to the condo board because we're not supposed to sublease. I wanted to sublease last year when I went on that Hong Kong cruise. The one I took Eunice on?" She was looking at me as if I was supposed to remember this.

"Sure," I said. "They wouldn't let you sublease."

Dottie didn't need much encouragement to rattle on forever about the vacation and never get back to the issue.

She cast a very annoyed glance at me for interrupting her again.

"Right. So, I was just a little peeved about the general being in Jeffrey's place and bringing that young man with him. And I was discussing it with Eunice. We were both about to complain. But that young guy, Jack? He was such a charmer. He talked us out of it. He said they weren't really subleasing from Jeffrey, they were just using his place occasionally. Of course, I didn't know the other man was the general then. I didn't recognize him. Eunice said she knew who he was all along, but I don't think she did. She's always claiming to know more than she does. You know people like that, don't you?"

I tried counting to ten while smiling and nodding.

I was so preoccupied by Dottie's message that General Andrews had at least one gay lover that I nearly missed Dottie's final bombshell.

But she hadn't recognized it as a bombshell. Dottie could have been hit on the head with an anvil without realizing what had happened.

I tuned in at the very end of the story.

"…So Eunice said maybe they'd had a fight or something. But I just didn't think that could be true because we would have known about it with them being right across the hall and all. There had to be some other reason they stopped coming here. Maybe just because Jeffrey got home."

"What?"

"Haven't you been listening?"

I rushed in so she wouldn't repeat the whole thing again. "Sure, but what does Jeffrey being home have to do with it?"

"Well, Jeffrey's place only has one bedroom. If he was back home for the winter, they wouldn't have had anywhere to sleep. So they must have had to use some other place. It didn't necessarily mean they broke up, does it?"

I missed the next few words because I was focused on General Andrews and his lover having terminated their relationship.

What caused that breakup?

Could the lover have killed him?

When I tuned back into Dottie's rambling, she was saying, "Eunice always jumps to conclusions like that. Just because she's divorced, she thinks everyone else has to be miserable. For instance, she can't stand the fact that my Arthur and I were so happy until he died. She believes I've been making that up."

Dottie was wounded by this idea, but I couldn't deal with one more story from her.

Besides, she'd already given me so much to think about that I had to go.

I pried myself from her grasp as quickly as I could. Dottie hadn't reported what she knew to the police or the media. I could only hope she'd remain in happy oblivion for a while longer.

CHAPTER SEVENTY-FIVE

Tampa, Florida
Sunday 9:30 p.m.
January 30, 2000

ALL THE WAY HOME, I kept the facts in my head. I noticed nothing as I raced toward my study. General Andrews was bisexual and he'd had an affair that ended just before his appointment. These facts, innocently supplied by Dottie, thrust a hole big enough to drive a truck through my theory of Thomas Holmes's death.

And supplied at least one other potential suspect.

The solitary nature of legal work usually suited me, but I'd rather have discussed the evidence and my conclusions with someone else. Unfortunately, there was no one I thought I could be completely honest with besides myself. George, Kate, Jason and Olivia were all inappropriate. Certainly, I wouldn't talk to Ben Hathaway or Michael Drake or, God forbid, CJ.

So I got to work. I sat at my desk with my journal and wrote down everything I'd learned today.

I had given each of the local suspects a page in my journal and listed what I learned about them as I learned it. I reviewed my notes now with the benefit of a strong drink to lubricate and elucidate my thinking.

First, I listed everyone whom I knew had a motive and opportunity to commit the murder, including some nut from one of the fringe groups opposed to General Andrews's nomination.

I still thought that would be the strongest and first choice simply because one of them had tried to kill Andrews on the final day of the confirmation hearings, but at the same time, I recognized that view as the wishful thinking it was.

My list included General Andrew's three children: Robbie, David and Donald. For completeness, I added Robbie's husband. In good conscience, I had to include the general's wife, Deborah, although I didn't really think she'd shot him. I also had to include Olivia because the same motives that made her want to defend Andrews's killer gave her a strong reason to kill Andrews herself. And I'd never been able to rule her out.

Lovers Andrews had had over the years should have been at the top of the list, but I didn't know who they were. Or at least, if I knew them personally, I couldn't identify them. I wrote Lovers? And more specifically, I wrote jilted lovers?

President Benson, Senator Warwick, his wife Tory and, to show myself how scrupulously fair I was, Jason Austin, were all included. I wouldn't explore whether I would let Jason be tried for murder if it meant I could have my husband back. The potential losses there were just more than I was willing to examine.

I refused to write George's name down at all.

But I had to accept, in my less impaired moments, that State Attorney Drake had enough evidence to authorize George's arrest and was working furiously toward an indictment. I wrote faster, as if mere speed would propel me to victory over Drake's ambition.

Next, I listed all the motives and opportunities for each of the suspects. Enough reasonable doubt to convince Drake not to indict George was all I needed. After that, someone else could find the killer. All I wanted to do was to save our lives as we knew them. Which meant George had to be exonerated. Fully.

I made my lists, refilled my drink twice, and got lost in the minutiae of the investigation thus far. I read the report of Thomas Holmes's accident again, and the death certificate. There was no mention of drugs. If a toxicology screen had been done, it wasn't mentioned here. Had he stopped using before he died? Or was he high at the time?

There were three other issues that I still had to resolve. How did George's gun get to the crime scene and where did that gray jacket fiber found on the bullet that killed Andrews come from? And where the hell was George when all this was happening, anyway?

Quite honestly, I was more than a little looped when I tugged at some memory in the back of my brain and it started to work its way out. The gin had relaxed me enough that I knew there was something stored on the hard drive of my brain that could help me. I just couldn't quite get at it.

When I'd finished, I was so exhausted, and it was so late, that I collapsed on my bed. Sleep claimed me in less than five minutes.

While I slept, my dreams were full of cats, beach houses, crashing waves, military uniforms, young boys and good-looking men.

Okay. That last may have been a reflection on the emptiness of my bed.

I tossed and turned and woke up several times with heart palpitations, sweating. What was my subconscious mind trying to tell me? I promised myself I'd think about it in the morning as I turned over and fell back into a deep sleep. I woke up with a jerk at three o'clock in the morning.

My head ached, my eyes were puffy, and my tongue felt like a furry animal had lain on it. But there would be no more sleep.

Stepping over a comatose Harry and Bess, I padded out to the kitchen in my yellow nightshirt. It was more than a little indecent, even thought it covered my arms and everything else to just above the knee. It was cotton, just not very thick cotton. Not that it mattered. Harry and Bess were oblivious and there wasn't anyone else here to appreciate the view.

While I scalded the milk, the kitchen filled with that heavenly aroma only fresh brewed coffee produces. It's too bad they haven't figured out how to get that smell into television commercials. Watching someone else supposedly enjoying the aroma isn't nearly as powerful as actually experiencing it. And it's no wonder a Saudi Arabian woman is allowed to divorce her husband if he refuses to provide coffee. That should be the law in all civilized countries.

The coffee and the milk finished about the same time. I pulled down a large mug that George had given me a couple of years ago, poured the milk through a strainer and then added coffee to create the right color. I poured four ibuprofen tablets into my palm and swallowed them without water. Acetaminophen worked better for headaches, but with the amount I drink, my liver can't take the risk.

The flat was chilly. I'd left the windows open and allowed the night air to come in. I indulged myself further with a small fire in the den's gas log fireplace.

Then I selected quiet piano nocturnes and turned on the stereo with the volume down, to avoid waking Harry and Bess. I wasn't worried about them having bags under their eyes or anything; I sought total peace and quiet. Unlike me, they are bundles of energy when they wake up. Of course, I didn't usually wake them at this hour, so who knew?

During fitful sleep, I had worked around a scenario that answered all the questions surrounding Andrews's murder, but two very big pieces of the puzzle were wrong.

I began to pace and talk to myself, trying to resolve the problems, as I'd done countless times before.

"George's fingerprints were found in Andrews's den. He had been there. But when? The night Andrews died? Or some other time?"

Then, I answered, "Without an alibi for the time of the murder, Drake could easily convince a jury that George was there the night Andrews died. You know juries. You work with them every day. They will believe hard evidence, like fingerprints and murder weapons and jacket fibers. Many a defendant has been convicted on less."

Turn. Sip. Walk.

"There must have been other fingerprints in Andrews's den, too. You need to see that fingerprint report."

Answer: "It's too early in the morning to call Ben Hathaway to get it. Besides, the mere presence of fingerprints by the other suspects won't exonerate George if he won't explain when and why he was there."

I paced a while longer, but I got nowhere so turned to the second problem.

"How did George's gun become a murder weapon? George loaned the gun to Peter, who brought it home from the gun club. How did the killer steal the gun from where Peter put it in Aunt Minnie's sideboard?"

Think it through, think it through.

"George loaned the gun to Peter a week before the murder. Peter put the gun in the sideboard two days before and forgot about it. He didn't check the gun at any time after that and then it turned up at the scene of the murder."

Turn. Sip. Walk.

"Right. So the question is, in those two days, who had access to the gun?"

The answer included George, me, and Peter. It also included everyone who worked at the restaurant and everyone who'd been a guest at the restaurant or visited us at home in that time frame.

"But most of those people had no motive to kill Andrews," I reminded myself aloud.

So I returned to all the names on my list of people who had been in the restaurant in those two days and had at least one motive to kill Andrews.

Everyone on the list had been in the restaurant the night Andrews was killed.

Except Olivia. Or was she there, too, and I just hadn't noticed because I didn't care about her then?

"Which one of the suspects with motive and opportunity had taken the gun? It could have been taken the very night of the murder," I reminded myself.

I went over each suspect carefully; none could be easily eliminated.

Exhausted from lack of sleep and pacing, I returned to the chair, allowed my heavy eyelids to close and visualized everyone at the restaurant that night. It was easy to do. The night was indelibly imprinted on my brain forever, even if the purple lump on my forehead had disappeared.

I imagined the guests as they sat at tables in George's dining room; I recreated the argument between the Warwicks and Andy;

saw Tory Warwick hurling the glass toward me and even felt its solid weight against my forehead. I raised my hand to the place where the lump had come up the next day. All traces gone.

What a shame internal wounds don't heal as quickly as visible ones.

Okay. Just for starters, I considered that the gun was taken sometime before the night Andrews died. Then, the possibilities were endless and I got nowhere.

So, consider whether someone in the room took it that very night. I looked at each of them closely in my mind's eye.

What were they wearing?

The gun was too big to conceal in a pants pocket, but it could have been tucked into a man's waistband or jacket pocket.

I visualized each of the men who were on the suspect list and present that night. All the men were wearing jackets. No one ever came to George's without a jacket. Any one of them could have slipped the gun into his pocket. No help there.

Or it could have easily been slipped into a handbag. Which one of the women had a handbag big enough to hold a .38 caliber revolver?

I was so startled when it hit me that I nearly spilled my coffee.

Of course! Now I remembered it.

One of those large, open feedbag types. The kind you could fit the kitchen sink in.

But, had I seen it that night? Did she have it then?

Despite what I had promised Ben Hathaway when he gave me the police file, I knew that nothing but a confession would do. Considering my previous failures with confessions, I should have learned my lesson. Hubris, thy name is lack of sleep. But how could I make her confess?

Mere suspicion was not evidence. I needed a solid plan.

And more information.

And some other suspects needed to be ruled out first, so that there was only one possible killer who wouldn't be George.

Michael Drake would insist on a solid case he could prove before he'd let George go, because it looked like Drake already had a winner.

I moved to the computer. I waited for the site to load. I'd read the Ask Dr. Andrews column daily, so I'd gotten a feel for Robbie's style. Her answers were pretty canned as well as increasingly harsh.

The usual questions on the usual topics comprised today's column. There were three letters about workplace issues involving sexual misconduct of one kind or another. The child-rearing queries were about sexual abuse. And the lovelorn letters were about sexual dysfunction.

Mine was the only letter of the day that wasn't about sex, but Robbie's answer was:

Research is conclusive. While even a bad marriage is good for a man, a bad marriage causes negative health effects and can literally kill the wife. If you stay with this man, you can expect further heartache.

You can't have a sexual relationship with a man who is in jail. If he's convicted, divorce him or resign yourself to infidelity.

Interesting take on the whole thing, Robbie. Kate says that we all teach what we need to learn. Maybe Robbie should take her own advice.

Robbie had sex on her mind.

Nor did she consider that Faithful Wife's fictitious husband really was innocent.

What was that about? Guilty conscience?

I hoped so.

I signed off and went back to my journal.

After a couple of hours of playing with one idea and then another, I thought I had it figured out. One step at a time, I'd get to the point where I could expose the killer.

But I needed to line up my evidence and nail it down.

Otherwise, Drake would never believe me.

CHAPTER SEVENTY-SIX

Tampa, Florida
Monday 6:30 a.m.
January 31, 2000

I ONLY HAD TO park outside Sheldon Warwick's house for about half an hour before he backed out of his driveway. I followed him to The Old Meeting house on Howard Avenue, in the district some clever marketer with a sense of humor had now dubbed "SoHo," meaning "South Howard."

I opened the door and walked through into history. On the left was the long counter. It was green Formica trimmed in chrome. Stools at the counter were round green vinyl, also trimmed in chrome. The waitress stood poised between the straw dispensers, taking orders for eggs over easy, country ham, and biscuits made with lard. Grits on the side. Sausage gravy smothered everything.

My mouth watered at the greasy smells as I took a seat at the counter and glanced above the open window to the kitchen for the blue plates that were displayed on the wall. Each plate reflected black handwriting that told diners what the supper special was for every day of the week. On Mondays, the special was bacon, lettuce and tomato sandwiches on white toast, cream of tomato soup, and a vanilla malt.

To say the Old Meeting House was reasonably priced was like saying it snows in North Dakota. People with old money in Tampa rarely spend it.

Warwick approached his buddies dressed for politickin'. He wore an old pair of khaki pants that looked like they'd need a patch any day now. The required beat-up deck shoes, sans socks, and a cloth belt with small fish on it that was ragged around the edges finished his bottom half. His golf shirt was a faded navy blue with a few speckles of paint on it. He'd probably snatched these clothes from his gardener.

Glancing over my shoulder, I saw Warwick was surrounded by several Tampa movers and shakers, all of whom were dressed exactly as unfashionably as he was, but they wore their own clothes. They dressed to be comfortable and because they weren't trying to impress anyone.

The difference between Sheldon Warwick and his companions was that they were all genuine and he didn't have a genuine bone in his body.

I skipped the lard, ordered scrambled eggs and coffee.

Warwick's crowd all recognized me, but theirs was not a gathering where women would be welcome or accepted. They didn't want to be rude, so they just acted like they hadn't seen me. Once acknowledged, the southern gentlemen's code of honor would have required them to include me. And be polite about it.

Seated alone at the counter, the waitress felt obligated to chat me up. We talked about the ice cream special of the day and the balmy weather. Warwick and his cronies laughed behind me while I savored the tastes of childhood.

After I'd finished my eggs, the tone of the conversation behind me sounded like Warwick was about to depart. I left a ten-dollar bill on the counter and followed him out to the parking lot where he tried to enter his fifteen-year-old Volvo. Another sign of old money around here was to buy cars as if they were priced per pound and never replace them while they still moved.

"Sheldon," I called to him over the noise of the traffic on South Howard.

He turned around.

"Oh, Willa. How nice to see you." He smiled for the crowds, or at least any crowds he thought might be looking at this hour. He held out his hand and took mine for the same reason. There was no warmth there.

"I didn't have the impression you'd be glad to see me again so soon after our last chat," I told him.

"You exaggerate, Willa. You always have." He turned to unlock his car door. "I do need to be going, though. Have a good day."

Before he could get seated inside the car, I moved closer to him and took off my sunglasses so that he could see the dark circles under my eyes as well as the seriousness of my intentions.

"Sheldon, I'm sure you know I'm not going to let this rest. Olivia Holmes told me that you have no alibi for the time of the Andrews murder."

Sheldon removed his sunglasses, too, five hundred dollar ones. I guess when he got dressed for his biscuits with the boys he must have neglected to borrow his gardener's old aviators.

"Look, Willa, I've indulged you because you're Jason's sister. But don't push your luck. I had no reason to kill Andy. As for my alibi, I don't need one. But I do have an appointment."

He sat down heavily in the car's worn leather seats. I grabbed the door handle, refusing to let him pull it closed.

His eyes were completely hidden by the sunglasses, but his tone dripped condescension. "If you're looking for a plausible alternative to George as murderer, you might consider your lawyer. Given her irrational hatred of Andrews, she had more motive to kill him than I did."

"You're too power-hungry," I said, trying out one of my late night theories, while holding onto the door handle and my temper. "Andrews was making you look bad, ruining your hearings, disrespecting you before your constituents. He embarrassed you, exposed your lack of political clout for the whole world to see. Men have killed for less, Sheldon."

He pulled the door out of my hand and slammed it, started the engine and backed out of the parking space, leaving me standing there holding nothing but the air and a fingernail broken down below the quick.

But I had him running, I consoled myself as I stuck my throbbing finger in my mouth.

I moved to the next step.

CHAPTER SEVENTY-SEVEN

Tampa, Florida
Monday 7:30 a.m.
January 31, 2000

JASON ENTERED THE PRIVATE room I'd reserved at the Tampa Club high atop the Barnett Bank building downtown. The club was mostly deserted and I figured there would be few opportunities to be interrupted.

While we gazed out over the southeast Tampa skyline, the Florida Aquarium, St. Pete Times Forum hockey arena, and Ybor City in the background, Jason ordered an egg white omelet and wheat toast. We talked family matters for a while.

It was pleasant to sit and talk with Jason about ordinary things. We hadn't had much contact in the past twelve years. He'd been living in Washington, D.C., but he was often out of the country on business for Senator Warwick or helping him campaign in election years.

Jason wanted to be Secretary of State some day. He had high political aspirations and he planned to run for Senator Warwick's seat when the senator retired.

I would have been proud to have Jason in the senate, but it was a waste of his considerable talent. I've made plain my view of the political process and everyone involved in it.

Time to get to the point. "I took your advice and investigated Thomas Holmes' death."

"I know. Sheldon told me."

I smiled. "What did he say about our interviews?"

Jason grinned, too. "That you are an impossible woman and it's too bad you already have a lifetime appointment. He said he can't get rid of you, but he won't support you for advancement to the Court of Appeals, either." Jason took a sip of his bourbon and water. "Sorry."

"Actually, unlike the rest of you, I don't have any aspirations to higher office. So it's not much of a hardship," I told him, even though losing the chance did sting me, a little. "Besides, if what I think is true, Senator Warwick won't be in a position to make a difference to my career if and when I change my mind about that."

He looked troubled, now.

It was always whose ox was getting gored, wasn't it?

Jason wanted Warwick to stay in the senate for another term and then retire, endorsing Jason to replace him.

Jason has had his life planned out in concrete progressive steps since he was eight years old. He wouldn't let anything upset the applecart at this stage of his career. He'd worked too long and too hard and kissed too many asses to get where he was.

Wasn't he just a little too satisfied to have George accused of murder?

Not that he wanted or expected George to be convicted.

But after George was arrested and the police stopped investigating, Jason as well as his boss gained a little more breathing space.

"So, what did you find out that upset Sheldon?" Jason still sounded like there wasn't any possible way that I could be a problem for the powerful Senator Warwick.

Maybe that's what prompted me to shake him up a little. My inner brat, as Kate calls it.

"I found out that President Benson asked General Andrews to get Thomas Holmes out of Charles Benson's life and shut him up. Permanently. And Sheldon Warwick not only knew about that, he arranged it." I said this as if it were a fact.

Judges don't actually lie.

Maybe I stretched the evidence a little, but I might be able to prove it, if and when the time came.

Jason almost choked on the ice that he'd just started to chew. The Heimlich maneuver might have been required, but for the fortunate thing that ice melts. Jason choked and coughed and his eyes watered as I sat and watched, making no effort to assist him.

Eventually, once he could talk again, he said, "Willa, you are barking up the wrong tree there."

"Maybe you better straighten me out, then, because unless I get some different information, this is the story I'm taking to Frank Bennett. I've only recently discovered what a powerful thing public opinion is," I said sweetly.

Jason is a tough political operator and I counted on that to inspire him to help me. Especially now that his career plans were at stake, too. He shook his head, amazed at my foolish conclusions.

He said, "I didn't mean to suggest that Thomas Holmes was murdered. His death really was an accident, just as the army said. Didn't you read the file?"

"Then why steer me in his direction?"

"Don't you believe his death was an accident?"

"No," I said. "But answer my question."

He gaped at me as if I were a few bricks short of a full load.

"You wanted to know why President Benson nominated Andrews to the Supreme Court. Andrews was no more qualified for that job than you are," he said, as if everyone with an IQ above sixty would have figured that out by now.

"Thanks."

He looked a little chagrinned. "You know what I mean. But Andrews hadn't wanted to retire from the army. The army was all he knew and he loved it. He'd have stayed forever."

Why Andrews retired? The public story was that he'd served his time and wanted to move on to other projects.

"Then why didn't he? Stay forever?"

"Because they made him go." Jason took a deep breath and got up and refilled his water from the serving cart. He stood with his back to me and drank a few sips of it before he walked back to the table.

He put the glass down and jammed his hands into the pockets of his khakis, leaned his butt on the edge of the chair and stuck his legs out straight in front of him. Stalling. I waited. It wasn't my turn. He took another sip of his drink.

"You've already figured out that Andrews was at least bisexual?" he asked.

So he gave me some credit, at least. I nodded.

He took another drink. At this rate, he'd be pie-eyed before he finished. "Sexual orientation, as long as you keep it private, is irrelevant in most circles, but in the army? Well, you know what the status of the world was there."

I sipped water. Slowly. Kept full attention on the facts. "Yes, Jason. Everybody knows. Andrews knew, too."

"Sure he did. Look, Andrews was a sorry S.O.B. Just being

bisexual wouldn't have been a big problem if he'd kept it to himself. But he couldn't keep it private. He was a general, nearly the top ranking army officer. Yet, he made sexual advances to junior army personnel."

An involuntary whistle escaped my lips. The army was, in many ways, just like any big corporation where bad apples, including sexual miscreants, could rise to the top, no matter how conscientious the organization was to try to prevent that from happening. Bad apples advanced in the corporate ranks, especially if they had powerful friends, as Andrews had. The army would have had the same vulnerability as Andrews was coming up, even though things had changed somewhat in recent years.

Still, even if Andrews was guilty of sexual misconduct, that couldn't be the whole reason he was forced to retire.

I said, "You're not trying to tell me that in an organization as large as the U.S. military, there aren't at least a few unauthorized sexual activities going on, are you?"

Jason wanted me to understand this now. "Even if his partners were willing, Andrews was so senior and had so much rank that you'd never know for sure." He took a deep breath and revealed the rest. "Some of his partners weren't consenting. At least, that's what several men said when they filed sexual harassment complaints against him."

"So the complaints were from men, not women?"

When I'd heard about the sexual harassment complaints the first time, I'd assumed Andrews's subordinate females filed them. Based on my own experience, I knew Andrews was a misogynist. It seemed natural that he'd be looking for sex in all the wrong places. I'd simply assumed it was heterosexual contact he'd been seeking.

Jason nodded. "There were both kinds. One particularly nasty event involving a man came to Warwick's attention. Sheldon went to President Benson and they told Andrews he had to retire. If complaints against him were revealed, they'd have ruined his career anyway. Andrews had no choice but to retire."

"Except?"

He gave me a look that said he didn't want to keep talking. But he did. "Except Andrews refused to go quietly."

"And?" I prompted again.

Jason gave me a look of resignation. "Andrews told Sheldon and the President that he would only retire if President Benson agreed to nominate him to the Supreme Court when the next vacancy came up."

"What?" I was, for the first time during this tale, actually shocked. "You have got to be kidding."

Now, I paced around the room, the steam fairly rising from my pounding heart to my flushed face.

"The President sold the most important job in the country to a man he believed was guilty of reprehensible conduct?"

"Calm down," Jason said, in the patronizing way that makes me want to throw a pie in his face. "President Benson said no and Sheldon said he wouldn't support Andrews either."

I felt a little better, but I remained standing and pacing and I could feel my blood boil.

For a couple of seconds.

Until he added: "And that's when Andrews told them both that if they didn't make sure he got on the Court, he would make sure the world knew about Charles Benson's drug use and how they'd all handled Thomas Holmes. Because it touched Sheldon personally, too. His son, Shelley, had been a part of that crowd."

Now, the lid blew off my composure completely.

"So we can add blackmail to Andrews's list of accomplishments now?" I shouted. "Warwick and Benson agreed to put that despicable character on our highest court for the rest of his life?"

I couldn't believe my ears. If I hadn't had such a low opinion of politics and politicians in the first place, this piece of information alone would have been enough to push me over the edge. I paced back and forth, berating Jason and his boss and the president and the system and on and on and on.

Then we heard a knock at the door to the private room, which preceded the entrance of an apologetic manager. "Is anything wrong, Judge Carson? Shall we call the police?"

The interruption threw cold water on my rage and embarrassed me into reassurance. He seemed mollified, but looked back to confirm no act of violence was imminent before he closed the door softly on his way out.

A few gulps of cold water and some time for thinking things through led me finally to ask Jason, "Would anyone care? Now? To find out that Charles Benson used drugs as a kid? I mean, really, lots of teenage kids experiment with drugs."

Jason, who had simply been waiting for me to vent, his gaze turned toward the far distances he could see from forty-two stories up, looked me directly in the eye now. "It wasn't just experimenting. Charles was a heavy user. He went into rehab after this. Besides that, Charles bought and furnished drugs to others. In the White House. That in itself is about ten federal crimes."

"So the President's kid was not just rebelling like other kids, maybe. Still, that was a long time ago."

"True," he said. "But the President, the man supposed to enforce the law of the land, knew his son and his son's friends were guilty of committing federal crimes in the White House. Benson covered it up. And that cover-up put Thomas Holmes in a place where he got killed."

I nodded now, seeing the larger scope of the problem.

President Benson, himself, was guilty of the cover-up. He covered up the drug use and Thomas Holmes's transfer, which led to Holmes's death.

In the court of public opinion, at least, Benson would be crucified. And he could have been prosecuted.

Sheldon Warwick and General Andrews were just as guilty. While the younger men might have been treated gently at the time, the adults had national responsibilities and obligations to enforce the law.

When they forced Andrews to retire, Warwick and Benson hadn't really had to do anything except make a promise that could, after all, turn out to be an empty one.

Since no Supreme Court vacancy had occurred in more than ten years, it was just as likely that Benson's term would have ended with no appointment made. Andrews's conditions would have been met but he would not have been named to the court.

Benson and Warwick had wanted Andrews to retire quietly and go away. By making the deal, Andrews's retirement would be voluntary and another messy military sex scandal avoided.

Not to mention that both Benson and Warwick would avoid criminal prosecution, assuming the statute of limitations on the cover-up hadn't expired.

Forcing control of my anger, I said, "Okay. I get your point."

Still, there were missing pieces to this puzzle, too. "What if Benson and Warwick had refused? How did Andrews coerce them?"

Jason ignored me.

"Seriously. I gather Andrews's threats were not hollow. Andrews would have had to prove the blackmail? With Thomas Holmes dead, how would Andrews prove Benson and Warwick were complicit without disclosing his own participation? Andrews had as much at stake, didn't he?"

Jason looked down at his hands and didn't answer me immediately. Then he sighed, as if he'd accepted that the only way to get me off this train of inquisition was to tell me the whole sordid story.

"Andrews had surveillance tapes of Charles Benson and Thomas Holmes using cocaine at the White House together. Andrews told Warwick and Benson that he destroyed the tapes when the incident first occurred. But he'd kept them. And he threatened to release the tapes to the press if Benson refused his requested nomination."

One picture, as they say, was worth a thousand words; incriminating video was apparently worth a Supreme Court appointment.

"What did Benson do?"

"What choice did he have? Charles has apparently straightened his life around. He's married now. Got a couple of kids. Shelly Warwick, too, is doing well. Fathers will do things to protect their kids that they'd never do for themselves."

My ears warmed again. Did he think he could sell me that altruistic crap? "And of course, going along with Andrews saved Benson and Warwick's own asses."

He ignored me. "Benson said he'd think about it, but Warwick and Andrews both knew Benson would appoint Andrews, and Warwick would have to do his part, too. If the opportunity came up," Jason finished, his own weariness now obvious.

As much as Jason had high ambitions, I hoped he was appalled at the pure self-preservation in which these corrupt politicians had engaged. At least, I hoped he was a fraction as appalled as I was.

I wrapped up the loose ends. "So you were all hoping there wouldn't be another court vacancy before Benson's term finished out next year and you'd never need to pay the piper. If Benson's term ended without a vacancy, Benson would leave office and Rumpelstiltskin wouldn't get the Kings' first born sons."

"But then Chief Judge Miller announced his retirement and there you have it." Jason drained his glass and sat there, both palms up, as if there had never been a more obvious conclusion.

Now I knew why Andrews had been appointed to the Supreme Court and I felt certain that appointment was related to his death, even though I still believed he would never have been confirmed.

But I could prove none of it.

Yet.

The nomination was too controversial from the start and after President Benson's midnight emissary told the Democratic senators they could vote against Andrews without being disloyal to the chief, there had been very little chance that Andrews would be confirmed.

All of which didn't answer the big question.

"Jason, we both know George didn't kill Andrews," I started, but Jason interrupted me and stood up to leave.

"I'd like to help you, Willa, I really would. You know I love George as much as everyone else does. I hope he didn't kill Andrews. But if he didn't, then I don't know who did."

"If you knew, would you tell me?"

"I guess that would depend on who did it." Jason was nothing if not honest.

As much as his answer pissed me off, it also made me believe him. Go figure.

Jason headed toward the door. When he placed his hand on the doorknob, I called his attention back.

I had one last thing I wanted to know.

"Where were you the night Andrews was killed?"

He shook his head slowly, from side to side, beyond the point of being surprised by anything I had to say, I guessed.

"I can't tell you that."

I cajoled and argued and threatened for another fifteen minutes before he simply walked out and I was forced to give it up.

CHAPTER SEVENTY-EIGHT

Tampa, Florida
Monday 9:10 a.m.
January 31, 2000

I HAD TO RETURN to my day job, but the missing pieces of the Andrews murder still careened around in my head like a set of billiard balls on the opening break. By sheer force of will, I could concentrate on something else, but not for long.

The jurors had arrived and the litigants were set up in the courtroom. I asked my Court Security Officer to go in and tell them they could take a short coffee break and I'd be ready to begin at nine-thirty. No one dared to question a federal court judge's trial schedule. But I felt guilty anyway.

There was no way I could reschedule the status conferences for three hundred asbestos cases, so I did the first group of ten, simply agreeing to the previous scheduling order and then sending the lawyers away. Asbestos cases rarely went to trial anyway. The important thing for me was to be sure I got rid of these quickly and then avoided getting assigned to any more.

Olivia had left several messages at my office, each with a more demanding tone. The last one said she'd meet me at three. I'd tried to reach her several times previously, but she'd not answered her cell or returned my calls. Now, I had no choice but to ignore her calls as I struggled to get a handle on my workload.

I glanced at the rest of my pink message slips, quickly reviewed my notes from the last trial day, slipped into my robe and walked slowly into the courtroom. I hoped they thought I made a stately entrance and the day would go smoothly, but that was too much to ask for.

During the Newton trial, paying attention had become a real struggle. I had so many things to do and so little time to accomplish them. The testimony had been long and tedious. There were few evidentiary arguments I had to rule on. Even the jury was bored.

Why did people still go to law school? If every prospective student was required to sit through a month-long trial before they took the LSAT, law school admissions would be down at least fifty percent. The rest of the applicants were just masochists.

I worked furiously through the break, signing orders, responding to telephone calls and e-mail. I gulped down my tuna sandwich and returned to the courtroom, head down, without even replacing my lipstick.

Looking up from my seat on the bench, I saw that the gallery was full of reporters again. If the CJ walked in, he'd blow a gasket. I recognized at least two from each newspaper as well as the local and network news stations. And I saw Frank Bennett in the back. Whatever was expected, it was big news if Frank was here to cover it personally.

Before we brought the jury back, I called counsel to the bench.

"What's up?" I asked them both simultaneously, covering up

my microphone with my hand so the question and answer wouldn't be broadcast at six and eleven.

"I have no idea, Judge," Newton said. I believed him. We were still in the middle of the plaintiff's case.

I turned to Tremain. "Well?"

"Me neither." He looked me right in the eye. I wished I was a better judge of liars. I was pretty sure Tremain's was a whopper, but aside from public flogging, I had no idea how to get the truth out of him.

"In my chambers. Both of you. Alone." I looked up and said, "The court will stand in recess for ten minutes."

Both lawyers followed me back, leaving the goslings twittering around at the defense table. I signaled the court reporter to remain in the courtroom.

Our conversation would be off the record.

CHAPTER SEVENTY-NINE

Tampa, Florida
Monday 12:00 p.m.
January 31, 2000

WHEN WE WERE SEATED, each of the lawyers in one of the bilious green client chairs, I moved aside a tower of files that had appeared in the center of my desk in the last ten minutes and turned to face them. "I know you've got something up your sleeve here. I don't know what it is, and I'm not continuing this trial until I find out."

They kept looking at me, neither one of them volunteering so much as a chagrinned expression. I ran my hand through my hair and felt it move into a style resembling an angry rooster.

"So, you can tell me now, or you can all go home."

Tremain thought it over. Newton looked merely curious. I'd entered a gag order in the case, and besides, if Tremain had already spilled the beans to the press they wouldn't be here *en masse* to find out what the story was.

So I guessed Tremain had only announced that there'd be big

news today. He'd have to send the reporters home, in which case they might not come back, or he'd have to tell me what he had planned and risk ruining his show.

I began to flip through the tower of new files, throwing each one on the floor beside my predecessor's throne as I saw what kind of case it was. Asbestos. *Splat.* Asbestos. *Splat.* Asbestos. *Splat.*

As the files landed on top of one another, my annoyance at the CJ grew. If he'd walked in at that moment, I might actually have thrown one of the files at his toady little head.

Meanwhile, the two lawyers played chicken with each other, neither one being willing to blink first. I'd made it all the way through the tower of files before Tremain said, "Mr. Newton plans to present the Court with a motion this afternoon for an injunction preventing us from publishing his tennis club membership list."

"Why do you want to use his tennis club list?" I asked, standing up to retrieve another stack of files on the left side of my desk and beginning to flip through those and drop them on the floor.

"Because I have a witness, a member of the club, who will testify that the club is all-gay," Tremain told me.

I glanced at Newton, who seemed prepared to deny the claim, but he surprised me slightly when he took a different tact. "The names of the people on that list include men who are not publicly out, Judge. These matters are of the most sensitive nature. Only a first rate scandal rag like this defendant would ever consider publishing such a thing."

I rubbed the throbbing that had started between my eyes again, reminding me of the list of things I still had to do for George. I didn't have the mental acuity to deal with this issue today. I doubted I ever would.

I turned to Tremain, "Putting aside for the moment how you got the list if it's so top secret, why is it relevant to this trial?"

Tremain looked at me as if I was the last idiot on earth. "Because Mr. Newton's name is on it, your honor. It's an all-gay club and he's a long-term member. The list establishes our truth defense."

I thought about it, and it seemed he was right. At least, the list was evidence of the truth of the matter, clearly relevant. The list would provide Tremain with the facts he needed to get the case to the jury.

"What's your response to that?" I asked Newton.

Now he was the one who seemed uncomfortable. "Judge, the prejudice of this document is unfair. If you allow him to publish this list, even say that the tennis club is not just a men's club, as everyone believes, but a gay men's club, a number of innocent people will be irreparably harmed, including me."

I considered the matter for what I like to think was longer than it would have taken me if I'd been a little more with it. "What exactly are the issues here? In short sentences, please."

Newton started. "Judge, this list is information that is completely unrelated to any legitimate purpose. Its only value is to justify public curiosity about people who are not even parties to this case. If you disclose this list, everyone on it will be thrust unwillingly into the full glare of bigotry, with no corresponding benefit to the public."

Good point. I looked at Tremain for his response.

"Mr. Newton has alleged two things in this case. The first is that whether or not he is gay is a private fact that *The Review* should not have printed in any event. The second is that he is not gay and the article is defamatory as untrue."

He seemed to be winding up, instead of down. "This list is evidence of the truth of the "Mr. Tampa" article. Beyond that, whether Mr. Newton is gay is newsworthy, and the list goes to our defense."

Tremain stopped to take a breath, and I hoped he was finished. No such luck. "This is a question of fact and it can only be determined by the jury's informed weighing of the competing interests involved. Mr. Tampa had the tennis club list at the time she wrote the article Newton has sued us over. If we are precluded from using the list, the policy you'll be espousing is that the media should always skirt trouble by completely avoiding any possibly sensitive area. Surely, that is a chilling effect on the First Amendment."

I hated to admit it, but he made a good point, too. Perhaps he really was worth the $850 an hour he was getting paid, even though the possibility gave me a stomachache.

"Look, the only way I'm going to be able to resolve this is to look at the list. I presume you both have law on this subject?"

"Yes, Judge," they said in chorus.

Of course, they did. They knew there would be a fight over this point. Nice of them to give me notice. Lawyers.

I tossed the last file on the floor and buzzed one of my clerks to come and take them all somewhere else, where I wouldn't have to look at them.

"Ok." I stood up and gestured that they both should rise as well. "What we're going to do is to go back out there. I'm going to put an innocuous statement on the record and call the jury in and dismiss them for the day. You're going to submit your briefs and the list, and I'll consider the issues."

Ignoring everything else on my desk, I promised, "You'll get my ruling tomorrow morning."

They glanced at each other, probably realizing that they each had an equal chance of victory and defeat.

Wanting no misunderstandings, I admonished them both, "Between now and then, if one word of this appears anywhere outside these four walls, you two will be spending some quality time together in close quarters, do you understand?"

So that's what we did.

When I got the paperwork from them, I recessed the trial for the day.

After that, I served the lawyers in the asbestos cases like a butcher at a meat counter, handling each case in line and giving them scheduling orders, until all of them were gone.

I was mindlessly marking time, trying not to worry about what Olivia might have to say.

CHAPTER EIGHTY

Tampa, Florida
Monday 4:30 p.m.
January 31, 2000

BY THE TIME I'D driven over to meet Olivia, I had worked myself up into a bundle of anxiety that I hoped had to do with excess caffeine consumption and not news that Drake had obtained his indictment.

Ybor City is a unique enclave in Tampa and a good example of the fickle nature of popularity. The area began as a cigar manufacturing community populated with Cuban expatriates. Cigars eventually went out of vogue and the community declined. In the late 1980s, the area was rediscovered and became a thriving nighttime destination. Teens cruised Seventh Avenue under the canopies of twinkle lights until the residents finally insisted on a curfew and an anti-cruising ordinance.

Nightlife doesn't start in Ybor until ten o'clock and it carries on until the wee hours, getting progressively more wild and loud. I had signed an order dismissing a case last week brought by a tourist against a fictitious "John Doe." The Tourist actually got shot while cruising the bars and didn't even know it happened. There was so much noise in the bar, no one heard the gunshot. She was so drunk, she didn't feel her missing tiny phalange until two bars later.

The case had to be dismissed because the tourist couldn't identify which bar she'd been shot in, let alone who shot her. At least she had a vacation story to tell that would top most of the others for the folks back home in Toledo.

The rough brick-paved streets rumbled under the wheels of my car as I searched for a place to park. Mid-afternoon on a weekday, the streets were sparsely populated, but there was no parking allowed on the picturesque Seventh Avenue. I circled the block twice and finally found an open parking meter on the other side of the street. I pulled in and parked. Standing on the sidewalk facing my car to put eight quarters in the meter, I didn't realize I'd parked illegally, facing oncoming traffic, right in front of a police sub-station.

I hustled over to meet Olivia at a trendy place called Bernini where the food is unusually good and patrons can smoke cigars during dinner in the upstairs dining room. With its dark wood paneling and neoclassical wood furniture, Bernini reminds me of a few places that George and I have a fondness for, like the Gotham Grill, in New York City. For some reason, Bernini's door handle is a huge bronze bumble-bee. Adds to the mystery, I guess.

Olivia waited for me on the lower level at a corner table in the back, impatiently tapping the pointed toes of her chic four-inch-high heels. After greetings and small talk, I asked her where she'd been.

"You don't own my time, Willa. I needed a break. You probably did, too."

"I did need a break. But I needed to talk to you, too."

"Well, I'm here now. What did you want?"

The hell with her. I'd defended my home from a rabid State Attorney and struggled through my workload, high on anxiety and tension. I was in no mood to put up with her attitude.

"I wanted to ask you whether you killed General Andrews."

She held up her hand, palm facing me so that I could see the gold and platinum rings that adorned each finger and the backs of her expertly manicured nails. "Okay. Okay. I'm sorry I didn't call you back. It won't happen again. Don't get your panties in a wad."

She smiled, trying to cajole me into a nicer tone at least.

I was placated, a little.

After a couple of seconds, I said, "I accept your apology."

No reason to be too obsequious just because I'd made my point, though. "But it's a good question, anyway. Did you kill him? Like a lot of other people, I'm finding out, you certainly had good reason to."

I was no longer belligerent, but I watched her reaction when she answered the question.

Olivia looked me right in the eye, unwavering, as she'd done hundreds of times to juries, witnesses and convicted felons, and applied the defense lawyer's creed: deny, deny, deny.

"I did not kill General Andrews. If I was going to kill him, I would have done it a long time ago. And if I had killed him now, I would have simply kept quiet and let George take the rap for it, don't you think?"

Was she lying? I had no better luck divining her veracity than I'd had this morning with Tremain.

"Do you have an alibi?" I asked her.

She looked at me through narrowed eyes. I heard incomprehensible shouting from the kitchen and somewhere behind me, a tray of dishes dropped onto the floor, shattering the quiet as well as the crockery. Louder shouting ensued, in Spanish, chastising the clumsy one, apparently. Another pair of late lunchers entered the front door and waited at the hostess station for a table. I simply waited.

Eventually, Olivia relented. "As it happens, I do. I was in Tallahassee. With the governor and about five hundred other lawyers. At a conference. Feel free to check."

Olivia must have wanted to kill Andrews, though. I think I would have wanted to, in her shoes.

"Why didn't you kill him?"

She looked away, sipped her wine and reviewed the menu. Olivia signaled the waiter, a tall, thin man wearing the smallish gray-framed glasses that are popular with the twenty-somethings these days. We both ordered salads and decided to share the excellent fried calamari.

When the server left, she spoke. "Look, Willa, this is totally non-productive. Why don't we just bring each other up to date and get back to work? My psyche isn't at issue here. I don't owe you any explanations for my actions. You can believe I killed Andrews or not. You can investigate me or not. But you and I need to get George cleared before that indictment comes down. Why don't we concentrate on that?"

So, for the remainder of our meal, we did. Since she'd been recharging, she claimed, Olivia didn't have much to report. I told her what I wanted her to know. We noodled for a while and then went our separate ways. I had a lot of work to do tonight and I needed to get started.

CHAPTER EIGHTY-ONE

Tampa, Florida
Monday 6:30 p.m.
January 31, 2000

ONCE I FINISHED MY after work routine, I got out the pending motions for the Newton trial. The parties were expecting an answer in the morning. I thought I could get it out of the way quickly and then turn to the Andrews murder.

Placing my reading glasses on my nose and with coffee for fortification, I began to review the list of club members that Tremain provided. I understood the legal arguments fairly well and I knew the decision was mostly a matter of judicial discretion. What that means is that the judge can do whatever she wants. This sounded easier than it actually was. It's not always easy to figure out what I want.

The title of the document was simply, *The Men's Tennis Club Membership List*. It consisted of four pages of names, all men. The addresses included San Francisco and Key West, but also Indianapolis, Kansas City and other Bible Belt areas.

There was an actor, several lawyers and doctors, a recently divorced state governor running for congress, and more than one law enforcement officer. A few military men were listed. Indeed, all occupational groups seemed to be represented. Many of these men, I knew, were married. Some of the older ones had been married several times.

The list wasn't arranged in any particular order that I could discern. Not obviously alphabetical, regional, or occupational. Two single-spaced columns contained names, job titles, business and home addresses and telephone numbers. A double space between each listing, as if the list was used to print mailing labels. Plenty of ammunition here to ruin more than a few lives.

My fingers kneaded the space between my eyes, trying to rub away the dull headache that had begun there as I wondered why any group of otherwise intelligent men would create such a potentially explosive document.

I read the first two columns carefully, feeling like a voyeur. This list was a private matter. It was true that many of the men on it were public figures who, for the most part, were not as protected by libel laws as ordinary citizens, even if their names were erroneously placed there.

But the potential destruction of lives that would occur from making such sensitive information public without the knowledge or consent of the participants was overwhelming and offensive, to say the least. Did no one understand the concept of privacy anymore?

My mind wandered as the headache became increasingly severe. Merely rubbing the place where the hurt started was ineffective. I got up, walked around, and then used the last of my cold coffee to help me swallow a few acetaminophen tablets, hoping for the best with my liver.

When I returned to the work, I tried to focus. After a while, I realized that I was reading a list of partners. A casual reader, without knowledge of the secret these men shared, might think this was a list of tennis partners. Which, of course, was the idea. But without a witness to testify that the tennis partners were all gay men, the list would be harmless and not probative of anything in the Newton trial. Without a live witness, the list was meaningless.

But, the problem of needing a witness could be easily solved. All Tremain had to do was to call Nelson Newton himself to the stand and ask the right question. Tremain could prove his defense from Newton's own mouth. That would likely be a slam-dunk winner as far as the jury was concerned.

The problem for Newton was that, with or without the list, Tremain could simply call Newton to the stand and ask him whether he'd engaged in homosexual conduct. Now that I'd seen the list, and knew what the meaning of the list was, Newton would not get away with a lie in my courtroom. He'd be forced to admit the truth.

My years in the legal biz had confirmed something one of my law professors had taught me years ago: Any evidence the jury hears from the witness stand, they may choose to believe. But if they see the evidence in a document or a picture, they will never believe anything else.

With this list, Nelson would surely lose this case. But if I admitted the list into evidence, at least fifty other prominent men and their families would be the victims of a violation of their privacy. I would, in effect, be outing them, against their will.

It was then that I noticed the date at the top of the list. October 11, which was National Coming Out Day.

My eye continued to travel down the second page and I recognized more and more names. By the time I got to the third page, I had almost stopped registering the information.

That was when I saw it.

On the third page, near the bottom. Both names together.

A. Randall (Andy) Andrews and John (Jack) Williamson.

And then, the dots that should have connected when Dottie told me about the general and his lover, "Jack" with the prominent white widow's peak, followed a straight line into my exhausted brain.

General Andrews was having an affair with his son-in-law, Jack Williamson.

And then maybe, or maybe not, depending on whether we believed Dottie or her equally nosey friend Eunice, Andy and Jack broke up.

Once the truth settled in, I realized not only what my decision about the list would be, but how I would resolve my personal problem as well.

Taking a full glass of gin and tonic along with a fresh Partagas onto the veranda, I stood in the light evening breeze and tried to let it cleanse away the sordid facts I'd learned when I lifted the rug of politics and looked at the rubbish underneath.

I knew what I was going to do, but I wasn't happy about it.

The whole thing sickened me. Andrews wasn't murdered because he was bisexual, although I believed he just narrowly missed being killed for having an affair with his daughter's husband.

None of the Andrews clan had told Olivia what they were all fighting about that night. But now, I felt sure that the argument was about the affair.

What a despicable man Andy had grown to be in the years since we'd known him. George thought Andrews had become mentally unstable and that much was clear. But Benson and

Warwick nominating such a man to the Supreme Court was morally corrupt, done primarily to hide criminal conduct. Andrews was not fit to be a Supreme Court Justice. Nor was he fit to be an army general or a father and husband, for that matter. The trouble was, at this point there was nothing to be served by bringing Andrews's participation in the entire squalid mess into the public's awareness. Andrews was already dead. Society couldn't execute him again.

My mother, or George, or what Kate calls my spine, or maybe even my subconscious had already decided what I would do in this circumstance before I ever even knew the problem existed. Privacy may not actually be a Constitutional right, as many scholars insist. But I believe in the value of privacy. I believe in dignity and morality, too. There is a struggle between free speech and privacy and that struggle, when I have to resolve it, means that personal privacy wins.

What people do with their personal lives, in sexual matters between consenting adults that harmed no one, was not going to be the subject of dinner table conversation in Tampa because of any decision that I made.

Maybe if Andrews was still alive, the public would have had a right to know that he was a bisexual, guilty of sexual harassment, before he was settled on the Supreme Court for life. And, if those had been his only faults, he might have been confirmed anyway. It's happened before.

But Andrews was already dead. No public purpose would be served by revealing his sexual privacy information now. I, for one, did not subscribe to the theory that the public had a right to know everything about everyone.

Secrets can be corrosive, but even if I do behave like Mighty Mouse sometimes, I know some secrets must also be respected.

The older I get, the more I understand the benefits of just being kind.

The Tennis Club list would not be made public. I didn't know where Tremain had gotten it, but the private lives of consenting adults were going to stay private in this trial. If Tremain chose to ask Newton about the list on the witness stand, then Newton would admit his participation in the club or face contempt sanctions. But the list would not be released. I prepared an order sealing the list and requiring Tremain to dispose of all existing copies of it. None of which would prevent someone on the list from disclosing it again in the future.

But there were bigger issues to resolve.

As Olivia had said a few days ago, two people can keep a secret if one of them is dead.

CHAPTER EIGHTY-TWO

Tampa, Florida
Tuesday 8:30 a.m.
February 1, 2000

WHEN THE NEWTON TRIAL reconvened the next morning and I announced my ruling on the list, there was great gnashing of teeth at the defense table. Then, both parties advised they had reached a conditional settlement overnight and agreed to a voluntary dismissal.

Neither of the litigants offered me a reason for their decision and the terms of the settlement were not disclosed. Newton's sexual identity was never proved, but neither was the item about him retracted by *The Review*.

Although the case was over, the privacy issues it raised lingered with me for quite a while. Celebrity comes with a very high price tag. If Charles Benson hadn't been the President's kid, his youthful drug use and stint in rehab would have passed under everyone's radar. General Andrews would never have been given the bargaining power to demand his

Supreme Court nomination, and he might still be alive.

I crossed the Newton case off my docket, improving my statistics. I turned my attention to the rest of the asbestos cases and finished up my last status conference.

At about two o'clock, Margaret interrupted me for a call from Olivia. She had posted a young lawyer at the Hillsborough County Courthouse to keep tabs on the proceedings.

"I thought you'd like to know. Drake only has three more witnesses this afternoon. Then he'll give George's case to the grand jury."

Worry gnawed at my stomach. "Are they going to finish today?"

"I'd say that's likely," Olivia told me. She didn't have to say what the outcome was going to be. We both knew.

"Okay, thanks." I stood up and shrugged off my robe, reaching at the same time for my purse and my car key. I lifted the receiver away from my ear to hang up.

"Willa?" I heard Olivia's voice as the receiver was almost back in its cradle.

"Yes?"

"If you've got anything else up your sleeve, now would be a good time to get it over here," she told me.

I replaced the receiver and jogged out to the car.

CHAPTER EIGHTY-THREE

Tampa, Florida
Tuesday 3:30 p.m.
February 1, 2000

I'D HAD A WHILE TO think about how I would handle the denouement. It seemed to make the most sense to cover the matter alone. I couldn't do it in my office, the place I felt safest in the world. Since the Oklahoma City bombing, Federal courthouses are guarded like the Crown Jewels. It would be next to impossible to get a gun, knife or other deadly instrument into my chambers.

But I'd never get the killer to go for that, anyway. So I had to go there.

I reviewed my props and my dialogue. I thought I had worked out all the possible snags. Even the knotty little problem of proving what I was sure I'd hear had been gone over carefully.

One more thing to do first.

It took Greta and me about twenty minutes to get to Jetton Street. The house was closed up tight, just like the last time. The uninitiated might think no one was home, but I knew better. I parked down the street and waited until the Gorgeous Gargoyle left. Then, I got out and walked up to the front door.

I didn't bother to ring the bell. I now knew it didn't work. I just turned the knob.

Locking the door is a habit and we only think we do it most of the time. Actually, I'd sentenced many a burglar who walked into homes where people left doors and windows unlocked.

I wasn't looking to steal anything and I wasn't breaking any laws. Not really. Michael Drake wouldn't see my actions this way, but after all, I was a family friend. At one time, anyway.

I heard the sound of computer keys clicking and followed them down the hallway to the third door on the right, facing the back of the house. The door was open.

She was sitting at the keyboard. Concentrating intently on the screen, she didn't sense me standing there for quite a while. It gave me a chance to look around the room.

The only window was closed and the drapes drawn to keep the light from reflecting off the computer screen. When I saw the couch, I wanted to laugh. Even an online psychologist has to have a couch, I guess. There were two end tables and the only light was from the two small table lamps.

The computer desk, a tall bookcase, and the very large chair Robbie sat in completed the furnishings. Not much room for a physical struggle. Not that I thought there would be one. Anyway, I could take her. Right. She outweighed me by at least a hundred pounds.

Finally, Robbie looked up, startled. "Did Juanita let you in?"

If she had, she'd be looking for a new job tomorrow.

"I knocked. No one answered and I let myself in."

"I guess I'll have to talk to Juanita about keeping the doors locked, then. I'm working. And I said all I've got to say to you already. Please show yourself out." Robbie turned back to her screen.

I guess she intended to ignore me so I'd go away.

"I'm not leaving, Robbie, until you talk to me. You can do it now or ten years from now. But we are going to talk."

She looked at me with such contempt that I nearly lost my resolve.

For a while, she continued to ignore me, but eventually she must have tired of staring at the screen and pretending to work.

She finally turned around and got up.

Even standing, Robbie was a good foot shorter than I am. "What do you want?"

"May I sit down?"

"No. You don't have anything to say to me that you need to sit down for."

"All right. I'll say this standing up."

I leaned my side against the left doorjamb and propped my right arm against the right jamb, effectively blocking her exit.

"I've discovered that your husband and your father were having an affair. I know who killed Andy."

I watched her closely.

She was controlled. She hesitated, maybe trying to decide how to handle it. That she was deciding told me more than any instant reaction would have.

Robbie knew about the affair. And she'd known for some time. The information was no surprise to her, which made me wonder who she'd told about it. Even though Robbie was the keeper of other people's secrets, I thought she wouldn't have kept this secret of her own.

Secrets were something I now knew more than I wanted to know about. I had my own secrets, which I guarded carefully. But they were the tame variety. The kind a woman in public life has to be vigilant about. Over the past few days I'd learned that most people have secrets of one kind or another. And the lengths to which they'll go to protect them were farther than one might think.

"That's preposterous. If you're through slandering my husband and my father, you can leave now. You'll hear from our lawyer." Robbie came toward me and I think she really expected me to let her through the door.

I braced my right arm hard against the doorjamb and she stopped before she ran into it. Now, she stood about eighteen inches from me.

"Is there something else? Surely you don't want to continue with this?" She was still forceful, belligerent.

I had trouble keeping hold of the sympathy I'd felt for her last night. "Don't you want to know who killed your father?"

I asked her softly. I didn't need to get into a shouting match with her. Besides, if you're quiet, sometimes they listen.

"Why would I believe you? You just lied to me and I already know you can't be trusted. Get out." Robbie started toward me again.

I stood up from my slouching position and filled the doorway as completely as I could. Since she couldn't step through unless I moved, she stopped about two inches from my face.

To shake her up, I said, "I think I understand why you killed him, Robbie. He was a mean, vicious and vindictive man. He never loved you. He stole, in the end, the only thing you ever thought you had: Jack."

As the words left my mouth, I felt the crushing weight of George's arrest for murder and his impending indictment settle on my shoulders.

It's simple to have principles and values when you live in a safe world, surrounded by people who love you and take care of you. Many of us never put those principles to the test. I resented Robbie and the whole damn situation for making me learn that lesson.

As I confronted Robbie, I became so filled with resentment that I actually wanted to hurt her. My entire body shook with barely suppressed rage. I wanted her to try to brush past me, to give me an excuse to hit her.

Since childhood, I'd never knowingly harmed another human being. The desire to do so now frightened me to my toes.

Robbie had turned my entire life inside out and upside down. I wanted to have compassion for her, but there was none in me.

Fortunately for both of us, Robbie didn't try to move me by force. Instead, she just sat back down and cried, making her pathetic, the situation abominable.

And I really believed, in that moment, that a jury might have excused her if she'd done more.

My anger evaporated like dry ice.

General Andrews wasn't just a lousy husband and a lousy father. Andy had never loved Robbie and he had taken from her everyone she ever thought had loved her: he had driven her mother to alcoholism, her brothers away from home and ultimately, he'd stolen the affections of her husband.

How much was a human supposed to withstand?

A colleague told me once that men are animals, civility just barely keeping their hostility under the surface. I'd scoffed at the time.

Life was just one big learning experience, wasn't it?

"I didn't kill my father, Willa." Robbie sat down heavily in the chair across from me. "Not that I didn't want to. I would have. I went out there that night to kill him. I even took George's gun with me." As I'd already guessed. "Only, I didn't know it was George's gun until later."

"How did you get George's gun?" At last, the thing I really came here to confirm.

Her answer seemed unresponsive. "I like antiques. You maybe noticed the ones I've collected?"

Her home was filled with furniture that even I recognized as valuable and quite old. I'm not a collector, but in the years we've inhabited Aunt Minnie's house, I've learned a few things about antiques. I nodded.

"So, that night, I was looking at the sideboard at the restaurant. It's got a very unusual carving on the back. I'd seen a similar one a few years ago, at an auction house, but I couldn't afford to buy it at the time."

I listened without interruption.

"I wanted to know who manufactured it. Sometimes, they stamp the drawers." She looked down now, maybe, finally, a little embarrassed. "I opened the drawer and there it was."

"The manufacturer's stamp?"

She sighed and shook her head. "The gun. I picked it up and put it in my purse. I don't know why I did it. I guess I just wanted to see if I could get away with it. And I did."

Of course she did. George would never expect a guest to steal from him. No one at Minaret would have expected it.

But Robbie's taking the gun was a piece of information I'd never have been able to prove without her admission. This last block of the case I had built finally fell into place.

I was still curious about a couple of things.

"Why had you decided to kill Andy that particular night?"

Any other time, and George would have had his usual alibi;

he'd have been in the restaurant with half of Tampa to confirm his presence.

She looked up at me as if I'd finally lost my last marble. "You already know the reason. His affair with Jack. It had been going on for years. Even when we lived in Colorado. Jack only wanted to move here to be near Dad."

"How long had you known?"

"A long time. I'd tried everything. I'd threatened Jack, argued, pleaded. I'd pled with Dad, too."

"Made threatening phone calls?"

It was the only explanation I had for the messages Deborah Andrews had told me she heard on the answering machine. Anonymous phone calls seemed to be Robbie's speed more than anyone else involved in this mess.

Her eyes widened, then narrowed.

"I told you to stay away from my mother," the snarling Robbie had resurfaced. She'd changed as quickly as flipping a light switch. It was hard to feel pity for the snarly one.

"So, why that night? If you'd known about the affair for years, why kill him now?"

She sighed and her shoulders drooped. "You already know we were all arguing that night?"

I nodded.

"We fought over my threats to tell the world about Andy being gay. The family was outraged with me." She waited a couple of beats. "Families keep a lot of secrets, Willa, for a lot of dysfunctional reasons."

She sighed and blew out the air through her mouth. "When the limo dropped us off at home, Jack called my bluff. He told me he loved Dad. More than me. And if I told the world Andy was gay, they'd be free to be together. And he said they would."

I made a mistake, then, I let my pity blind me to her instability. I let my guard down.

She continued, "I could live with a bisexual husband. But, the only way to keep him was to eliminate the competition."

"What happened when you got to Andy's house?" I asked her. I remembered the snakes and the gators in the backyard. There was no way Robbie would have followed Andrews out to that fishing boat in the dark, no matter how angry or threatened she'd felt.

"I went around to his den. He was getting ready to go fishing. I knocked and he looked up and waved me in. I took George's gun out of my purse and went in pointing it at him. I had every intention of killing him. I wanted him dead. I'm glad he's dead." She'd started to tremble now, remembering the confrontation.

Robbie's face suffused red and tight white lines stood out on either side of her pursed lips. Her emotional state was volatile and unpredictable. My pity seemed sorely displaced now.

"But I wanted to tell him what I thought of him first. That's where I made my mistake," she said, defiant as any teenager.

"What did you say?"

"I told him to leave my husband alone. I told him he was a lying, despicable person and a worse father. I said everything to him I've ever wanted to say. Everything I'd said in therapy for years. And do you know what he did?"

She became even more enraged.

Her memory of the confrontation took on a life of its own. I suspected that she had relived this humiliating scene at least a hundred times since the night Andy died.

"What did he do?" I whispered into the void.

"He *laughed*. He said, 'Put the gun on the desk and go home, Robbie.' Just dismissed me! Went back to his fishing tackle! I wanted to shoot him. I wanted to. I really did."

She started to cry, then. Huge, wrenching, uncontrollable sobs that shook her entire body.

"What did you do with the gun?"

I needed to know. This was perhaps the most important part of her story to George. Merely removing the gun from the sideboard and taking it to Andy's house wasn't enough. Someone had used it to kill.

"I put it on the desk, like he said. I left the suicide note I'd written for him there, too. I just left. I didn't do anything to him at all."

The mental cost of not following through on her desire to kill her father might have been more than Robbie could cope with. She might kill herself instead, I thought. I couldn't leave her alone because I had no idea what she might do.

While I was trying to figure out what to do next, she pushed right past me. I had my guard down. I hadn't realized that while I was feeling empathy for her, she was intent on getting away from me. I wasn't prepared.

She pushed past me, shoving me so hard that she knocked me to the floor. My body fell awkwardly. I landed somehow on my ankle and felt a sharp pain shoot up my shin.

I rolled over in time to see her run, more quickly than I'd believed possible. I tried to jump up. When I got to my feet, pain pierced my leg and I cried out with the shock of it. By the time I righted myself, Robbie had made it down the hallway and out the front door. Belatedly, I realized what she had in mind.

I hurried out the door, limping after her, fresh pain shooting up my shin with every step. I cried out, "Stop! Robbie stop!"

The next time I saw her, she was in her car with the door locked, backing down the driveway.

I hobbled after her, pounded on the hood and shouted again for her to stop the car. Robbie turned her face to me then, and I saw tears still streaming down her large, round cheeks and mucus pouring from her red nose. She glared at me as if pure hatred could strike me down, as her car backed out into the street.

Limping quickly down the block, calling after her, I tripped on one of Tampa's damned uneven sidewalks. I got up, still limping on my sore ankle, ignoring the bleeding scrapes on my arms that burned as if I'd scooted about fifty feet along the concrete. I pulled out my key and managed to get into Greta.

Next time I looked up, Robbie was gone. I had no idea where she went. I pounded my hand on the steering wheel and said a few very unjudicial, not to mention unladylike, words. It didn't help me find her, or ease my burning limbs.

Guilt ridden, afraid I'd pushed her so far that she would hurt herself, I picked up the phone and called Chief Hathaway.

Not in his office.

Why is it that you can never find a cop when you need one?

Not knowing what else to do, I left Hathaway a long voice mail, explaining that I'd had an argument with Robbie Andrews, she'd left me very upset and I was concerned that she might hurt herself. And I told him where I was going next.

I hung up feeling impotent to prevent another tragedy.

But I now knew what I needed to finish the General Andrews business, once and for all.

I dialed Olivia on my way. When she picked up, I got straight to the point. "What's the status now?"

"One witness left, then Drake's summation."

"Can you stall him?"

"How long?"

I glanced at my watch. "An hour?"

My cell phone started to crackle and sputter as I drove through a dead spot in the invisible airwaves that connected us. I couldn't hear all of what she said.

Just the one word: "Doubtful."

CHAPTER EIGHTY-FOUR

Tampa, Florida
Tuesday 4:30 p.m.
February 1, 2000

I DIDN'T WANT TO catch him at home. I wanted a nice, public place and some fresh air. I'd asked Jason where I could find the senator this afternoon and, to his credit, Jason had told me. Conveniently, Senator Warwick was playing golf at Great Oaks. Alone.

The symmetry appealed to me. I'd been playing golf at Great Oaks the day I learned Andrews had died.

Now, if I handled him correctly, I might collect enough evidence to prove my theories. I'd battled wits with Warwick several times recently and I'd come out the loser. This time, I planned to change that.

I parked Greta myself and limped over to the pro shop where I picked up a driver, a five iron, and a putter. I held the clubs across my lap as I drove one of the carts toward the ninth tee.

Sheldon Warwick stood on the fairway of the ninth hole, just in the middle of his backswing on what was probably his second shot. The ninth hole was a straight par three. The idea was to keep you playing, so your last hole on the first nine should be a fairly easy one. The senator was a good enough golfer to get on the green in one from the tee. Since he hadn't done so, he must have flubbed his drive. Something on his mind, maybe.

As he was walking back to his cart, his second shot having landed on the green where the first one should have been, I drove up to Warwick and stopped.

"Hello, Senator. Mind if I join you?"

He glanced up and noticed a foursome behind him and a pair of male golfers in front, realizing he was effectively stuck in the middle with me. "Is there any way I could stop you?" he asked.

He was a fast learner, anyway. "We could go into the clubhouse to have this conversation," I offered.

"Not likely."

We drove both carts, me following him, up to the ninth green. He took his putter and I limped along without a club, just to watch. After three putts he managed to sink his ball. Neither of us said anything.

We approached the tenth tee. I took out the driver I'd borrowed from the pro shop and put a ball down. I hadn't hit a golf ball since the day of the Blue Coat. Usually, I take some warm-up shots, but I wasn't here to impress anybody.

I swung and hit the ball a respectable 150 yards, straight. Warwick took his time and hit his ball a little further. As we walked back to the carts, I said, "I thought you'd want to know that I've figured out who killed General Andrews. I'm on my way to Michael Drake's office."

"Are you now?" he responded, as he got into his cart and headed off toward my ball, which was about twenty yards from his.

"Either that, or Frank Bennett," I told him. So I'd offered him the choice: tell me the truth or I'll tell the media what I know and let the public sort it all out.

Apparently Warwick was unwilling to get out in front of me on the fairway. Wise man. He sat in his cart, and after I hit the ball with the five iron, he sped off, leaving me standing there.

I caught up to him as he walked back following his second shot, pulled in between him and his cart and got out. "Here's the time for us to talk about this and get it over with."

"Willa, for God's sake. First you invite yourself to join my game. Then you get in the way. And now you want to hold up that foursome behind us, too? Where's your professionalism?"

He stepped around my cart and got into his. As he'd done before, he sped away and stopped at my ball in the fairway. His shot had landed on the green.

I followed him.

When I got within hearing range, he said, "Hit the ball, Willa. We'll talk at the pin where we're not making a public spectacle of ourselves."

I hate it when men act so condescendingly to me. Who the hell did he think he was anyway? I had a pretty good weapon in my hand and he didn't know I wouldn't hit him with it, knock that attitude out of him.

When we reached the green, he putted his ball in first. Then he stood by waiting for me.

He said, "It was just a matter of time before someone killed Andy. He had cheated death a hundred times and there are at least that many people who are not sorry he's dead. Maybe Andy's not even sorry. He was a twisted, unhappy guy."

Takes one to know one, I thought.

"If he'd been the first one out of his limousine the last

Thursday of the hearings, he'd have been shot instead of Craig Hamilton right then. What difference does it make now who killed him?"

I didn't answer. Instead, I put my ball down in two strokes and we drove separately to the eleventh tee.

Again, Warwick arrived before me. I had beat him on the last hole, but he swaggered up and went first anyway, putting himself ahead of me, just like he'd put himself ahead of George and Deborah Andrews and Jason and everyone else.

Gripping my club tightly, I felt a little of the way Robbie Andrews had felt the night she hadn't killed her father, but wanted to.

"It makes a difference to me, Sheldon."

I could have gone straight to Drake or Bennett, but I didn't have enough to nail Warwick. I needed more. I glanced at my watch. Most of the hour Olivia had estimated had already elapsed.

"Why? You know George didn't kill him, don't you? Drake will never be able to convict him. Let it alone. Justice has already been done."

That much, based on everything I'd heard, was mostly true. "Not good enough. I don't want my husband to go through a trial or risk a conviction. Things go wrong when cases are put to a jury, you know that."

I hit the ball, taking a cue from one of my friends who visualizes the heads of her enemies when she hits a golf ball. I imagined Sheldon Warwick's disgusting smirk, grinning up at me from the tee and I hit that ball with all the strength of my indignation. It worked. This time, my drive was much longer than his.

Who'd have thought being unwilling to pulverize my enemies was a golf handicap all these years?

We rejoined at Warwick's ball. I didn't tell him how I'd hit mine so much farther, but it frightened me a little to acknowledge to myself that I felt a little calmer.

I had no proof of my theories that would be admissible in court. There are two types of admissible evidence: direct and indirect. Physical, documentary and testimonial evidence is direct. Circumstantial evidence is indirect. And conclusions, such as the ones I'd come to based on deductive reasoning, as far as the law is concerned, are simply fiction.

If I couldn't prove Warwick killed Andrews, it didn't happen. The only way I'd be able to hand Michael Drake the man who killed Andrews, and convince Drake to let George go, was to get a confession. Or, I could allow Frank Bennett to do the rest of the work for me. I worried that Warwick wouldn't answer my questions, and I was a little surprised when he did.

"How'd you get George's gun?" I asked Warwick as he hit his second shot about a hundred yards off to the right. The fairway doglegged to the left. Not his day. Next we met at my ball.

As he watched my second shot, he said, "I didn't get George's gun. Andy had it. I think Robbie brought it with her when she meant to kill him." Warwick smiled knowingly. "Andy laughed about it. He said Robbie had never done anything right in her life. She couldn't even hold on to her husband. I picked the gun up off his desk and put it in my jacket pocket when he wasn't looking, before we walked out to his fishing boat."

He seemed to enjoy taunting me with the details. Was he crazy, too? Or was it just arrogance? He probably felt safe because he knew I'd never be able to prove anything he said if he denied it under oath. I'd discovered no forensic evidence to tie him to the general's murder and there had been no witnesses.

Rage borne of impotence flooded my body and I gripped the

golf club so tightly my hand began to throb. The intensity of my emotions shocked me. I really might have hit him. I imagined myself swinging the club upward to knock him down, knock that smug look off his face and that entitled attitude out of him.

I wanted to do it. I really wanted to. Only forcing myself to put the club head on the ground and press it there kept it from flying toward his head until he returned to his cart. That, and knowing that if I didn't get him to confess, George would be indicted for murder.

We'd both need another fairway shot on this par five hole, so once again, we met at my ball. My anger hadn't abated. This time, his ball was just a short distance away. I set up and hit. He hit a few seconds later. Both shots landed on the green, although his was closer to the pin.

"Why'd you shoot him, Sheldon, if all you had to do was wait and let some anti-abortion nut do it for you? Or one of his kids or lovers? Why get your hands dirty? It's the end of your career, you know." He sank his putt and it was my turn.

As I set up, he grinned at me. His arrogance was amazing. He actually thought he could commit murder and get away with it. But then, so far, he'd been right. "Timing, Willa, timing." We both knew he wasn't talking about the golf game.

He leaned both hands on his club and waited. "He did it to himself. I finally realized that if Andy had been confirmed and gotten on the Court, he'd only have been satisfied for a while."

He walked a few steps, knelt down and eyed the supposed trajectory of the ball. "But his confirmation was not going to happen. Mostly because of his own belligerence and foolhardiness."

"Why did that bother you?"

"I told him that night that I was voting against him," Warwick said. "He said if I did, he would destroy us all. He said he'd frame me for the murder of Thomas Holmes. Which, of course, I had no part of. Except that he'd blackmailed me into keeping quiet about it after I found out he killed Thomas."

This story wasn't what I'd expected to hear. I'd thought Andrews had threatened to expose Benson and Warwick's own criminal conduct in covering up Charles Benson's drug activities. "How was Thomas Holmes's death a part of all this?"

Warwick stood at the ball, leaning on his club, talking as if we were discussing the weather. His blasé, patronizing attitude was infuriating. "Andy made a pass at Thomas, but Thomas wasn't gay and he had an immediate, visceral, irrational response. Panicked, I guess."

"Why?"

He shrugged. "Thomas was high at the time, of course. On cocaine. He had a gun in his hand and threatened Andy with it. They struggled. Andy was stronger and quicker and a better shot."

He acted as if what Andrews had done was nothing more serious than a social gaffe. "He killed Thomas and then he covered it up."

If it really happened like that, I thought, the verdict could have been self-defense. But the problem would have been explaining Andy's sexual advance toward Thomas. For that alone, Andrews would have been court-martialed.

Warwick shrugged again. "I swear, I didn't know he was going to kill Thomas before he did it."

"But, when the other sexual harassment complaints came out during the hearings, you and Benson sabotaged Andrews, didn't you?"

He shrugged again. "I wouldn't put it that way, exactly. I went to talk to Andy, to try to persuade him to withdraw his nomination.

He wouldn't hear of it. He was raging, irrational. We argued. That was when he threatened to frame me for Thomas's Holmes's death."

"And how would he have done that?" The idea seemed too far out, even for Andrews.

Warwick looked directly at me now. "Andy said he'd tell the world that I had asked him to kill Thomas to keep him away from my son. He would have done it, too. He said he could supply enough evidence that people would believe him."

And then it clicked. The surveillance tapes. They must have shown Shelly Warwick as well as Charles Benson and Thomas Holmes using drugs. Andrews still had them, after all these years. That must have been why Warwick helped with the initial cover-up. To keep his own son out of jail. That, and to keep from being personally embarrassed. It was the only thing that made sense.

I'd never understood how Andrews got possession of the tapes in the first place, but this time, Andrews must have threatened to use the tapes to prove Warwick had a motive to kill Thomas Holmes. If Warwick was in Korea at the time Holmes died, the motive tape might have been enough to embarrass Warwick out of office. The report I'd read had not said exactly where Thomas Holmes's body had been found. Somewhere that both Andrews and Warwick could have been, too, obviously.

Without clear proof, Andrews's threat might not have been strong enough to push Warwick to murder, unless both Andrews and Warwick believed the revelation would also open the old criminal case and its cover-up.

Warwick said, "He laughed when I said I'd kill him first. He laughed at me. Me. Andy was laughing at me. Can you imagine?" His indignation was almost comical, except that he was so deadly serious.

I could imagine, actually. I'd felt something like the same level of rage at Warwick just a few moments ago, myself.

If Warwick was to be believed, Thomas Holmes had tried to kill Andrews, and failed. And Robbie Andrews had been goaded to take a gun to face her father's condescension. I recalled how Andrews had baited Warwick and led both Tory Warwick and George to violence the night he died. Not to mention the heated argument the entire Andrews family had both on the way to dinner and on the way home that same evening.

The general was more than capable of inspiring violent rage in others, even taking pleasure in it. In the end, Andrews pushed one man too hard. Andrews had inspired Warwick to kill him.

Warwick, though, could have been discussing his last appearance on Meet The Nation. "So the world is better off. End of story."

He gestured to the foursome behind us, waiting for us to finish on the green. Was he insane? Had something in his brain simply snapped? His behavior was far from rational and an involuntary shiver made me glad we were in a public place.

I glanced up to see the foursome advancing on us. "And what about the surveillance tapes? What did you do with them?" The tapes were tangible evidence I could use. I needed to find them.

Warwick's face flushed red again and he struggled to get himself under control. But he didn't answer my question. Instead, he said, "Of course, you won't ever be able to repeat any of this. Even to free your precious George."

Warwick had to think I'd go to the media with what I had figured out on my own to save George, even if disclosing Warwick and Benson's secrets would cause their destruction. What choice did I have?

As if he'd read my very thoughts, he told me why he'd bothered to confess his involvement to me.

"You have no corroborating evidence and I'll deny it all."

His smug derision caused me to retaliate, too soon. "Where's that beautiful gray cashmere jacket I saw you wearing the night before Andy died, Sheldon? The one that must have a very inconvenient bullet hole in the pocket?"

I'd asked Ben Hathaway to get a search warrant for Warwick's house when I left the voice mail message on my way to the golf course. I'd also told Olivia about it. I expected that we'd find the same gray fibers in Warwick's jacket that were stuck to the bullet that killed Andrews. The jacket and the tapes would free George.

Warwick's face flushed full with color now. He clenched his teeth and his nostrils flared. The short fuse, especially for ridicule, that had triggered his murderous impulse toward Andy was obvious. For the second time, I was glad there were lots of people around.

Then, he laughed again, wickedly this time. "The trash truck picks up in our neighborhood on Saturday morning, Willa. Isn't that convenient?"

I remembered a trash truck behind me as I sat at the curb after the golf tournament that Saturday when I'd first heard about Andrews's death on the radio, and my heart sank. If I'd known about the jacket then, maybe Ben Hathaway could have found it. Now, locating the jacket in the landfill would be impossible. And Hathaway's search pursuant to the warrant would turn up nothing in Warwick's closets.

"Then I'll testify," I said, belligerent.

"I doubt it," he replied, smugly. His confidence was unshakable. He never expected to be called to account. Not for any of it.

"How are you going to stop me? Shoot me, too, right here on the golf course? That would be a little awkward wouldn't it?" I taunted him.

I learned another lesson at that point. It's best not to be sarcastic to a murderer sitting in a golf cart when you're on an injured foot.

He gave me a narrow-eyed glance that quelled my sarcasm.

"Think about it," he said.

Then, he sped off in his cart toward the clubhouse. By the time I caught up with him, he'd left the cart with the bag boys and escaped into the men's locker room. I couldn't very well chase him in there, so I leaned up against the wall near the entrance and waited.

After a while, he came out. With the mayor, Michael Drake, the CJ, and two other politicians. CJ looked at me as if he couldn't believe I had time to play golf, with my heavy caseload. The others nodded at me, said hello, and went out to their cars. Drake gave me a smug look. He held up his pager and waved it at me to let me know he'd be called the moment the grand jury returned his indictment, any minute now.

I wouldn't have spoken to Drake on a bet. But I couldn't separate Warwick without accusing him of something we both knew I couldn't prove. I'd look like an even bigger fool if I tried and failed.

As I stood there deciding what to do, Jason drove up in a Mercedes sedan, Warwick got in and Jason waved at me as they drove off toward the airport.

By the time I found Greta and followed the car, both Warwick and Jason had entered the Senator's private plane. I watched it taxi down the runway, probably on its way to Washington.

I'm not sure how a woman looks with her tail between her legs, but that's exactly how I felt. Full of impotence, I fished around in my bag for my cell phone and dialed Chief Hathaway. He still wasn't in.

What a mess.

CHAPTER EIGHTY-FIVE

Tampa, Florida
Tuesday 5:35 p.m.
February 1, 2000

WHEN I GOT HOME, George was there. I decided to come clean and tell him the whole story, including my confrontation with Warwick, the botched attempt I'd made to get a confession out of Robbie and that I now did not know where she was. He was, as always, a lot of help.

"Call Ben Hathaway," he suggested.

Not knowing what to do next, I ignored him and went in to the shower. The water stung my scraped elbows and my ankle had begun to throb again. The pain was a reminder of how badly the day had gone.

When I returned, he'd poured me a Sapphire and tonic. After I lit my cigar, George casually mentioned that Ben Hathaway had called and was on his way over. I was sitting there with my hair wet, no makeup on, in my bathrobe. Great. Hathaway knocked at the door and George went to let him in.

I heard George lead Ben into the living room and offer him a drink. Always the consummate host, even to a man who has accused him of murder. When they made my husband, they definitely broke the mold.

We only had one chair big enough for Chief Hathaway to sit in, so I knew where they were. When I walked into the room, George got up, as he always does when a woman enters. Ben, not to be outdone, heaved his bulk out of the chair. I'm sure he expected me to excuse him from the courtesy. He'd have to think again.

"Good evening, Ben," I said, not shaking his hand but taking my customary seat near George on the sofa. I had already warned George that I would do all the talking. The last thing we needed was him making admissions we'd have to deal with at trial if I couldn't persuade Hathaway to convince Drake.

We hadn't asked Olivia to join us.

Hathaway sat back down with a thump, settling his big butt on the delicate seat. I wondered how long that chair would last. Aunt Minnie's mother had owned it, but the spindly legs wouldn't survive if Hathaway continued to visit us.

"Well, Willa, suppose you tell me what you've been up to. I understand you have some theories about who killed General Andrews. Besides George, here, I mean." He turned his head and winked. And George actually laughed. Men are so impossible.

I gritted my teeth and drew my bathrobe together. It was hard to maintain my judicial dignity with wet hair and no clothes on.

I told Hathaway almost everything, ending with a description of my encounters with Robbie and Warwick this afternoon. He raised his eyebrows a few times during the telling, but maintained his silence until the end. When I'd finished, he pulled out his notebook and made me tell it all again.

Our conversation lasted several hours, well into the night. Hathaway naturally had a lot of questions. It took him awhile to accept my answers, but when I could respond to each objection he raised, he finally began to piece the puzzle together for himself.

It helped, of course, that he knew me. He already realized that I was what lawyers called a credible witness.

I shared almost everything I knew, but I didn't tell either of them about the Men's Tennis Club. Andrews's affair with Jack Williamson, which Jack had admitted to Robbie, established that Andrews was bisexual and helped to explain why he'd killed Thomas Holmes. Still, I didn't need to disclose the tennis list of partners to get the point across. After all, I had Dottie's eyewitness account of the love nest, as she'd described it.

When I explained what happened to George's gun, why Robbie had taken it and left it at her father's house, and how Warwick had used it to kill Andrews, I expected it to be the final blow to Hathaway's skepticism.

Chief Hathaway could interview all the witnesses himself to confirm the stories I told him, before he took the evidence to Drake. I didn't care how he got Drake to agree to drop the charges against George, only that he got the job done.

Yet, Hathaway wasn't totally convinced. Maybe because my husband's life was at stake and I wanted so desperately for someone else to have killed Andrews. He made me no promises, other than to "look into it."

I told him he had until tomorrow morning. Then, I'd call Frank Bennett and tell him everything.

But would I? With Andrews dead and President Benson in the last few months of his last term, would I set Frank Bennett on a course that would cause so much personal pain to the Benson and Warwick families as well as public pain to the entire country?

I'd told George about Charles Benson's drug crimes and his father's criminal cover-up. George had shared my outrage. But what we would do about it now, neither one of us had decided before Hathaway arrived.

Hathaway frowned now. "It's amazing what kind of mischief people will get into," he twirled his hat in his hand. "I can't believe none of Andy's enemies got him. Why does it always have to be a friend or a member of the family?"

"Let's not speak ill of the dead, Ben," George admonished. "Andy was a good man once. Life dealt him some harsh blows." I was about to interrupt when George held up his hand to stop me. "I know he did some despicable things. But judgment is not for us to make, Willa. That's someone else's job."

"Actually, I am a judge and I make judgments all the time. Forgiveness may be divine. I'm not." I turned to Ben Hathaway and suggested that he might want to get started finding those surveillance tapes, since they were the only hard evidence that remained to support my theories.

"What about George's fingerprints in Andrews's den?" Ben asked us both.

"I'm sorry I can't answer that," George said, making me want to strangle him. "I gave my word."

But the question stirred my memory. Something I'd seen or heard was buzzing around, just out of reach. The fingerprints. In the den.

"There were other fingerprints in Andrews's home office, weren't there?" I asked.

But I was still preoccupied. What had I seen there? What was I thinking?

"All of which are accounted for, Willa, including Robbie Andrews and Sheldon Warwick." Ben replied. "George's are the only fingerprints that remain unexplained."

George and Ben debated George's refusal to prove his alibi and I barely listened. Something about Andrews's den. What was it?

Unable to persuade George to say more, Ben prepared to go. Before he left, Ben said, "Warwick's out of the jurisdiction now, Willa. And he's right that we have no evidence to connect him to the murder. You've seen the forensics, just as I have."

Ben held his hat in his hand.

"I'll testify against him," I said again, the tone of my voice rising of its own volition. "This is outrageous. The man is guilty of murder and he has to stand trial."

Ben shook his head. "Warwick will deny the murder, pitting your credibility against his. With no corroboration, it's just he said/she said. The despicable nature of Andrews's character will come out and tarnish Andrews's reputation further and hurt his family." He stopped a couple of beats. "Is that what you want?"

Of course, he was right. But I couldn't let it go. My whole life was about serving the judicial system. I did my job every day, as best I could, under a caseload so heavy it sometimes seemed as if I was drowning in sludge and would never, ever find my way to the top of it all.

"Well?" he asked me again.

The problem was that I knew all the reasons why Warwick would never be convicted. I saw all the holes in the evidence, all the missing proof. Hathaway was right. Warwick would keep going right on with his life, no matter what. I could simply accept that, or I could go down swinging, causing a lot of pain to a lot of people in the process.

So, after one more weak protest, I gave in. For now.

"I don't want to hurt Deborah and her family any more than

they've already suffered. But I want George out of trouble and I want his name cleared. How are you going to do that if you don't arrest Warwick? And we can't leave the man in the Senate, for God's sake!"

"I'll talk to Drake, tell him your story," Hathaway started.

"It's not my story, Ben, it's the truth," I interrupted him, hotly.

"We'll check it out. Drake will need some political favors from Warwick one day, if he doesn't owe some already. The investigation will remain open, the case unsolved." He looked at me squarely now. "Assuming I can get enough corroboration to get George's indictment dismissed, will that do it for you?"

At the words George's indictment, my stomach twisted with those same maggots that seemed to have taken up permanent residence since George was arrested.

I hadn't realized the indictment had been returned by the grand jury. Ben probably had it in his pocket right now. The knowledge took the last of the fight out of me.

Ben's solution was far from perfect, but it would take care of most of our problems. "That doesn't clear George's name, though. I want you to release a statement saying that George's gun had been stolen before the murder occurred. I want you to say George is no longer a suspect and you made a mistake. I want you to say you're sorry."

Ben sighed. "Okay, Willa. If Drake approves, I'll do that."

George said, "That'll be fine, Chief. We appreciate your help."

Ben turned to the door. "I'm really sorry for all the trouble this has caused you," he said, in our general direction. "You understand I had no choice but to arrest George. I knew the real killer would turn up sooner or later."

I resisted the urge to throw something at him as he left the room.

And then I remembered the dirty fireplace. Where Warwick must have burned the old surveillance tapes showing Thomas Andrews, Charles Benson, and Shelly Warwick snorting cocaine.

If they were still there, the residue would provide corroboration for my testimony.

EPILOGUE

IT WASN'T EASY TO tell Olivia about what had happened to Thomas. She'd already expected the worst and she'd gotten most of it right. I think telling her about Thomas's real relationship with Charles Benson, Shelley Warwick and their drug use was the right thing to do, but I'm not really sure. Before I told her, Olivia thought her brother was a wonderful young man who had been murdered by a cold-hearted general. Tarnishing the image of the dead in the name of honesty may not always be the right choice.

The charges against George were dismissed after we explained the facts of life to Drake ourselves. What made Drake do the right thing was the certain knowledge that he'd never have gotten George convicted at trial and he didn't want to face the public humiliation or ruin his perfect record. If he'd openly opposed Warwick and Benson to pursue who I thought was truly guilty, his career would have been over.

I'd told Drake my hunch about what happened to the surveillance tapes. Whether he checked it out or not, I didn't know. We waited for Warwick to be indicted, but that never came. Nor was President Benson ever exposed. Whether Drake owed

Warwick any political favors was a question I didn't want answered.

Frank Bennett was still sniffing around the story. He might put the puzzle pieces together for himself, eventually. I stashed my journal away in our safe deposit box, in case I ever needed a contemporaneous record of my investigation.

I'm a judge and a lawyer. I know that in a court of law, if you can't prove it, it didn't happen.

After the charges were dropped, George and I had several long conversations about the investigation and the events leading up to his arrest. He finally admitted that he'd been at Andrews's home the night of the murder and that's how his fingerprints came to be in Andy's den. He'd joined Warwick and Benson there, trying to convince Andrews to withdraw his name from the confirmation process. Of course, Andrews had refused.

George left before Robbie arrived that night, so he hadn't known what happened later. His mere presence in Andy's study on the night of the murder would have given Drake more ammunition anyway. George had refused to reveal his whereabouts because he'd given his word to keep the meeting confidential, to the President, the leader of the free world, a man I now thought of as a common criminal.

During the morning hours, when I was at the Blue Coat, George told me he'd met with President Benson, Senator Warwick and Jason to discuss how to defeat Andrews's confirmation and the President's sabotaging emissary. As I suspected when I first heard about it, the President had fully intended his actions to be revealed after Andrews was rejected by the committee. He planned to prove that he'd withdrawn his support for Andrews once Andrews was rejected.

What George told me was information I'd never have obtained

any other way, and I'd promised not to reveal. With these revelations, George and I began to communicate better and I felt happy that I'd regained some of my marital privilege; I now knew things I couldn't be forced to reveal. But I was still shaken by the magnitude of the secrets George had kept from me as well as the secrets I'd learned about the marital relationships of others.

Even after I told him that Warwick was a murderer, Jason continued to work for Sheldon Warwick because he claimed Warwick was going to retire and endorse him for the next senate race. I thought there was still more to the Benson, Warwick and Andrews story than I knew and I suspected something was going on with Warwick that I hadn't discovered.

I doubted any promises Warwick made to Jason could be relied upon and I was sorry to hear that Jason's ambition was as great as I had feared. Ambition is like electricity: it can be helpful or destructive. It looked like Jason was going down the destructive path, but he wouldn't listen to me or to George when we tried to dissuade him. All we could do was hope for the best.

George moved back into our house and things pretty much returned to normal between us. By normal I mean we went back to our usual routines. We ate together, slept together and were our joint best friends. I knew he was grateful that I'd helped him, but if he admitted it, then he'd have had to acknowledge how close he'd come to prison and destroying our marriage. Both of us tiptoed around that.

But our relationship had changed. It would be some time before we found our way around each other again. Now, picking up the pieces and reassembling our life would take time. As Kate said, one privilege of marriage is handling the surprises.

THE END

ABOUT THE AUTHOR

Diane Capri is a *New York Times*, *USA Today*, and worldwide bestselling author.

She's a recovering lawyer and snowbird who divides her time between Florida and Michigan. An active member of Mystery Writers of America, Author's Guild, International Thriller Writers, Alliance of Independent Authors, and Sisters in Crime, she loves to hear from readers and is hard at work on her next novel.

Please connect with her online:

Website: http://www.DianeCapri.com
Twitter: http://twitter.com/@DianeCapri
Facebook: http://www.facebook.com/Diane.Capri1
http://www.facebook.com/DianeCapriBooks

If you would like to be kept up to date with infrequent email including release dates for Diane Capri books, free offers, gifts, and general information for members only, please sign up for our Diane Capri Crowd mailing list. We don't want to leave you out! Sign up here:

http://dianecapri.com/contact